Down to the Woods

M. J. Arlidge has worked in television for the last twenty years, specializing in high-end drama production, including prime-time crime serials *Silent Witness*, *Torn*, *The Little House* and, most recently, the hit ITV show *Innocent*. In 2015 his audiobook exclusive *Six Degrees of Assassination* was a number-one bestseller.

His debut thriller, *Eeny Meeny*, was the UK's bestselling crime debut of 2014. It was followed by the bestselling *Pop Goes the Weasel*, *The Doll's House*, *Liar Liar*, *Little Boy Blue*, *Hide and Seek*, and *Love Me Not*. *Down to the Woods* is the eighth DI Helen Grace thriller.

@MJArlidge

Down to the Woods

M. J. ARLIDGE

MICHAEL JOSEPH
an imprint of
PENGUIN BOOKS

MICHAEL JOSEPH

UK | USA | Canada | Ireland | Australia
India | New Zealand | South Africa

Michael Joseph is part of the Penguin Random House group of companies
whose addresses can be found at global.penguinrandomhouse.com

First published 2018
001

Copyright © M. J. Arlidge, 2018

The moral right of the author has been asserted

Set in 13.5/16 pt Garamond MT Std
Typeset by Jouve (UK), Milton Keynes
Printed and bound in Great Britain by Clays Ltd, Elcograf S.p.A.

A CIP catalogue record for this book is available from the British Library

HARDBACK ISBN: 978—0—718—18387—5
OM PAPERBACK ISBN: 978—0—718—18388—2

www.greenpenguin.co.uk

MIX
Paper from
responsible sources
FSC® C018179

Penguin Random House is committed to a
sustainable future for our business, our readers
and our planet. This book is made from Forest
Stewardship Council® certified paper.

I

She reached out, but found only emptiness. The silky fabric was cool to her touch, which confused her. Where there should be a warm, sentient being, there was just . . . a void.

Unnerved, Melanie Walton hauled herself upright. Immediately she regretted it, her burgeoning headache slapping into her forehead. Every time she and Tom went camping it was the same. Plans for a relaxed, *restrained* evening soon gave way to unbridled hedonism – a roaring fire, loud music, then the inevitable bourbon-fuelled sex. In truth, Melanie wouldn't have it any other way – she could still feel Tom's presence on her skin, which made the emptiness next to her even more confusing.

Their tent was old and cramped – a poky two-manner Tom had picked up in a clearance sale – and Melanie was used to having her fiancé's reassuring bulk next to her. True, he snored, but the bourbon helped block that out and she loved the feeling of the pair of them snuggled up together under the stars. Usually the thought made her smile, but not tonight – as she craned around to peer through the darkness, the sight of Tom's empty sleeping bag confirmed what she already knew. She was alone.

Darting a look to her right, she saw that the tent flaps were open, swaying gently back and forth in the breeze. Immediately she felt a stab of irritation – it was just like Tom to stumble off to the toilet block and forget to close them. She'd taken him to task about it before. She wasn't naturally fearful, but they weren't the only people on the campsite and anyone could wander in. The fact that a zipped-up tent provided little protection against a determined intruder was beside the point – she just didn't like the idea of someone being able to see into their little sanctuary.

Melanie stayed seated for a couple more minutes – listening for signs of Tom's stumbling progress, rehearsing a good-humoured barb for his return – but it remained doggedly quiet outside. Cursing, she gave up the wait, tugging on her jeans and flip-flops before crawling out of the tent.

It had been a warm summer's day, but the cool night air made her shiver as she emerged from her cocoon. It caressed her shoulders and neck and she wrapped her goose-pimpled arms around her as she scanned the campsite. Earlier the place had been lively – it was the first sustained period of good weather and dozens of campers had abandoned Southampton to pitch tent at this New Forest site – but now it was deathly quiet. All that could be heard was the murmuring of the breeze and the occasional satisfied snore.

'Tom?'

Her gentle plea drifted away on the wind. Where *was* he? Often during his night-time sorties to the ablutions Tom would hum to himself, the refrain of earlier tunes cannoning around his brain, but tonight she could hear nothing. Nor was there any light coming from the toilet block.

'Tom? Are you there?'

Louder this time – her anxiety overcoming her fear of disturbing others – but still there was no response. Was he playing a trick on her? Waiting to jump out and surprise her? It was not his style – normally he was dead to the world at this time of night – but what other explanation could there be?

'If this is supposed to be funny . . .'

She was careless of her volume now. She just wanted to find him, give him a bollocking, then return to the tent.

Their night, which had been so pleasant, was swiftly turning sour.

'I mean it, Tom. If you're there, if this is some kind of trick . . .'

Her voice quivered, distress and fear mastering her. If it *was* a game, surely Tom would have brought it to an end by now? He wasn't cruel or hurtful. He was sweet, loving, kind . . .

'Please, Tom. You're scaring me,' she continued, tears pricking her eyes. 'Where *are* you?'

But her words fell away, dying quietly in the darkness.

2

She crept through the gloom, taking care not to make a sound. The terrain was unfamiliar and she had to tread carefully to avoid a bed post, a chair, some discarded clothing. She suddenly realized that she was holding her breath. Stupid really, but if it lessened her chances of detection, so be it. She was determined to escape unmolested.

Bending down, Helen scooped up her underwear, her clothes and finally her biking leathers. These were the hardest to slip on discreetly – they were old and battle hardened, creaking noisily as they encased her. But the well-built man slumbering peacefully in the bed a few yards away seemed not to notice. Exhaling a sigh of relief, Helen took a couple of quick steps towards the bedroom door, grasping the handle gratefully.

'Jane?'

Helen stopped in her tracks, then turned slowly.

'Early start. Sorry . . .'

If he saw through her weak lie, Daniel didn't show it. Running a hand through his tousled hair, he gazed at her happily, memories of an enjoyable encounter still fresh in his mind.

'So . . . can we do this again some time?'

'Sure thing.'

It was said too quickly, sounded unconvincing, which was stupid, because a part of Helen *would* have liked to spend another night with this attractive stranger. Things had been so turbulent recently – the inquest into DS Sanderson's death in action and Helen's subsequent (in her view unwarranted) exoneration – that it had been liberating to cut loose for a night.

She had met Daniel at a new club off Lime Street, singling him out as the only person there strong enough and brave enough to give her the pain she craved. Their session had been unremitting and gratifying and it was no surprise to Helen when they tumbled into his flat shortly afterwards. Nor, depressingly, was her desire to flee, as soon as their encounter was over.

'Can I get your number then . . . ?'

It was said casually, but did Helen detect a firmness behind the request? A desire not to be treated as a one-night plaything? Helen hesitated before responding. She wasn't sure she was ready to go there and, besides, handing over her personal details would reveal that she had been lying all night – about her background, her job, her name . . .

'Jane?'

His soft voice cut through her absorption, underscoring her mendacity. And perhaps if they had had this conversation in bed together, naked and intimate, she might have confessed, might have been *persuaded*. But here she was, dressed in her battle armour and ready to go.

'I'll see you at the club.'

Daniel knew it was a brush-off and, to his credit, didn't challenge her as she slipped from the room. Angry with herself, Helen marched away, her pace rising with each step. Having done the deed, she just wanted to find her bike and go home. But even as she charged along the corridor, familiar doubts, familiar questions confronted her. Busy as she was, committed as she was to leading Southampton's Major Incident Team, there was no denying that she was lonely. She needed a release, she needed company, she needed *life* to counter the darkness that consumed her, within and without, so when it was offered to her, why did she push it away? What was wrong with her?

Why did she always *run*?

3

He crashed through the undergrowth, tearing wildly at the foliage. Pain coursed through him as the thorns ripped at his skin, but on he went, charging blindly forward. He had no sense of where he had come from, nor where he was heading, only the conviction that he had to keep going.

He was dressed in boxer shorts and T-shirt, but even these flimsy garments conspired to frustrate him, the gnarled bushes catching at the fabric, tugging him back towards danger. It was as if the forest itself were his enemy tonight, but fear drove him on and, summoning his strength, he burst forward once more, emerging from the dense foliage onto solid ground. For a moment, the way seemed to open up for him – was that a track ahead, amid the gloom? – and he took full advantage, sprinting away. But as soon as he did so, a savage pain tore through him, bringing him to an abrupt, juddering halt.

He had been making good progress, but suddenly realized he was unable to put any weight on his left foot. Casting an anguished look behind him, Tom bent down to examine his sole. To his horror, he saw a large, jagged thorn – an inch long at least – embedded in the soft flesh. Already the skin was puckering up, pink and angry, as blood oozed from the deep wound. An anguished whimper escaped his lips, but he swallowed it down. He dared not make a sound.

Gritting his teeth, he fixed his fingertips around the end of the thorn. A silent count of three, then he tugged hard, ripping the thorn clean out. Another gasp of agony, then a brief rush of relief, before a dull, nagging pain reasserted itself. Could he walk on it? Could he *run* on it? It seemed impossible, given the pulsing ache, but he had to try.

Scrambling behind a gorse bush, Tom scanned the woodland around him. He was out there somewhere . . . the question was, where? Tom had been fleeing for ten minutes, maybe more, and his pursuer had been a steady presence all the while, dogging his footsteps. Occasionally he heard him – the snap of a twig, the rustle of a bush. Sometimes he glimpsed him – a tall, shadowy figure – but it was his presence he could feel the most – malevolent, menacing, relentless.

Suddenly, movement to his left. Tom turned sharply . . . but it was just a small rodent darting across the forest floor. Turning his gaze back to the murk in front of him, he screwed up his eyes, peering into the darkness for signs of his pursuer. But he was nowhere to be seen. The forest was quiet.

Part of Tom still wanted to believe this was all a bad dream, that before long he would wake, restless and hungover, next to Melanie. He knew, though, that this was too vivid to be a dream. But how was that possible? How could he have ended up *here*? He had gone to bed happily drunk, next to the woman he loved . . . and he'd woken, confused and half naked, in a strange part of the forest, a shadowy, hooded figure ordering him to run.

Breathing deeply, Tom tried to calm himself. If he was to survive, he would have to be smart, to make the right choices. Swiftly, he cast around him – hoping to make out his pursuer, but also searching for an escape route. Some sign as to which way to run. There was a faint track behind him, but there was also something that looked like a path a short distance away to the right.

Which one should he choose? How could he be sure that

either would deliver him to safety, when he had no idea where he was? There was no sign of the campsite, any habitation, indeed any human presence nearby. Could he even be sure he was still in the New Forest?

Panicking, he flicked his gaze between the two paths. He was suddenly gripped by indecision, aware how costly the wrong choice would be. He didn't know why he was being hunted, which way he should go, nor what kind of agonies lay in store for him.

All he did know was that death was stalking him tonight.

4

A piercing scream rent the air. It was shrill, agonized, fearful, jolting Charlie awake. Immediately, she was on the move, but her body struggled to keep up with her brain and she half fell, half stumbled towards the door. Pulling it open, she hurried across the darkened landing, pushing into Jessica's bedroom.

Her daughter was sitting bolt upright in bed, her eyes wide with terror. Stricken, Charlie went to her, wrapping her arms around the petrified four-year-old.

'It's ok, sweetie. Mummy's here.'

An elbow flew out, catching Charlie in the neck. Stunned, she gasped, robbed of breath, as her daughter thrashed in her arms.

'No, no, no . . .' Jessica moaned, seemingly determined to fight off her mother.

'Jessie, it's me. Everything's ok . . .'

But tears were already filling Charlie's eyes. The shock of being struck mingling with a profound sense of helplessness. Things were very far from ok. This was the fifth evening in a row that Jessica had suffered from night terrors.

'She all right?'

Steve had now entered, looking bleary as he stumbled towards her in his baggy pyjamas. Charlie didn't trust herself to speak, so simply shook her head. Steve joined them, wrapping his arms around the frantic child. Gradually, the struggling subsided, Jessica's eyes slowly drooping, and eventually she allowed herself to be lowered onto her bed.

'I want to go to sleep now,' she announced drowsily, turning away from them.

Still shaking, Charlie pulled the sheet up around her shoulders, tucking her daughter in. Incredibly, Jessica was already asleep, slumbering peacefully as if nothing had happened. Charlie's nerves were still jangling, however, and she remained stooped over her child, as if expecting her to rear up again.

'Come on, let's go to bed.'

A gentle tap on the shoulder, nudging her towards the door. 'She's fine,' Steve persisted gently. 'Let's get some sleep.'

'Two minutes.'

He padded away. Charlie suspected he'd swallowed a sigh, which she was grateful for. She couldn't handle any censure right now – she felt bad enough as it was. Each night was the same – an episode of unmitigated terror, then hours of peaceful sleep. In the morning, Jessica had no recollection of the night's events, nor any explanation of what had scared her.

In snatched moments at work, Charlie had trawled NHS websites and family health guides, trying to get some information on the causes of Jessica's nightly anguish. But guidance was scant and far from reassuring – the terrors seemed to have no obvious cause, nor a proven way of making them go away. At some unspecified point they would just stop.

Charlie had her own suspicions regarding the cause, however. Jessica was nearing the end of her first full year at school and, while things had gone well initially, recently she'd started complaining, attempting to wriggle out of going to school by complaining of tiredness, even illness. Perhaps she was telling the truth – it was exhausting for a nursery child to move into full-time education – but Charlie couldn't help wondering if there was more to it than that. Was it a problem with the teacher, Mrs Barnard, whom everyone thought strict? A friendship problem with one of the other children? Was it even possible that Jessie was being bullied?

The clock ticked loudly on the wall. Looking at it, Charlie was surprised to find she'd been standing there for over ten minutes. No doubt Steve would be getting irritated – though he loved and supported Charlie, he always accused her of over-thinking things. He was probably right, annoyingly, but she couldn't help it. They could have held Jessica's start back a year, but had chosen not to. This was partly because she was a mature girl who'd seemed ready, but also to make their working lives easier. Had they made a mistake? In trying to make things better, had they ended up making everything *worse*?

Jessica hadn't mentioned any problems at school, so Charlie was left to guess at the cause of her disquiet. For the first time since Jessica was born, Charlie felt powerless to help her. Which meant they probably had many more nights of agonized screaming ahead. Looking down at her daughter, slumbering in the bed below, Charlie suddenly felt tearful, anxious and scared.

5

He remained frozen, gripped by fear. His pursuer was now just a few feet from him.

Torn as to what to do, he'd remained hidden in the sanctuary of the gorse bush, ignoring the persistent prickling from its numerous spines. He'd continued to scan the gloomy forest, debating which direction to head in, when suddenly the shadowy figure had emerged from the darkness, heading in his direction. Instinctively, Tom had tried to make himself smaller, curling up into a ball. But his pursuer continued his steady progress towards him.

Half of Tom wanted to close his eyes, the other half knew he had to keep them open. He had to *know* if he'd been spotted. So he kept his gaze fixed on him, finding, then losing him amid the trees. On he came, looming ever larger, like some figure from a grotesque nightmare.

Reaching the bush, the figure paused. Tom wanted to scream and shout, to bellow out his fear and alarm, but he reined in his terror. He had been holding his breath for over a minute now – his lungs were heaving and he was desperate to breathe out. But his lips remained clamped shut, his nostrils clenched, fearful of emitting even the tiniest noise. Should he be discovered now, there would be no hope for him, trapped as he was in the bush.

Ten seconds passed. Then ten more. Then the figure turned, looking straight at him. Tom braced himself for a bark of triumph, for a sudden lunge towards him, but to his surprise his pursuer now moved on, padding away from the bush, spying out the forest for his prey. Faint with relief, Tom held his breath for a few more seconds, then exhaled, releasing the trapped air slowly and silently.

He counted another minute, watching the figure disappear into the forest, then eased himself onto his feet. Casting wary looks around him, he pressed down on his left foot. Pain seared through him, but he swallowed it down. If he was to escape this ordeal, he had to move fast.

He headed for the faint path he'd glimpsed earlier. Perhaps the moon was emerging from behind the clouds, perhaps he was becoming accustomed to the darkness – either way he could now make out his way more clearly. To his enormous relief, the path became more defined and he stumbled along it, half running, half limping. Inexplicably, he wanted to laugh, a sudden burst of optimism and relief threatening to erupt from him. Dismissing this crazy thought, he ploughed on, treading quickly along the path, taking care to avoid the fallen thorns and shadowy rabbit holes that punctuated the track.

He was making solid progress, putting good distance between him and his pursuer, but now he slowed. The path, which hitherto had seemed well defined, suddenly petered out. Sweating, he looked left and right. Nothing, nothing, nothing . . .

Closing and opening his eyes, trying to quell the panic, he tried again. And this time he made out something to his left. It wasn't a clear path, but seemed to be some kind of continuation. The bushes had been flattened, a few flowers trampled . . .

He moved on, following the outline of this track as best he could. He lost it, hesitated, then found it again. Over and over again this happened – his flight which had been swift up to this point was beginning to falter. And now, once again, he lost the path all together.

'Shit, shit, shit . . .'

He breathed the words, hoping they would soothe his pounding heart. But fear was assailing him, making his limbs shake and his brain ache. There had to be a way out of here. There had to be a way . . .

Desperately, he surveyed his surroundings. Was that another path off to the left? He didn't really want to head in that direction, but what was the alternative? Stumbling through bush and briar, frightening the wildlife and drawing attention to himself? Even as he thought this, a pheasant took flight nearby, calling out in raucous alarm.

This decided him and Tom plunged towards the path. He was careless now of the pain in his foot, sprinting as fast as he could down the flattened track. Yes, this was more like it. This was a proper path that would lead him to safety, back to normal life, back to his beloved Melanie . . .

With each step his speed increased, adrenaline driving him on. He would be ok, he would get out of here. Then he would finally be able to make sense of this nightmare. All he had to do now was keep going.

He rounded a bend, hoping to find a widening of the path, a light glimmering through the trees, anything. But instead he skidded to a halt by a large gorse bush. Faltering slightly, he stared at it. It looked familiar and, yes, there was a tell-tale stain of blood beneath it. This was the same bush he had sheltered in earlier. He had just run around in a large circle.

A twig snapped loudly behind him. His heart in his mouth, Tom turned. He knew what he would find, but still the sight took his breath away. The hooded figure was now just twenty feet from him, blocking his path.

'Please . . . I haven't done anything . . .'

His pursuer took a step forward. Then another. As he did so, the moon broke free of the clouds, illuminating the hunter, who now came to a halt just short of his prey.

'Who are you? What do you *want* from me?'

He screamed his question, but the figure didn't react. Screwing up his eyes, Tom strained to make out his pursuer's face, to understand what evil he was facing, but he could discern no human features at all within the hood.

Only darkness.

6

The wind battered her body as she roared along the road. It was a pleasant sensation, making her blood pump faster, energizing her for the day ahead. Crouched over her Kawasaki, Helen felt her spirits soar. It had been a restless night, but a new day always seemed to bring fresh hope.

Swinging onto Southern Road, she drifted gracefully to the left, hitting the indicators and gliding into the bike park. It was early and Southampton Central had yet to spring into life, allowing her free choice of the dozen or so spaces reserved for solo travellers. Bringing her bike to an elegant stop, she killed the engine and flicked out the stand. This had been her daily routine for as long as she could remember and it felt good.

Sliding off her helmet, she undid her leathers. Then, retrieving her phone and bag, she turned towards the imposing limestone and granite building in front of her. As she did so, however, another bike slid past her, coming to a halt a few spaces along. Curious, Helen hesitated. This was not a bike, nor indeed a rider, she recognized, which made her suspicious. In these days of heightened security, anything out of the ordinary was worthy of investigation.

To her surprise, the rider, who had now dismounted, gave her a cheery wave. Seconds later, his helmet was off and he approached her, a friendly but respectful smile on his face.

'Morning, ma'am.'

'DS Hudson,' Helen replied, concealing her surprise. 'You're keen.'

'Wouldn't you be?'

Whether it was a compliment or a genuine question, Helen couldn't tell. But it was true that she always turned up for work at Southampton Central full of enthusiasm. And it was one of the things that had impressed her during Joseph Hudson's job interview. He had worked a number of difficult patches in his career – South London, inner-city Liverpool – but he retained an energy and an optimism that were refreshing. Many of those who'd climbed the ranks were ground down by the experience. But not him.

'Well, seeing as you're here bright and early, why don't I give you the tour? I'd hate a newbie to get lost on his first day.'

'I think I can probably take care of myself,' he replied, suppressing a smile. 'But, if you can spare the time . . .'

Trotting up the stairs, they passed through the central atrium. First stop, inevitably, was Jerry Taylor, who had been working the front desk for as long as Helen could remember. Jerry guided Hudson methodically through the various security protocols, dotting every 'i' and crossing every 't' with rigour. As he did so, Helen took the opportunity to appraise her new DS.

For a long time, Helen had resisted interviewing for Sanderson's replacement. Her brutal murder still made Helen feel sick – she blamed herself for pushing Sanderson too hard, propelling the young woman to put herself in the line of fire – and the idea of 'replacing' her seemed obscene. Nevertheless, there remained a hole in the team – something Superintendent Simmons, the new station chief, was at pains to remind her of. So, they had placed the advert. Predictably, they had been swamped by applications – despite the dangers inherent in the job, Helen's unit was prestigious and popular – but in truth Hudson had stood out from the very first interview. A strong academic background, with specialist training in cybercrime, allied to many years' operational experience targeting organized crime, sex trafficking, drugs and worse, gave him a head start. But it was his attitude, personality and bearing that swung it for him. Fit, healthy, with a handsome, open countenance, he was insightful, incisive and refreshingly good company. Not every police officer had a sense of humour, but Hudson clearly did, tinged with a dash of rebelliousness and cheek. He was one of those guys whose straight face was undone by the smile in his eyes, which was something Helen appreciated. He would have to work closely with both Helen and Charlie in leading the team and she instinctively felt that he would be a generous and engaging colleague.

'Ok, I think we've verified that he's not working for the Russians,' Jerry intoned, with his best attempt at a cheeky wink.

He was a fossil, but a nice one, so Helen thanked him and moved on, guiding Hudson into the main body of Southampton Central. Minutes later they were striding along the seventh floor – Helen's home from home.

'You'll have time for the full tour later. For now, I'll just give you the highlights. Human Resources is on floor two, the canteen on three, the armoury – should you ever need it – is on the first floor and the gents' locker room is on the floor below us. Ok so far?'

'Two, three, one, six,' Hudson responded.

'Seventh floor is mostly given over to MIT, but remember this door well. If you're here you've either messed up or done something noteworthy.'

They had paused outside Superintendent Simmons's office, her name etched in gold on the mottled glass. Simmons was an old friend of Helen's – her mentor in fact – and Helen felt sure she would give their new recruit a warm welcome. But that would have to wait – Simmons was in conference and Helen wanted to acquaint Hudson with the inner workings of the Incident Room. The sooner he was up and running the better.

Buzzing through, they pressed on into the inner sanctum. Helen had spent more hours than she cared to mention in this room – some very pleasant, some decidedly not – but it always felt good to return. Crime never died and was constantly evolving, meaning there was always a job for Helen to do.

'This is where you'll spend most of your time. Data analytics are over there, the main body of the team here,' she continued, pointing to various groupings of dog-eared desks. DC Ellie McAndrew could be seen finishing a phone call at one of them.

'I'm over there – I'm the only one who's allowed a door – and you'll be there, sharing a station with DS Charlene Brooks. Everyone calls her "Charlie" and she's a first-rate colleague . . . but don't talk to her first thing in the morning. She has a little one and takes a few coffees to warm up.'

'Noted.'

'Good, now let me give you an overview of what we've got on the books.'

She was about to lead Hudson towards the incident board, when she noticed DC McAndrew hurrying towards her. She and Helen had had their ups and downs over the years, but McAndrew was a skilled, professional officer who wasn't easily shocked. Which was why her pale, flustered expression alarmed her.

'Sorry to interrupt, ma'am. But something's come up.'

It was obvious from her tone that this 'something' was decidedly out of the ordinary. Instantly, Helen knew that a day that had started so brightly was about to get a whole lot darker.

7

She gripped her hand tightly as they hurried along. This was partly because they had to cross roads, but mostly because they were late. Charlie had eventually drifted off to sleep around 2 a.m., inevitably slumbering through her alarm, waking just before eight. This necessitated a rushed breakfast, during which Charlie remembered that it was the conclusion of the school's Space Week today – meaning that Jessica had to attend school dressed as something 'intergalactic'.

Fortunately, Jessica had been convinced by Charlie's argument that a couple of cardboard tubes fixed to her flanks, topped off with a pointy hat, was sufficient to make her resemble a rocket and the pair had departed with a fair chance of making it to school before the bell. Drained as she was, Charlie set a decent pace and before long Skyswood Primary came into view. Chancing a look at her watch, Charlie realized that, miraculously, they had three minutes to spare.

Slowing her pace, Charlie glanced down at Jessica, who was ambling beside her. She seemed content enough today, but now began to drag her heels as they approached the gates.

'Should be a fun day today,' Charlie said gamely. 'Bet you don't do any maths or literacy. It'll just be dressing up, games and mucking about.'

Jessica shrugged, as if not bothered either way. She seemed more interested in her rainbow shoelaces.

'What do you think you'll be doing? Competitions? Space travel? Do you *actually* get to go to the moon?'

Jessica shook her head gravely, as if this were a possibility. They had come to the gates now and Charlie released Jessica's hand. As she did so, she saw Jessica pause, as if nervous to cross the threshold. Turning to follow her gaze, Charlie took in the playground, which was teeming with kids, dressed as all manner of aliens and astronauts. It should have been heart-warming, but today it made Charlie feel decidedly odd. Jessica was young for her age, but still the other kids seemed *so big*. From here, it looked as though she would be swallowed up by them.

Crouching down to her daughter's level, Charlie stroked her back reassuringly.

'You know, sweetheart, if there's anything that's worrying you, you can always tell me . . .'

Jessica said nothing, still seemingly engrossed in her shoelaces.

'If someone's said something, or scared you, or hurt you in some way . . .'

The thought made Charlie feel a bit sick, but she carried on.

'. . . then it's ok to tell me, so we can deal with it. Mummies can make anything better, you know that, don't you?'

Jessica nodded, smiling briefly, and for a moment Charlie thought she might be about to say something. But at that moment the bell went and, picking up her bag, Jessica trotted towards the throng.

'Love you lots,' Charlie called after her, realizing too late that she had forgotten to give Jessica her customary goodbye kiss.

She watched her daughter go, feeling a knot in her stomach. If there was something wrong, if something was bothering Jessica, it would remain a secret.

Jessica was now lost in the throng and Charlie strained to make her out, lingering unnecessarily. But as she did so, a piercing ring tone filled the air, wrenching her attention away

from the playground. Flustered, Charlie pulled out her phone, to find it was Helen calling. Immediately, Charlie felt her body tense. When Helen called this early it meant only one thing.

Trouble.

8

Emilia Garanita looked at the screen . . . to see herself staring back.

She was at her desk, scrutinizing a publicity shot that was due to appear in one of the national dailies, alongside a puff piece about her. As ever, she found fault with her appearance, with the historic scarring that marred the right side of her face, even though in reality this was one of the better photos.

There had been a lot of them recently. Emilia's abduction by Daisy Anderson, the spree killer who'd terrorized Southampton for twenty-four hours, had served the journalist well. She'd done numerous TV interviews, written countless profile pieces and now, nine months on, her book about 'her time with Daisy' was due to be published. Hence the picture on her screen.

Spinning on her chair, Emilia tore her gaze away from the computer to take in the newsroom around her. It was a view which continued to give her satisfaction. In addition to the notoriety and money that her brush with Anderson had generated, she had also used her heightened profile to leverage her position at the *Southampton Evening News*. Threats of resignation, and defection to more august publications, had proved enough to force her editor to restore her to the position of Senior Crime Reporter, at the expense of the incompetent time-server who'd briefly filled the role. In Emilia's mind, this restoration of rank was long overdue and, to be fair, Martin Gardiner had promoted her with good grace, even though his hand was being forced. As Emilia surveyed the staff members working with her, and under her, she sensed that at long last all was finally well in the world.

The only fly in the ointment was her inability to actually *create* the stories. There had been the usual slew of unpleasant, predictable crimes in Southampton recently. The odd sexual assault, a racially motivated attack in a nightclub and a spate of aggravated burglaries, which continued to unnerve home-owners throughout the city. But there was nothing that really got the juices flowing – after the drama and bloodshed surrounding Daisy Anderson, everything else seemed *beige*.

Turning back to her desk, Emilia picked up her pen and chewed the end, trying to summon the enthusiasm to finish her piece about burglary prevention. She should have finished it half an hour ago – it was the kind of fear-mongering piece she could write in her sleep – but instead she'd allowed herself to be distracted by the chatter on the police radio which she listened to while working, quietly absorbing the domestic incidents and traffic accidents that Southampton's finest were being called to.

She seldom took in the details – the familiar voices detailing the units dispatched providing a soothing background to her deliberations. But now she suddenly sat up, riveted. Five units had been scrambled to the New Forest to secure a crime scene. More interestingly, the Major Incident Team had been deployed, with DI Helen Grace as the SIO in charge.

A smile crept across Emilia's face. Things were seldom dull when Grace was involved. Scribbling down the location, she rose quickly, yanking off her headphones. Picking up her jacket and phone, she hurried from the newsroom without a glance at her colleagues, who continued to beaver away, unaware of this surprising development. Teamwork, Emilia had always felt, was overrated.

This one she was keeping for herself.

9

The trees swayed above her, casting long, sinister shadows in the early-morning sun. Helen picked her way carefully through the forest, her eyes sweeping it for broken vegetation, footprints or scraps of clothing. She was diligent, observant, but kept moving quickly. Initial reports of the crime scene were so alarming that she wanted to get there as soon as possible.

A forestry worker had discovered a body deep in the New Forest National Park. The call had come in just after 8.30 a.m., the police controller somehow managing to make sense of the terrified woman's reports – and Helen had immediately dispatched the team. The corpse had been found in a remote part of the park, in an area of untouched woodland between the hamlets of Blissford and Fritham. As soon as Helen had heard the news, her mind had rocketed back to another body found in the depths of the forest – one of the victims in Helen's first big investigation – but she'd swiftly pushed those macabre memories aside to focus on the case in hand. If initial reports were accurate, they were dealing with something very unpleasant.

There were no roads, houses or campsites near the crime scene – Helen had had to park half a mile away on Abbots Well Road – so how had the victim ended up in such a remote part of the forest? And, just as importantly, why? Helen's eyes darted about her as she followed the faint path in front of her, but there was little in the bucolic surroundings to engender alarm or explain the morning's strange developments. The ground was dry and unyielding, so footprints wouldn't help and the vegetation in this part of the forest appeared undisturbed. In fact, the forest looked as beautiful as ever this morning, which made the brutal slaying seem all the more unreal.

The path widened slightly and Helen glimpsed activity up ahead – the familiar, fluorescent jackets of the uniformed officers. Quickening her pace, Helen reached the end of the track, emerging into a large clearing, which was already teeming with police officers and CSI investigators. Nodding to Meredith Walker, Southampton Central's Chief Forensics Officer, Helen came to a halt, bracing herself as she turned to take in the body.

Helen was not easily shocked, but she had never seen anything like this before. A young man – late twenties, perhaps early thirties at the most – was hanging from the branches of an oak tree in the middle of the clearing, his face contorted with terror. The man's feet had been tied together, then the rope had been looped over a thick branch, hoisted up and secured to the trunk, so the naked, brutalized body hung upside down, its outstretched arms reaching hopelessly towards the ground below. The man looked like a piece of strange fruit, gore-smeared and lifeless, hanging from the ancient branches.

Worse still was the manner of his death. Helen could make out three arrows protruding from deep wounds to his chest, neck and back. Moving closer, positioning herself directly underneath the body, she realized that actually they were crossbow bolts. It looked very much like a close-quarters execution, given the depth of penetration . . . but that hardly explained the strange staging of this brutal murder.

Questions flooded Helen's mind. Why here in a remote clearing that few knew of? And why a crossbow? Attacks of this sort were extremely rare. Moreover, why had the victim been left like this, prominently displayed for some unfortunate rambler or park worker to discover?

Stepping away, Helen glanced across the clearing to the portly, middle-aged woman now being interviewed by DC McAndrew. Janice Smith was dressed in the familiar green of the New Forest Park Association, but that was the only colour about her – she looked deathly pale and was clearly in shock. They would glean what details they could from her – she would have to account for her presence here and the discovery of the body – but Helen feared there would be little in the way of solid information. She would not have been strong enough (and seemed an unlikely candidate) to suspend a grown man from a tree, and given the time of her call she was unlikely to have been a direct witness to the attack. Smith had called Southampton Central under an hour ago, but the blood on the victim's wounds was already congealed and crusted over. Meredith Walker and Jim Grieves, their truculent Chief Pathologist, would provide more details in time, but Helen already suspected this was a night-time slaying. The thought sent a shiver down her spine.

Returning her attention to the body, Helen found herself looking at Graham Ross, their most experienced crime scene photographer, who was hard at work. Raising a friendly eyebrow at Helen, he got out of her way, moving around the body to take close-ups of the victim's legs and feet. Helen was grateful – she needed a clear sight of the body to try and read the meaning of this horrific murder.

There had been no attempt to dispose of the body – quite the opposite: great pains had been taken to display it – which presumably meant that some message was being sent. Was it a warning? An act of retribution? Could it even be an occult killing, given the elaborate staging and timing of the attack?

Or was the victim's killer merely flexing his or her muscles, displaying their prowess and handiwork to the wider world?

Helen's mind continued to turn on these alarming possibilities as she stared at the butchered man, her eyes inexorably drawn to the large pool of blood that now stained the forest beneath the slowly revolving corpse.

10

'What's happened to him? Where is he?'

Melanie Walton stared intently at Charlie, tears filling her eyes. She had reported her fiancé missing at first light, but the significance of this had not become apparent until the discovery of a body in the forest shortly afterwards. The photos of Tom Campbell on her phone and her description of the victim's distinctive signet ring strongly suggested that her fiancé *was* the unfortunate victim.

Helen had dispatched Charlie and DS Hudson to the Woodland View campsite, an impressive new facility on the fringes of the forest, while she explored the crime scene. Charlie had barely had time to say two words to her new colleague, but he seemed pleasant and responsive enough, happy to organize the witness trawl, while Charlie interviewed Campbell's anguished fiancée.

'A body has been found in the forest,' Charlie replied soberly.

'Oh my God . . .'

'We can't say for certain who it is, until there has been a formal identification. That may be something we ask you to do in time. Would you be willing, and capable of doing that, if called upon?'

Melanie nodded mutely, before dropping her gaze to her hands. She examined them intently as if trying to find some meaning, some explanation there.

'Can I ask how long you two have been together?'

'Five years or so . . .'

'And how old is Tom?'

'Twenty-nine . . .'

Helen had estimated the victim to be in his late twenties – another small detail suggesting that they were on the right track.

'Do you often go camping?'

'Sure.'

'To this site?'

'No, it's pretty new.'

'So why here?'

'I don't know. We got a flyer through the door and liked the look of it. Tom loves his camping, so . . .'

Melanie petered out, the present tense tripping her up, revealing the dark fears swirling around her mind.

'What time did you arrive last night?'

'Around seven p.m. We both had to work, so . . .'

'And when did you last see Tom?'

Melanie paused, rubbing her hands with her face.

'Around midnight, I guess. We had a few drinks and a smoke, then we went to bed . . .'

She shivered slightly, as if the memory haunted her.

'Then what?'

'Well . . . we . . .' Melanie faltered, colouring, before continuing: 'We . . . made love and then went to sleep. That's kind of how it always goes.'

'Was it consensual?'

'Of course,' she retorted angrily.

'No problems? No arguments?'

'No, nothing like that. We're engaged to be married, we're *happy* . . .'

A tear slid down her cheek. Charlie could feel Melanie's anguish – the dawning realization that her world was about to be turned upside down – and she sympathized. More than that, she believed her. Family members and lovers are always the prime suspects, but there were no marks on the beautiful young woman and the campsite manager had confirmed there had been no disturbances during the night. Moreover, her emotion, her shock, appeared genuine.

'So, tell me again what happened. Slowly, if you can . . .'

Melanie's initial reports had been garbled, but now she tried to gather herself, aware of the importance of her testimony.

'I woke up in the middle of the night.'

'Can you remember what time?'

'Not really. Two? Three perhaps? I'm sorry . . .'

'It's ok. Carry on.'

'Tom had been sleeping beside me, but he wasn't there any more. I went looking for him – at the toilet block, by our car – but . . .'

'Did you try phoning him?'

''Course, but his mobile was still in the tent. So I waited until morning and when there was still no sign of him, I went to the camp manager.'

'And you didn't hear him leave?'

'I was asleep.'

'You've got no recollection – even a vague feeling or memory of movement, of a disturbance, of the tent being opened . . . ?'

'No, no, nothing. One minute he was there beside me . . .'

Melanie looked up at Charlie, fear writ large on her face.

'And the next, he was gone.'

'Nobody saw or heard anything.'

Clearly DS Hudson had been hoping to give Helen better news.

'I've spoken to the other campers, but to be honest they're pretty bemused by the questions. A couple of them met Tom Campbell last night, but they say they all spent a peaceful evening here, weren't aware of any problems.'

'We'd better run the rule over them anyway. See if any of them had connections to Tom Campbell or Melanie Walton.'

'Sure thing. I've also asked them to surrender their phones, for an hour or so. Before we let them go, I want to check if anyone has footage from last night, anything that might give us an idea of what went on.'

'Good idea. What about Campbell's car?'

'It's where he parked it last night.'

Hudson indicated an Audi saloon on the far side of the campsite.

'The keys are still in the tent,' he continued.

'Any sign of another vehicle? Near their tent or by the car?'

'There are numerous tyre tracks to be honest – you have to drive past the edge of the site to access the car park – but nobody heard a vehicle, so . . .'

Helen digested this. Had Tom Campbell willingly abandoned the campsite to plunge into the forest then? It seemed improbable, but, on the face of it, appeared to be the most likely explanation.

'Keep on it. Let me know if you find anything.'

'Yes, ma'am.'

Hudson headed off to join a crowd of anxious campers, who were huddled together by the picnic tables. Helen moved in the opposite direction, towards a harassed-looking man, dressed in faded cords and a brown fleece.

'Mr Robinson, I'm Detective Inspector Grace,' Helen announced, flashing her warrant card. 'I know you've already talked to my DS, but I'd like to ask you a couple more questions.'

'By all means . . .' Robinson stammered.

'You manage the campsite?'

'Manage and own it.'

'Since?'

'I've had the site for over a year. But we only opened four weeks ago – took longer than expected to plumb in the waste pipes, build the shower block.'

'Because?'

'Builders. What else?' he replied ruefully.

'I see.'

Helen surveyed him carefully as she formulated her next question. Nigel Robinson was trying to keep calm, but looked flustered and ill at ease, sweat creasing his brow. Whether this was because he feared the negative headlines the murder would generate or because he was simply unused to being interviewed by the police, Helen couldn't say.

'Do you sleep on site?'

'At the moment. When we're fully up and running, I'll hire someone else to do it, but I want to stay on top of things for now.'

'And you weren't aware of any trouble last night?'

'Nothing at all.'

'And before? Have you had any issues? During construction? When you opened?'

Robinson shook his head. 'The people who come here are good sorts. So are the guys who work for me, despite their tardiness. This is a peaceful, family site, a nice place to –'

'That's all for now,' Helen interrupted, keen to avoid the full advertisement. 'Please stay on site. We may have more questions.'

Robinson nodded vigorously – he clearly wasn't going anywhere while there were police officers crawling all over the place. Helen took her leave, intent on conducting a circuit of the campsite. It was a large facility, with a number of pristine log cabins, in addition to the brand-new toilet block, shop and bar. Robinson had clearly spent some money on it. Whether this would prove to be a wise investment was now open to question.

Helen bent her steps towards Campbell's tent, examining the exterior, before poking her head inside. It was nothing special – tatty and worn – and there was little inside: a few items of clothing, two sleeping bags, an expensive-looking camera and a near-empty bottle of bourbon. How drunk had Tom been last night? Was it possible he'd had one too many? Lost his way and wandered off into the forest? That seemed more likely than forceful abduction in the circumstances, though he would have had to be pretty far gone. Had he been *lured* into the woodland then? Was there something in that part of the forest that he wanted?

Straightening up, Helen continued her tour. The shop was well-stocked and smelled of fresh paint, the bar's spirit bottles were nearly full, though the grille was now down. Moving on, she reached the fringes of the forest. This was the point where manmade habitat met wilderness, but even here there were signs of Robinson's industry. A dozen trees had been chopped down to make room for a small playground – the rides almost entirely made of wood to suit modern tastes – and several

34

more had been sacrificed to give bar dwellers an unobstructed view of the lake. In fact, the whole perimeter area seemed to have been altered for the pleasure of the paying guests.

All except a handful of trees that loomed over the toilet block. Looking at them, they immediately struck Helen as odd. Nothing else had been allowed to stand in the way of progress, but these seemed to crowd in on the campsite. They had had their branches cut back to spare the toilet block roof, but the trees themselves had been allowed to remain in situ, despite the likelihood that their roots would eventually threaten the stability of the new building. Helen found herself walking over to them, curiosity drawing her on. Skirting the pristine facilities, she found herself at the base of the first tree. Running her hand over it, she soon found something unnatural embedded in the bark.

A metal spike had been driven into the tree – so forcefully that just the face of it was visible, making it impossible to remove. Further investigation revealed five more spikes, driven into the tree at different heights. Helen moved on to the second tree. It was the same here, as it was with the third.

Helen's mind was already whirring, a number of possible scenarios presenting themselves, as she turned back to look at the campsite. She didn't know which of these would prove correct, but as she took in the campsite manager, who'd been following her progress intently from afar, she knew one thing for certain.

Nigel Robinson had been lying to her.

'What the hell do you think you're doing?'

Emilia froze, cursing silently under her breath. She turned towards the approaching police officer, a look of innocent confusion on her face, as she dropped the police cordon she'd been in the process of lifting.

'Sorry, sorry,' she answered, trying her best to sound ditzy and flustered. 'I was just going for a walk when I came across this . . . tape.'

'And I'm Brad Pitt.'

'Sorry?'

'I know who you are and why you're here. So hop it. You'll have to go through the usual channels if you want any information.'

He was staring at her, arms folded across his chest, oozing self-importance. Emilia was sorely tempted to tell him where to go, but instead replied:

'Fair enough. You've got me bang to rights.'

Turning away, she took stock of the surrounding woodland, wondering how far she would have to go before she could drop out of sight and access the cordon from another angle.

'And in case you're tempted to try elsewhere, I should warn you we have officers stationed all around the perimeter. I'm going to radio them now to inform them of your presence.'

Now Emilia really did want to punch him. But reining in her temper, she pivoted and approached him once more.

'Look, I said hop it –'

'And I heard you, but I can't go back to the office empty-handed, so let me ask you a couple of questions.'

'No can do.'

'I presume it's a body you've got in there?' Emilia carried on quickly.

'I can't comment on that –'

'And I'm guessing it's a murder?'

'You can guess all you like.'

'You don't scramble a CID team to a suicide, do you?'

Now the officer faltered, wrong-footed by Emilia's knowledge of their deployment.

'How bad is it? What are we looking at?'

The officer said nothing, but looked uncomfortable.

'Had the body been there for some time? This is a pretty remote bit of the forest. Or was it a recent killing?'

'You'll get nothing from me,' the officer countered, darting a look either side of him, as if looking for – hoping for – reinforcements.

'I appreciate you're toeing the party line, Officer . . . ?'

'You don't need to know my name.'

'But I've said I can't leave empty-handed and I meant it. Honestly, I can carry on like this for the rest of the morning. So, unless you want to arrest me for wasting police time . . .'

Clearly this was not something he fancied. There was little to be gained by taking on such a notorious, and spiteful, member of the local press.

'A body was found this morning, ok? That's all I can say.'

'I'm guessing it was found by a camper, or a hiker . . .'

'Well . . .'

'At the start of the season too. Please don't tell me it was a family, that there were *kids* involved –'

'No, there weren't,' the officer responded forcefully. 'So,

don't you go writing that. It was a forestry worker, if you must know. Nothing more dramatic than –'

'Man? Woman?'

'Enough!' he spat back, taking a step towards her. 'You've got what you came for. Now go!'

He virtually shouted his last instruction. Would his voice carry to the next officer, inviting more scrutiny? Either way, Emilia knew it was time to retreat. She hadn't got the full picture, but she had got what she wanted – confirmation that a murder had taken place and a means of getting more information on it, *without* having to go down the usual channels. This was one story on which Emilia was determined to be ahead of the curve.

Thanking the officer, she turned on her heel and hurried away, disappearing from view amid the dense woodland.

13

'The victim's name is Tom Campbell. He's twenty-nine years old and lives in Winchester with his fiancée, Melanie Walton.'

Helen and the team were now back at Southampton Central, huddled around the incident board. DC McAndrew was still at the crime scene, supervising the fingertip search, but Helen had pulled every other officer back to base to review the latest developments.

'He is a senior biochemist with the Nexus group, which may have a bearing on his murder.'

'Who are Nexus?' DC Bentham asked gamely.

'They manufacture petrochemicals and oil products. Fourth-biggest company of its kind in the world. Their new headquarters in Lyndhurst caused a lot of controversy when it was built a year or so back –'

'I remember,' DC Osbourne overlapped. 'We had to send uniform down there to break things up.'

'There were protests by environmentalists and local pressure groups,' Helen replied, nodding, 'because of the amount of forest clearance the new base required. Some of the protests were peaceful, some were not, but in the end Nexus got their way, because of the jobs they would bring to the area.'

'Money talks,' DC Reid drawled, to general agreement.

'Hampshire Council have approved a number of controversial planning applications recently,' Helen continued, talking over the murmurs, 'allowing developers and businesses to develop on or near the New Forest Park. They're trying to build their way out of the downturn and, on the whole, they've been pretty successful, but the encroachment into previously protected woodland has provoked a strong reaction.'

'And Robinson's campsite was one of these new businesses?' Charlie asked, picking up on Helen's theme. 'He seems to have been pretty liberal with his use of the chainsaw.'

Helen nodded, turning to pin some photos up on the board.

'I counted at least two dozen trees that had been cut down, but the three in these pictures have been "spiked".'

She indicated the close-ups of the metal spikes, driven hard into the tree.

'It's a staple technique of eco-protection, or eco-terrorism, depending on your point of view. It makes it impossible to cut the trees down, as you risk breaking your saws and endangering your workers, as the spikes splinter on contact.'

'Do we know who's responsible?' DS Hudson asked, cutting to the chase.

Helen turned to the board once more, this time pinning up an e-fit of a man's face. Instinctively, the group craned forward to take in his features – the unkempt beard, the craggy forehead, the piercing eyes.

'Contrary to his initial testimony, it turns out that Nigel Robinson *has* had trouble on his site since day one. It started with threatening letters, then escalated to a dead fox left hanging in the site office.'

'Jesus.' DC Edwards winced.

'Then things got serious. Construction workers were threatened and a log cabin was burnt down. Robinson should have contacted us at that stage, but instead he hired some heavy-duty security to protect the site. Things went smoothly after that, but before paying guests arrived Robinson had to dispense with the heavies.'

'Making the site vulnerable again,' Charlie concluded.

'Robinson glimpsed this man on a couple of occasions recently, loitering in woodland near the site,' Helen continued, gesturing at the e-fit. 'He's ninety-nine per cent sure it's the same guy who threatened his workers, left the rotting fox.'

'Do we think that Tom Campbell was *also* targeted by this guy?' DC Bentham piped up. 'Was specifically chosen because he worked for a company who'd created environmental carnage elsewhere in the New Forest?'

It was a good question. One which Helen couldn't answer.

'That's what we need to find out. DS Hudson will lead further examination of the victim's private and professional life. Campbell doesn't seem to have any obvious enemies and, apart from a minor possession charge, has a clean record. He's not a local, journeying down from Winchester to camp in the New Forest, so let's find out who knew he was coming, who might have known his plans. Let's also see if he was involved in any of the clashes at Nexus.'

Hudson nodded, as Helen turned to DC Reid.

'DC Reid will co-ordinate a wider search of local weapons enthusiasts, shooting clubs and the like. We need to know if anyone's been making threats recently, been expelled from clubs, been arrested for threatening behaviour. The rest of you will assist myself and DS Brooks, as we take a look at this guy . . .'

Helen turned to the board for a final time, pinning up a police mugshot directly next to the e-fit. Another murmur rippled through the room – there was a striking similarity between the photo and the sketch.

'Nathaniel Martin. Fifty-two years of age. Convictions for drugs, hate crime and aggravated assault – he attacked a police officer with an iron bar during a protest in the late nineties. Did time for it, but came out even more extreme. Graduated from Greenpeace to more aggressive groups advocating direct action, before cutting his ties with them a few years back. Been a solo player ever since, sending letters to developers and council members with choice phrases such as . . .' Helen consulted her file. '. . . "If you build, we will burn" and "If you harm the Mother, her children will strike back." He is currently wanted for questioning about an assault on an official at City Hall, on a warrant dating back over two years.'

'Where the hell's he been?' Reid queried, sounding genuinely stunned. 'He can't have just vanished.'

'We have a last known address for him – a former girlfriend – but beyond that nothing. No ATM withdrawals in the last eighteen months, no benefits claimed, no phone calls, no tax returns, no new offences. Perhaps people thought he'd gone soft, or died, or lost his mind, but I think he dropped off the map intentionally, turned his back on his old life –'

'There *have* been rumours of a hermit, a wild man, living in the forest,' Charlie interrupted.

'And if it's Martin, we need to bring him in. This guy is dangerous, possibly delusional, and has an animus against Robinson, Tom Campbell and others like them. I want him in custody before things escalate. So, let's go to work.'

The team sprang to their feet, hurrying off to their stations. As they did so, Helen turned to look at the sketch of Martin once more. Executed in stark black-and-white, the image was particularly haunting. The sallow features, lifeless eyes and hooded expression combined to chill the blood.

It was a face from your worst nightmares.

14

McAndrew suppressed a shiver as she watched the paramedics wheel the body away. She hadn't relished remaining on site – she'd have preferred to be back at base, rather than in the shadowy, sinister clearing – but she had executed her duties professionally, organizing the search teams and liaising with Graham Ross about his coverage of the crime scene. And while she had been surrounded by familiar faces, she'd managed to ignore the growing disquiet she'd felt ever since she'd first set eyes on the devastated corpse. Now, however, she was all alone and distinctly ill at ease.

Was it the memory of the victim's hideously contorted face that made her anxious? Or was it the creaking of the ancient branches, the murmuring of the leaves? The latter sounded like a chorus of whispers, as if a group of unseen beings were out there, watching her. She wasn't prone to flights of fancy, but today the forest seemed to be alive, full of mystery and menace. McAndrew was a city girl and, truth be told, she'd never much liked woodland. She had always found it unnerving, rather than beautiful, could never shake the sense that if you came to grief here, no one would be the wiser. Even as she thought this, her eyes were drawn to the crimson stain on the forest floor.

'Come on, girl, get it together.'

Attempting to shrug off her anxiety, McAndrew checked her watch. The search teams had been picking their way through the forest for over two hours now, starting a mile away and working inwards towards the crime scene. They would shortly be returning to report what, if any, evidence they'd uncovered, but before they did so McAndrew wanted to do one last circuit of the crime scene. DI Grace and Meredith Walker had done preliminary inspections on arrival, but it was her job to make sure nothing had been missed. Grace valued the input of CSI operatives – their evidence had been crucial on many occasions – but she also put great stock in the experienced eye of a seasoned detective. Which was why McAndrew, one of the longest-serving members of her team, had been left in charge.

Sticking closely to the common approach paths, McAndrew moved swiftly round the perimeter of the clearing. Previously, her gaze had been riveted to the body and thereafter the forest floor, looking for footprints, discarded weapons or snagged clothing. Having found nothing of any interest, she allowed her eyes to wander, taking in the branches, the trunks, the birds, even the forest canopy, which continued to sway in the breeze.

She moved forward briskly but carefully, her eyes constantly roving, hoping to find something, however minor, that might shed light on this brutal crime. But there seemed little out of the ordinary in this quiet, bucolic setting and the forest background seemed to blur into indistinctness the more she looked at it. Now she understood what not seeing the wood for the trees *really* meant.

She was halfway round the perimeter, already thinking forward to finishing her circuit and connecting with her teams, when she spotted something away to her left. Many of the trunks had creepers running up them – the trees here were several hundred years old – and they all had a similar brownish hue. But one particular tree seemed to have an unusual addition – it looked like a creeper, but the colour was wrong. It was too green, looked manmade, and McAndrew hurried over to it, her curiosity aroused.

It was a cable. Bending down, McAndrew pushed aside the foliage at the base of the tree to reveal a small plastic box from which the cable originated. From here, it ran twenty feet up the trunk, before vanishing into a hollow. Straightening up, McAndrew followed its progress with her fingers, feeling the tacks that held it in place. This had obviously been put in place recently, given the unblemished nature of the cabling, but this was not the work of their killer. It was a bird cam.

Suddenly, McAndrew felt a shiver of excitement. There were several such cameras dotted about the forest – was it possible that this one had been recording last night? That it might have captured something? Stepping back, McAndrew surveyed the tree, trying to work out her line of attack.

There were several low branches and McAndrew was soon on the move, stepping onto the thickest and hauling herself upwards. The next obvious branch was thinner, so she paused to check it could bear her weight. Reassured, she pushed down hard, climbing higher. The hollow was only another five feet away now, but the branches were more spread out, necessitating a little leap onto the next one. McAndrew knew hesitation would be fatal – she wasn't keen on heights – so she took flight, landing safely on the branch and clinging on to the trunk for safety. Exhaling with relief, she craned up to peer into the hollow.

There, as expected, was a small bird's nest, with two eggs tucked inside, and just above it a tiny camera. Generally, the cameras were behind the nest, pointing outwards to record the mother's arrival, as well as the eggs themselves. And that would have been the case here, offering McAndrew the tantalizing possibility of CCTV-style footage of the forest below, had the hinge of the camera mounting not been damaged. Instead, the camera was pointing uselessly down into the depths of the hollow, recording only darkness.

15

'My name's Annie Brewster. I'm calling from the *Southampton Evening News* . . .'

The lies tripped effortlessly off Emilia's tongue.

'I work for the Social Affairs team here. We're currently doing a Southampton-wide survey on productivity levels in the workplace. Could you spare me two minutes of your time to answer a couple of questions?'

The HR manager at the New Forest Park Authority seemed unsure – Emilia sensed there was a lot going on at their HQ today – but soon consented, under the weight of Emilia's enthusiasm for the subject.

'Can I ask you how many of your workers are currently off sick?'

There was a brief pause, as records were checked. Emilia listened to the computer keys being tapped with a sense of satisfaction – a successful deception was always fun.

'We currently have seven employees on sick leave,' the manager eventually said, in her office monotone.

'And how many of those are long term?'

'Five' was the swift reply, as if each one was a malingerer costing the organization.

'I see. So, the other two –'

'Short term, usual stuff,' she replied crisply, shutting down that avenue of enquiry.

'Male, female . . . ?'

'I'm not sure I see how that's relevant,' the manager replied, suspicion creeping into her tone for the first time.

'I just want to get the most accurate picture we can of long-term trends in productivity.'

'Both female, but I wouldn't say that signifies a trend.'

'And are these field officers or clerical staff?'

'Field officers.'

'I'm guessing they work unusual hours, are out in all elements, more prone to bouts of illness?'

Emilia continued to ask questions, but was barely listening to the answers. She was too busy crossing off names on her list of Parks Authority staff. The organization was still dominated by men, especially when it came to field work, making her task considerably easier. There were only five women who regularly went out into the field and Emilia was confident it wouldn't take her long to find out which one of them had been signed off work, following their unpleasant discovery this morning. In the age of social media, shared databases and the (occasionally inappropriate) use of private data, digging into people's private lives had never been easier.

Which was one of the many reasons Emilia loved being a journalist. In her world, nobody was safe.

16

Eleanor Brown watched on nervously, as Helen prowled the cramped space.

The dingy attic was piled high with books, treatises, pamphlets and manifestos, many of them dog-eared and defaced by erratic, spidery handwriting. It was like walking into someone's brain — the small room was a treasure trove of environmental radicalism, dozens of tomes on Gaia, Mother Earth and the New Utopia, mingling with manuals on anarcho-primitivism, 'rewilding' and anarchy in action. Prominent on top of the nearest pile of books was a biography of the Unabomber — the daddy of all eco-warriors. Leafing through it, Helen was not surprised to find that many of the pages had been heavily annotated, passages underlined in thick blue biro.

'When did you last see Nathaniel?'

She didn't look up, but she knew Eleanor Brown was close by. Nathaniel Martin's ex-girlfriend had been loath to let a police officer into her ramshackle house and certainly wasn't going to let her have free run of the place.

'About eighteen months ago. When I kicked him out.'

'How come you've still got all his stuff?'

'He said he'd come back for it, but . . . but he was sectioned a month or so after we split, so . . .'

Eleanor shrugged, as if he were of no importance to her. But she looked unsettled. Was it fear undermining her attempt at nonchalance? Or guilt?

'Why was he sectioned?'

'He'd had mental health problems for most of his life. His dad was violent, used to beat up his mum. I think that was one of the reasons Nathaniel was so *angry*.'

Putting the book down, Helen spied a discarded photo on a rickety desk. It was of Martin and Brown in happier times. Taking it in, Helen realized for the first time how *big* Martin was – six foot four at least and broad with it. He dwarfed his girlfriend, making her look like a fragile bird.

'And the drug use didn't help . . . He could be very paranoid, very hostile . . .'

'Was he ever violent towards you?'

'What do you think?'

It was said defiantly, but her voice shook.

'When I told him to go, he became very aggressive. Afterwards, he was upset, inconsolable really. I wasn't surprised when he was taken in.'

'How long had you two been an item?'

'A year or so, but he only lived here for a few weeks.'

'Domestic life not suit him?'

Brown laughed, long and bitter, surprising Helen. She turned to look at the 48-year-old, taking in the neat, hand-printed headscarf, the make-up-free face, the long, angular body.

'Domestication was the problem. The root of all evil . . .'

'Meaning?'

'Meaning it was unnatural. In his mind. All this . . .' Brown continued, gesturing at the walls around them. '. . . houses, buildings, roads, railways, construction, mechanization, industrialization . . . they were all ways of perverting nature, taking it away from its original state.'

'He wanted to live in paradise?'

'He wanted to turn the clock back, to go back to the old ways. The idea of him living in a two-up, two-down was laughable. It was just a place for him to dump his stuff.'

49

She gestured at the congested attic.

'You don't share his views?'

'I believe in the environmental cause, any intelligent adult would,' Brown replied sharply. 'But I was never an extremist.'

'And he was?'

'What does it look like? He left Greenpeace cos they were pussies, couldn't stand all those wankers dressing up as penguins. Then he joined Earth First, because they were up for direct action. But even they were too soft for him, so he joined the Earth Liberation Army, which was when he got into trouble.'

'The attack on the police officer?'

Brown shrugged, but couldn't carry it off. Helen sensed this violent attack on a young police officer troubled her.

'They kicked him out after that. But he didn't care. He'd given up on organized resistance, teamwork, was happy to face the world alone.'

'And you took him in?'

'Silly cow that I am. But it was never going to last. Nathaniel was the genuine article. A *real* anarcho-primitivist, went on and on about rewilding –'

'Sorry, you're going to have to translate.'

'It means going back to our original state. No organized agriculture, no industry, no machinery, a return to the hunter-gatherer life. Living off what Mother Nature provides, what you can kill, forage or grow.'

'Does he still hold these beliefs? In your view?'

'Probably, but who knows? Word was he'd pretty much lost his mind by the end. I had friends who saw him living on the streets – drunk, dirty, abusive – before he finally disappeared. So, who can say?'

Her voice shook a little now. Was there still some affection there, despite her anger?

'Either way, he's not here. So, if you've got what you came for . . .'

'I'm going to have to take a few items away with me. If you would like me to give you a recei—'

'Take what you want. Means nothing to me.'

Thanking her, Helen busied herself, bagging a selection of Martin's personal effects, paying particular attention to his handwritten manifestos on rewilding. Following his recent mental health crisis, had Martin retreated to the depths of the forest, hoping to live in total isolation, away from the rapacious spread of modern urbanization? If so, what would he have made of the sustained attack on the forest by housing developers, campsite owners and leisure companies? And how would he have reacted?

There were many questions still to answer, many leads still to chase down, but a disquieting image was forming in Helen's mind, one she found hard to shake.

Nathaniel Martin padding through the forest, doggedly hunting his prey.

17

'No serial number, no maker's mark, no Kitemark ...
nothing.'

Charlie stared at Meredith Walker, who held the crossbow
bolt up for her to view.

'The bolts weren't bought in a shop or online,' Meredith
continued. 'I'd say they were homemade, cannibalized from
other bits of metal. There were three in total, and all show
subtle differences in shape, weight, density.'

'So, they're homemade?' Charlie replied.

'Looks that way.'

Meredith handed one of the evidence bags to Charlie. The
pair were in the CSI labs in Woolston, surrounded by dozens
of forensic operatives, but Charlie had eyes only for the
gnarled crossbow bolt in the palm of her hand. The weight
of the thing unnerved her – she suddenly had a vision of
what it must feel like to be struck by one of these deadly
missiles.

'Any prints on it?' Charlie said, gathering herself.

Meredith shook her head.

'And the DNA on it belongs to Campbell. If you can find
where the bolts were fashioned, we might be able to make a
link, but that's the best I can do.'

Charlie nodded, trying not to show her disappointment.
She'd hoped for more, but wasn't surprised. Nothing about
this case seemed straightforward.

'What about the rope?'

'Nothing special. It's old, so probably wasn't sourced recently, but it's very strong.'

Another image shot into Charlie's mind – Campbell's lifeless body being hauled up into the air.

'We haven't checked all of it yet, so we might get lucky on prints or DNA.'

It was a sop to Charlie, something to engender a smidgen of optimism, but it fooled neither. They were dealing with a calculating, resourceful killer here – someone who could fashion their own instruments of torture, someone who didn't intend to be traced. Nevertheless, Meredith's findings were important, underscoring the possibility that their killer was someone outside the mainstream, someone who knew the forest well and was using this to their advantage.

Charlie left shortly afterwards, leaving Helen a brief message with her findings, before hurrying back to her car. Their priority now was to find Nathaniel Martin, but where should they start? None of the usual methods would work – financial tracking, known associates, an appeal for witnesses. All they had to go on was Robinson's sketch and the knowledge that somewhere in the depths of the New Forest lurked a malign spirit, a phantom who could lure an innocent man to his death. Charlie often felt at sea in her private life, but she was beginning to feel the same nagging anxiety at work too. She was meant to lead, to help Helen drive the team forward, to guide DS Hudson as he established himself at Southampton Central. But what were they supposed to do now?

How *do* you find someone who has vanished into thin air?

18

'Why would someone do this? I don't understand . . .'

Melanie Walton was staring directly at Joseph Hudson, entreating him to help her. He understood her grief, her shock, her need for answers – he'd seen it many times before – and his heart went out to her. But he had nothing concrete to offer her and there was no point dressing it up.

'Honestly, we don't know yet. Which is why we need your help.'

Melanie didn't respond. Instead, she tugged at her engagement ring, turning it round and round her finger. The sight of it clearly upset her – the beautiful diamond ring was the last present given to her by her murdered fiancé – but her nervous tic was somehow keeping tears at bay. Hudson suspected that she would break down completely if she stopped.

'Melanie?'

'I've said I'll help you, but I don't know how I can . . .'

The shock of the morning was giving way to helplessness and despair. Following her interview at the campsite, Melanie had been escorted to the police mortuary. There, supported by an FLO, she had formally identified the victim as Tom Campbell. Afterwards, she'd been driven back to her flat, Joseph deciding it would be better to talk to her in familiar, comfortable surroundings than in the station's austere interview suites.

Now he was wondering if he'd made the right call. Tom Campbell was clearly a keen photographer – endless photos of Melanie, beaming happily back at her lover, covered every inch of wall space. Smiling, happy photos, images which seemed to mock the bereaved woman now.

'We just need some info on Tom. His background, where you met . . .'

Bland, general questions first. He needed to get Melanie talking.

'He's a south coast boy, always has been,' Melanie eventually responded, sniffing loudly. 'Southampton born and bred. I met him at a sailing club. We were both into it and just hit it off.'

Another few turns of the engagement ring.

'What did you like to do together?'

'Hiking, camping, cycling. Tom loved the great outdoors, loved his camera too, always brought it along on our trips.'

Joseph darted another look at the photos on the walls.

'He was never happier than when he was snapping away. And I loved to watch him. He seemed so excited, so happy . . .'

She dropped her gaze to the floor, a couple of quiet sobs racking her body. She was trying very hard to hold it together, but the strain was beginning to tell.

'When did you get engaged?' Hudson persisted gently.

'Six months ago, should have done it earlier really, but we wanted to wait until Tom was settled at work.'

'Did he enjoy working for Nexus?'

'Sure. Being a biochemist was all he ever wanted to do. I don't understand it at all, but to him it's like poetry . . .'

'Did he have any trouble during the protests?'

'Not that he told me about. They were pretty short-lived and the company brought in security so . . .'

Hudson suspected that things were actually much heavier than Melanie was letting on, but he let it go. Perhaps Campbell had shielded her from the truth, to save her from worrying.

'So, he was never targeted personally, at home or at work? No threatening letters, no damage to the house or car?'

'No, he was a scientist, not management.'

'What about his private life? Any problems? An ex-girlfriend? An ex of yours?'

'No, we've been together nearly six years. There was no one serious before that.'

'Money problems?'

'No, he's well paid. Always has been.'

'What about drugs?'

'What about them?'

'Did he take them recreationally?'

'In the past, maybe . . .' Melanie replied hesitantly.

'I noticed he has a conviction for possession.'

'He was *eighteen*. Wrong time, wrong place. He had too much going on to be part of *that* scene these days.'

'Did he drink much?'

'No more than you.'

It was said defiantly, angrily, as if Joseph were slandering her fiancé.

'And this trip you decided to take – to the Woodland View campsite – was it planned a long time in advance?' Joseph said, moving the conversation on.

'A week or so.'

'Who else knew you were going?'

'Well, my folks, I suppose. But nobody else.'

'Did you post or tweet about it?'

'Sure, but only once we got there. The site was really nice and the sunset was beautiful, so . . .'

Joseph knew that both Tom and Melanie were enthusiastic contributors to Facebook. He had looked through their recent offerings at the station and it was hard not to feel a stab of sadness. Pretty much every selfie and photo was of the young couple, happy, carefree, in love.

'It was perfect, the whole thing was just perfect,' Melanie

continued, climbing inside the memory. 'We'd even talked about maybe getting married in the forest, at one of the nice hotels in Lyndhurst, with a reception somewhere nearby. We were making plans that night . . . and now all *this*.'

She threw out an arm in a hopeless, helpless gesture, as she looked up at Joseph once more, confusion and despair all over her face. Her life had seemed so sunny, so optimistic – she had plans, hopes, dreams, but they had all gone up in smoke. She had lost her fiancé, no, she had had her fiancé snatched away and it was this that was tearing her apart.

Dealing with the reality of Tom's death was one thing. Facing up to the fact that he had been brutally murdered, then hung out for the birds, was something else entirely.

19

Helen stared down at Tom Campbell corpse, sickened by what she saw. The grey, lifeless skin, the puckered, encrusted arrow wounds, the livid, raw patches where his ankles had been bound – these were bad enough, but it was the sight of the young man's face that really upset her. His mouth was open, his lip curling upwards. It was an expression of pure terror, one which made Helen shiver. What had he endured to provoke this sort of reaction?

'Gets to you, doesn't it?'

Helen lifted her gaze to find Jim Grieves approaching. She had worked with Hampshire Police's Chief Pathologist for several years now and he seldom confessed to any emotion. But this one seemed to have affected him.

'You can see pain in his face,' Helen replied thoughtfully. 'But something else too. Fear? Horror?'

'It's not a pretty sight, that's for sure, but let me give you what I've got,' Grieves replied, keeping his tone businesslike.

Whether he was busy or just wanted to get this over with, Helen couldn't tell. Either way, she was glad of his professionalism.

'As you can see, there are numerous abrasions on the body. The clothing I removed from him was extensively torn, so I think it's fair to assume he'd fallen into a bush or been running through the forest. The state of his feet would certainly indicate the latter.'

He gestured Helen towards the end of the slab.

'You can see the soles of his feet have been lacerated numerous times, with a single, deep wound here . . .'

Helen craned down to take in the angry hole in the middle of his left foot.

'Given the cleanness, depth and curve of the wound, I would guess at a large thorn, but it's hard to say for sure.'

Helen shuddered, could suddenly see Campbell running for his life, the thorn embedded deep inside.

'A wound like that would have hindered his progress, making him an easy target perhaps. The bolt wounds were all good, clean hits – all occurring at the same time by the looks of things – so when he *was* finally stopped, he was stopped suddenly.'

'Would they have killed him?'

'You'd hope so, wouldn't you? But in this case, I'd say no.'

Helen looked up at him, surprised.

'Three major wounds to the torso. Massive haemorrhaging and blood loss, but the bolts missed the major organs. If they'd hit the heart, the lungs, even the kidneys, he might have been a goner, but as it was . . .'

Helen digested this. She had been hoping for a quick death, but in fact Campbell's agony must have been extreme and sustained.

'Look at the dried blood on his torso,' Grieves continued, pointing to the thick lines starting at each of the wounds and running up his body towards his neck and face. 'And on the arms. By the looks of things, I would suggest that the victim was strung up while he was still alive.'

'How can you be sure? Blood would have seeped from the wounds anyway surely?'

'Not in this quantity if his heart wasn't beating. Also, look at his ankles, there is no way they would be so swollen if the victim was dead when hoisted into the air.'

An image of Campbell twisting desperately on the rope darted into Helen's mind, but she pushed it away.

'So, cause of death? Time of death?'

'Hard to be exact on the timings. After midnight but before dawn is the best I can hazard. Cause of death? Well, that's pretty simple. He bled out.'

Helen nodded, but could hardly take it in.

'It would have been long, slow and distressing. Like a gradual suffocation.'

Helen wondered, was this accidental or deliberate? Did Campbell's killer watch on, as the life leached from his victim?

'Anyway, those are my preliminary findings. I've got the toxicology reports for you – plenty of alcohol in the bloods, but no drugs or medicine of any kind.'

Grieves continued briskly, reeling off his discoveries, but Helen's eyes remained glued to the corpse, following the lines of blood that ran from his wounds to his fingertips. What must it have been like to feel the life ebbing from him? And why had he been made to suffer so? Was it simply for his attacker's enjoyment? Was it a deliberate punishment for Tom's unwitting 'crimes', whatever they might be? Or was there a deeper meaning?

Was it possible that the copious amounts of blood that flowed from the stricken victim were an offering to the forest itself?

20

Emilia pressed hard on the doorbell, holding it down for several seconds. The modest suburban house in front of her was quiet, but she could see lights within. *Someone* was inside and Emilia was determined to talk to them, despite their concerted attempts to ignore her.

This was the last address on her list. So far, her search had proved fruitless. The first three women she'd approached seemed surprised to have been contacted by a journalist. They had clearly been out in the field all day, at various sites around the New Forest, and had not yet heard about their colleague's distressing discovery. There was no word from the police yet, thus nothing in the mainstream media; nor had the company's internal rumour mill reached them. Emilia wondered how tightly the Park Authority's top brass were guarding their nasty little secret. It was hardly something they'd want to shout from the rooftops, just as peak tourist season was swinging into life.

Movement now within and Emilia released her finger, stepping away from the door to appear as unthreatening as possible. The fourth woman on her list hadn't been very welcoming either – she was suffering from a bad head cold. Emilia had swiftly worked out that she'd been off work for three days now, so hadn't detained her, hurrying on to the final address on her list.

The door swung open and a middle-aged man appeared. He looked Emilia up and down, his irritation clear, but even as he did so his decidedly hostile attitude seemed to waver, surprised and discomfited perhaps by the heavy scarring on the right-hand side of Emilia's face.

'Well?' he barked, trying his best to sound unwelcoming.

'Sorry to bother you so late. My name's Annie Brewster, I'm from the *Southampton Evening News*.'

She flashed her ID quickly enough to conceal her real name. But the surly gatekeeper barely looked at it – he seemed unnerved to be facing a journalist.

'You must be Mr Smith?'

'What of it?'

'I wonder if I could have a word with your wife?'

'What about?' he demanded.

'We're doing a survey on productivity and sickness in the workplace. I understand your wife was signed off work today?'

The man narrowed his eyes, but said nothing. He appeared to be trying to work out what question was really being asked of him.

'So?'

'Well, I just wanted to find out whether it's a short-term illness, a cold perhaps, or something more seri—'

'It's none of your business' was the terse reply, even as Smith retreated into the doorway once more.

Sensing the door was about to be slammed in her face, Emilia stepped forward, planting her foot on the threshold.

'Here, what do you think you're doing?'

'It'll only take a second, then I promise you I'll be on my way,' Emilia insisted, looking over his shoulder into the gloomy house beyond.

'Absolutely not,' Smith replied, squaring up to her.

'If she's bed-ridden, we could do it over the phone.'

'It's nothing like that.'

'What then?'

Emilia's tone was incisive, penetrating, which seemed to surprise her opponent. He was clearly torn as to what to do for the best.

'Look, she's had a nasty shock, that's all. And she doesn't want to talk to anyone, least of all a journalist. So perhaps you'd do me the courtesy of heading back where you came from . . .' He angrily kicked Emilia's foot off the sill. '. . . and leaving us in peace.'

Emilia took a step back as the door slammed in her face. She could hear footsteps walking softly away, then an anxious female voice inside. Slowly, a smile spread across her face. She might have been repelled, but she'd got what she came for. She now knew the identity of the key witness and she intended to act on it.

She had a long list of questions for the unfortunate Mrs Smith.

21

'Did she say anything to you? Was something worrying her?'

Charlie and Steve were intertwined on the sofa, a bottle of wine in front of them. Having checked in with the team, Charlie had decided to head home. They had a big day ahead of them tomorrow and she felt utterly drained – the cumulative lack of sleep over the past week taking its toll.

To his credit, Steve had been waiting for her, with a home-cooked lasagne and a bottle of Barolo. He had already got Jessica off to sleep – another missed bedtime for Charlie – and seemed intent on making the most of their evening together. They had eaten, caught up on the day's events and now lay together, Steve gently massaging Charlie's feet. It was relaxing, it was comforting, and yet, try as she might, Charlie couldn't shake her anxiety about Jessica.

'No,' Steve replied cautiously, not keen to be dragged into a long discussion. 'She'd had a fun day at school, enjoyed Space Week. She was in good spirits.'

'She didn't say anything about what might be worrying her?'

'You know what she's like,' Steve countered good-humouredly. 'She tells you what she had for lunch and that's pretty much it. But she seemed fine in herself, so try not to worry.'

He was right of course – Jessica generally did come home from school exhausted but content – yet still Charlie couldn't shake the feeling that they didn't know the full picture, that something *was* wrong.

'I just don't understand where this is coming from. Things seemed to be going so well at school.'

'And maybe they still are. Maybe there's no connection at all between what happens during the day and her night terrors.'

'Maybe . . .'

'You know what all the websites say — there's no rhyme nor reason to these things.'

Not for the first time, Charlie wished she had Steve's unshakeable optimism, not to mention his stamina. He seemed to cope with the lack of sleep far better than she did.

'But if there is a root cause, something we don't know about —'

'Then it will become apparent, in time. If there is a problem, we will find out what it is and deal with it, right?'

It was said kindly, but was a clear invitation to move the conversation on.

'I suppose . . .'

'Good. Now how about we finish this bottle of wine?'

Charlie was happy to oblige, suspecting where this was heading. And sure enough, once the bottle had been drained, Steve scooped her up and carried her upstairs, stealing cheeky kisses every step of the way. Tiptoeing past Jessica's room, they made it to the bedroom and moments later were under the covers, naked, entwined.

Stroking the hair away from her face, Steve kissed her on the neck, on the earlobe, the tip of her nose.

'I've been thinking . . .'

Charlie opened her eyes, intrigued by his tone.

'Why don't you forget to take your pill tomorrow?'

'Are you serious?'

'Let's make babies, Charlie. You know we're good at it . . .'

'You must be joking.'

'Jessie needs a little sister. Or brother.'

'Not yet she doesn't.'

'And I promise you we'll have fun along the way. But I do need your assistance.'

'Sorry, no can do. This is purely recreational.'

For a moment, Charlie thought he was going to argue back, but instead he whispered:

'I love it when you talk dirty.'

He moved in for the kill, pulling her towards him, then rolling on to his back, so that she was now on top. Charlie closed her eyes and gave in to the moment, revelling in his touch, shivers of excitement pulsing through her. Later, as she lay next to Steve, listening to his gentle, satisfied breathing, she tried to let sleep take her, but she remained wide awake. Despite the pleasurable distraction of the evening, Charlie couldn't switch off, couldn't quell her anxiety about Jessica.

So she lay there in the darkness, frustrated and upset, waiting for the cries that she knew were coming.

22

A sharp rap on the door made Helen look up. She expected it to be Joseph Hudson – he was the only officer left in the incident room, gamely proving his enthusiasm on his first full day. But, to Helen's surprise, Superintendent Grace Simmons now entered, closing the door gently behind her.

'Got a minute for an old lady?'

'Absolutely. I was going to call in on you before I left anyway.'

Seating herself, Simmons took in the interior of Helen's office, her eyes fixing on the commendations hanging on the wall, the case files littering the desk, the empty coffee cups in the overflowing bin.

'I thought I'd see what life was like at the sharp end. When you've been stuck in boardrooms for as long as I have, it's nice to see where the real police work is done.'

Superintendent Simmons had been in charge at South-ampton Central for six months now. In her early sixties, she should have retired from the force by rights, but at the eleventh hour top brass had persuaded her to take the job of station chief on an interim basis, following their failure to find a suitable permanent replacement for Jonathan Gardam. Helen had been covering two jobs up until then and was grateful to have a replacement, especially as Simmons was someone who had always been very dear to her.

Following her parents' murder, Helen had been shuttled around various care homes, eventually ending up at an establishment in Basingstoke. The things Helen saw there – the things she *endured* – would stay with her for ever, but Simmons's intervention, then just a lowly WPC, proved crucial in helping Helen escape. Thereafter, Simmons had kept a close eye on her, guiding her, supporting her, eventually mentoring her when Helen decided to join the force. Indeed, her influence on Helen had been so profound that she'd borrowed Simmons's Christian name – Grace – when choosing a new identity for herself.

Helen was therefore delighted when Simmons took over at Southampton Central. Where Gardam had been obsessive, vengeful and manipulative, Simmons was honest, supportive and kind. It was the first time Helen had ever had a boss she got on with. Which was why her door was always open to her.

'You're too modest. You've forgotten more about policing than we'll ever know,' Helen replied, pleased to be ending a difficult day on a pleasant note.

Simmons waved away the compliment – she was a plain-speaking woman who didn't need to be stroked.

'So how are we getting on?'

'Well, we have a person of interest – Nathaniel Martin – but no obvious way of finding him. He's been completely off grid for eighteen months now.'

'No sightings at all?' Simmons replied, surprised.

'Nothing confirmed. We think he may be hiding out in the New Forest, so the whole team are heading there tomorrow. I could do with some extra bodies though, as the area we are covering is pretty vast.'

'Of course, take whoever we can spare.'

'Thank you. Also, an operation of this kind is inevitably going to attract attention, so what would you like to do about the press?'

'What do they know?'

'Media liaison have released a statement saying a body was found in the New Forest this morning. But there are no details as to the manner of the death.'

'Let's keep it that way for now,' Simmons confirmed decisively. 'I'd like to know what we're dealing with, before terrifying the holiday hordes.'

'Of course.'

'That's that, then,' Simmons said, rising. 'I take it you'll be calling it a day soon?'

Helen shot a look at the clock – eleven o'clock – then back at Simmons. She suspected this was the real reason for Simmons's impromptu visit.

'Ten more minutes.'

'No more than that, please. This place will still be here in the morning.'

People marvelled at Helen's workrate and commitment, but Simmons wasn't fooled. She knew that Southampton Central, that her role here, was Helen's sanctuary, a retreat from a world which had always treated her harshly.

'I know you love this job, Helen,' Simmons continued. 'That what you do *matters*, but you have to give yourself a break every now and again.'

'I do. It's just that there's always so much going on –'

'It's not your job to take the world's woes onto your shoulders. I know you feel bad about what happened to Joanne, that you think working all the hours God sends will somehow make up for that.'

The mention of DS Sanderson set Helen's nerves on edge.

'It's not about that.'

'Isn't it? You did everything you could at that inquest to get yourself disciplined, even fired. Assuming full responsibility, publicly lacerating yourself, questioning your operational decisions –'

'And I was right to do so –'

'No, you weren't. You did nothing wrong, Helen. Which is why you were cleared of any culpability. This is a dangerous job, you know that more than most. So, it's time to forgive yourself and look forward.'

She was probably right, but it was easier said than done. Joanne Sanderson had died in Helen's arms and the memory was hard to shake.

'I mean it, Helen. Don't cling to the past. Or it will eat you up.'

She rose and headed to the door, but as she opened it, she concluded:

'You deserve a life too, you know.'

With that, Simmons departed, leaving the door ajar for Helen's departure. Helen watched her go, reflecting on her words. She *did* need to get out there again, to engage with the world, but to what end? What was out there for her?

Gathering up her files, Helen rose from her desk, shooting a quick look into the incident room – only to find Joseph Hudson staring directly at her. How long he'd been looking at her, she couldn't say, but embarrassed to be caught out, he quickly dropped his gaze, busying himself with his work. For a moment, Helen stared at *him*, intrigued by his curiosity, but Simmons's words were still ringing in her ears, so, turning to walk to the door, Helen killed the lights, plunging the room into darkness.

23

Heavy clouds hung above the forest, blocking out the sun. It was just after dawn, but the day had yet to rouse itself, and the Woodland View campsite was bathed in an insipid, milky light. Charlie hopped from foot to foot, clutching her latte, hoping the steaming coffee would bring her brain and body to life. After another sleepless night, she felt as washed out as the weather.

The team were gathering at the campsite, awaiting Helen's arrival before the big push into the woods. Bentham, McAndrew and Reid were on site, as was Joseph Hudson, who stood with Charlie now, sneaking one last cigarette before battle commenced. The new boy seemed to be gelling well with the team, taking the time to talk to the junior officers, as well as some of the uniforms, but he cleaved close to Charlie this morning, keen to get the lie of the land from one of his most experienced colleagues.

'So, what's she like to work for?'

'Helen?'

Hudson nodded, as if the answer were obvious.

'Good. Better than good, in fact.'

'Because?'

'Because she cares. Because she works harder than anyone else. Because she gets the job done. And . . . because she's loyal.'

'You two been working together for a long time?'

'A few years.'

'Can't do your prospects any harm, working with someone like DI Grace.'

71

'Sure, but that's not why I do it. I do it because she makes me a better police officer. If you want to learn, you've come to the right place.'

'Amen to that.'

He took a final drag on his cigarette, before stubbing it out and tossing it into a nearby bin.

'She's never been tempted to move on? Get promoted to a new patch?'

'She likes Southampton.'

'Does she have family here?'

'No.'

'A husband?'

'I expect you know the answer to that. But, no, she doesn't. Helen doesn't do relationships. How about yourself?'

Hudson looked up at Charlie, smiling, as if amused by her concerted move to turn the spotlight back on him.

'I *was* married. When I was working in London. But it didn't work out and I never really made a connection with anyone in Liverpool. Didn't speak the lingo, you know.'

Charlie nodded. She assumed the handsome DS would be a catch anywhere, but it was true his well-spoken, southern accent would have made him stand out.

'Well, maybe you'll have better luck here. We don't mind posh boys.'

Charlie finished her coffee, but continued to cling to the cup, keen to harvest what warmth she could. Try as she might, she just couldn't shake off the cold this morning.

'And is it true?'

Charlie looked up at Hudson and was surprised to see him hesitate for the first time.

'Is it true what they wrote about her? About what she went through in prison? About all that stuff with Robert Stonehill?'

Charlie's eyes narrowed. She was naturally protective of Helen and didn't like anyone prying into areas which were hurtful to her. The newspapers had taken great delight in regurgitating all the details of Helen's relationship with murdered dominator Jake Elder, of her dangerous tussle with her vengeful nephew Stonehill, which had landed her in HMP Holloway. Over the numerous days of their coverage, they had added all manner of detail that was salacious, misleading or untrue, meaning every man and his dog thought he knew Charlie's old friend inside and out. The real Helen was very different to the newspaper caricatures – but Charlie was not prepared to share this with someone she barely knew.

'You don't want to go believing everything you read,' she shot back. 'But if you're really curious, why don't you ask her yourself?'

Charlie nodded over his shoulder towards Helen, who had parked her bike and was now striding over to them. Charlie was amused to see Hudson straighten up, dropping his cheeky smile, like a private awaiting inspection.

'Everyone ready?'

'Sure thing,' Charlie replied, turning to Helen as she approached. 'I'm leading Team A to the north. DS Hudson will take Team B south and you're on point with Team C.'

'Everyone got their maps, the prescribed route?'

'Yup, and radios have been checked and distributed. We're on band three.'

Charlie handed Helen a radio. She took it swiftly, flicking the frequency to the required band.

'Then let's do it.'

Turning, Helen marched off towards the fringes of the wood, where the rest of the officers were now gathered. Hudson followed close behind and finally Charlie too. Normally, big operations of this kind excited her but today she couldn't shake a nagging feeling of unease. Perhaps it was the scale of the task, perhaps it was the menacing clouds, but something seemed to be taking its toll on her mood today. She tried her best to slough off her anxiety, but even as she put her best foot forward, the rain started to fall. Sharp, spiteful rain. It was as if the weather itself was conspiring against them, mocking their endeavours.

Was it the gloomy vista of the forest that depressed her? Or the memory of Martin's haunting face? Whichever, there was no way she could let her feelings show, so, marshalling her team, she led them forward, driving into the depths of the forest, hoping that concerted activity might quell her growing fears.

24

She tugged anxiously at the curtains, peering outside. The journalist who'd appeared on her doorstep last night hadn't reappeared, but Janice Smith couldn't shake the feeling that she was out there somewhere. Her cover story of a workplace survey was obviously nonsense – it was no coincidence she'd turned up at their house on the same day that Janice had made her shocking discovery. She was after her story, pure and simple.

The very thought of this made Janice feel queasy. Because it meant it was all real. She still couldn't really fathom it, couldn't process what had befallen her. She had gone out to work as usual yesterday – up with the lark to check on the nests. It was the part of her job that she enjoyed the most, striding through the forest at first light, the dew fresh on her shoes. She loved the stillness early in the day, the sense that the world was just awakening. Few ventured where she did, into the hidden recesses of the forest, and she often wandered along the faint tracks in a world of her own. Yesterday morning had been the same – until she'd been brutally yanked from her daydreaming.

She hadn't been able to take it in at first, assuming it must be some kind of prank. Students mucking about. A local artist perhaps, with a weird sense of humour. Even a TV show with hidden cameras. But inside she knew the sight in front of her was too macabre to be any of those things. Creeping slowly towards it, her heart thumping in her chest, she had taken in the arrow flights, the thick, clotted blood around the wounds. And then she knew.

It was the first dead body she'd seen, barring her parents of course. But they had been serene, peaceful, beautifully presented for their wakes. This body was brutal and ugly and Janice had felt the nausea rising in her as she stared at it. Turning away, she stumbled from the clearing, scrabbling for her phone. Panicking, flustered, she dropped her mobile on the forest floor, and even when she did have it in her hands again was all fingers and thumbs. It took her several attempts to successfully dial 999.

Everything that had happened since then had been pro-gressively more unreal. Giving her statement to the police. The phone calls with senior management. The journalist ringing her doorbell . . . Fortunately, David had been on hand to comfort and support her, hurrying from work to pick her up. He had been by her side throughout what had become an increasingly distressing day and he had held her close last night, as they strived in vain for sleep. This morn-ing he'd insisted on staying at home, but she had shooed him out. It would have been nice to have him with her, but they couldn't afford for him not to work and what was there to say? She'd given her statement and hoped that would be an end to it. She would take a few days to get her head straight – HR had insisted on that – then she would return to work. Simple as that.

Now, however, she regretted pushing him out of the house. She'd done the housework, watched a bit of TV, tried to keep herself busy. But that awful image kept intruding – the half-naked corpse rotating back and forth . . . She tried to shut it out, but it lingered, insistent, horrifying. Suddenly she longed for company, for distraction. The walls seemed to be closing in on her, but she refused to bother David again – he seemed to spend most of his life propping her up. She refused to be *weak*. No, she would have to deal with this herself, by going about her life as normal, getting on with things. Which meant going out – to Tesco's, to the garden centre, anywhere.

Peering out, Janice searched the close, looking for anything out of the ordinary. As usual, everything was quiet. There was a red Corsa she didn't recognize, parked a few doors up, but the woman inside seemed to be engaged on a phone call and paid their house no heed. So, summoning her courage, Janice snatched up her coat and shopping bag and hurried outside, hoping to lose herself in the real world.

25

It was like nowhere else on earth.

Helen had ventured into the New Forest on many occasions, but it still surprised and overwhelmed her. It was not just its scale, nor its unique character, the thousands of wild horses and donkeys that roamed its many miles of woodland giving the place an untamed, even mystical feel. It was the sense of history you felt as you walked under the towering trees that always struck Helen most forcibly.

She was working her way east from the campsite, her team spread out around her, eyes peeled for any sign of human presence. They had started early, as the tourists, hikers and campers would be active later, and for now the forest was eerily quiet. As she padded through the hushed woodland, Helen's mind turned on those who had gone before. The path she was following had been walked by Celts, Romans, Vikings, Normans and more. Thousands, possibly hundreds of thousands of souls had sought sanctuary in the forest over the years, had lived, died and perhaps even been buried here. Layers of history, real lives, were literally under her feet, concealed beneath the forest's ancient soil. How many secrets were hidden from view, tantalizingly close, yet for ever obscured? As ever in life, the truth lay just beneath the surface.

Helen's mind flashed back to a crime committed centuries ago. William Rufus, son of the famous Conqueror, shot and killed by an arrow in this very forest. It was an uncomfortable coincidence – local legend suggesting Rufus's ghost still stalked the forest, seeking his killer – but not one Helen had shared with the team. She didn't think it had any bearing on the current investigation – that was too far-fetched, wasn't it? – but there was no denying the continuing legacy of that infamous death on the landscape.

Murder or hunting accident? The debate continued in academic circles, but today tourists could visit the Rufus stone, the alleged spot where the arrow struck. Or wade through Tyrrell's Ford, the stream the king's killer, the unfortunate Walter Tyrrell, crossed when fleeing his pursuers. It was a crime that was imprinted on the very fabric of the forest, a disquieting echo of the present-day barbarity. Was it possible the killer was aware of this parallel? Or was there another reason he or she had chosen such an unusual weapon?

The truth was they wouldn't know until they found Nathaniel Martin, until they engineered a break in this troubling case. Motive, opportunity, the very nature of the attack itself – so many aspects of this crime remained shrouded in mystery, which was why today's operation was so important. If they were wrong, if Martin wasn't hiding in the confines of the forest, what then? News of the crime would break soon enough and Helen was determined to have solid progress to report before then.

But a breakthrough seemed a long way off. The vista in front of Helen was serene, birdsong the only disturbance amid the deathly calm. The three teams had been at work for an hour already, the officers patiently stalking the quiet landscape, searching in vain for a sighting, a clue, anything. But perhaps this was how it was always going to be in a forest that kept its secrets close.

26

Charlie crested the fallen tree, landing deftly on the other side. As she did so, she scanned the way ahead, her eyes darting here and there. She and the team had walked in total silence for over an hour now, probing and evaluating everything they saw. They had searched thick foliage, peered into deep holes and even cast their eyes up the mighty trunks that towered above them. But they had uncovered nothing of interest and Charlie now raised a hand, signalling for the team to halt. Slowly the officers gathered around her, seeking temporary shelter from the increasingly heavy rain.

'Let's take five. You've all got water and cereal bars. For those of you who need a loo break, there are loads of bushes around.'

A couple of officers hurried off, while the rest refreshed themselves. Taking a swig of water, Charlie pulled her radio from her belt.

'Team C, this is Team A,' she said, clearly but quietly. 'We've reached our first rest point. Nothing to report, over.'

There was a pause, then Helen's voice crackled through her handset.

'Ditto. Stay in touch. Over.'

Charlie turned the volume down, as Helen checked in with Hudson's team, who had little to report either. Turning away from her colleagues, Charlie took a step deeper into the forest, her eyes wandering over its rich, green fabric. The others were grateful for the rest, an opportunity to break the tension by sharing a joke or two, but Charlie didn't feel like small talk. The truth was she felt indescribably anxious.

This was natural enough, she told herself, they were sweeping the forest for a suspected killer. But it was more than that. Charlie had a strong sense that they were the weaker party here, that their quarry had an advantage. While attempting to be silent in their progress, it no doubt sounded like they were crashing and lumbering about to anyone who knew the forest well. Indeed, they had already disturbed numerous birds, advertising their presence to anyone lurking close by.

Charlie told herself she was being paranoid, but right from the off she'd had the strong sense that they were being watched. On a number of occasions, she thought she felt a presence close by – to the side, just behind, in the bush to the left. She had spun, hoping to catch sight of this voyeur, only to find the forest staring back at her. Was she mad? Or was someone – or something – out there right now, watching them?

'DS Brooks?'

Charlie jumped, startled by the sudden intrusion. Turning, she found one of the uniformed officers staring at her.

'The boys are ready to crack on, if you are.'

'Of course.'

Charlie tried to retain her professional front, but the officer knew he'd spooked her. Her heart pounding, Charlie signalled to her fellow CID officers to follow the uniforms' lead. It was time to resume the hunt.

On they went, Charlie taking point, as they spread out to cover the widest area in the shortest possible time. Gradually her heartbeat began to slow, the sweat on her brow receding, but the sense that they were being watched wouldn't go. It gnawed away at her, her brain fighting her strong instinct that she and the team were in danger.

There was nothing to do but press on, however, so she strode boldly forward, looking this way and that, even as the rain continued to beat out the rhythm of her anxiety.

27

She was biding her time, waiting for the right moment to strike.

Emilia had pretended to be on a heated phone call, lingering in her car as the timorous Janice Smith emerged from her house and scurried away down the road. She had given her a head start, then hopped out of her car in pursuit. Emilia enjoyed tailing people – she was good at it now – and this morning's assignment presented few challenges. The nervous middle-aged woman was scuttling along quickly, but had no idea she was being followed. Better still, she was alone.

Before long they were on the high street, Janice passing the time of day with an acquaintance, before darting into Sainsbury's. Emilia was close behind, feigning interest in the magazines, while Janice dithered in the fruit and veg section. Eventually, however, the forestry worker moved on, heading deeper into the supermarket. Now Emilia came alive, shadowing her prey until finally Janice Smith came to a halt in a deserted aisle.

She was in the freezer section, a place shoppers tended not to linger because of the icy chill. This suited Emilia perfectly – she didn't want an audience – and she strode forward to intercept the unsuspecting woman.

'Janice?'

She looked up from the frozen peas, confused.

'Sorry?'

'Janice, I'm Emilia Garanita. Senior Crime Reporter from the *Southampton Evening News*.'

She handed Janice her business card.

'I was wondering if I could have a very quick word? I understand you've had a terrible shock.'

The woman stared at her, stupefied.

'There's a café here. I could buy you a cup of tea, something to eat perhaps?'

Emilia gently removed the peas from Janice's hand and placed them back in the freezer.

'How do you know about . . . ?' Janice finally stammered.

'The police have made an official statement,' Emilia lied, lowering her voice as she continued, 'naming the victim, the circumstances of the murder . . .'

None of this was pre-planned, it just came naturally, which pleased Emilia immensely. She was always able to lie instantly and with total conviction.

'I don't know, I . . .'

'Janice, I appreciate it's hard to talk about. You had an awful shock yesterday, something you were totally unprepared for. It's no surprise you're still coming to terms with it. I would be just the same, believe me.'

She laid a comforting hand on her arm.

'But it is best to talk about these things. And, being honest with you, it's best to do it now. The story is out there, which means the press are going to want to know who found the body, why they were there. I'm afraid you're going to be the subject of *considerable* interest . . .'

Janice Smith looked horrified at the prospect.

'. . . and the best way to protect yourself, and your husband, is to get your story out there as soon as possible. Once it's done, it's done. There'll be nothing there for the journalists and they will move on. They're not stupid . . .'

Janice was clearly wavering, shocked by Emilia's sudden approach, but also partly convinced by her argument.

'I'm not sure I can . . .' Her breathing was getting quicker, she seemed flustered, upset. 'I'm not sure I *want* to talk about it. It was so awful . . .'

'I know, but trust me, Janice. You'll feel better for it. Now why don't I take that for you . . .' She took the heavy shopping basket from her. '. . . and let's get that cup of tea. I know I could do with one.'

It was over, the battle was won. A shaky Janice allowed herself to be guided down the aisle towards the café. She seemed simultaneously nervous but grateful for the support. Emilia was happy to offer it, confident now that Janice Smith was going to give her exactly what she wanted.

28

Charlie stole a look at her watch and was dismayed to find that several hours had passed. It was approaching noon and still they had nothing to show for their endeavours. All three teams were deep in the forest now, scattered over a wide area of virgin woodland, but their constant searching had failed to locate Campbell's route to the clearing or any evidence of his attacker's whereabouts. With each dogged step, a tiny sliver of optimism seemed to evaporate – Charlie could tell that her team were cold, dispirited and, above all, soaked, the rain continuing to pour down on the unfortunate party.

Some of the back markers were beginning to drag their feet and Charlie knew that she should probably call time for lunch, give her bedraggled team some time to dry off. But something stopped her. Was it just frustration? Her desire to have something positive to report? Or was it that little voice inside her, reminding her that an important discovery could be just around the corner? She had listened to that voice before and been proved right, though never in circumstances as forlorn or hopeless as this.

She picked up her pace slightly, anger mingling with determination. Ten more minutes. She would give it ten more minutes and then –

Suddenly, she saw it. Movement up ahead. It was concealed by dense foliage, but she felt certain she had seen a shape moving. Something sizeable, something dark, shadowing their progress. Acting on instinct, she changed direction sharply, sprinting towards the bush. Immediately, the shape reacted, darting away fast. Haring round the bush, Charlie was just in time to glimpse a tall figure disappearing into the trees.

'Over here!' Charlie shouted over her shoulder, her eyes glued to the retreating form. 'Suspect at two o'clock.'

Then she was off, slaloming through the trees, desperate not to lose sight of him. For an awful moment, she thought he'd vanished, but then a flash of movement to the right, followed by the loud squawk of a pheasant. Now Charlie had a bead on her quarry and she powered forward. All thoughts of her morning tiredness were gone – she was focused, full of energy.

The fleeing shape knew the forest well, changing direction sharply, constantly disappearing from view, before suddenly reappearing far ahead. But Charlie kept pace, clutching her radio in one hand, her baton in the other, as she hurdled the fallen branches that littered the dense woodland. She suddenly felt convinced that Martin – for surely it must be him? – would soon be in custody, that despite his natural advantage there would be no escape.

Ducking a low branch, she came across a small stream. She crested it without difficulty, landing gracefully on the other side. As she did so, she looked around for signs of the fleeing figure, but he was nowhere to be seen. Where the hell had he gone?

Pad, pad, pad. Charlie froze, certain she could hear something. Yes, there it was again. Somewhere in the quiet woodland, she could hear footsteps creeping away. Straining, she tried to locate the sound. Turning slowly, she followed the direction of the river – and then she saw him. Or at least his shadow, skirting the edge of the stream. Carefully, she took a step towards him, then another. And suddenly he was off again. Despite her caution, she'd been spotted.

Charlie exploded into action, hurling herself along the

riverbank, eating up the yards between herself and her prey. Was he tiring now or had he hurt himself? Either way, Charlie felt certain she was gaining on him. She clutched her baton in readiness, bracing herself for a fight.

On they went, hunter and hunted straining every sinew. The fugitive stumbled on a log, allowing Charlie to close the distance . . . then she too lost her balance, catching her foot in a rabbit hole and crashing down onto the path, raking her palms and knees on the rough ground. Even before she had come to a halt, however, she was scrambling up again. She raced forward, around a huge oak, before coming face to face with a dense bank of gorse.

The fugitive was nowhere in sight, but Charlie felt sure he must have come this way. And now, as she moved forward, she saw a gap in the seemingly forbidding barrier. It was large enough for an adult to squeeze through and was an attractive escape route. Crouching down to avoid the vicious spines, Charlie pushed through.

The bush was large and dense, clawing at Charlie, but eventually she emerged from it, to find herself in a small clearing. She was alone, but to her surprise she glimpsed a dwelling on the far side, perfectly camouflaged, yet visible from her vantage point.

Charlie cast warily around the clearing. It was the perfect spot for someone who wanted to remain hidden, surrounded on all sides by dense foliage. If there *were* any paths in this part of the forest, you could happily follow them without ever spotting this discreet spot. But where was its occupant? Had he retreated inside? Or was he hiding in the bushes, waiting to strike?

A faint crackle from her radio. Charlie hesitated, then turned the volume down. She daren't risk announcing her presence and, besides, she had no idea where she was, even if she had wanted to summon help. Raising her baton, she moved forward, taking a cautious step towards the hut, which she now realized was made entirely from forest materials. The frame and roof were made of wood, while animal hides hung down over the door and windows, shielding the interior from view. Outside, hanging over a smouldering fire, was a small cooking pot, containing some kind of porridge or oatmeal. And around it, running in a perfect circle as if protecting the pot, were a series of stakes, proudly displaying future meals. A skinned rabbit hung on the nearest one, its flesh livid and pink, its glassy eye staring at Charlie. A couple of birds hung on the next, their feet bound together, their beaks touching as if in an embrace. And, beyond that, was something that looked like a weasel, its mouth hanging open as if it was about to laugh.

The sight sent a shiver down Charlie's spine, the presence of death unnerving her. Her eyes cautiously reconnoitring the clearing, she moved forward, hoping for a glimpse of her fugitive, but he remained hidden. She took a step towards the hut. Then another. Immediately, something sprang up at her, smashing into her calves. Charlie let out a howl of pain, her baton falling from her hand, as she stumbled wildly, before managing to right herself. Looking down, she was aghast to see that she had stepped on a mantrap. The spring had triggered and its vicious metal jaws were now clamped around her leg.

Reaching down, she tried to jam her fingers between her flesh and the metal. The pain was unbearable, the pressure seeming to grow with each passing second, but the trap resisted, mocking her attempts to prise it open. She tried again, digging her fingers into her flesh . . . but it was impossible.

And now she became aware of something else. Footsteps

approaching her. Instinctively, she lunged for her baton, but she was too slow. A boot kicked it away, the baton skittering away into the undergrowth. Jerking back, Charlie reared up to defend herself.

To find herself face to face with Nathaniel Martin.

Joseph Hudson spun around. He felt certain he had heard something, something that sounded like a human scream. But could he be sure? The forest was teeming with birds, foxes and deer, whose cries and calls often sounded mournful, even despairing. It was easy to be fooled in this mysterious environment . . . and yet his instinct was that it was a genuine cry of alarm.

'Team A, this is Team B,' he rasped, squeezing the transmit button on his handset. 'Do you have eyes on DS Brooks? Over.'

'Negative' was DC Bentham's swift reply. 'We think she was heading north-east, but we lost her at a small stream. Over.'

Hudson clicked off, peering intently at his surroundings. The forest seemed to be taunting him today, clouding his mind with unfamiliar sounds and sights, but he knew he had to stay focused. If Charlie *had* cut north in pursuit of a suspect, then that would have brought her into his area of operation. Could the scream have come from her? Was she even now being attacked? Gesturing to the team to follow, Hudson made his decision, cutting south towards Bentham and his colleagues, now desperately searching for their leader.

Why had she run off like that? He knew the MIT had a reputation for acting first and asking questions later – Grace's influence no doubt – but still it was a crazy thing to do, given the unfamiliar terrain. To him, there could be only one explanation for such foolhardiness – Charlie Brooks had spotted

Nathaniel Martin and had been determined not to let him escape. But where had her desperate pursuit taken her?

He moved steadily forward, listening for further cries . . . but all was quiet. He would have to act on instinct now, guessing where he *thought* the sound had come from and he drove the team on.

'Eyes and ears open,' he barked at them. 'And stay together.'

They didn't need telling twice. Hudson could tell his fellow officers were desperate to find Brooks too, but none were willing to mirror her impetuousness and risk ending up alone in a strange part of the forest.

Pushing his own fears aside, Hudson marched on, scanning the woodland ahead of him. He was scared, but also excited too. The adrenaline was coursing through him, his senses in overdrive. Anxious though he was – for Brooks, for his team – there was also a part of him that thrilled to be in on the chase. He had become bored with the familiar routine of life in Liverpool – the same old faces, the same old crimes – and he had applied to Southampton Central, hoping to find himself in situations just like this. This was life at the sharp end. This was where policing *mattered*.

It had been a long time since he'd felt revitalized by his profession, but he was feeling it today. A colleague was missing, a suspect was on the loose, danger threatened on all sides. And now that it was a matter of life and death, Joseph Hudson was determined to make his presence count.

30

'Charlie, this is Helen . . . Can you hear me? Over.'

Helen had dispensed with the formalities, repeatedly appealing to Charlie by name. But, as before, she was met by silence. Where could she be? And why was she not responding? Perhaps she had dropped her radio, or turned it off to avoid giving away her position? The alternative was that she was being prevented from contacting them by something, or someone. Charlie was an experienced, battle-hardened officer, who was more than capable of taking care of herself, but suddenly Helen was very concerned.

She was half jogging, half sprinting, determined to find Charlie, but conscious of the need to keep her team with her. However worried she was about her old friend, there could be no question of losing one of her own, leaving them isolated and vulnerable. In police work, you had to deal with what was in front of you, what you could influence, and Helen knew she had to keep the pack together during their desperate hunt.

They drove deeper into the forest. Helen had lost her bearings now – the map had proved to be unfit for purpose and her GPS was struggling to keep up, but the Compass app on her iPhone helped her gauge her rough direction and she bent her steps north. With Hudson heading south, she was hoping they would eventually converge on Charlie, but it was hard to be confident in such unfamiliar surroundings. They might miss each other entirely, miss Charlie – with potentially disastrous consequences.

Where was she? Helen had a sickening feeling that something terrible had happened to her old friend. Unbidden, an image of Jessica popped into her head, Charlie's only child and *her* godchild, but she pushed it away. If her friend was in danger, she had to keep alert, had to suppress her fears. There was no point imagining the worst until confronted by it.

The path seemed to peter out now and, acting on instinct, Helen veered left. The forest seemed to be less dense in that direction, meaning they could maintain their steady progress. She could hear a few of her team stumbling behind, tiring now, but Helen urged them on and now, through the bushes ahead, she spied clear ground – a clearing of some kind, not one she'd noticed before. Ducking low, she pushed through the spiky bush and emerged into the open – only to stop dead in her tracks, stunned by the sight in front of her.

Death had visited this remote part of the forest – a body lying prone in the middle of the clearing. But it was not that of her colleague and friend. In fact, it wasn't human at all. As the rest of the team joined her, Helen took in the felled pony that lay rigid and lifeless on the forest floor. It was hard to think that something – or someone – would willingly slay such a graceful beast, but they had. The horse lay on its side, staring placidly up at the forest canopy, three vicious-looking crossbow bolts embedded in its flank.

Bending down, Helen felt a sudden rush of anger, of sadness. There was something about the sight of the prone horse that felt profoundly wrong, as if someone had killed a unicorn. The wild horses that grazed the forest were an integral part of its habitat, helping to keep the forest in good condition. They harmed no one and visitors to the New Forest were charmed by them. But someone had hunted this one down and butchered it, leaving it to rot in the heart of the forest. The horse had not yet started to decompose, so had presumably been killed relatively recently, but the early signs of decay were there. A good deal of flesh was missing from one of the horse's legs, presumably taken by a fox. Maggots too were forming in the wounds, even as the flies buzzed round the horse's eyes, nostrils and mouth, seeking sustenance.

Straightening up, Helen turned to DC Reid.

'Stay here and call it in. We need Meredith Walker down here, asap.'

Reid nodded, pulling out his phone and holding it high in the air, desperately searching for a signal. Helen, meanwhile, gestured to the others to continue their drive north. Charlie was in danger and every second wasted increased the chances of her coming to harm.

The clock was ticking now.

31

A bead of sweat slid down Charlie's cheek. Her captor had barely said a word since his sudden appearance, merely staring at her as he took in her predicament. Whether he was enjoying her pain or trying to divine her reasons for intruding, she couldn't tell. His face was devoid of emotion.

'I'm Detective Sergeant Charlie Brooks,' she blurted out, ignoring the throbbing pain in her leg. 'I'm here with dozens of other officers from Hampshire Police –'

'Where are they then?' he replied calmly.

'Here, in the forest,' Charlie insisted, gesturing around her. 'Big place . . .'

His tone was knowing, even triumphant. Walking past Charlie towards the hut, he paused by a block of wood. Charlie had noticed the hatchet already, had been alarmed by its large blade. Even more so now, as Martin picked it up, toying with it a little, before slamming it down into the wood. Charlie winced at the impact, watching with alarm as the axe split the wood in two.

'Guess it's just you and me for now.'

'That's right, Nathaniel. And I'd like to talk to you.'

Martin reacted, looking puzzled, even a little angry.

'There's nobody of that name here. That guy died a *long* time ago . . .'

'Ok, if you'd like me to call you something else –'

'Shhhh . . .'

He put his finger to his lips as he hissed out his order. Even as he did so, he laid his hand on the axe, wrenching it from the splintered wood. His back was to her now and Charlie slid two fingers inside her jacket pocket. Her radio was nestling there and if she could hit the transmission button –

'I'll take that.'

Charlie froze. He wasn't even looking at her, yet somehow he *knew*. Turning, he walked towards her. In one hand he carried the axe, the other reached out to her, gesturing to her to comply. With half an eye on the axe's wicked blade, she teased the radio out of her pocket and handed it to him. Dropping it on the floor, he stamped on it, once, twice, the radio disintegrating under the weight of his attack.

'And the rest?'

He gestured to her again.

She reached inside her jacket.

'Careful now . . .'

Deliberately slowly, she removed her pepper spray from her pocket, then her warrant card.

'That's it.'

A quick sniff of the spray, then he tossed it aside, concentrating on her ID instead. He looked at her photo, then pulled her business card from her wallet.

'DS Charlene Brooks. Major Incident Team . . .'

He wrapped his mouth around the last three words, as he slipped the card into his pocket. Immediately memories of his brutal attack on a police officer – snapshots of the young man's fractured skull – shot into Charlie's mind.

'What are you doing all the way out here, Charlene?'

The way he said her name was unnerving. Part of her wanted to scream and shout, but the mantrap held her firmly in place and there was no way help would arrive before the axe came crashing down. She needed to keep him talking.

'I was looking for you.'

'Looking for *me* . . . ? Why would you be doing that?'

He turned to face her. Charlie felt the heat of his gaze, his desire to intimidate her, but she met him head on, refusing to be cowed.

'Because someone was murdered, in the forest.'

There was no point dressing it up. He would smell lies.

'Does that surprise you?'

His question certainly did. She had been expecting a fierce denial or a tacit admission of guilt.

'Yes.'

'It doesn't me.'

'I don't understand –'

'Look around you, Officer Brooks, the evidence is under your nose.'

Charlie's eyes flitted from Martin to the axe, to the lifeless animals skewered on wooden stakes.

'We are under siege. Mother is hurting . . .'

'You mean the forest?'

'Mother is hurting, her children too. They cut us. Cut, cut, cut . . .'

The axe swung back and forth in time with his anger.

'Slash, burn, slash, burn. Mother used to be beautiful, but now she is ugly, she is *defaced*. The rot started a long time ago . . .'

He took a step closer. Charlie tried to shuffle backwards, but the metal jaws pinned her to the soil.

'Is that what all this is about? You want to protect yourself? Protect the forest?'

She was talking as much to quell her fear, as to keep him engaged.

'Everybody has the right to defend themselves. Against *intruders*.'

His eyes were fixed on her, but Charlie's were riveted to

the axe. She was in range now and had no means of defending herself.

'Is that why you did it? Is that why you targeted Woodland View? Because they had invaded your territory?'

A shadow passed across his face, a reaction to the mention of the campsite, then he crouched down, so he was now eye level with Charlie. He reached out to her and instinctively Charlie jerked backwards, expecting him to grab her head and stove it in. But instead, he ran a grimy finger down her cheek.

'That's what you do in the wild, Charlene. When you see vermin . . .' His finger rested on her mouth, teasing her lips open with his dirty fingernail. '. . . you exterminate it.'

32

The thorns ripped across her face, roughly jagging her skin. Helen came to a juddering halt, regretting her decision to plunge through the wild roses that had blocked her path. Swallowing down the pain, she disentangled herself carefully, then ran her fingers across her neck and cheek. Fresh blood, rich and crimson, stained her fingertips. Wiping it angrily on her trousers, she tugged at the bush, ripping the offending branches clean off, opening up the way ahead.

They were keeping up a desperate pace, but at each turn the forest frustrated them. First, they had stumbled across a pool that was too deep to wade across. Then one of the uniformed officers had sprained his ankle, requiring one of his colleagues to remain behind. The rapidly diminishing band had soldiered on, but the bushes and branches tore at them, hampering their progress, challenging them to give up the chase. There was no question of that, but morale was dipping fast.

There was no sign of Charlie, nor her team. Hudson's group also continued to elude them, so Helen yanked her radio from her belt once more.

'Team B, this is Team C. What's your location, over?'

There was a long pause, then Hudson's voice crackled into life.

'Uncertain. We've been heading south-east for twenty, twenty-five minutes. There's no sign of Officer Brooks, nor her team, over.'

'Can you identify any landmarks? Anything we can place you by?' Helen replied desperately.

'We've just had to go around a large pool. We lost some time there . . . but it was too deep to cross. According to the map, I think it's called Florian's Cup, but I can't be sure, over.'

Helen swore under her breath. She was sure this was the same pool her team had recently circumnavigated – heading in the *opposite* direction.

'Stop where you are. Head due east. It's the one area we haven't tried, over.'

'Roger that, over.'

Gesturing to the rest of her team, Helen turned tail, heading back in the direction they had come. There were a few suppressed groans, but Helen didn't care. Thanks to her incompetence, they had failed Charlie, losing her in the wilderness, to face her fate alone. They had one last chance to make a difference, one last part of the woodland to explore and she would sweat blood until they had done so.

It was now or never.

33

Charlie writhed on the ground, desperately trying to keep her captor in view. He was circling her slowly, enjoying her fear. The axe rested lazily on his shoulder, its blade pointing up in the air.

'Please don't hurt me . . .'

Martin said nothing, continuing his lazy circle.

'I have a child, a little girl . . .'

Her captor waved this away, as if it was unimportant. Charlie knew Martin didn't have any children and was estranged from his parents.

'I haven't done anything wrong . . .' she moaned, desperate now.

'But you're trespassing, Officer Brooks. This is my *home*,' he replied, gesturing at the camouflaged hut. 'You are an intruder. And the law says I can defend myself against intruders, doesn't it?'

Charlie felt a sharp spike of fear, as Martin came to a halt in front of her.

'Please, Nathaniel, look at me . . .'

Martin shook his head quickly, as if wishing his name away.

'I am a human being, a mother . . .'

She stressed the last word, hoping it would have some effect on him.

'And I'm defenceless. There's no law, natural or otherwise, that can justify harming someone who is at your mercy.'

She was gabbling now, but she had to puncture his defences somehow. Martin seemed unmoved, however, shrugging gently, as he took a step towards her.

'Even so, it's time the boot was on the other foot . . .'

As he spoke, he raised his right leg, pressing down hard on Charlie's left shin.

'You people have been chipping away at me for years.'

Charlie's ankle was trapped, immobile, the pain building steadily as Martin increased the pressure. One hard push now and her ankle would snap. The pain was intense, making Charlie feel dizzy and faint.

'Please . . .' she murmured.

'You've abused me, attacked me . . .'

'Please, Nathaniel, don't do this . . .'

'. . . tortured me. Have you any idea what I've been through?'

Charlie could hazard a guess – anyone who's taken an iron bar to a serving police officer could expect a rough time in prison.

'I'm sorry if we hurt you,' Charlie gasped. 'But that wasn't me, I would never –'

'Never what? You came to arrest me, didn't you?'

'Yes, but –'

'Then you're no better than the rest of them.'

He put his full weight on her leg. She tried to resist, but the pain, the pressure was unbearable.

'And you're going to pay for it,' he continued savagely.

Charlie gasped in pain and terror. Any second now her ankle would break and the axe would come down on her head. This was it then – the day she'd often feared would come.

Then suddenly shouting. The voices were close by, but Charlie couldn't tell where.

'DS Brooks?'

Martin paused, instinctively easing the pressure on her leg.

'DS Brooks? Can you hear me?'

Charlie recognized Hudson's voice.

'I'm here,' Charlie screamed. 'I'm over here!'

Martin turned to her, furious. Their private hell had been penetrated and she was no longer at his mercy.

'I'm here, help me, please!'

Several voices answered her, their volume growing all the time. Bodies could now be heard crashing through the bush. Martin glared at her, naked anger contorting his expression. Without warning, he suddenly spat in her face. Then he raised his axe above his head, but as he did so, Hudson crashed into the clearing, looking determined and energized.

Immediately, Martin dropped the axe and ran. Sprinting hard across the clearing, the fugitive pushed through the animal hides into the hut, disappearing from view. Charlie watched him go, relief tumbling over her fear.

She had survived.

34

A moment's hesitation, then Joseph Hudson raced over to his colleague. Other members of his team were still emerging from the undergrowth, breathless and confused, unnerved by the strange sight in front of them. It was as if they had stumbled on the dark heart of the forest.

'You ok?'

Charlie nodded mutely. Casting his eyes down to check for injuries, he winced as he took in the wicked metal jaws clamped around her left ankle.

'Get that off *now*,' he roared at a pair of uniformed officers, who rushed over to assist.

Straightening up, Hudson gestured to the others.

'The rest of you, with me.'

They moved swiftly across the clearing. Hudson had seen Martin drop the axe and pelt into the hut. He knew it was his duty to bring him in, but he slowed as he approached his bolt-hole. He had no idea what might be inside and couldn't risk putting himself, or his colleagues, in danger. He could imagine Martin waiting for them, his crossbow primed and ready, and had no desire to be in the firing line.

'Spread out. Form a circle.'

Reid, Osbourne and the remaining uniforms responded, surrounding the cannibalized dwelling. There would be no escape for Martin now – the only question was whether blood would be spilt before he was in custody. Pulling his radio from his belt, Hudson hit the transmission button.

'Team C, this is Team B, over. We have the suspect

trapped, but have no eyes on him. Should we proceed or wait, over?'

A brief pause, then Helen's voice responded.

'If it's safe to do so, bring him in, over.'

'Roger that. We are in a clearing five minutes east of the pool. Officer Brooks is injured, but safe, over.'

Clicking off, Hudson returned his attention to the hut.

'Nathaniel, I'm DS Hudson. You are surrounded now. You have one minute to exit, with your hands on your head.'

He was met by silence.

'If you have not complied by that time, then we will have no choice but to forcibly apprehend you. Do you understand?'

Still nothing. Was Martin sweating in there, cowed and contemplating surrender? Or was he raising his crossbow? Hudson fervently hoped it was the former.

'Thirty seconds, Nathaniel.'

Hudson shot a glance at DC Lucas, who looked as tense as him. Hudson slowly counted down in his head. Ten, nine, eight, seven . . .

But he knew Martin wasn't coming, the minute elapsing with no sign of movement within. Bracing himself, Hudson crept forward. The other officers followed suit, closing in on the hut. Ushering them to stay to the side, out of the direct line of fire, Hudson took a further step towards the entrance. It consisted of a large animal hide hanging down in front of a gap in the wooden frame. Carefully taking hold of the bottom edge of the hide, Hudson whipped it open, lurching to the left as he did so, shielding himself from view on the other side of the wooden door frame.

But the expected counterattack didn't materialize. What was Martin doing in there? Was he hunkered down? Cowering in the corner? Was it even possible he had taken his own life to avoid capture? Craning his neck round the doorpost,

Hudson tried to peer inside. But the gloom was hard to penetrate and he could only make out shadows. What should he do, stick or twist? It would be safer to wait, but it would take ages for an armed unit to arrive, even if they could find the clearing. Besides, something told him that this was his first big test.

He darted to the other side of the open doorway, making it across unscathed. He could see little from this side either, so turned to DC Lucas, whispering:

'Follow me and stay low . . .'

He mouthed a silent countdown, then swung into the hut, keeping his head down. He was crouched ready to spring, his baton clasped in his hand . . . but the hut was empty.

Nathaniel Martin had vanished.

35

'Maniac loose in the forest.'

It wasn't her most inspired headline, but it would do the job. Whether you were a local planning a weekend in the forest or a tourist arriving for a week's camping, you couldn't help but be alarmed by the *Evening News* banner headline.

Emilia had expected something juicy, but still Janice Smith's testimony had knocked her for six. Racing back to the office, Emilia had texted David Spivack, her mole at Southampton Central mortuary, to confirm the identity of the victim, before phoning Gardiner, telling him to hold the front ten pages. Pleasingly, he had complied, shelving everything else to ensure the story had maximum impact. Thanks to Janice Smith, Emilia had detailed knowledge of the facts – the location, the weapon used – not to mention a horrifying, first-person description of the body itself. Emilia had majored on this aspect, lingering on the details of the corpse, riven with arrows, hanging helplessly in that eerie clearing. She had had to exercise a little artistic licence, of course, having not actually visited the crime scene herself, but that was not a problem. Embellishment and exaggeration were her stock in trade. Her editor had been delighted, Gardiner giving her a manly slap on the back, which she assumed was his version of a compliment.

Emilia was now keen to capitalize on her success, certain there was more to cull from this extraordinary story. The killer was still on the run, in possession of an unusual but lethal weapon – who's to say he wouldn't strike again? They would go into detail on campers' worries, legal controls on crossbows, speculation on motive and more, but their main thrust would be the hunt for the killer. Gardiner had already approved the establishment of a dedicated hotline for tip-offs or information regarding the perpetrator, while Emilia had updated their Facebook page *and* started a Twitter strand from her own account: #newforestkiller. It had a pleasing ring to it. Hopefully, it would soon become a repository for gossip, speculation, even leads, as well as a space for her to promote herself by dropping juicy nuggets about the on-going police investigation.

Emilia could only imagine what DI Grace and her colleagues would make of it. She had been on decent terms with the local police recently, a brief truce following her ordeal at the hands of Daisy Anderson. But she knew that her decision to write a book about the teenage killer had not gone down well at Southampton Central, as it raised ghosts that they would rather banish. How would they react now, as Emilia broke this new story before the police had even put out a press release? Tut, tut, Emilia thought to herself. The early bird catches the worm . . .

Her editor would no doubt receive the customary phone call, reminding him of his responsibilities. And Emilia herself would get the cold shoulder too. She would be accused of sensationalizing the story, of fear-mongering, but she would ride it out. If the police weren't prepared to protect the public, to warn them of the killer in their midst, then it fell to honest journalists to do it for them. Taking in the banner headline once more, Emilia felt a surge of satisfaction.

This was public service journalism at its very best.

36

'Police are appealing for witnesses to an arson attack on a church in Cromwell Road. It follows a similar incident at a synagogue on Duke Street last month. Elsewhere, residents from Bitterne Park and Harefield are meeting with police to seek reassurances following a spate of burglaries in –'

She switched stations, cutting the newsreader off. She couldn't handle more bad news today, so flicked through the musical offerings instead, settling on Heart Extra. Anodyne, cheesy and uplifting – it was what she needed.

Moving away, Lauren Scott left the shelter of the gazebo and returned to her boyfriend, who was labouring to put up their tent in the driving rain. Matteo had been bugging her for ages to go camping and she had resisted at first, arguing for a weekend in Rome instead. She was done with tents and, besides, she'd fancied something more surprising, more exotic. But Matteo was nothing if not persistent and eventually he'd ground her down. Now, however, she was having her doubts – the heavens had opened as soon as they'd arrived and a trip which had seemed romantic on paper risked becoming a damp squib.

Braving the elements, she sidled over to him, tugging at his sleeve. Matteo had been humming happily to himself, in spite of the deluge, but now stopped as he turned to her, concerned by her expression.

'Everything all right, honey?'

'Yes . . .' Lauren replied carefully, wary of bursting his bubble. 'I'm just wondering if this is a good idea, given the weather . . .'

'I'm nearly done,' Matteo countered, smiling gamely.

'It's just that the forecast says it's likely to rain all night.'

'The tent's brand new. We shouldn't have any problems.'

'And the temperature's already dropping.'

'Then we'll just have to snuggle up a little closer, won't we?'

He slipped an arm around her waist, pulling her to him.

'Get off me, you're all wet.'

But Matteo ignored her, planting several wet kisses on her lips. Lauren struggled, but it was half-hearted and she soon gave in, wrapping her arms around him. Kissing her once more, Matteo removed a stray hair from her face.

'You know I've been looking forward to this all week, that I want to spend the night with you under the stars,' he murmured. 'But . . . if you want to go home, we'll go now. Straight away. Because I love you . . .'

He kissed her again.

'And I want you to be happy . . .'

Another stolen kiss.

'So, tell me, what do you want to do . . . ?'

Lauren looked at him, then at the carefully assembled tent. Matteo had bought it at the weekend – a ridiculously expensive four-manner – and had been itching to give it a go ever since. His excitement had been obvious – he was like a small boy going to Scout camp – which pleased and moved her. Matteo had done so much for her, had sacrificed so much to get her back on her feet, that it was great to see him doing something for himself for a change. Even the awful weather hadn't shaken his mood. It was teeming down, but Matteo was happily sodden, having previously promised to whip off his clothes – and hers – as soon as they were in the tent.

'Ok, just this once,' she relented, reluctantly. 'But next time, we *are* going on a city break . . .'

'Scout's honour.' Matteo winked, disengaging to finish his task.

She had no choice really, despite the cold and rain. Matteo would have been as good as his word, would have packed up their things there and then, if she'd insisted on going home. But how could she do that to him, after everything he'd done for *her*? He had saved her, there was no other way of putting it. So often during her life she had truly hated herself and yet here she was with a man who loved her, who supported her, who *believed* in her. It was dizzying and heart-warming, almost making her believe that happy endings were possible. Which was why she was prepared to swallow her serious misgivings and spend a night with him in the forest. Perhaps she was wrong to be so fearful, so negative.

Perhaps everything was going to be all right, after all.

37

'Are you sure you're ok?'

Helen was crouched down by Charlie, who was sheltering under a tree, wrapped in Hudson's coat. She was finally free of the mantrap, but the vicious jaws had left their mark. Charlie's leg was badly bruised and she was clearly very shaken. Helen had never seen her look so pale.

'I'm fine, really.'

'The paramedics are on their way. They will take you to South Hants for a check-up, then it's straight home.'

'I've said I'm fine –'

'You can barely walk, Charlie. And you've had a nasty scare, so this is not a request. You need time to recover.'

Helen was being firm, but her guilt would not let her do otherwise. From initial reports of her encounter with Martin, Charlie had had a narrow escape.

'No arguments, please.'

Charlie nodded, grateful for Helen's concern. Patting her affectionately on the shoulder, Helen rose and crossed the clearing towards the hut. She'd told the rest of the team not to touch anything – Meredith would be on site soon – instead sending them to search the surrounding woodland for their fugitive. He was probably long gone, but if they could work out which direction he'd taken, perhaps they could resume their hunt. In all honesty, nobody had the energy or appetite for it, but they had to try.

Pausing on the threshold of the hut, Helen took in Martin's impressive construction. There was no cement, no steel, no bricks – no manmade materials of any sort. A wooden frame and roof were supported by pillars made entirely of clay, providing a perfect, waterproof cocoon to live in. There were small openings for windows, covered by animal skins, which could be drawn across to let in light and air. It was an attractive set-up, but even more impressive on the inside. Venturing within, Helen's gaze stole over the hut's fixtures and fittings. There was a bath in the corner that appeared to be made of wood and a sturdy bed in the corner. Moving over to it, Helen tested the mattress, which she was surprised to find was made from compacted leaves. Shaking her head at his ingenuity, Helen surveyed the rest of Martin's possessions – berries preserved in jars, blankets made of rough wool and several ecological tomes, now brown and weather-worn – before turning to take in his most impressive modification. At the back of the hut, near the rear wall, was a deep hole. An animal skin, which had presumably concealed it, had been flung off, allowing Helen to crane down and peer into the abyss. The hole was in fact the mouth of a tunnel, which had been well excavated. Tall, wide, supported by wooden posts, it was easily big enough for a six-foot-plus man to scurry down.

Martin had expected this moment would come and planned accordingly. Eleanor Brown thought her former lover had lost his mind, but this strategic thinking suggested otherwise. Violent, erratic, misguided perhaps, but Martin was clearly a devious and dangerous adversary, one who would not be taken quietly. Despite a heavy police presence in the forest, he had managed to elude them.

As Helen looked around the spartan dwelling, she felt once more the weight of their failure. They had been right to target the forest, but that was all that could be said for the morning's operation. Protocols had broken down, an officer been put in danger and what had they achieved? There were no trophies from Martin's crime here or any obvious evidence linking him to Campbell's murder. Nor was there any sign of his crossbow. Worst of all, there was no sign of Martin himself.

He was out there right now, lurking in the forest, ready and primed to strike again.

38

He remained stock-still, his body rigid with tension. His pursuers were close, so close they could almost reach out and touch him.

He cursed himself for his stupidity. He had been enjoying himself so much with Brooks that he had been blind to the danger he was in. She hadn't been bluffing about her fellow officers, half a dozen of them crashing into *his* clearing moments later. Fortunately, his reactions were still quick and their caution had bought him time to make his escape.

Taking advantage of his head start, he had darted down tracks that only he knew, changing direction frequently to throw off his pursuers. But he had no idea how many there were, nor whether he risked running into a second wave of officers. So, at the first suitable opportunity, he had ended his headlong charge through the bushes. He had lived in these woods long enough to have identified numerous hiding places, logging them for the day he would need them. He was glad of his foresight now, climbing inside the husk of a rotten tree that had fallen long ago and been colonized by other forest plants. Snuggling low into the hole, he pulled the surrounding foliage close around him. And then he waited.

At first, nobody came. For a brief while, he dared to believe that they had given up the chase. But then he'd heard noises. Hushed voices, tramping footsteps, the crackling of radio handsets. And then slowly they'd loomed into view – a group of officers, four, maybe five in number, moving steadily forward.

Their gaze scoured the wood, raking the ground, sweeping the bushes, even darting up to the forest canopy. They looked tense, as if fearing an attack. Part of him would have loved to oblige, but the odds were not in his favour and he had been on the wrong end of police brutality before. So he remained where he was, watching and waiting.

The group were only a foot from his hiding place. Had they turned, investigated the foliage, they would surely have found him. But they remained locked in earnest conversation, debating what to do next. One of them now broke away, pivoting in his direction. Gently, Martin closed his eyes. He was dressed in greens and browns, colours culled from the forest, and he was perfectly camouflaged for his surroundings. But the whites of his eyes could still give him away, so he kept them clamped shut. He could hear his own breathing, could hear his heartbeat – both seemed monstrously amplified. But he held his nerve, held his breath and was now rewarded with the sound of footsteps moving away.

Still he kept his eyes closed, imagining himself dissolving into the fabric of the forest itself. As he did so, he felt a surge of power, of confidence. His pursuers had no affinity with the forest, nor any idea of how to harness it. He did and he would use that to his advantage, blending in seamlessly with his surroundings.

The forest had been his home for a long time. Now it would be his saviour.

39

Meredith Walker shivered as she looked around her. She had attended many unusual scenes in the course of her career, but nothing like this. The angry sky was still spitting at them, the water dripping heavily off the sodden leaves, and the temperature had dropped markedly as night fell. She realized now that she'd dressed too lightly for this assignment, her forensic suit keeping out the rain but not the creeping chill.

The sun had dipped below the horizon, so they'd had to set up arc lights to illuminate the clearing. The powerful beams threw crazy shadows everywhere – the forest that usually looked so beautiful appeared sinister and menacing tonight. The steady drip, drip, drip of the rainwater, the scurrying in the brush, the occasional hoot of a wood owl all served to underline Meredith's sense of isolation. There were other officers present, but Meredith felt very small tonight, as if she were surrounded on all sides by something powerful and malign.

'How you getting on?'

Though she would not normally chivvy a fellow professional, Graham Ross was being unusually slow tonight. He liked to do a thorough job, reminding anyone who'd listen that the devil was in the detail, but to her mind he was lingering unnecessarily, shooting frame after frame of the unfortunate animal.

'Just a couple more,' he replied, without looking up, moving around the horse to find a better angle.

Suppressing a sigh, Meredith watched him finish. Eventually, he turned to her, a broad grin on his face, as he tucked away his camera.

'All yours.'

She was glad someone could remain upbeat. She, by contrast, went to her task with a heavy heart. This was not normally her area, but they had no veterinarian on the payroll, so it fell to her to recover the evidence herself. Sliding on latex gloves, she knelt down by the horse. The ground had softened considerably in the last few hours and her knees sank into it, sucked downwards by the greedy mud. She had no worries about disturbing the scene – her initial sweep had revealed no obvious footwear marks, not surprising given that the pony must have been killed several days ago when the weather was warm and the ground hard. Nor had she found any fabric strips, discarded items or obvious excretions, so the most interesting clues no doubt lay *within* – the three crossbow bolts sticking out of the deceased horse's right flank.

It defied belief that someone could do something like this. Meredith had always had a soft spot for animals, had ridden a lot when she was a kid. What kind of person could stand over a prone horse and unleash an additional couple of bolts? The animal would have been in great distress – bemused and in pain – but it had been shown no mercy. What sort of kick did someone get from this? From deliberately butchering such a sweet, beautiful creature?

Swallowing her repugnance, Meredith slid her fingers into the wound. The bloody fissure sighed quietly and she teased it open, delving inside. Her fingertips followed the length of the shaft, until she found the head. It was barbed, as she'd expected it would be, and she had to use all her strength to loosen it. The pony was in full rigor mortis now, the frozen flesh gripping the vicious bolts. Patiently, methodically, Meredith worked away, taking care not to cut herself on the sharp ridges. Eventually, she gained enough leverage, easing the bolt from the wound and dropping it into an evidence bag. Pausing, she straightened up, stepping away from the body to hold the bolt up to the light.

It was made of iron, with a rough, uneven surface. Though it was hard to tell with the blood still on it, the bolt appeared to be homemade, smelted together from different sources perhaps, given the ridges and bumps on the shaft and head. Furthermore, the shape of the bolt was familiar to Meredith. A sharp, thin bolt head, then a curving barb on either side, uneven in length and shape to each other. It reinforced her feeling that this was not the creation of a factory worker. They would have to do more tests at the lab, but there was no doubt in Meredith's mind that this bolt was a match to the ones used on Tom Campbell two days ago.

Shivering, Meredith looked around her. It seemed improbable, but it was true. Something evil was stalking the forest. Someone cruel and pitiless. Someone who was still at large. Casting a wary look at the darkened forest, Meredith returned to her work, anxious to conclude her investigations.

Suddenly she was keen to be anywhere but here.

40

'What the hell happened?'

'It's my own stupid fault,' Charlie lied quickly. 'We were pursuing a suspect and I got my foot caught in a rabbit hole.'

'A rabbit hole did *that*?'

Steve gestured to the dressing which swathed Charlie's lower leg. She had just returned from South Hants hospital and, though she had been given the all-clear, her heavily bandaged leg was quite a sight. She was resting on the bed, Steve looming above her.

'You can barely walk on it.'

'It's just a bad sprain. And a major source of embarrassment,' Charlie replied gamely, adding her best attempt at a smile, as she shifted her position.

'Who was this guy you were chasing?'

'I can't say.'

'Was he dangerous?'

'Potentially, but I had people with me, so it wasn't an issue.'

Charlie hated lying to Steve, but she knew he would go crazy if he knew the seriousness of the situation she had found herself in. Had Martin really planned to harm her, kill her even? Or was he just toying with her? Charlie didn't know and, in all honesty, didn't want to think about it. Despite the hour or two spent decompressing in A&E, she still felt badly shaken by the experience, constantly replaying Martin's threats in her mind. The image of his contorted face was hard to shake.

'So, what now? Are you going to take time off?'

'I'll see how I feel in the morning.'

From his reaction, Steve could tell he was being fobbed off, that Charlie would find a way to make it in to work. He was about to respond when the conversation was cut short by the appearance of Jessica, clutching a pair of soft toys.

'Hey, what are you doing up?' Charlie chided gently.

'I brought you brown bear and teddy,' Jessica replied, matter-of-factly. 'To help you sleep.'

Charlie felt a sudden rush of emotion. She had downplayed her injury to both Steve and Jessica, painting herself as victim of her own foolishness, but in their different ways they had both been alarmed by her appearance as she hobbled through the front door, swallowing down the pain. The truth was that, despite the powerful painkillers she'd been given, her leg still hurt like hell, throbbing angrily beneath the dressing.

'That's very sweet of you, honey.'

Smiling, Jessica handed her the bears, then pulled back the duvet.

'Hey, what's this?'

'I want to sleep with you tonight.'

'You've got your own bed.'

'But I want to . . .'

Charlie hesitated, angling a look at Steve, who shrugged, batting the decision back to her. Jessica had to sleep in her bed – that was the rule. To relent now, giving in to the tyranny of the night terrors, would be a major mistake. One which might take days, even weeks to undo. But Charlie couldn't face another night of screaming, not after everything that had happened today.

'Just this once then,' Charlie relented, allowing the four-year-old to snuggle up next to her.

She knew she was being weak and that she would regret it – three to a bed was seldom restful. But tonight she was willing to make an exception.

Tonight, she wanted to hold her child *close*.

41

His eyes never left her as she slid across the room. Helen paused briefly to talk to Ellie McAndrew, then turned to the team.

'Thank you, everyone, for your work today. It was much appreciated by myself and, of course, DS Brooks. She should be back with us tomorrow, fit and well, and we'll go again. Thank you.'

Hudson had dropped his gaze, keen not to be caught watching her. But now, as she hurried towards her office, he raised his eyes once more, watching her slender form recede, until she eventually disappeared from view.

'The rest of you can head off now,' he said, as her office door closed. 'I can handle anything that comes up.'

The assembled officers muttered their thanks and began gathering their things. Joseph Hudson wanted to appear generous – he was aware how tired, damp and cold everyone was – but he was also keen to underline the fact that he was in charge when Helen and Charlie were otherwise engaged. Experience had taught him that it was important for him as a new DS to assert himself, gently, but quickly, to let people know that he would not be manipulated or overlooked simply because he was new. It was one of the reasons he'd stayed so late the past few nights – there was no question of him being a weak link.

But there was another reason for his diligence. As the team departed, Hudson returned his attention to his computer. During the working day, there was no time for personal research, partly because of workload and partly because of the risk of detection. After hours, however, it was a different matter. Maximizing his window, he looked at the search results. A long list of operations, all of them with the same SIO. It amazed him that Helen Grace had tackled so many complex operations, but the sober reports confirmed it, underlining the heroism, selflessness and dedication she'd exhibited in bringing them to a successful conclusion.

The lengthy reports on the investigation into the deaths of Jake Elder, Max Paine and Amy Fawcett were particularly interesting, not just for what they revealed of Helen's private life, but because they illuminated the complexity of her relationship with her sole remaining relative – Robert Stonehill, who now languished in Winchester Prison. Did his hatred burn as strongly as ever? Had she ever found it in her heart to forgive him? Were the pair in contact? Questions, questions, questions . . .

Police reports are written in dry, official prose and, during his late-night sessions, Hudson had often abandoned the police database in favour of Google. The stories he found there were much more sensational and entertaining – 'The DI and the Dominator', 'Detective's Prison Hell', 'Twenty-Four Hours of Carnage in Southampton' – but in truth he knew the details by heart. He had made a point of preparing diligently for his interview with Helen, in case she tackled him head on about her past cases, to see if she could intimidate or embarrass him, or in case it became clear during the interview that there were areas she expressly wanted to *avoid*. In the end, the preparation had proved worthwhile – the interview had gone smoothly and he had got the job he craved – but it meant his searches now felt repetitive.

He continued to sift, trying every variation of her name, both real and adopted, as well as putting together key words relating to her personal and professional history. But each time he hit a brick wall, finding himself directed to articles he'd read a dozen times. There were other sources of information that could have proved fruitful, but they were close allies of Helen – DS Brooks and, according to rumour, Chief Superintendent Simmons – and hardly likely to open up to him. Meaning all he could do was sift and hope, going around and around in ever decreasing circles.

It was time to leave, he knew that, but still Joseph Hudson remained seated. Failure was something new to him, arousing complex emotions. His hunt was persistent, dogged, but his quarry remained elusive. If the infamous detective inspector genuinely wanted to remain an enigma, she was making a good fist of it, no question about that. She had no control over what others wrote about her, of course, but she jealously guarded her own privacy. She had no dependants, no interests, no causes she favoured, no events she regularly attended. No Facebook status, no Twitter handle, even her mobile phone seemed to be unregistered – a breach of police rules which the powers that be seemed happy to overlook. He had never seen anything like it before. She had *no* personal footprint at all, online or in life, her office containing only work files and official commendations. This frustrated him, intrigued him and, if he was honest, excited him a little too.

42

Helen remained in her office, the door shut and the blinds down.

Normally, she left her door open, to encourage the free flow of information, but tonight she needed to think. This poky office was her sanctuary, a place to retreat to when she needed some calm amid the storm. Often Charlie joined her to sift the leads and review their progress, but she was at home, having been signed off by the hospital doctors. Nasty bruising, perhaps a slight sprain, but nothing that would keep her from returning to work. Helen was glad of it – she had the unnerving feeling that the investigation was drifting badly off course. She would need her friend's insight and assistance in the days ahead.

A pack of Marlboro Gold lay half hidden by a casefile on her desk. Helen was tempted to grab it and head for the yard. But she was trying to cut down and was determined not to crown a disastrous day by giving in to temptation. Charlie would be fine, which was a blessing, but other than that things couldn't have gone much worse. True, they had discovered Martin's bolt-hole – police dogs now had his scent and two units were currently sweeping the forest in search of him – but the man himself was still at large and Helen's gut told her he would be hard to track down. It was possible he had been living in the forest for nearly eighteen months, sighted fleetingly and then only when he wanted to be. He, more than anyone, would know how to vanish into the forest's depths, to disguise his scent, to blend in with his surroundings. If he wanted to disappear for days, even weeks, what chance would they have of finding him?

Rising, Helen strode around the room, angry and frustrated. They had come so close to catching Martin today, but he had slipped through their fingers. He would no doubt have proved to be an unpredictable and aggressive interviewee, but Helen would have loved to have him in front of her nevertheless. There were many questions for him to answer – about his past conduct, his reasons for disappearing into the forest and, of course, his capture of Charlie. Helen longed to know how he would have justified himself.

There was no doubt about it, Nathaniel Martin *was* a good fit for Tom Campbell's murder. He had targeted Woodland View before – Charlie had confirmed his strong reaction to her mention of the name – and was exhibiting behaviour that was unstable, violent, even deranged, fighting a one-man war against those who defiled Mother Nature. He was a man adept at living by his ingenuity, fashioning whatever he needed from things he found. It was true he favoured natural materials, but there were iron objects in his camp – cooking pots, utensils – and it was not beyond the realms of possibility that he could have smelted some of these down to manufacture a deadly weapon.

And yet there were things that troubled Helen, things that argued against his guilt. According to Charlie, Martin had had the opportunity to confess his crimes, but had not, despite the fact that Charlie was completely at his mercy. Moreover, there was no concrete evidence that he possessed the murder weapon. He could have taken it with him, of course, and any additional bolts, but if he had been fashioning these armaments himself, wouldn't you expect to find some tools, some remnant of their manufacture, on site? They could have been made elsewhere, obviously, but Martin was not itinerant – his camp would have taken a long time to construct and the jars of preserved fruit, the well-appointed 'bathroom' and comfortable bed all pointed to him having lived there for some time. So where was the evidence of his deadly craft?

More than this, it was the murdered pony that worried Helen. Martin had a long history of violence and had no problems with killing to eat – the dead hares and stoats impaled at his camp suggested he was an efficient hunter. Yet, here again, there were problems. These animals appeared to have been trapped rather than shot and, besides, there was nothing perverse or unusual about Martin targeting them. Forest-dwellers had been bagging hares for centuries.

The pony was something else, however. Martin was determined to turn back the clock – his avowed philosophy of rewilding necessitating that he live like our pre-industrial ancestors. In practice, this meant adapting to the character of the forest, following its lead, eating what was provided – berries, mushrooms, vegetables, tubers and herbs – and hunting what could be spared, the odd hare, bird or squirrel. The ponies were part of the fabric of the forest, part of its natural, regenerative rhythm, their itinerant grazing providing a natural pruning service which kept the forest healthy. Targeting a pony would actually *harm* Mother Nature and ran counter to the essential tenets of Martin's philosophy.

In his world view, you harvested what you needed to survive. Indiscriminate desecration or destruction was not part of his lexicon. Killing the horse served no purpose – no meat or skin was taken, its hooves, teeth and tail hair were untouched. It was a harmless, useful member of the forest community, so what would be the point of killing it?

It was possible that Martin had used the horses to hone his hunting skills. After all, killing a human being was a different proposition to trapping hares. This made more sense to Helen. The horse would then have been target practice, might even have been a necessary step on the road to murder – Martin testing his mettle by killing a horse, before escalating to taking a human life. But, still, Helen's knowledge of Martin's credo and beliefs gave her pause. Martin was far gone, for sure, but his continued presence in the forest and his exchanges with Charlie suggested his belief in the importance of protecting Mother Nature remained as strong as ever.

So were they right in believing Nathaniel Martin was the perpetrator? Or was it possible that something even more sinister, even more malign, was responsible for this awful crime?

43

'Please, God, let me wake up. Please, God, let me wake up . . .'

She repeated the mantra breathlessly, praying that she would be propelled out of this hideous nightmare. Back to her tent, back to Matteo . . . But when she opened her eyes, she was still in hell.

Lauren shivered, clutching her arms around her. She was frozen to the bone, her T-shirt and knickers sodden with rain, and racked with terror. Closing her eyes once more, she moaned softly in despair.

Why was this happening to her? What was going on? She and Matteo had spent a loving evening together, then she had drifted off to sleep. Only to awake, cold and confused, in the darkness. At first, she thought their tent might have blown away. But then she realized that she was in the heart of the forest, surrounded on all sides by towering trees and lush vegetation. She had called out Matteo's name – once, twice, three times – but to no avail. Initially she was met by silence, the soft whistling of the wind the only accompaniment to her distress. Then she had heard footsteps.

She had turned, gasping with relief, hoping to see Matteo. But the sight that greeted her chilled her blood. A tall, hooded figure was walking directly towards her.

She could barely make out his contours in the gloom – he was perfectly camouflaged – nor could she see his face. But she knew with absolute certainty that he intended to harm her.

'Run.'

The command was barked at her. Immediately, she turned

and fled, crashing straight through the nearest bush. Thorns tore at her arms and thighs, but she ignored their savage sting, charging on, on, on. She had no idea why she was running, nor whom she was running from, but instinct told her that hesitation would be fatal. She *had* to get away.

But how could she? When she had no idea where she was, nor which direction to head in? The forest seemed to be crowding in on her – every time she darted one way, she came up against a solid wall of vegetation. Darting another, she would stumble over a hidden obstacle or glimpse *him*, pacing quietly towards her.

Swallowing down her terror, she fought on, clawing at the foliage, fashioning a way forward. But her body seemed to be revolting against her – her head was pounding, her throat was dry, her lungs were starved of oxygen. She was fit and healthy, so why did she feel so bad? Was this what terror did to you?

Blundering through the brush, she glimpsed a path ahead and tore towards it. Immediately, her right foot hit something unyielding and she felt herself falling. She crumpled to the floor, her head connecting sharply with the ground, even as a savage pain ripped through her knee. Shocked, confused, she looked around her – to discover she had tripped over an exposed tree root, smashing her left knee on one of the exposed wooden tentacles as she fell.

Tears filled her eyes as agony took hold of her body, making her feel nauseous and faint. Even so, she found herself stumbling to her feet and limping on, determined to keep going. With each step, she tried to go faster, ignoring her protesting knee, struggling forward through the gloom.

But he was close by now, she could sense it. He had gained on her, was perhaps even now shaping to attack. In her fear, Lauren suddenly had to know. She wanted to be able to defend herself or perhaps, if God was on her side, cheat death? Craning around, she peered over her shoulder, as she stumbled on.

He was only thirty feet from her now. The figure, who had been cloaked in darkness, was now illuminated by the moon as it broke free of the clouds. Lauren slowed still further, desperate to know who her pursuer was. His clothes were dark green, possibly black, and smooth with it, glistening in the moonlight. His hood was made of a similar material, but it was its contents that interested Lauren. Who *was* this guy?

Peering into the void, Lauren gasped in confusion and horror. This hunter did not have a human face. She could make out no features at all, apart from two huge, lamp-like eyes.

'Please, no . . .'

Terror gripped her. What was this thing? Some evil spirit? A shade raised from hell to torment her? Convinced now that she was stuck in a living nightmare, she scrambled on, desperate to put some distance between herself and her pursuer. But despair was robbing her of hope, fear conquering her will to survive. She was being hunted by something monstrous, something unreal.

And at any moment she expected death to descend upon her.

44

She wrenched back the throttle and roared along the empty road.

After a difficult day, Helen wanted to put some distance between herself and Southampton Central. It was not a desire to be back home that spurred her on – the same unanswered questions would nag her there – but a thirst for speed. When assailed on all sides, Helen sometimes resorted to pain to expiate her anxiety, but on other occasions she opted for the adrenaline that only speed can provide. It was late now and the roads were empty, allowing Helen a clear run home.

On leaving the incident room, she had called in on Superintendent Simmons. It had been useful to update her, but their discussion hadn't allayed Helen's fears or furthered their thinking, so in the end she had headed to the bike park. Before long she was on the ring road, crouched down against the roaring wind, angling her weight into the bends. She had first ridden a motorbike at the age of fifteen – thirty years on it still gave her a rush.

But she was not reckless, nor a speed freak. She pushed her bike, her body, hard, but she was always in control, risking only her own life and limb, as she ripped along the road. She kept her senses alert, constantly checking the way ahead, as well as what lay behind. And now, as she looked in her mirrors for the umpteenth time, she noticed something.

A bike was speeding along the road about a hundred yards behind her. It hadn't been there when she'd checked a few seconds ago and she hadn't slowed for traffic lights for some time, so the rider must be setting a blistering pace. Why were they going so fast? And where were they making for in such a hurry? Intrigued, Helen dropped her speed, drifting slightly to the left to allow the bike to pass.

To her surprise, the bike slowed, keeping a safe distance from her. Immediately, her body tensed. Was this bike following her? She dropped her speed still further, her eyes glued to her mirrors. The rider responded, copying her, telling Helen everything she needed to know – except for *who* was pursuing her, and why.

Her nerves were jangling. She had been hunted too many times not to be on her guard. But she could do little until she knew what she was dealing with, nor did she like the idea of being anybody's quarry, so, making an instinctive decision, she tugged hard on the brakes.

This took her pursuer by surprise, who shot towards her, before suddenly killing their speed. But it was too little, too late. The bike was a popular, nondescript model, but Helen *did* recognize the helmet and the distinctive winged angel on the side. It was Joseph Hudson.

Helen's mind spun. From memory, he *did* live out this way, so there could be an innocent explanation for his presence. Perhaps he was hanging back because he didn't want to smash the speed limit in front of his new boss or because he wanted to avoid being recognized, for fear that it would look like he was following her.

But Helen wasn't convinced by either of these explanations. His pursuit was not intimidating, he was not bearing down on her, trying to bully her out of his way. No, there was something circumspect about this pursuit, even a little coy. Was he checking her out from a distance? Perhaps, but if so it was a clumsy pursuit. Was she *meant* to see that he was following her, then? Was it possible the handsome DS was flirting with her?

Inappropriate though that was, Helen hoped it was this and nothing more sinister – memories of Robert Stonehill were still fresh. Either way, she was not going to be the supine object of his attention – she had never played the game by anybody else's rules before.

She slowed still further, almost to a standstill, then, as Hudson did likewise, ripped back the throttle. Her bike leapt forward, the needle moving wildly on the speedometer, as she hit 40 mph, then 60 mph, then 80 mph. Roaring on, she angled a look over her shoulder. Hudson had responded to her sudden move, but too late.

The race was over.

45

Lauren plunged through the forest, never daring to look back, hoping her relentless momentum might deliver her from harm. She knew he was still behind her, could hear her pursuer's progress as he ripped through the brush, but miracle of miracles, she was still alive. Her knee throbbed horribly, but in the last few minutes she had found a way to deal with it, pushing through the pain as she broke into a sprint once more.

Her lungs burned, her breath was short, but she powered on. Her eyes had become accustomed to the darkness and she was better able to avoid the pitfalls that littered her path. She no longer had a thought for who might be doing this or why, she just wanted to survive, to be reunited with Matteo. Summoning all her energies, she sped on, daring to hope. Had she surprised her pursuer with her stamina and determination? Was it even possible that she had opened up the gap between them? The thought spurred her on and she hurdled a fallen log with ease, touching down gracefully on the other side.

She felt hysterical, even slightly euphoric now. She knew that she was injured – the soles of her feet were sticky and sore, no doubt cut to ribbons by the fallen thorns on the forest floor, but she didn't care. She was making progress, cutting through the forest, driving on, on, on. From nowhere, she suddenly felt as if she could go on for ever, outrun anyone, *survive.*

And now she glimpsed it. Light up ahead. She screwed up her eyes, fearful her senses were deceiving her. But there could be no doubt about it, the forest was thinning. Hope surged through her. If she could get out of this desolate darkness, perhaps she could find a road, flag down a motorist, find a house to seek refuge in.

She was insensible to what was behind her now, sprinting towards salvation. She was forty feet away, thirty, twenty. With a roar of triumph, she broke free of the gloomy woodland, running out into open pasture. A little way ahead there was a low stone wall and she raced towards it, her feet springing off the wet turf. Clearing it easily, she ran on, scanning the horizon for signs of life.

But even as she ran, fear stole over her. She could make out *nothing* ahead of her. No lights, no shapes, nothing. How was that possible? Instinct made her slacken her pace and seconds later she skidded to an abrupt halt.

For a moment, she thought she might fall, teetering on the edge of the vertiginous cliff. But throwing her weight backwards, she righted herself, staggering away. She had saved herself, but now her head was spinning. She'd had no idea she was so far south in the forest – she must be *miles* from the campsite. She chanced another look over the edge. The drop was awful – a hundred feet or more into the swelling sea, which was crashing angrily onto the rocks. But what was the alternative?

She turned, knowing full well what she would see. The hooded figure was walking towards her, but now there was no hurry. Her pursuer seemed neither breathless nor troubled, gliding eerily in her direction, utterly confident of victory. Shaking, she looked all around her, seeking some means of salvation, but there was none. She was stuck between the devil and the deep blue sea.

'Please . . .' she whimpered.

But she knew there would be no mercy. Spinning, she

took a step forward towards the cliff edge . . . but once again the pounding surf made her pause.

'Please . . .'

She was talking to herself, tears streaking down her cheeks, but she knew it was no use now.

It was time to die.

46

Alice stared into the depths of her coffee cup, filled with a terrible sense of foreboding. In spite of the early-morning sunshine, which poured in through the floor-to-ceiling windows, the dark liquid mirrored her mood. She felt heavy, downcast, lost in the fog.

What should she do? What was the right call? Every time she thought she'd hit upon a course of action, she was undone by hesitation, the potential pitfalls presenting themselves as she interrogated her scheme. Part of this was justifiable circumspection, even a sensitivity towards her daughter's feelings and well-being, but part of it was honest-to-God cowardice. She felt guilty, terribly guilty, uncertain how to make amends.

She had turned her back on her daughter. There was no point dressing it up, that was what she had done. And though there were extenuating circumstances, she knew that people judged her. They never said it to her face, but they all believed that a parent should *never* cut off their child, no matter the circumstances. Part of her felt that too, but if they could have glimpsed inside her soul, if they had *seen* her turmoil, they might have been a bit more charitable.

The truth is that you cannot truly cut yourself off from your own flesh and blood. Once you've carried a child to term, given birth to them, nurtured them, there is a bond there that never disappears, whatever else may happen. In spite of everything, it still exerted a strong pull on Alice, thoughts of her estranged daughter constantly in her mind, obsessing on all that she had suffered, all she might *still* suffer.

This was why she was prone to these bouts of darkness, why she often felt so blue. And this was why she had to do something. Difficult as it would be for both parties, she had to act. The alternative – going gently mad, day by day – was unthinkable. It was time to seize the nettle, time to make amends.

She just prayed she wouldn't be too late.

47

'Why don't I come to work with you?'

Charlie couldn't help smiling, despite her discomfort.

'I'd love that, sweetheart, but you have to be a bit older before they give you handcuffs and a warrant card . . .'

Jessica's face fell and she returned to pushing her Weeta-bix around the bowl.

'But I'll tell you what. About every six months or so kids get to come down to the police station and look around. You can meet the sniffer dogs, talk to real police officers. Why don't we do that instead?'

'I want to go *today*,' Jessica persisted sulkily.

'I know and that's very kind. But I think I can manage, even if I have to hop.'

Charlie hopped from the table to the sink, hoping to elicit a smile. But she got nothing and was rewarded instead with shooting pains up her left calf. Though she could just about walk on her injured leg, it was still very tender. Part of her knew she should stay at home and rest up, the other half knew that if she did her fears would only grow.

'I don't want to go to school.'

Charlie's heart sunk still further.

'Why not, honey? Is something wrong?' she replied, limp-ing across to her.

'I want to look after you.'

'But I've said I'm fine . . .'

'I don't want to go,' Jessica persisted.

'Look, sweetie, I know it's hard. School can be a scary

place sometimes – all those big kids, those new faces. But the teachers are nice and –'

'I don't like her.'

'Who?'

'Mrs Barnard.'

'Why?'

Jessica said nothing, pushing her bowl away from her. Charlie noted she had barely touched her cereal or her apple juice.

'Did something happen? Did she say something that upset you?'

'I don't like her. *Please* can I come to work with you . . . ?'

Irritation now flared in Charlie. She was exhausted, strung out, trying to make the best of a difficult situation. But nothing she said seemed to make things any better.

'I've explained why you can't do that, Jessie, and we *are* running late . . .'

Charlie shot a nervous look at the clock. They would have to drive if they were to make it on time today.

'. . . so if you've finished your breakfast, let's grab your book bag and go.'

Jessica stayed where she was, looking disgruntled and a little lost. Suddenly all irritation evaporated, as Charlie felt anxiety master her once more.

'If there was a problem, you would tell me, wouldn't you?'

She couldn't suppress a slight wobble in her voice.

'Sweetie . . . ?'

Jessica considered this for a little while. Then she looked up at Charlie and said:

'I don't want to go.'

48

They traipsed out of the house in single file – mother, daughter, then dad. They were carrying the standard paraphernalia of the morning run – book bags, PE kits, recorder – and seemed to be in a hurry. Doors were flung open, bags thrown inside, the engine fired up. They went about their task in earnest and with practised slickness, unaware that they were being watched.

Helen took a step back, fearful of being spotted. There was little chance of that in truth – she had chosen her vantage point well – but she didn't want to freak them out. Nor did she want her presence detected. Christina would definitely remember her and wouldn't take kindly to her sudden appearance at her home. Helen never brought anything but bad tidings to this family.

It had been years since Helen had laid eyes on Christina, but she looked well. With expensive clothes, glossy hair and artfully applied make-up, she was doing a good job of middle age. Elsie also looked in good form. Predictably, Helen was surprised by how much she'd grown – not just in stature, but in maturity. The toddler she remembered was now a young lady, pushing teenage years. She looked sparky, intelligent, talkative – a far cry from the surly child she had known. Helen felt a brief spark of shame at having been away for so long.

Helen had had a brief relationship with her father, after Christina had kicked him out. Mark was struggling with the breakdown of his marriage, with being a part-time father, and had turned to drink. He was Helen's principal DS at the time, so she had taken him in hand, helping him beat the booze. In the process, lines had become blurred and they had started seeing each other. It was a mistake which had catastrophic consequences, Mark dying in action, partly because of his connection to her. Helen had felt hugely guilty, her heart breaking for Christina and Elsie, both of whom were poleaxed by his death, and she'd resolved to keep an eye on the pair of them, aware of the long, hard road they had to travel.

She had honoured her promise for a couple of years, but inevitably, as life grew more complicated, her unheralded visits had tailed off. She had heard on the grapevine that Christina had remarried, but this was her first sight of him. He was what she expected – Christina liked the people in her life to be handsomely turned out – but there seemed to be a kindness to him too. He was affectionate and good-humoured with Elsie, teasing her as he chivvied the dawdling child into the car. Their relationship seemed warm and relaxed. They looked *happy*.

It was a far cry from those early days, after Helen had broken the news of Mark's murder. Christina had been in pieces, her residual love punching through despite their split, and Elsie had just been uncomprehending, at a loss to understand why she wouldn't see her daddy again. It had been bitterly hard to watch and Helen was cheered to see how they had rebuilt their lives. It proved that there was hope after all.

Helen had spent another restless night, her mind turning on Joseph Hudson's pursuit, but also on Grace Simmons's words to her. 'Don't cling to the past, or it will eat you up.' They came back to her now as she watched the family drive off, chatting and laughing together. Something had driven Helen here this morning. Was it to honour the ghost of Mark, the last person she had a serious relationship with? Or was it to reassure herself that it was possible to recover from tragedy? That it was possible to *move on*?

Helen was still pondering this, when her phone started buzzing. It was Hudson. A moment's hesitation, then Helen hit receive.

'DI Grace.'

'Sorry to disturb you early,' he said breathlessly. 'But I thought you'd want to know . . .'

He paused, before delivering his punchline:

'Someone's just reported their girlfriend missing from a campsite in the New Forest.'

49

'You're becoming vain . . .'

Emilia breathed the words as she stared at her reflection, barely suppressing a smile. She was in the ladies' loos at work and quite alone. It was not customary for her to talk to herself as she touched up her make-up, nor for her to feel anything other than dismay as she surveyed her scarred face, but she was feeling buoyant this morning, even a little skittish.

Last night's edition had been one of the fastest selling in the paper's history. It had flown off the shelves, newsagents and supermarkets struggling to keep up with demand. Most of the city's inhabitants were in the midst of making summer plans, a sizeable chunk of them planning to head for the New Forest. But not any more – not while a homicidal maniac was stalking its confines. Locals had drunk in the detail – the shadowy clearing, the hanging corpse, the crossbow bolts – then hit social media, the panic spreading virally. Not bad for a day's work.

The continuing radio silence from the police had further helped her cause. In the absence of any other concrete information, media outlets had turned to her for insight. She was well known following her brush with Daisy Anderson and once again she seemed to have the inside track on a breaking story. Always keen to bolster her profile, Emilia had been happy to oblige. She had already done two radio interviews and was due to put in an appearance on BBC South shortly. The thought made her smile. Radio was all very well, but every print journalist dreams of having their moment on the small screen.

Tucking her foundation away, Emilia checked her lipstick once more, before gathering her things. Leaving the toilets, she hurried down the corridor, aware that her taxi would be arriving shortly. As she did so, she pulled out her phone, checking WhatsApp, before opening Twitter. She was immediately intrigued to find a large number of tweets featuring #newforestkiller. Most of them were idle speculation and scaremongering, but they were all reacting to a tweet written earlier that morning.

'Commotion at our campsite this morning. Random woman gone missing. Should we be worried??? #newforestkiller'

It was tweeted by Squeakybum74 and featured a couple of smiley faces, so presumably the sender wasn't too concerned. It was just a joke to her, but Emilia was taking it very seriously, scanning the photo which accompanied the tweet. It was of an unshaven man with riotous, curly black hair, speaking to uniformed police officers. The pictures were snatched and from a distance, but even so it was clear that the man was very distressed.

Gripping her phone, Emilia hurried to the exit, tweeting as she went. She would contact the sender, find out where the campsite was and advise her not to send any more messages until she got there. It was a simple plan but one which might pay dividends, if the killer *had* claimed his second victim. Running towards the exit, Emilia felt that familiar thrill, that excitement as a new lead broke. Suddenly all her plans for the morning were up in the air, but she didn't care one bit.

Her spot on BBC South would have to wait.

50

'Tell me what happened.'

Helen's tone was gentle, but firm. She was closeted away with Matteo Dominici in the manager's office at the Sunnyside campsite. He had reported his long-term girlfriend, Lauren Scott, missing first thing this morning and was still in an emotional state. Distracted, anxious, pale, he ran his fingers through his thick hair, while casting around him. It was as if he expected Lauren to pop up somewhere in the office, but the young woman had not been seen for several hours, despite leaving all her possessions and clothing in their tent.

'Please, Matteo, I need you to focus.'

'I'm sorry, I don't feel good . . .'

'Can we get you something? Water? Nurofen?'

'Both, please. I feel like shit,' he croaked, rubbing his forehead with his hand.

'Heavy night, was it?' Helen replied, trying to keep the conversation light, as she signalled to the uniformed officer to get the painkillers.

'No way. Nothing like that.'

He looked almost affronted, which surprised her. Matteo obviously clocked her reaction, because he now expanded:

'We don't drink. Or do drugs, if that's what you're thinking. We're both recovering alcoholics.'

'I see.'

'That's where we met, at AA. We've been dry for over two years now.'

'I'm pleased for you,' she replied genuinely, all too aware of the devastation alcohol can wreak. 'And how long have you been together?'

'Eighteen months. Took me a while to pluck up the courage to ask her out, but we've been inseparable ever since. She's one in a million.'

Helen smiled, trying to push away the images intruding on her consciousness – images of where Lauren might be, what might have befallen her.

'And what happened last night?'

'Nothing. Nothing unusual anyway . . .' he replied slowly, as if trying to make sense of events. 'We turned up in the driving rain, set up camp, then spent the night in our tent. It was too wet to do anything else.'

'Did you meet anyone? See anyone near the tent?'

'No, we were alone all night.'

'You went to sleep around . . . ?'

'Eleven, eleven thirty.'

'And when did you realize she was gone?'

'Just after sun-up. The light woke me up, or maybe the birds . . .'

'And?'

'And she was gone. All her stuff was there, but the tent flaps were open and there was no sign of her. I did three circuits of the camp, then sat and waited for an hour, in case she'd gone off to the village for some reason.'

'What about a car?'

'Don't have one. We came here on the bus.'

Helen made a mental note to check this. There was a hop-on, hop-off bus running during tourist season that would have delivered them to the campsite, but every last detail would have to be investigated.

'And you called the police just after eight thirty . . .'

148

'Sure. She'd been missing for nearly three hours by then. I thought I might be overreacting, but . . .'

Helen nodded sympathetically.

'What's happened to her?' He was looking at her directly now. 'Even I know they don't send this many police officers for a missing person.'

'I don't know yet,' Helen answered truthfully, privately glad Matteo hadn't seen last night's *Evening News*. 'But I intend to find out. Tell me, Matteo, do you often feel unwell when you wake up? Do you have any medical conditions or –'

'No. Having a clear head is one of the perks of not drinking.'

'So how would you account for it?'

Helen saw his eyes narrow, as if scenting disbelief.

'I've no idea. We went to sleep as usual, sober, clear-headed, but when I woke up, I felt dreadful. Dizzy, nauseous, with a cracking headache.'

'And, during the night, can you remember anything that disturbed you? Any noises? Movement of any kind near the tent?'

'No, not really,' he replied hesitantly.

'Anything at all?'

'No, I mean I didn't hear her leave or anything like that.'

'But . . .'

'But . . . I think I heard a car at some point. I can't be totally sure, it was pretty faint, but it sounded like a car. A low, steady purr . . .'

'You didn't see the vehicle?'

'No, I only half remember it, to be honest. I was so knackered last night, I don't think I opened my eyes once . . .'

He looked crestfallen, as if his lack of vigilance was to blame for Lauren's disappearance. Taking advantage of the return of the attending uniformed officer, Helen left Matteo taking his Nurofen, promising to be back with him shortly.

Exiting the office, she headed straight for Matteo's tent, which was now taped off. Elsewhere on the site, Helen could make out Charlie and Hudson conducting interviews, the former hobbling from tent to tent. But she didn't linger, lifting the cordon and approaching the tent. This time she didn't bother with the interior, running a rule over the outside instead. Tom Campbell's tent had been in a shabby state, old and torn, but Matteo Dominici's tent was brand new, looking box fresh. Sliding a gloved hand over the fabric, she probed the surface, testing it for weakness. But it seemed to be in mint condition, able to repel the rain and anyone who might want to penetrate the interior. Rounding the tent, she continued her search, convinced that there must be a breach somewhere. But the far side seemed fine too, so she proceeded to the rear. Here she slowed, taking great pains to check every seam and join, fearing now that her search might yield nothing.

And now she found it. A small tear in the fabric of the tent. No, not a tear, it was too neat for that. It was an incision. Someone had slid a knife or scalpel down the seam, opening it up, allowing access to the tent. It was small, no more than ten centimetres in length, but it would be wide enough to accommodate a hose or length of tubing.

Right from the off, Tom Campbell's seamless disappearance from the tent had worried her, anxieties that had only increased with Lauren Scott's inexplicable disappearance. But in his own stumbling way, Matteo Dominici had provided a possible explanation. They had been gassed. Melanie Walton hadn't realized it, thinking she was suffering from a hangover, but Matteo knew something was amiss. And the cut in the tent proved it for Helen.

Moving away from the tent, Helen searched the ground for tyre tracks. In recent years, there had been a spate of crimes in which campers and caravan owners had been targeted by organized gangs, usually as they travelled through France. Their tent or campervan would be breached, then carbon monoxide from an idling vehicle would be pumped inside, rendering the inhabitants insensible before they were robbed. Was their killer doing something similar?

It was risky – if you overcooked it, you could kill – but it had the benefit of rendering everyone within the tent unconscious. Furthermore, some enterprising thieves had started modifying their vehicles recently, adding padded, aluminium shields to dull engine noise, bolstering their chances of carrying out the attacks undetected. Was this what had happened here? Matteo Dominici had described the noise he heard as 'a low, steady purring' which to Helen sounded very much like an idling vehicle.

The ground was saturated, her feet springing off the turf. And ten feet away from the tent, Helen found tyre tracks. They were deep and wide – a 4x4 perhaps – and they seemed out of place. Matteo had said they'd travelled here by bus and the car park was on the other side of the camp, near the entrance. So there was no reason for a vehicle to park up here.

Unless you had an interest in the inhabitants of the tent.

51

The car bounced over the grass, as they drove slowly but steadily along the verge. Joseph Hudson had been in the middle of questioning a bemused camper, when Helen had summoned him over. Explaining her findings, Helen had left Charlie to continue the hunt for witnesses, asking him to requisition a vehicle instead. The pair then headed off, him driving, while she kept her eyes glued to the tyre tracks.

They led away from the campsite, following a track that took them towards the forest, rather than back towards the road. Hudson drove purposefully but carefully, making sure to avoid the tracks themselves, which might prove to be crucial evidence. They drove in silence, intent on their task, but both were aware that a clearer picture of these crimes was taking shape. One which left them both feeling unnerved.

'Stop the car.'

Hudson reacted, braking sharply. The car slid to a stop and Helen was out in a flash. Killing the engine, Hudson climbed out, hurrying round to join her.

Helen was down on her haunches, examining the tracks.

'Same tracks, but they're deeper here. Way deeper . . .'

Looking more closely, Hudson saw that she was right.

'You're thinking that the killer *stopped* here?'

'Could be,' Helen replied, rising. 'Let's find out.'

Moving away from the tracks, she walked cautiously to the trees nearest the tracks. Hudson followed, examining the ground for trampled grass. The grass on the verge was long and wild and it was hard to be sure, but there *did* seem to be some flattened areas approaching the thick vegetation.

'Here.'

Helen was now at the edge of the woods, her finger directing his attention to a tiny scrap of white material caught on a tree branch.

'Her T-shirt? A vest?'

She shrugged, stepping under the branch and proceeding carefully into the forest. Hudson followed, scouring the gloomy woodland for clues.

'There.'

He'd spotted it instantly – a broken branch hanging limply, ten feet or so further on. Examining it, Helen nodded and they pressed on. Their progress was swift – they found two more broken branches, a larger snag of fabric and then a small patch of blood. They had almost walked past the latter, but Helen had grabbed Hudson, pointing out the crimson stain that had suddenly caught a beam of sunlight on the end of a vicious-looking branch.

On they went, following the discreet trail of devastation, until eventually the path opened out into a clearing. Helen was still on point and Hudson heard her little gasp of horror, just before she ground to an abrupt halt. Summoning his courage, Hudson emerged into the clearing and looked up.

To find Lauren Scott's corpse hanging from a nearby tree.

52

Matteo Dominici. Lauren Scott.

Emilia's finger hovered over their names. There was no doubt about it – this was the unfortunate couple.

On arrival at the Sunnyside campsite, Emilia had kept a low profile, leaving her car some way off and approaching the camp via the woods. There was still a major police presence and plenty of activity. A group of campers were being interviewed in the picnic area and, as she cautiously approached the site office, she saw the distressed-looking guy with the unruly hair being ushered away by a solicitous family liaison officer. Emilia's first instinct was to follow them, perhaps try and grab a picture with her phone, but it would be hard to do so without being detected and, besides, she needed hard facts. So instead, on instinct, she'd darted into the deserted site office.

Crossing to the front desk, she reached over and picked up the guest register. She took a quick photo of the names, then got to work. Keeping one eye out for police officers or site workers, she started Googling the names on the list, looking carefully at the images for each name. At the seventh attempt, she got lucky. Matteo Dominici – with his bushy black crop of hair – was very distinctive. A number of the photos featured him with his arm around a pretty young woman. Sifting the Facebook offerings for 'Lauren Scott', she quickly confirmed his girlfriend's identity.

So, this was the missing woman. None of the campers being interviewed resembled her and, given Dominici's distress, she *must* be the one. Had the police already found a body? Or was she still missing? Emilia knew she was getting ahead of herself, but the similarity between Tom Campbell's murder and Lauren's disappearance was too striking to be a coincidence. She felt certain the New Forest killer had struck again.

Emilia stared at the woman's profile photo. Her trusting, open countenance, her slender, pretty face, even the clothes she was wearing – a pink Race for Life T-shirt – made this the perfect image for tomorrow's front page. The photo had obviously been taken at the end of the run, when Lauren was exhausted but happy, a broad grin spread across her face. It would tug at the heartstrings of their readers – here was a kind, spirited young woman who contributed to society – and provide a chilling counterpoint to her abduction.

The story was already taking shape in Emilia's mind, but she needed more details. Perhaps some of the campers would talk to her. Or maybe she should approach a uniformed officer – see if one of the young ones could be intimidated or encouraged into talking to her. But as Emilia darted a wary look out of the window, she was surprised to see that the police team was on the move. A couple of uniformed officers remained with the unnerved campers, but all the others – CID particularly – were hurrying to their vehicles. Though 'hurrying' was perhaps the wrong term to describe DS Brooks, who was limping rather awkwardly across the site. Emilia wondered if she had sustained this injury in action. Perhaps in some kind of confrontation?

Engines were now starting up, doors being slammed. Snapping out of it, Emilia knew she needed to make an instant decision. Stick or twist? Staying put might yield some interesting information, but surely a mass departure could only mean one thing.

Dropping the register, Emilia fled the office, hurrying back through the woods towards her car. If she could get there as they were securing the scene, there might be some good photo opportunities, not to mention a chance to target the team when they were off guard. The thought sent a shiver of anticipation through her. When it came down to it, there was nothing she enjoyed more than the thrill of the chase.

53

Helen marched back towards the car, her phone clamped to her ear.

'Is it the same guy? The same MO?'

Simmons sounded focused but concerned. Another killing so soon suggested a perpetrator who was fearless, reckless, or both.

'Yes,' Helen replied quickly. 'The forensics team will be on site shortly . . . but I've no doubt this is our second victim. It looks very much like Scott was abducted, hunted down, then left to bleed out.'

There was a brief pause, then Simmons's voice punched through again.

'What do you want to do?'

'Well, that's your call really,' Helen answered. 'But I don't think we can sit on it. Not after last night's headlines.'

There was a brief silence on the other end. Both women had been surprised and angered by Emilia Garanita's inflammatory article, and dismayed by the panicked response to it. The incorrigible journalist was clearly enjoying her moment in the sun, having called Helen's mobile twice this morning, seeking an official comment – calls which Helen had resolutely ignored.

'You think we should put out a general alert, talk to the national press?' Simmons responded.

'There'll be hundreds of holidaymakers descending on the New Forest this week. If they're at risk, we need to let them know.'

'Do we want to name Nathaniel Martin as a suspect?'

'Not yet. The public won't help us flush him out – that's down to the search teams – and naming him might deter people from coming forward with other information.'

'Ok. I'll get media liaison on to it straight away. We'll advise the public to review their plans, to exercise caution. Would you like me to handle the press conference?'

Simmons knew her too well. Helen loathed being harangued by journalists, when she could be doing something more useful.

'That'd be great. I'll keep you up to speed.'

'Please do.'

Simmons clicked off, but before she did so, Helen heard her asking her PA to summon media liaison. It was one of the reasons she admired her new boss so much – she was no-nonsense, practical, purposeful – and it behoved them to follow her lead. Gesturing to Hudson to join her, Helen climbed into the car.

'Where to?' Hudson said, sliding into the driver's seat and starting the engine.

'Southampton Central.' Helen's tone was grim but determined. 'We've got work to do.'

54

'So, we're saying that the victims were gassed?'

The team was back at base, gathered together in the incident room. Helen had brought them up to speed on her findings and, predictably, they were full of questions. On this occasion, it was DC Reid who'd got in first.

'Looks that way. We don't know for sure what they used, but my bet would be carbon monoxide.'

'Because it's convenient if you've got a car,' Osbourne suggested.

'And it doesn't leave any lingering trace in your blood or your organs,' Helen added. 'So it's hard to find.'

The assembled officers digested this. As long as you didn't overdo the dose, there was no question that exhaust fumes were a simple and discreet way of pacifying your intended victims.

'Then what? They are let loose in the forest?'

'Presumably,' DS Hudson answered. 'The trail we followed looked very much like a pursuit. But the victim wasn't killed where she was found. The trail continued to a cliff edge roughly half a mile further on.'

'And then she was dragged back to the clearing?' DC Edwards enquired.

'We didn't see any drag patterns, so it looks like she was carried,' Helen replied. 'We only found one set of footwear marks – a size eleven combat boot of some kind.'

Helen punched a few buttons on her phone and her snatched image of the boot print sprang up on the screen.

'It's rough and ready, but it'll have to do until we have Ross's photos. Interestingly, we also saw what looks like a single boot print on the victim's T-shirt. Perhaps the perpetrator stamped on the victim. Or just pinned her down, while discharging one of the bolts . . .'

One of the younger officers shuddered, but Helen pressed on.

'Given the size of the boot, the strength required to transport and hoist the body and the fact that there appears to be only one set of footwear marks, I would suggest that we are looking for a lone male, someone of considerable size and strength. Unless we find concrete evidence to the contrary, I want us to proceed on that basis.'

The team nodded. It hardly narrowed the field down, but they had to start somewhere. Helen scrolled through her photos once more, pulling up another.

'This is a close-up of the tyre tread left by what we believe to be the perpetrator's vehicle. DC McAndrew has already done some work on this.'

She nodded at McAndrew. As one, the team turned to look at her.

'It's a wide, heavy-duty tyre, which suggests off road. Looking at the tread pattern, I'm pretty confident we can say it's an Avon Rangemaster. They're expensive and relatively rare tyres, but they were standard issue on the Land Rover Defender.'

'They've stopped making Defenders, right?' DC Edwards, their resident petrol head, piped up.

'Land Rover stopped production a couple of years back,' McAndrew confirmed. 'But I think this vehicle is older than that. The tread pattern is from one of the early iterations of the Rangemaster tyre and, besides, it's very faint and uneven, suggesting the tyre is worn. So, we might be looking for a

Defender that's seven, eight, nine years old or more. DC McAndrew has the latest DVLA lists. There are fifty-three registered Defenders in the Hampshire area. Now, maybe the vehicle is unlicensed or stolen, but our first job is to trace these vehicles and run the rule over the owners, focusing on possible motives and, crucially, their movements during the last few days.'

'Does this mean we're discounting Martin as a suspect?' DC Edwards asked, gesturing towards his mugshot. 'I mean, we don't think he has a car and he doesn't like using machinery anyway.'

'We rule nobody out at this stage,' Helen countered decisively. 'Martin still has questions to answer, about his animus against Woodland View, about his attack on DS Brooks, but we have to consider other possibilities –'

'We're looking for anyone with concrete connections to Tom Campbell and Lauren Scott,' DS Hudson cut in. 'And clues as to the choice of MO. We're looking for hunting enthusiasts, weapons obsessives, anyone who would know how to source, construct and operate a crossbow. We need to deepen our trawl in this area to see if anyone connected to this type of vehicle has form for assault with a deadly weapon, aggravated assault or threatening behaviour. Also, has anyone been buying or trading crossbows online, either conventionally or via the dark web?'

The assembled officers nodded soberly, the scale of their task only now becoming clear.

'I will break you up into smaller units and apportion specific tasks,' Helen resumed. 'Some of you will be investigating the areas DS Hudson has just outlined, others will be assisting DS Brooks to explore the victims' backgrounds and personal history.'

Charlie rose, wobbling slightly as she did so.

'So, principal question,' she said, steadying herself, 'is why were these two individuals targeted? Does our perpetrator attack campers simply because they are vulnerable or because he has a particular animus against them?'

'I bloody hate camping,' DC Edwards drawled, to a mixture of muted chuckles and groans.

'Were they chosen at random?' Charlie continued, unabashed. 'Or were they targeted specifically? Are they connected in some way?'

'Do they know each other?' Osbourne asked, picking up Charlie's thread.

'Not that we can see from our preliminary trawl. They are both from Southampton originally, but other than that there is very little overlap. Campbell was nearly thirty, Scott was twenty-seven. She's a middle-class dropout, he's a grammar school boy made good, with a well-paid job, a fiancée, an expensive house in Winchester. Lauren Scott by contrast has a history of petty crime, drug abuse, even the odd caution for prostitution. She had cleaned up her act recently, but is estranged from her parents and lives with her boyfriend in a flat in Thornhill.'

'It may be that there's no connection at all,' Helen added. 'She was an alcoholic and drug addict who was never able to hold down a job. He was a well-educated scientist with the world at his feet, but if there *are* any links, we need to find them. At present, the perpetrator's choice appears random – the victims are different genders, from different backgrounds and were taken from different campsites – Campbell's campsite was near Godshill, Scott's was much further south, near South Baddesley. So, what's driving his choice? The victims or the locations? Let's pull apart the personal histories of the victims, but also look again at the campsite owners. Has anything occurred recently at either location that might explain why Campbell and Scott were abducted? What is driving our killer?'

Helen broke up the briefing shortly after this, dividing her team into working groups and sending them on their way. Her last question hung in the air, preying on everyone's minds, as they tore apart the fabric of this case. What was the meaning of these attacks? And what had precipitated them? Did the killer have a specific motive?

Or did he just enjoy watching his victims suffer?

55

He was staring directly at her, challenging her to take him on. Arms folded, chin jutting out, this macho idiot seemed determined to thwart her.

'I'm an accredited journalist,' Emilia hissed, barely containing her fury. 'I have every right to drive down this road –'

'You're a pain in the arse,' the smirking officer replied. 'And this is a crime scene. Authorized personnel only, I'm afraid.'

What was it with young police officers these days? In the past, Emilia had always been able to work them somehow – through flattery, veiled threats or outright bribery. But the new breed seemed impervious to temptation or fear, toeing the official line with a zeal that bordered on the obscene.

'I need to speak to DI Grace,' Emilia demanded, hoping her knowledge of the SIO would buy her some slack. 'Or DS Brooks. I know their unit is here –'

'They left an hour ago.'

Emilia cursed under her breath. On leaving Sunnyside, she had followed the flotilla of vehicles towards South Baddesley, maintaining a safe distance, while always keeping it in view. All had been going well until, right at the death, a tractor had slipped into the gap, crawling slowly along the road for almost half a mile, before diverting into a field. By the time Emilia rounded the lumbering tractor, the police vehicles were long gone.

This wasn't necessarily a disaster, as the road was a dead end, petering out by a cliff edge. So she knew where she was heading. Her problem became clear a mile further down the road, when a fluttering police cordon came into view, hovering a few metres in front of a police roadblock.

Slewing her car to a stop, Emilia had considered her options. Really, she had none – other than to try and circum-navigate the roadblock by penetrating the thick bushes to the right or traversing the steep meadow to her left. Sensibly, she had attempted the latter, only to find a pair of uniformed officers stationed at the top of the hill.

Now she had no option but to drive down the road and see if she could talk her way through the roadblock or, at the very least, garner some information about what was going on. But the fresh-faced officer remained tight-lipped, seem-ingly enjoying frustrating her.

Having been ahead of the game, Emilia suddenly found herself behind the beat. Angry, frustrated, she was about to leave, when she noticed something in the distance. A man, with a bag on his shoulder, walking slowly away from the forest. Now Emilia paused. There were no other vehicles – police or ambulance – to help her piece together the narrative, but perhaps this lone survivor might tell her something. Not literally of course, the world and his wife seemed to know who Emilia was these days, the curse of her current notori-ety. But there was more than one way to skin a cat.

Returning to her car, she dawdled casually, smoking a cig-arette and pretending to send some emails. And, sure enough, five minutes later a black Volvo estate crawled by. Busying herself with her phone, Emilia nevertheless angled a surrep-titious glance at the driver and was rewarded with the sight of Graham Ross driving by. She had seen the crime scene photographer at several other crime scenes over the years and recognized him instantly. The car, however, was new to her, so she didn't hesitate, zooming in to take a close-up of the number plate.

All was not lost, it seemed. Emilia had a contact at the DVLA who could slip her his home address. She did not know Ross personally, but she felt certain she could work on him. He had always seemed a little isolated, a team member in name only. Would he not welcome some stimulating female company?

If Helen Grace, and her loyal colleagues, would not talk to her, perhaps Graham Ross would.

56

'I need to speak with him urgently. Can you tell me when he will be back?'

Joseph Hudson's tone remained courteous and professional, concealing his growing frustration.

'He's at a cattle auction in Dorset. Should be back around ten o'clock.'

'It is important we contact him, Mrs Druce, so if you could give me his mobile number?'

'Oh, I couldn't do that. How do I know you are who you say you are?'

'That's easy. If you ring Southampton Central Police Station and ask for DS Joseph Hudson, they'll put you through.'

'No, thank you.'

'I'm sorry?' Joseph retorted, unable to conceal his surprise.

'This could be one of those scams you hear about.'

'I can assure you it's not. You can look me up online if that would put your mind at –'

'I don't trust the internet. Never have.'

She hung up shortly afterwards, leaving Joseph simmering with irritation. The elderly farmer's wife was clearly determined not to help, despite Joseph's evident desire to track down her husband, who had owned a Land Rover Defender for a number of years. She was not alone either – Joseph had around twenty names to check and in only three cases had he actually managed to talk to the car owner. None of those had seemed like legitimate suspects – they were by turns too old, too ill, abroad on business – leaving him with precisely nothing to show for two hours' work.

Looking up, he realized that his colleagues were faring little better. Ellie McAndrew and a couple of junior officers were sifting the web for weapons nuts, perusing an endless parade of muscle-bound thugs brandishing all manner of offensive weapons, while his own officers were as bogged down as him. He could see them drawing thick lines through potential suspects, at best occasionally adding a question mark, if they had been unable to contact the car owner over the phone or if the vehicle had been reported stolen.

It was a pretty depressing picture and prompted Hudson to take action. Grabbing his list, his phone and his jacket, he hurried over to his colleagues. If the mountain won't come to Mohammed, as his mother was fond of saying, it was time to get moving. There was nothing to do now but hit the streets and try and track these owners down personally. It would be tiring, it would be laborious, but it was a chance he would have to take.

In cases such as these, the devil was often in the detail.

57

She stared at the corpse, her eyes crawling over the skin.

From Southampton Central, Helen had biked straight over to the mortuary, keen to glean what she could from Jim Grieves. The pathologist was even more grumpy than usual, complaining that he was still in the initial stages of his examination, that nobody afforded him the respect he deserved. Helen was happy to weather the storm of his complaints – Grieves always did this – as his insights were often significant.

They were standing in the viewing area, at a safe distance from David Spivack, who was still hard at work on the body, his hands currently deep in the victim's abdomen. Lauren Scott's blood-soaked clothing had been removed and sent to Meredith for analysis, allowing Helen a clear view of their second victim. She was quite a sight, not because of her shoulder-length black hair or her lacerated feet, which were pointing almost directly at Helen, but because of the sheer number of markings on her body. She had several tattoos – none of them particularly pleasant – and a plethora of small cuts. The latter seemed to cover her torso, upper arms and thighs.

'Are those all from last night?'

'No,' Grieves replied firmly. 'There are dozens of historic cuts, some of which have been there several years.'

'Self-harming?'

'I'd say. They are all in places that can be easily concealed.'

Helen's eyes lingered on one of the tattoos – a snake devouring a baby's head, just beneath her left breast. What frame of mind had Lauren been in?

'Are they all old?'

'No, some are more recent. I'd say she was pretty committed to it.'

'How about bloods? Any drugs? Alcohol?'

'Clean as a whistle.'

Helen digested this – Matteo Dominici had clearly been telling the truth, when he insisted they were both dry and clean.

'Anything else, Jim? I know your time is precious.'

'Very similar wounds to Tom Campbell's,' Grieves pressed on, ignoring the attempt to butter him up. 'Lacerations to the feet, scratches and jagged cuts on the arms, neck, face, all consistent with thorns, vegetation and so on. Three major wounds caused by the crossbow bolts. The impact areas are more severe than with Campbell, the haemorrhages greater, meaning she would have bled out more quickly.'

This was something at least. Perhaps Lauren's nightmare had had a mercifully quick end.

'We've obviously removed the bolts and sent them to Meredith, but they look similar to me.'

Confirmation, if it were needed, that the same perpetrator was responsible for the two murders. Turning, Helen replied:

'Ok, well, keep me up to speed –'

'There was one more thing,' Grieves interrupted, his eyes still glued to the corpse on the slab. 'Though it's nothing to do with the circumstances of the attack.'

Helen paused, intrigued.

'She was pregnant.'

Helen's heart sank.

'Very early stages, but no question about it. Thought you'd want to know.'

Thanking Grieves for his work, Helen left the mortuary shortly afterwards. She wandered to her bike, deep in thought. Matteo Dominici had not mentioned the pregnancy when they spoke. True, he was distracted, frantic with worry, but surely he would have mentioned it, had he known? Extra pressure to bring to bear on the police to find her? Did this mean he was unaware? And what of Lauren? If she was in the very early stages, it was possible even *she* didn't know.

The thought stopped Helen in her tracks. This baby could have been Lauren's future, her legacy to the world, something good to come out of what had obviously been a difficult life.

But now it would never be.

58

'Sorry, do I know you?'

Graham Ross had jumped out of his skin when Emilia approached him. His mind was elsewhere – he hadn't seen her coming – but now confusion was giving way to suspicion.

'We've not met, but I know your work,' she replied winningly. 'I'm Emilia Garanita, from the *Southampton Evening News*.'

'Of course . . .' Ross replied slowly, recognition kicking in. 'You're the one who's been terrifying Southampton with your ill-judged headlines.'

'Just reporting the facts, Graham,' Emilia replied breezily. 'Talking of which I'd love to have a quick word with you, if you can spare the time.'

'What about?'

'The case, of course. I'd be very interested to get your take on it.'

He looked at her, appraising her, appraising the situation. As he did so, he pulled nervously on the strap of his camera bag, which was slung over his shoulder.

'How did you know I'd be here?'

'This is your office, isn't it?' she replied, gesturing to the flat-cum-studio nearby, where Ross lived and worked. 'A friend at Southampton Central said I'd find you here.'

In fact, a mole at the DVLA had confirmed his home address – once the requisite cash had been promised. But Emilia hoped mention of a friendly face at the station might put him at his ease.

'I don't think I can. I'm supposed to be at a meeting in an hour or so —'

'Just a quick drink,' Emilia countered, laying a hand on his bare forearm. 'I promise I won't take up too much of your time.'

Ross looked at her hand, then up at Emilia. He seemed amused, even a little intrigued.

'Why should I?' he replied, challenging her good-humouredly.

Emilia flashed her widest smile.

'Because I'm buying.'

'I can't tell you anything that's not in the press release.'

They were cocooned together in a local pub. Emilia didn't generally drink during the day, but had made an exception on this occasion – Ross seemingly eager to quench his thirst with a pint of IPA.

'That hardly told us anything,' Emilia complained. 'But that's nothing new.'

News that Hampshire Police were putting out a general alert, warning campers to steer clear of the New Forest, had filtered through as Emilia was idling in her car, waiting for Ross. For a moment, she had been tempted to hotfoot it over to Southampton Central to hear the details, then thought better of it. Grace never fielded press briefings herself and whoever did would be evasive, so Emilia sent a colleague instead. She was more interested in Ross.

'That's the game, right?' Ross said with a crooked smile, enjoying their banter.

'Maybe. But this game just got serious, so a bit of candour would be appreciated. You photographed Campbell and Scott, right?'

Ross reacted, clearly surprised that she knew the identity of the second victim.

'What makes you say that?'

'There's no need to be coy, Graham. I know the MIT team was at Woodland View two days ago and at Sunnyside this morning. I'm assuming Scott's body was found in woodland near South Baddesley?'

Ross stared at her, clearly intrigued to know how she was so well informed.

'I managed to have a word with her boyfriend, Matteo Dominici,' Emilia lied. 'But he was obviously very shaken and didn't want to discuss the details. I'm assuming that she was also murdered with a crossbow?'

Now Ross smiled.

'You don't give up, do you?' he said, finishing his pint.

'God loves a trier.'

'Then I'll tell you what I'll do,' he continued, somewhat magnanimously. 'You can ask me questions and I'll nod or shake my head.'

It was beyond childish – a sad, lonely man's way of playing at being a mole – but Emilia was happy to play along.

'Sounds good to me.'

'But first, I need a slash. Why don't you buy me another pint while you're waiting?'

With that, he sidled off to the Gents. Emilia rose too, but as she did so, her eyes alighted on Ross's camera bag, tucked discreetly under his chair. A moment's hesitation, then she pulled it out and unzipped it. Removing the camera, she switched it on. It was not dissimilar to the SLR she used and she quickly found the playback mode.

'Oh my God . . .'

A close-up of Lauren Scott's blood-streaked face filled the screen.

Breathlessly, Emilia scrolled through. Long shots, mid-shots, then detailed shots of the arrow wounds, the torn feet, the raw ankles. The images were horrendous, but amazing. She darted a look at the Gents – there was still no sign of Ross – then reached into her own bag. From the inside pocket, she retrieved a data stick, which she swiftly plugged into the port on the camera.

Selecting a dozen of the most shocking pictures, she pressed 'transfer'. Immediately, a little hourglass started spinning on the camera's screen. One photo, two, three . . . It was efficient enough, but seemed to be going slowly, too slowly. She darted another look at the Gents and was horri-fied to see Ross emerging.

Five photos, six, seven . . .

She would surely be caught. Any minute now, he would round the corner.

Nine photos, ten . . .

To her intense relief, Emilia saw Ross stop to chat to the barmaid. She obviously knew him and didn't seem offended by his amateurish flirting.

Eleven, twelve.

The camera pinged as the transfer completed and, quick as a flash, Emilia retrieved her data stick and popped the camera into its case. She was sliding it back under the chair as Ross finally approached.

'Sorry, work call,' she said, rising, waving her phone at him. 'Let me get you that drink.'

She skipped off to the bar happily. Sometimes she resented other people getting drunk at her expense, but not today. Two pints of beer was a small price to pay for the plethora of hor-rifying images that were now safely tucked away in her pocket.

59

'Can you confirm that both victims were killed in the same way? With the same weapon?'

It was the tone of the question that irritated Grace Simmons. The journalist, a cub from one of the local free sheets, was trying to sound sober, but couldn't hide her excitement about the exotic brutality of the murders.

'A crossbow was used in both instances,' Simmons replied calmly. 'It's too early to say if it was the same weapon.'

She turned away from the young woman and immediately a dozen more journalists took their chance, firing questions at her. All the local media outlets were present, plus a few freelancers who worked for the nationals, who'd managed to scramble to the press conference, scenting a major story. And all thanks to Emilia Garanita's stirring. They would have had to share news of the murders with the media eventually of course – it was their duty to do so – but they would have done so properly and responsibly. Garanita was only interested in creating hysteria, something she seemed to have achieved handsomely, given the ridiculous number of journalists crammed into their modest briefing room.

'Do you have any idea as to motive?' a local radio broadcaster was asking.

'We're keeping an open mind on that at the moment –'

'Suspects, then?' the journalist persisted. 'Do you have any names in the frame?'

'None that I'm willing to share, but the public can be

reassured that we are making swift progress and should be in a position to say more shortly.'

'Are you looking for an individual? Or a group of suspects?'

'I'd rather not comment on that for now.'

'Is an arrest imminent?'

'Like I said, our investigation is ongoing –'

'We'll take that as a "no" then,' one of the assembled wags commented, to general amusement.

Simmons stared directly at the offender, until he looked away. She would have loved to call him out, but sensibly bit her tongue. Still, it beggared belief that people could find humour in such a situation.

'Are you declaring the forest a no-go zone?'

This time the question came from a local TV reporter.

'Of course not. Thousands of people use the New Forest every week, for work, for pleasure. What we *are* saying is that people should exercise caution, avoiding remote areas of the forest, and consider postponing non-essential visits.'

'Is it true there's a wild man in the forest?'

'Not to my knowledge,' Simmons countered dismissively.

'There have been several reports of a crazy hermit living deep –'

'Every *significant* lead will be investigated, but we're not in the business of engaging with wild speculation and gossip –'

'What measures *are* you putting in place to protect the public?'

Simmons was taken aback by the speed with which the questions kept landing. It was as if the assembled throng scented blood.

'There is an increased police presence in the forest and we will be keeping the public up to speed with the latest developments via the Hampshire Police website and local media outlets. We have also set up a dedicated hotline for anyone with information about these crimes –'

'Is the public safe? Can you hand on heart say that you can keep us safe, when there is a maniac stalking the forest?'

'We will do everything in our power to ensure public safety *and* a swift resolution to this case.'

'And what about DI Grace? Does she retain your confidence? There've been two murders and no concrete developments, no tangible leads,' the journalist from the *Evening News* now piped up.

'Yes, she does. And I'm surprised that her competence should be in question, given her exemplary track record.'

It was said pointedly, even a touch aggressively, cowing the interrogator. But Simmons knew this was only a temporary reprieve. While the killer remained at large, while they struggled to get a handle on these baffling crimes, the questions would continue to come.

60

'Are you sure? Are you absolutely sure?'

Matteo Dominici was visibly distraught, so Charlie sat down beside him on the sofa, resting a supportive hand on his shoulder. Having received Helen's update from the mortuary, she'd been keen to share the terrible news with Dominici before he heard it from another source. So they were now alone together in the flat he used to share with Lauren Scott.

'We are, I'm afraid. She was about two months along.'

Dominici's whole body shook. Charlie felt awful delivering such devastating news, when he was already raw with grief, but she had to be straight with him.

'She never mentioned anything . . .' he murmured eventually.

'Do you think it's possible she knew?'

'I don't know . . . Her . . . her periods were incredibly irregular, so she may not have assumed that she was . . .'

He couldn't say the words, so Charlie helped him out.

'If she *did* know, it's possible she was waiting until the three-month mark, until it was safe to share her news.'

Charlie had no idea if this was true, but wanted to say something to ease his pain. Dominici nodded, as if it made sense, but said nothing.

'When we first spoke, Matteo, you said you and Lauren had been together for around eighteen months.'

Another nod.

'During your time together, were you aware that she was self-harming?'

'Of course. She . . . she was secretive about it, tried to hide it from me. But when we were together, in bed, in the bath, it was hard to hide . . .'

'Do you know why she did it?'

'No, I asked her a million times, but she just said that when the mood overcame her, she felt compelled to. She hated herself, thought she was unworthy, that the world would be better off without her. I know she had contemplated suicide in the past, but we managed to get past that. Once she was dry, once I was dry, it was possible for us both to see a way forward.'

'Can I ask why you drank, Matteo?'

'Why I was an alcoholic, you mean?'

Charlie had seen this from ex-alcoholics before – a fierce determination not to dress up their behaviour.

'Marriage breakdown. Got hitched too young and it ended messily.'

That would need to be checked out. It was not beyond the realms of possibility that Dominici might be connected in some way. Though his pain, his distress, seemed genuine, they only had his word as to what happened that night.

'And now *this*,' Dominici said, looking up. 'Why did this happen just when she was getting her shit together?'

'I don't know, but we will find out, I can promise you that.'

'Dear God, this is all my fault,' Dominici moaned, seeming not to hear Charlie at all. 'All my fault . . .'

'Why do you say that, Matteo?'

'Because she didn't want to go,' he replied, shaking his head.

'What do you mean?'

'Camping was my thing, not hers. She wasn't keen, didn't like the idea of sleeping outdoors. But I went on and on at her.'

'And in the end she agreed?'

'I'd just bought a new tent, wanted to try it out. Then we got this leaflet through the door for Sunnyside. Maybe I put pressure on her, I don't know, but she said she'd come because . . . because she loved me and wanted me to be happy.'

Now he wept openly.

'This is not your fault, Matteo. None of this is your fault.'

'But if I hadn't made her go, she'd still be alive . . .'

'You don't know that,' Charlie replied quickly, though she couldn't fault his logic.

'Dear God, what have I done?'

She was losing him now, despair consuming him.

'Matteo, I won't take up any more of your time, but I do need to ask you one more thing.'

He looked up, bewildered as to what Charlie could possibly want to ask, given the circumstances.

'We think Lauren's murder might be connected to another death, a few days ago.'

Blank astonishment.

'So I'd like you to look at this photo and tell me if you recognize the man in it, if Lauren might have known him socially or through her support networks.'

She handed him a photo of Tom Campbell. It had been taken at a recent family gathering and showed the young man smiling broadly – happy, relaxed, full of life. Dominici stared at it for what seemed like an eternity, taking in the details of the man's features.

'No, I'm sorry . . .' He looked up at Charlie, handing her back the photo. '. . . I've never seen that guy before in my life.'

61

The metal screamed as the claws descended, twisting and contorting under the intense pressure, before eventually being crushed flat. It was hard to watch – the car, which had presumably once been someone's pride and joy, flattened like a pancake – yet oddly it was hard to take your eyes off it. It seemed so overwhelming, so *final*.

Tearing his gaze away, Joseph Hudson pressed on, pushing deeper into the scrapyard. He was a practical man – had always been interested in constructing weird and wonderful machines from spare parts – and in other circumstances would have enjoyed exploring the sprawling site, taking in the dismembered fridges, cars, computers and TVs. But he had a job to do so, ignoring the mammoth towers of metal which surrounded him, he bent his steps towards the manager's office.

'Terry Clarke and son, scrap merchants'. The battered sign above the door looked tired and forlorn, mirroring Hudson's mood. He had spent the past three hours trawling Southampton, knocking on doors, having terse, irritable conversations with car owners, who bridled at his intrusion. His presence was welcome nowhere, but he had pressed his case and, through his persistence, had now ticked off most of the names on his list. DCs Bentham and Edwards were doing likewise elsewhere in Hampshire, but had turned up nothing so far. Hudson told himself that this would be his last call of the day – perhaps tomorrow would bring him better luck.

Knocking on the door, he was greeted by a grunt. Taking

this as an invitation to enter, he stepped inside. A burly, unshaven man in overalls looked up at him, surprised and suspicious. There was obviously something in Hudson's bearing that made it clear he was not a customer.

'Terry Clarke?'

'S'right.'

'I'm DS Hudson,' he replied, showing the owner his warrant card. 'I wonder if I could have a quick word about a Land Rover Defender – registration number DB09 OLF?'

'Why? What's this about?'

'Do you still own the vehicle?'

'Sure, but I don't use it.'

'I see . . .'

'I've got a Freelander now. My son drives the Defender.'

'And his name is . . . ?'

'Dean.'

Hudson scribbled the name down.

'Is he here?'

'No, he's just popped out.'

'And the car?'

'S'out back.'

'Could I take a look?'

It was said with a smile, but Hudson's tone revealed that this was not a question.

'What's happened? Is this about speeding or . . .'

He petered out, knowing full well that you don't receive home visits for speeding offences. Hudson could see the scrapyard owner's mind turning, sifting the possibilities.

'Why don't we just take a look at the car?' Hudson replied amiably.

Clarke's definition of 'out back' was generous. It took them ten minutes to pick their way through the maze of wrecked cars and discarded appliances, before they eventually reached a shabby warehouse at the rear of the site. Had the owner been the least bit hostile or menacing, Hudson might have felt apprehensive, isolated in the sprawling yard on the edge of Woolston, but Terry Clarke was out of shape, wheezing as he struggled along.

'Keeps it in here,' Clarke gasped, heaving open the door to the warehouse.

Stepping inside, Hudson was immediately struck by the smell – part rotting wood, part bird droppings, part engine oil. It was a heady combination.

'Just there,' Clarke continued, gesturing towards the black Defender, parked at the back of the dusty space.

Hudson moved forward, intrigued. Why did Dean Clarke feel the need to hide the vehicle away in such a remote part of the site?

Approaching the vehicle, he took in the battered wings and dirty windscreen. This was not a vehicle that was much loved – it was a functional, off-road beast which was clearly being driven into the ground.

Bending down, Hudson examined the front tyres. They were Avon Rangemasters, as he had expected, and they were virtually bald, the tread worn down by age. Intriguingly, mud caked both tyres, filling in the space between the soft rubber ridges. Hudson ran a finger over it – it was dry but firm, refusing to crumble – suggesting it was relatively fresh.

'How often does your son use this vehicle?' Hudson asked, straightening up.

'Often enough,' Clarke replied evasively.

Nodding, Hudson continued his circuit of the vehicle. There was no question that it had seen some action – the body had numerous dents and the paintwork was severely scratched.

'And what does he use it for? Work or play?'

'He uses my van for work, this is just for getting about.'

Hudson continued his circuit, peering into the boot of the car. Some of Clarke's possessions were in there, but it was impossible to say what they were, as a thick blanket covered every inch of the boot. Curious, Hudson tested the handle, but was not surprised to find it locked.

'Any idea what he's got in there?'

Clarke shook his head, looking tense. Hudson suspected he wanted to know what this visit was all about, but was fearful to ask.

'And when are you expecting him back?'

'Not sure, to be honest. He doesn't tend to hang around after his shift's finished.'

'I could call round later, to the family home?'

'You won't find him there.'

'He's got his own place?'

'No, he lives with me, but . . . but he's not around in the evenings much.'

'Does he have a partner? Mates?'

'Not to speak of.'

'So where does he go?'

'Out.'

Hudson looked at Clarke, who could barely meet his gaze.

'Maybe . . . maybe he finds it a bit suffocating at home. Just me and him . . .'

'You've never asked him where he goes?'

'No, I'm not his keeper. He can do what he likes.'

It was said with bluster, but rang hollow. The scrapyard owner was clearly rattled, which made Hudson wonder. Where was Dean Clarke? What was he hiding from his father?

And where did he go at night?

62

The cigarette smouldered in her hand, unnoticed. On returning to Southampton Central, Helen had eschewed the incident room, instead heading for the yard. She told herself she needed a smoke, but actually she needed some time, some *space*, to think. Few ventured here – it was a forgotten part of the station that Helen often fled to, a good place to let your mind turn on a troubling case.

But today Helen was not the only person seeking its sanctuary.

The door groaned and Helen looked up sharply, but it was only Charlie, one of the few people who always knew where to find her. Pocketing her cigarettes – Charlie was not a fan – Helen turned to face her colleague.

'How did you get on?' she said, as brightly as she could.

'Not good,' Charlie shrugged, seeming a little downcast. 'You?'

'Nothing. We're chasing down every possible angle, but there's no sign of a link between the two victims so far.'

'You're sure the murders *are* connected?' Charlie asked, sounding suddenly doubtful. 'I mean, if the evidence isn't there . . .'

'I hope so, for all our sakes,' Helen emphasized. 'Otherwise, we're going to have the devil's own job finding the perpetrator.'

Charlie nodded, but looked distracted.

'I think we need to look deeper into Lauren Scott,' Helen continued. 'Her history of self-harm, her relationships, her drug abuse . . .'

'Right . . .'

'It may be something, it may be nothing. But it's a line we can work with. Tom Campbell is just so . . . clean. It's hard to think why anyone would want to harm him.'

Charlie nodded once more.

'How did Dominici respond to the photo of Campbell?'

'He didn't recognize him, but to be honest, he was too devastated to respond to *anything*.'

Helen could tell Charlie was upset and reached out to her. There were no barriers between them after all these years.

'It's so cruel . . . Life seemed set fair for him,' Charlie continued, falteringly. 'For both of them. And now he has a double funeral to plan . . .'

Charlie was staring at her shoes, emotion bubbling to the surface. Helen looked at her friend with concern – she had been tired and anxious of late.

'Look, why don't you head home, Charlie? Rest that ankle of yours?'

'I'm fine,' Charlie said, grimacing as she rotated her swollen foot to show off its capabilities. 'To be honest, I think I'm safer here.'

'Meaning?'

'Oh, it's nothing,' Charlie said, sounding embarrassed. 'It's just Steve is set on having another child. He's probably putting the wine on ice as we speak, lining up his Barry White playlist . . .'

'But you're not sure you're ready?'

'Part of me wants to, of course. For Steve, for Jessie, but . . . what if that's just me being weak? Taking the easy way out, because it's what *they* want?'

'Have you spoken to Steve about it?'

'Not properly and I'm not sure I want to.'

'Because?'

'Because I will sound paranoid. And scared.'

Helen stared at Charlie. Her friend was always absolutely candid with her, a quality she admired enormously. But she did seem frightened and unsure of herself tonight.

'I just can't get what happened to Joanne out of my head.'

'I know.'

'Whenever I think of the next step, of having another child, I think about that day . . .'

She didn't need to spell it out – Charlie was one of the first on the scene, after Joanne Sanderson had died in Helen's arms.

'I still visit her mum, you know.'

Helen felt a sharp stab of guilt – her visits to Nicola had tailed off.

'And I see how it's affected her, how it's affected the whole family . . . and it makes me think – what if it had been me? What if I'd come face to face with Daisy and . . .'

'We've all thought that.'

'I know,' Charlie said, angrily wiping an errant tear from her eye. 'I know you feel it worse than me, which is why I feel so . . . stupid.'

'You're not stupid. This job is dangerous and if you ever feel –'

'I *don't* want to step away from my job, that's not what this is about. But Joanne has made me . . . appreciate what I'm risking. It makes the idea of having another child seem crazy, but that's stupid too.'

'Charlie . . .'

'Because I can't put my life on hold – our life on hold – because of something that happened to someone else. It's not fair to deny Jessie a sibling – she'd love a little brother or sister – and yet . . .'

'If you're not ready, you're not ready,' Helen said firmly.

'Obviously, I know nothing about these things.' Helen smiled, aware of how absurd it was for her to be dispensing domestic advice. 'But I'm sure when the time is right, you'll know. Until then you have to allow yourself to grieve for your friend and process what happened in whatever way comes naturally. Don't force yourself to feel that you're over it, if you're not.'

Helen knew she was also guilty of obsessing over Joanne's death, but nevertheless she felt that what she was saying was true.

'It happened. It's horrible, but it happened. And we all need to deal with it, however distressing or troubling that might be.'

'You're right, of course you're right,' Charlie said, flashing a smile of gratitude at Helen. 'And thank you.'

'Now get off home, you've had a long day.'

'I will do, if that's ok. You never know, there might be some football on to distract Steve.'

Smiling ruefully, Charlie departed, leaving Helen alone. Her encounter with Nathaniel Martin had clearly amplified Charlie's fears, reawakened all the doubts and anxieties she'd experienced after Joanne's death, but Helen was glad to see her leaving with a smile on her face. Watching her go, Helen reflected that they had both been affected by Joanne's murder, albeit in differing ways. Charlie at least was engaging with the world, trying to build a life for herself and her family. Helen, by contrast, was alone in the smokers' yard, toying idly with a packet of cigarettes. It was a perfect picture of isolation, which made Helen feel suddenly empty.

Charlie might have her problems, but she had made her mark on the world, with Steve, with Jessie. If Helen died tomorrow, what would be her legacy? Who would mourn her?

Not for the first time today, Helen found herself unable to answer a simple question.

63

'No, no, no. And that's my final word on the matter.'

Emilia was tempted to point out that 'no, no, no' was actually three words, but thought better of it. She had to pacify Gardiner, her editor having already worked himself up into a lather.

'I'm not talking about any of the graphic shots,' Emilia replied, gesturing at the crime scene photos spread out on the desk. 'I was thinking we could use one of the long shots. You can see the outline of the body hanging from the tree, but you can't see her features, her injuries, or any flesh. In fact, it's a rather beautiful shot. The way the trees frame the crime scene . . .'

Martin Gardiner looked at Emilia as if her idea of 'beautiful' was beyond perverted, but she persevered.

'And think what a sensation it would be. Grace, Simmons, they're all guilty of treating the public like kids, of hiding the true situation from them. Well, we could bust it right open –'

'You're talking like a comic book hack,' Gardiner shot back angrily. 'And before you go any further, let me remind you that this is a local paper.'

'How could I forget,' Emilia muttered, low enough for him not to hear.

'People read this paper for the property pages, the recipes, the crossword. The news they want is local news –'

'This *is* local, it's on their bloody doorstep.'

'By which I mean, council elections, school fetes, fun runs . . .'

'This is going to be a *big* story. And we could steal a march on everyone . . .'

'By publishing graphic crime scene photos – photos that you *stole*.'

'We can say they were leaked –'

'And when we get taken to court, when we have to prove that? What then?'

'It wouldn't be down to us to prove anything. *They* would have to prove that we'd obtained them illegally. Besides, they'd never go down that route. It would make them look totally incompetent.'

Gardiner was about to interject, so Emilia carried on quickly.

'Look, we're wasting time. If we can agree on which shot to go for, then I can give you a thousand words by close of play.'

'Emilia,' Gardiner replied, just about controlling his temper. 'You don't seem to understand what I'm saying, so let me try and be clear. We are *not* publishing crime scene photos that will repel the vast majority of our readers – not on the front page, not on the centre pages, not in the bloody horoscopes.'

Emilia again tried to interrupt, but Gardiner wasn't finished yet.

'Nor am I going to have my arse sued off to further your career.' He began to gather up the photos. 'We shall put today's error of judgement down to youthful enthusiasm and pretend it never happened,' he continued, thrusting the sheaf of photos into Emilia's hands. 'Is that crystal clear?'

'Yes.'

'Good, then get on with your article. Your description, the facts that we have, will be chilling enough, trust me.'

But the problem was Emilia didn't trust him. Didn't trust

his judgement, nor his instincts. As she stalked back to her desk, cursing under her breath, she reflected that she had never seen eye to eye with Gardiner – who seemed threatened by her gender, her youth, her talent. But she refused to be cowed by him. She had taken quite a risk obtaining the photos and there was no question of them going unused.

Which meant that once again she would have to take matters into her own hands.

64

His fingers slid across the keys, typing in commands. Moments later, a photo sprang up on screen. It was of a young man in a khaki vest and camouflage trousers, staring directly at the camera.

'That's him. I recognized the name as soon as you said it.'

Hudson shot a look at the name tagged to the photo – 'Hellmanned2008' – then turned to DC Reid. The latter read his confusion.

'It's Dean Clarke's online alias, a bit of word play on Helmand. He served there from 2007 to 2010.'

'Right . . . Where did you come across him?'

'Lots of places, he posts quite regularly. Mostly on weapons sites and survivalist forums. It's a lot of beefed-up guys bragging to each other about how tough they are, how they would be the only ones left standing if society collapsed. It's all pretty homoerotic, if you ask me.'

Hudson let that one go – he was still getting a handle on DC Reid's unusual sense of humour.

'He also contributes to several forums, plus he has his own website.'

The welcome page for *Lastmanstanding.co.uk* now filled the screen. It featured a close-up of Clarke's piercing, emerald eyes, framed by darkness.

'The welcoming image is designed to intimidate, I guess. The rest are fairly standard shots to excite military obsessives and muscle worshippers.'

Reid pulled up the gallery shots, some of which featured

Clarke stripped to the waist, his bulging muscles and tattoos on display. Hudson let his eyes run over the latter, most of which were military in character.

'We're sure he was in the army?' Hudson asked, surprised.

'He says he was in the Special Forces and claims to have over a dozen service kills to his name. He goes into quite a lot of detail about those – his use of automatic weapons, knives, his bare hands on one occasion . . .'

Hudson's gaze fell onto Clarke's meaty palms, which seemed a giant's in comparison to his.

'He also talks a fair deal about what will happen when the walls come tumbling down. How he and others like him will need to be ready. My guess is he's been watching too much *Walking Dead.*'

'Does he have many followers? Who reads this stuff?'

'It's fairly popular. Some ex-soldiers of course, but it's mostly teenage boys and young men who are angry with the world. Some of his followers sail pretty close to the wind, condoning racist killings in America, sending death threats to politicians and celebrities. It's a fairly toxic bunch, to be honest, and I think I've had my fill for one day, so . . .'

Rising, Reid gestured to Hudson to take his seat. Thanking his colleague, Hudson continued to scroll, pulling up a picture of Clarke in full battledress, right down to the camou-flage gear, flak jacket and blackened face. Staring at this disquieting, aggressive image, Hudson found himself more and more intrigued by Dean Clarke. This was a young man who used to have purpose and prestige, but was now working for his father in a low-rent junkyard. He was a practised killer, living locally, full of anger, suspicion and hostility. An elusive figure too, with a keen interest in weapons, regularly dis-appearing for night-time excursions. Was it possible that he was their man? That the unusual weapons used to hunt down

Tom Campbell and Lauren Scott could have been fashioned from the discarded metal that surrounded him at work?

It was an intriguing possibility and one which Hudson was determined to run to ground. Reid and the others could go – he would remain where he was. Now that he finally had a scent, there was no way he was abandoning the hunt.

65

His eyes never left him, but he said nothing.

Terry Clarke sat opposite his son, who was devouring his dinner with an intensity that was unpleasant to behold. Since his wife passed away, Terry often ate on site, a stock of ready meals on hand. Occasionally, Dean joined him, but he wasn't much of a companion, eating and leaving as quickly as he could. These brief encounters made Terry feel strange – it was depressing how little he knew his son these days, how lifeless their shared dinners were, yet he was loath to give them up. They reminded him of happier times, when the three of them used to eat together in the family home. He had promised his late wife, Nancy, that he would continue to keep an eye on their errant son and it was not a pledge he intended to break.

'Had the police round here earlier . . .' he said, pushing his plate away from him.

Dean's fork froze momentarily, then he resumed eating, consuming a couple more mouthfuls, before grunting a response:

'And?'

'They were asking about you. About your vehicle.'

Another brief pause.

'What they asking for?'

'You tell me.'

His son plunged a final forkful into his mouth. He chewed slowly, before eventually replying:

'Nothing to tell.'

'Then why did they come? We've never had the police around here before –'

'Right upstanding citizen, aren't you?'

His son's tone was mocking.

'I've cut corners,' Terry replied, irritated. 'But I have *never* broken the law.'

'Keep telling yourself that.'

Shaking his head, Dean rose.

'Where you going? We're not finished yet.'

'Yes, we are.'

Dean was on the move and Terry was quickly after him. Haring across the room, he grabbed his son by the shoulder, spinning him around.

'What's going on, boy? What you got yourself into?'

Anger flared in Dean's eyes. Unnerved, Terry took a step back, but the anger suddenly dissipated. To be replaced with something worse – disdain.

'Don't ever lay a hand on me again.'

'I just want to know what's going on. If you're in trouble, I can help. Your mother would have wanted that.'

'There's no trouble.'

'Then why did they come here? What's in that vehicle?'

Dean's hand shot out, grabbing him by the throat, and Terry now felt himself spinning. Half a second later, he slammed into the wall, the breath knocked from him. Stunned, he blinked wildly, as Dean moved in close.

'Be careful, old man. Be very careful.'

'I . . . I don't mean to pry.'

But Dean held a finger to his lips, silencing him.

'And stay out of my business.'

It was not what his son said that unnerved him, though that was bad enough. It was the way he said it. Cold, detached, steely.

'Of course . . . I just worry ab—'

He didn't get to finish, his son flinging him roughly to the floor and stalking from the room. Terry watched him go, his heart pounding, at a loss to explain what had just happened. He had known for a long time that his son was aggressive, troubled, unpredictable, but he had never felt personally threatened by him. Had his wife's recent death unhinged his son in some way? Had he finally lost him?

Terry Clarke had felt many emotions over the years – regret, sadness and confusion chief among them. But tonight, for the first time, he felt scared.

66

Helen stared at the fragile face, searching for answers. The photo of Lauren Scott was a recent one and seemed to capture a moment in time. You could read the trauma, the neglect in her features – the deep lines under her eyes, the stained teeth, the thinning hair – but also a sparkle of hope in her expression, a sense that life could be about to get better. How tragic this photo seemed now.

Helen had retreated to her office. Joseph Hudson was the only other soul present, but for once he seemed utterly absorbed in his work, so Helen took his lead, poring over the details of Lauren Scott's life. The pressure for progress was growing. Simmons had handled the press conference adroitly, but the questioning – about the nature of the attacks, the lack of leads, the competence of the team – was aggressive and sustained. Simmons had worked hard to reassure the assembled journalists, while still withholding some of the more unpleasant details of the attacks, but the sense of rising panic was unmistakable, both in the station and in the wider city.

Why? Why had these two innocent people been attacked? This was what everyone wanted to know, but still Helen couldn't fathom it. There had to be a clear motive, some obvious connection between the two, but, if so, it was hard to discern. They had both been born in Southampton, but other than that there seemed no overlaps. There *was* a possible drugs link, but in truth even this seemed tenuous. Tom Campbell had one possession charge from his teenage years, a lucky escape given he had enough on him to warrant an intent-to-supply charge, but this paled into insignificance compared to Lauren Scott's history of offences. Lauren had fallen off the straight and narrow early in life, while Tom Campbell seemed the very definition of it – sober, hard-working, successful.

And yet . . . was it really possible they had been targeted at random? This wasn't a drive-by or chance encounter. Their abduction and murder had been premeditated, calculating, precise. Having been spirited away from their tents, they had been driven to remote parts of the forest, where they could be hunted down without fear of detection or interruption. These murders had been well planned and efficiently executed, without a single clue as to the killer's identity. The local press, Emilia Garanita in particular, might be portraying the perpetrator as some kind of maniac, but in reality he was anything but. The killer knew exactly what he was doing and was adept, even professional, at it. Which made Helen feel that there had to be a connection between the victims, a reason as to why they were selected.

The perpetrator was taking great risks, abducting his or her victims while they slept next to their partners, in crowded campsites, in peak tourist season. Furthermore, the victims weren't swiftly dispatched – they were let go, given a chance to flee. The odds were against them, but still it was an incredibly risky game to play if the perpetrator genuinely had no interest in the identity of his victims. There were easier ways to isolate and abduct victims if it was purely a love of hunting, the thrill of the chase, that was driving these attacks.

Frustrated, Helen tossed the photo of Scott aside, picking up a company portrait of Tom Campbell instead. She took in his smooth skin, his confident gaze. At first, Helen had thought Nathaniel Martin had targeted Campbell because of his crimes against the forest, because of his connection to Nexus. This remained an active line of enquiry, but in truth there seemed little reason for Martin to target Lauren Scott. She didn't particularly like camping, seldom visited the forest and, as Martin was already being hunted by police search teams, would he really have taken such a risk, coming out into the open to strike again? It was possible, of course, but until the search teams smoked him out, they wouldn't know for certain.

Helen felt sure there must be a connection between Campbell and Scott, a reason why they were singled out for special treatment, but it remained hidden. She had pored over the details of their lives and found nothing, which made her now wonder if the connection might lie elsewhere. This was not something Helen had properly considered before, but picking up a holiday snap of Lauren and her boyfriend Matteo on a sunny Spanish beach, she wondered now if she had been foolish to overlook this possibility. The victims had been terrified and brutalized, almost beyond imagination, but memories of Melanie Walton's shock, of Matteo Dominici's distress now came back to her. Their suffering would be less acute than their partner's initially, but would be much longer lasting. They would carry the awful images of what had happened to their loved ones – hunted down and left to bleed out – for the rest of their lives. The after-effects of this kind of trauma, laced no doubt with survivor guilt, could be profound, could even drive people to suicide. Was it possible then that Walton and Dominici were the link?

They had scant information on their lives so far, but they would have to remedy that tomorrow. First thing, they would burrow deep into their pasts, seeing if there were any crimes or misdemeanours, any hidden links, that might cast a new light on these baffling murders.

In the meantime, they would continue to flounder in the darkness, searching for a killer who refused to be found.

67

He plunged deeper and deeper into the darkness, ever more alarmed by what he was seeing. Joseph Hudson hadn't moved since his colleagues left, his cold coffee sitting untouched in front of him, as he climbed inside Dean Clarke's world. Having exhausted Clarke's mainstream offerings online – bored now by his citations, medals and service kills – he had taken a walk on the wild side, using one of the team's Tor browsers to access the dark web.

In a previous posting, Hudson had spent eighteen months seeking out paedophiles, arms dealers and drugs gangs in its shadowy recesses. All manner of depravity and criminality lurked within and he knew he had to be focused to find what he was looking for. He searched first for weapons-dealing forums, concentrating on those which catered for exotic tastes – sites that sold samurai swords, studded maces, crossbows and the like. Twenty minutes' surfing yielded little, apart from a growing disquiet about the number of whack jobs in the world, but eventually he stumbled on Clarke. His online moniker was slightly different here – '2Helmandback' – but the shadowy close-up of his masked face was a replica of his online branding. Perhaps Clarke felt his piercing eyes were his best feature.

Clarke was a regular visitor to the dark web, making frequent contact with other weapons enthusiasts to discuss, purchase or trade weapons. Their exchanges were conducted openly, without codenames or subterfuge, the various participants talking at length about their need for – and the performance of – the weapons they were seeking. Clarke was more active than most, a serial trader in all manner of knives, swords and bows . . . there seemed no end to his interest or enthusiasm. By Hudson's estimate, he must have a small arsenal of weapons, something he was evidently very proud of. In a photo posted three weeks ago, Clarke could be seen licking the blade of a twelve-inch bullet knife, his eyes wide with excitement.

Many of these posts had links to other offline sites and these were even more disturbing. Hudson now found himself thrust into the dark world of military-themed torture porn, scrolling through posts featuring footage of war zones, battlefields and besieged cities. Some were decades old – Hudson was particularly chilled by footage of inmates at Auschwitz being abused by their SS guards – but most featured the recent conflicts in the Middle East. Predictably, the Allies were the good guys and the enemy – uniformly labelled 'ragheads' – were the victims. There were images of snipers chalking up kills, two US Navy Seals emptying their magazines into a grounded combatant, even a proud British infantryman standing above the body of a teenage girl. Worst of all were the pictures of those unlucky combatants who had been tortured for information and then killed – one young man hung upside down, while his captors posed and laughed next to him.

Dean Clarke was a regular contributor, sharing and commenting on the disturbing images. His racism was clear, as was his thirst for blood. His pride was also evident, Clarke going to great lengths to describe his *own* experience in this field, detailing the throats he'd slit, the insurgents he'd gunned down while at prayer. Nothing seemed too base for Clarke, nothing off limits – in his world it was dog eat dog, with no exceptions for age, gender or circumstance.

Throughout all of his postings, Clarke was keen to portray himself as a man of action, a warrior. It was an image decidedly at odds with his daily existence, working in the scrapyard under the watchful gaze of his father, and it made Hudson think. What was the relationship like between the two? Why was Terry Clarke so worried about his son? And why was Dean Clarke so *angry*?

It was getting late now and Hudson knew it was time to go home, but somehow he felt compelled to stay. He couldn't take his eyes off Clarke – his postings, his posturing – and even now his gaze was drawn to his latest offering on the *ModernWarrior* forum. It was a restricted site used by men with bloodlust in their eyes, many brandishing weapons they claimed to have used. Clarke's latest picture was newly added and it stopped Hudson in his tracks.

Flanked by a dark background, Clarke stood in full camouflage gear, his emerald eyes just visible through a black balaclava. He was in battle pose, arms raised and readied, his crossbow pointing directly at the camera.

68

It was first light, but the forest was alive with activity. Helen tramped through the thick brush, the dew clinging to her boots, aiming for the search officers huddled together in the clearing. She had received the call just after 6 a.m. and had raced across town.

'Can we clear the scene, please?'

The team reacted, parting to allow Helen through. They had resumed their search for Nathaniel Martin bright and early, but had not ventured far off the beaten path when they stumbled on the body of a pony, lying discarded and forgotten in the brush. As with the first horse, the beast had been laid low by human hand, five crossbow bolts jutting from its flank.

As the officers drifted away, Helen crouched down by the corpse. This was their second such discovery, but there was no doubting that this pony had been killed first. It was already in an advanced state of decomposition, the stench of decay strong. Maggots riddled the body, a significant part of which had been stripped to the bone by other forest dwellers. Both of the unfortunate creature's eyes had been plucked out, giving the horse a sinister, even demonic air.

Were there other ponies lying undiscovered in the forest? Or was this the first? If so, it was evidence of the perpetrator's methodical build-up to his crimes. The beast Helen had chanced upon had been efficiently dispatched, downed by three well-aimed bolts. This pony had suffered more – five bolts this time, only three of which could have inflicted a fatal blow, the other two being lodged in its back and rear leg respectively.

Staring at the corpse, Helen wondered if this was by accident or design. Were the errant shots the ones that slowed the beast, before it was dispatched? Were they just badly aimed? Or did this random scattering of shots signify something else? To Helen, it looked very much like overkill, as if someone had *enjoyed* themselves, loading and firing five times, unleashing the final bolts even after the horse was dead perhaps. Part of her hoped this killing denoted an amateurish beginning, but another part feared this was the work of someone with a taste for death.

'Ok, let's secure the scene,' Helen said, rising and turning to the assembled officers. 'As soon as Meredith gets here, you can resume your search.'

The officers got to work. Walking away from the ravaged body, Helen pulled her phone from her pocket, keen to inform Charlie of the latest developments. The pony's body had been found in woodland near Furzley, well away from the other crime scenes, opening up a new area for them to investigate. As she raised the phone to her ear, however, she paused. Her eyes had alighted on a tree at the edge of the clearing, which appeared to have a bright green creeper climbing up its trunk. Following its length upwards, Helen's eyes now alighted on something that made her heart race.

A birdcam, perched high up in a small hollow, staring directly down at the clearing below.

69

He could feel his father's eyes burning into him.

He had turned up for work early, keen to make a good impression and put last night's unpleasantness behind them. He cursed himself now for his violent over-reaction – he had obviously scared his father, which could only lead to trouble. Old fool that he was, his father was unused to being bested and wouldn't take it lying down. He would punish him, no question, but worse than that he would ask questions – questions Dean didn't want to answer.

His father had barely looked up as he entered the site office, merely grunting at him. Grabbing some tea and toast, Dean had slunk down in front of the TV. Better this than the heavy, hostile silence. The morning news was on and he'd sat through the weather, then the sport, and was now watching the local headlines. They led on the killings, this morning focusing on Matteo Dominici, the Italian who'd been in a relationship with Lauren Scott. Dean watched on, intrigued, as the harassed figure hurried from his flat to an awaiting taxi, suitcase in hand. The bereaved boyfriend had clearly been driven from his home by the constant attentions of the press and it amused Dean to hear the reporter relay this in sober, judgemental tones, as if she was no part of it. Liar, liar, Dean thought to himself.

The reporter tailed off and the anchor switched focus to less sensational news, moving on to a spate of burglaries. Dean didn't linger, flicking the TV off. He could sense his father watching him, staring at the back of his head as if trying to penetrate his skull, and it made him feel ill at ease. Finishing off his toast, he crossed to the tiny kitchen, slinging the dirty crockery into the sink.

'I'll crack on then.'

He darted a look at his father, but the latter nodded absently, turning away from him. Angry with his father, with himself, Dean departed, pushing through the door and out onto the site. There was a fridge that needed to be stripped down and he was suddenly keen to get on with it, to be away from the suffocating atmosphere in the office. But, even as he hurried away, he heard the office door creak open, his father following him out.

Try as he might to ignore the shift in temperature between them, it was clear that something *had* changed. His father was suspicious now, perhaps even sensed what lay behind his son's evasiveness, and appeared intent on finding out the truth. This made Dean intensely nervous, but there was little he could do about it. This was his father's site, his domain, and while Dean was on it, he would remain under surveillance.

70

'Are you sure?'

Hudson tried, and failed, to contain his astonishment.

'One hundred per cent. I've checked twice.'

'So, he couldn't have been a member of the SAS?'

'Obviously not,' the army sergeant continued, as if talking to a child. 'There was no one by the name of "Dean Clarke" enrolled in the Armed Forces during the years you mentioned.'

'Is it possible he enrolled under a false name?'

'Anything's possible, but our background checks are extremely thorough, for obvious reasons.'

'Of course,' Hudson replied, his mind turning on this strange development.

He'd called the British Army headquarters in Andover first thing, eventually being put through to Staff Sergeant Greta Smith. She was brisk and condescending, but not unhelpful, so Hudson decided to chance his arm again.

'Could I beg one more favour of you? There are a couple of things I'd like you to take a look at.'

Ten minutes later, Hudson had the full picture. He'd forwarded Sergeant Smith photos of Dean Clarke's citations and medals and was not surprised to learn that the former were fake, amateurish copies of the real things, probably signed by Clarke himself. The medals *were* the genuine article, but as there was a lively trade on eBay for ex-servicemen's gongs, these could very easily have been found elsewhere.

Hudson took his findings straight to McAndrew, who'd

been doing some further background checks, all of which reinforced his growing suspicions. Clarke, it appeared, had left school at sixteen, but after a couple of failed apprenticeships had started claiming benefits. These had continued to be collected during the years he was supposed to have been on overseas duty and coincided with a couple of police cautions for theft and affray. He had never been charged, hence his lack of a criminal record, but he clearly had led an unfulfilling existence during his early twenties, until the wheels eventually came off when his benefits were stopped for good, following a fraudulent attempt to claim disability allowance.

Hudson could guess the rest, the son falling back on his parents' charity, working at the yard, sleeping at the family home. Perhaps he had always been delusional, perhaps his mother's death had sent him over the edge, but it was clear that somewhere along the line Clarke had developed a split personality. On the one hand, he was a downtrodden worker, ripping apart other people's junk for his dad, on the other, he was a violent fantasist, living out a fabricated life as a battle-hardened warrior. The question was, how real was this alter ego, how much had he inhabited his delusions?

Clarke was a failure, isolated and angry. Would he have enjoyed exerting power over his victims, hunting them down? Would it have given him a thrill to pursue them through the woods, perfectly camouflaged and impossible to detect? Would it have fulfilled his fantasy of being a trained killer?

As Hudson drank in Clarke's litany of failure, and the improbable alter ego of an SAS assassin he'd created, Joseph Hudson was forced to ask himself how strong Dean Clarke's grip on reality actually was.

71

Everything was a blur.

Charlie was already knackered but, fortifying herself with several cups of coffee, she had set to work, investigating the minutiae of Matteo Dominici's life. Helen had initiated this new line of enquiry last night, then, having been called away to investigate a second pony's death this morning, had asked Charlie to run with it.

She was happy to do so and, having asked DCs Bentham and Osbourne to investigate Melanie Walton's life, she'd got stuck in. But the details were unremarkable – Dominici was second-generation Anglo-Italian, had lived in Southampton all his life and had spent most of that working in the family restaurant – a nice, friendly establishment in the city centre. He had no criminal convictions, paid his taxes and contributed to the local community. His Facebook posts were intermittent, but optimistic, his outlook on life sunny – in summary, there seemed to be no reason why anyone would have wanted to destroy his happiness or sanity. This line of investigation had the feeling of a dead end, and as Charlie scrolled through his recent posts, they started to blur, their repetitive, benign sentiments starting to merge into one.

'DS Brooks?'

Charlie snapped out of it, turning to see Helen gesturing her towards her office. Rising, Charlie hurried over, closing the door behind her as she entered. It was clear from Helen's demeanour that something important had come up.

'I was out near Furzley this morning,' Helen commenced,

eschewing the pleasantries, 'checking out the second horse fatality.'

'Is it our man?'

'No question, but I think this was a dummy run. The horse has been dead a week or more and the attack was less precise – five bolts this time.'

Charlie nodded, digesting this.

'While I was there, I spotted a birdcam. Fortunately, this one was working and with a bit of arm-twisting I managed to get the footage from the last couple of weeks.'

Charlie sat forward in her seat, as Helen turned the laptop towards her. She had slipped a USB stick into the port and now opened up the video player. Seconds later, the screen burst into life, the night vision camera providing an eerie, green-hued view of the nest and forest beyond. A timecode ran continuously along the bottom and Helen now scrolled the footage forward.

'I warn you, it's not very pleasant . . .'

Charlie braced herself for what was to come, staring intently at the small screen. A few seconds elapsed, then suddenly in the upper fringes of the image, there was movement. A pony entered the field of view, stumbling into the clearing. It was followed by a tall, shadowy figure, who walked up to the wounded beast, raising his bow and firing at point blank range.

The horse bucked wildly – Charlie flinching as it did so – but worse was to follow. The pony had now collapsed onto its knees, but its attacker showed it no mercy, booting the poor beast onto its side and pinning it down. Two more bolts followed, bringing the total to five. The horse was presumably in shock, its body rigid with fear, but gradually its head lowered and moments later it was still. Its killer lingered over it, however, drinking in his achievement, before turning away.

Charlie's eyes were riveted to him, as he crossed the clearing, drinking in the details. The thick, rubber-soled boots, the dark clothing and hood, the fact that the attacker was clearly left-handed, still gripping the crossbow as if expecting more bloodshed. A bird now flew past the camera and this seemed to startle the fleeing figure, who briefly turned to follow its flight.

As he did so, Helen punched a key, freezing the footage. The figure was now looking directly up at the birdcam and Charlie leaned in to try to discern his features. Involuntarily, she gasped. For where there should have been a face, there was just a void. She could make out no chin, no nose, no ears – just a sea of black with two white orbs where eyes should be.

Charlie looked up at Helen. She had expected a glimpse of their suspect, but instead she appeared to be looking at some kind of monster. Helen raised an eyebrow – she was clearly as unnerved and disappointed as Charlie – so the latter returned her gaze to the computer.

To find the figure still staring directly at the camera, his malevolence radiating towards her.

72

'Look me in the eye and tell me you weren't responsible.'

Superintendent Simmons's blood was up, her tone withering, but Emilia refused to be cowed.

'They're your photos, not mine. I've no idea how they got into the public domain.'

She gestured towards Simmons's laptop, which displayed Graham Ross's crime scene photos, now available for all to see on *Backchat*, an underground news website which specialized in the unusual and, occasionally, the illegal. The powers that be had tried to shut it down numerous times, but so far the site had risen above the injunctions, continuing its mission to inform, educate and appal.

'Well, forgive me if I don't believe you –'

'Superintendent Simmons, we barely know each other –'

'But I think I've got the measure of you. Your coverage of this case so far has succeeded in terrifying the public and heaping pressure onto my officers, who are already working around the clock.'

'Not that you'd know it.'

'And all in the interests of making your star shine a little brighter. I'm aware that you've acted illegally in the past in order to further your own agenda . . . which is why I had a little chat with Graham Ross this morning.'

Emilia regarded her, saying nothing.

'He said you shadowed him to a pub yesterday – despite his repeated attempts to dissuade you – and that you may have stolen these images while he briefly left his camera unattended.'

'Doesn't ring any bells,' Emilia replied blithely. 'I'm not in the business of following strange men into bars and, besides, I was busy at the office yesterday. You may be aware, there's a major story breaking –'

'I know it was you and I know why you did it. So, let me give you a little piece of advice . . .'

Emilia was tempted to continue her denial, but thought better of it. Strangely, she loved these dressing-downs, the impotent rage of the establishment struggling to come to terms with the digital world. How foolish they were to think that anything could be contained.

'You may think that this will help you,' Simmons continued, pointing at the gory images on screen, 'that this will make the story *bigger*. But this is not journalism. This is fear-mongering. And it could have serious consequences: for members of the public and for you too.'

Emilia raised a quizzical eyebrow. How many times had she been threatened before, in this very office, and lived to fight another day?

'Which is why I shall personally be looking into this data breach. If I find evidence that you *were* responsible, then you can expect your day in court.'

'If you want to make a fool of yourself, be my guest. Now, if there's nothing else . . . ?'

Emilia was determined to end this on her terms. There was no way she was walking away from their first confrontation with her tail between her legs. And, to her satisfaction, Simmons now terminated their meeting, albeit with ill grace. Emilia walked away in good spirits, confident that Simmons was powerless to do anything. She was pretty sure the pub had no CCTV; nor were there any witnesses to her crime. Moreover, it would be impossible to prove that *she* leaked them to the wider world.

That was the beauty of modern life, Emilia thought to herself as she sauntered down the corridor, you could do what you like these days, post what you like, protected always by the perfect anonymity of the internet.

73

'I want to know where he goes, who he meets, what he does.'

Helen had corralled the team together once more. Having consulted with Joseph Hudson about the latest developments, she was now ready to launch the next phase of their investigation.

'DS Hudson will lead, assisted by myself and by DCs McAndrew, Osbourne and Reid. Others of you may be called in – we need round-the-clock surveillance on Dean Clarke.'

'Are we saying he's our prime suspect now?' DC Bentham asked.

'He's our *main* suspect,' Helen replied. 'DC Reid and DS Hudson have done some deep digging on Clarke and he certainly fits the profile. A single white male, disaffected, angry, addicted to internet violence. The line between fantasy and reality is thin for these guys. Clarke is not a soldier – he never even applied, according to Army recruitment records – but he'll tell anyone who'll listen about his service kills, his awards for valour. Perhaps he's come to believe his own lies. Or perhaps there are others, as yet undetected, who are encouraging him, prompting him to commit these barbaric crimes –'

'Plus,' said DS Hudson over Helen, 'his vehicle fits the profile and he's a practical guy, with unfettered access to scrap metal *and* the tools to fashion them into something new. He is clearly someone with an unhealthy fascination with weapons and instruments of torture. I'm betting that if we raided the family home tonight, we'd find an arsenal of weapons, many of which have been used.'

'The circumstantial evidence is also intriguing,' Charlie added, pulling up the birdcam snapshot of the perpetrator. 'Height, build and note the face. The guy looks like some kind of evil spirit, but he's probably just wearing a mask or balaclava, plus camouflage gear. Note also that the guy is left-handed. It may be a coincidence, but in all the images Clarke has posted of himself he uses his left hand to pull the trigger.'

'The most important thing now,' Helen resumed, 'is to find out where he goes at night. We've been assuming that the attacks are nocturnal because the perpetrator wanted to enjoy the cover of darkness, but it might be that they *have* to take place after dark – his father keeps a close eye on him during the day. We need to find out where Clarke goes, and what he does. DC McAndrew will take first watch, then DS Hudson. In the meantime, I want us to keep up our exploration of the victims and their partners, to see if there are any patterns, any clues we're missing. DS Brooks?'

The team turned to face Charlie once more.

'We're going to continue to run the rule over Matteo Dominici and Melanie Walton – past relationships, internet history, any brushes with crime or criminality – but we're also going to keep up the heat on Lauren Scott. If there is a tangible connection to the perpetrator, we still feel she is the most likely access point, given her history. Her parents live in South Africa – I'm due to talk to her father shortly – but we need to target others who might have known her during her late teens or early twenties. Someone who might have sold her, or got her hooked on, drugs, might have targeted her as somebody weak and vulnerable. We'll also be looking at her numerous spates of rehab – and the people she met there – to see if there are any links there to criminality.'

'Have we interrogated her phone contacts, her digital connections?' Helen asked.

'We've got one possible lead there – a phone number that appears in both Campbell and Scott's call history – but we don't know what it signifies yet. We're talking to the phone companies, trying to identify the caller.'

'Impress on them the *urgency* of the situation,' Helen urged, before turning to DC Edwards. 'What about other weapons enthusiasts, particularly those interested in archery, historical weapons and so on?'

'There is one guy who might be interesting,' Edwards volunteered. 'Andrew Tucker. He's been a member of the Weston Archery club on Lever Street for many years now.'

'Go on.'

'Well, he's a bit of a loner, recently divorced, and four weeks ago he had an altercation with another member. Things got out of hand and he pinned the other guy down, held an arrow to his throat. He was kicked out and nobody's seen him since. I've rung him several times, been round his house, but no joy. There's nothing definitive linking him to these crimes but . . .'

'Keep on it. What about the hotline?' Helen continued, turning to DC Lucas. 'Have we had anything interesting from the public?'

'The phones have been ringing non-stop, well, since the crime scene pictures were leaked anyway . . . Nothing useful though. Just attention seekers or dog walkers who think they see homicidal maniacs every time a twig snaps . . .'

Helen didn't react, but privately cursed Emilia Garanita once more. Her sensational headlines and underhand tactics never helped their investigations, succeeding only in creating paranoia and panic. Superintendent Simmons was hauling her over the coals right now, though Helen feared it would have little effect on the journalist's behaviour.

'Stay on it. Anything comes up, I want to know about it.

That goes for all of you,' Helen continued, turning to the rest of the team once more. 'Whatever else you've got on, drop it. This is your sole priority now.'

She paused briefly, before concluding firmly: 'We need to bring this guy in.'

74

He came at her without warning, ambushing her as she neared her car.

Having survived her dressing-down, Emilia was keen to get back to the office. The leaked pictures were creating a storm on the internet and she wanted to take advantage of this – she had already talked Gardiner into running a specially extended edition of the paper, offering their readers the definitive guide to the New Forest Killer.

But as she reached her distinctive red Corsa, she felt a shadow fall upon her, then a hand dragging her back, spinning her around. Though startled, she was not surprised to find Graham Ross ranged against her.

'Look what the cat dragged in.'

His tone was even, but there was a coiled aggression underneath.

'Please don't tell me you've been working on that line, Graham. Because it's lame, even by your standards . . .'

'Simmons charge you?' he continued, ignoring the insult.

'Not at all. In fact, we had a nice girly chat,' Emilia drawled happily.

'Bullshit. She was incandescent when I was in with her. I only just managed to stop her cancelling my contract. But, then again, I'm the innocent party in all this.'

'And I'm the big bad wolf?'

To her surprise, Ross laughed, as if genuinely amused by the description.

'Something like that. Anyway, this is just a friendly chat to let you know how disappointed I am in you. I didn't have you down as a thief.'

'I've been called worse.'

'Still . . . I will say this for you. You've got a good eye for a photo. The selection you picked were . . . well chosen. The best of the bunch in fact. So, I suppose I should be grateful. They've created quite a stir, haven't they?'

Emilia was about to respond with a few well-chosen words, but Ross had clearly said his piece, turning now to walk back to his car. Emilia followed his progress, confused and intrigued by the strange, abrupt conclusion to their conversation. There was something knowing in Ross's tone, even a hint of smugness. Which made her wonder.

It was extremely naïve of a seasoned professional to leave his camera unattended like that. Also, his unexpected conversation with the barmaid had conveniently bought Emilia enough time to steal the precious images 'undetected'. Finally, despite his professed anger towards her, he seemed oddly relaxed today, even satisfied, at the way things had worked out.

Was it possible, then, that he knew exactly what he was doing from the off? That he had *wanted* her to steal the images, knowing they would be leaked without a stain on his reputation?

Was it possible that *she* was the dupe, not him?

75

From her seventh-floor window, Grace Simmons watched Emilia Garanita climb into her car. Their interview had gone as planned, but had done little to settle her nerves. And the subsequent conversation between Ross and Garanita worried her further. Was this meeting prearranged? Was it possible they were in this together?

If so, it could only spell trouble. The leaking of the photos had created panic in the city and a firestorm within the building. The Chief Constable had called her first thing this morning, the Mayor shortly afterwards, both of them pointing out that the leaking of such graphic images was unprecedented and risked public order. Simmons couldn't disagree, so had had to take the verbal beating, promising to run those responsible to ground. She felt she had already done this, in fact, but was powerless to do anything about it – the laws of the land struggling to keep up with the realities of an ever-changing world.

Garanita's car sped off down the street, the driver blatantly ignoring the 20 mph speed limit. Simmons pictured the occupant, smiling to herself at having got away unscathed, following yet another misdemeanour. Emilia Garanita was the type whom Simmons had always disliked – parasitic, without conscience, a free-market trader in other people's misery. Never mind that she herself had been the victim of violent crime on a number of occasions – these experiences had seemingly numbed the young journalist to other people's pain, rather than exciting her sympathies. But there was more to Simmons's anger and animosity than a simple dislike of the devious journalist. Helen Grace, her protégée, had come in for sustained criticism in the last few days. In spite of her incredible track record, the powers that be, not to mention the wider world, had questioned her competency, her ability to bring the case to a successful conclusion. Garanita's irresponsible actions had only fanned the flames licking at Helen's heels.

It was totally unjustified, of course, which only increased Simmons's ire. Emilia claimed to be engaged in public service journalism, but Simmons was sure she was just using this case as a stick with which to beat Helen, the two having never seen eye to eye. Instinctively, Simmons wanted to intervene, even though she knew that the experienced officer was capable of taking care of herself. Simmons had found that out a long time ago.

Yet the truth was she *did* want to protect her, to bat away the slingshots now aimed at her. It wasn't necessary, nor was it professional, Simmons letting her personal feelings for Helen cloud her judgement. Sometimes she tried to justify this to herself – one couldn't ignore their personal history, pretend they weren't friends – but most of the time she chided herself for her weakness. Perhaps, after all, it said more about her than it did about Helen.

Her husband, Ralph, had died three years ago. She had managed to get through that – his death was a release in the end – and while the boys were still at home she'd had people round her to provide support and company. But now that they'd moved out, she did feel a little at sea, rattling around in a family home that was too big for her. She had on occasion flirted with the idea of selling up, but had always backed off from this, confirming as it would the end of one stage of her life and the beginning of another.

No doubt about it, she was becoming sentimental in her old age, perhaps even a little indulgent. She'd never had favourites before, had always been scrupulously fair, but something about Helen's past experiences, and her own situation, made her want to save her from those who would bring her down.

Rightly or wrongly, she would continue to keep a close eye on her protégée.

76

He sped down the road, his eyes glued to his rear-view mirror.

Wherever he went today, he felt *watched*. While he was at work, his father's gaze seldom left him. He had endured it at first, then began to challenge him, looking up sharply to catch him in the act. But this scarcely seemed to register – his father would look away briefly, before quietly resuming his surveillance.

Eventually, Dean could bear it no longer and he'd headed to Greggs for an early lunch. But even here he felt as if people were reacting to his presence, regarding him with curiosity. He was being paranoid of course, there was no way they could *know*, yet he felt as if they were looking at him strangely. Moreover, he was convinced that on a couple of occasions he'd seen the same face behind him – a young woman he'd noticed earlier on his way into work. But surely that was impossible. His mind *must* be playing tricks on him.

Having endured the heavy atmosphere at work, during an afternoon which seemed to crawl by Dean eventually made a break for it, rushing to finish a botched job on the fridge, before heading off. He would have to do it all over again in the morning, but he didn't care, he had more important things to worry about.

Without a word to his father, he had roared off in the Defender. Even as he sped away from the yard, he half expected his father to loom into view in his rear-view mirror, dogging his progress in his old pick-up. But there was no sign of him – perhaps his curiosity was just that, the inevitable consequence of the recent police visit.

Of course, it was this that lay at the root of his paranoia. His father's suspicions he could handle. There was no way he would ever turn his son in. The influence of his mother, the oaths she'd made her husband *swear* on her deathbed, would see to that. But what were the police up to? And what did *they* know? The fact that they had shown an interest in the Defender made him nervous. Had it been spotted? Had they somehow traced it? Shooting another look in the rear-view mirror, he made a mental note to spend some time Googling new vehicles tomorrow. If it had aroused their suspicions, it would have to go.

The cars idling behind him in the city centre traffic seemed unremarkable – he didn't recognize any of them from earlier – so he returned his attention to the road ahead. Progress was slow, making him jumpy. Now he just wanted to get back to base, to prepare. It was possible his father might return home early, suspicion driving him there, and he was determined to avoid a scene. There was no time for that tonight.

Spotting a gap in the traffic, he gunned the Defender forward, darting down a quick cut-through. A few more manoeuvres and the way now opened up for him – ten minutes later he was back outside their ramshackle home. Avoiding the main street, he parked up in the alleyway behind, before creeping round to the front of the house. Emerging onto the street, he scanned left and right, searching for his father, an unfamiliar face, anything out of the ordinary. But the street was quiet, as lifeless and suburban as usual.

Shaking off his paranoia, he hurried up the steps, slipping

his key into the lock and hurrying inside. The door slammed firmly shut behind him, the key turning in the lock. Then all was quiet once more . . . save for the arrival of an unremarkable Ford Focus, coming to a gentle stop a few doors down from the Clarke residence. The young female driver appeared to be lost, pulling a road map from the arm of the door and leafing through it.

Yet oddly, despite her predicament, she seemed little interested in the map, her eyes never leaving the house across the road.

77

She didn't want to look, but somehow she couldn't help herself.

Following the team briefing, Helen had retreated to her office to dig deeper into Dean Clarke. McAndrew had gone out on surveillance, Charlie was chasing down leads on Lauren Scott and the rest of the team were hard at work, allowing Helen a moment to get the measure of their suspect. Joseph Hudson had joined her – he seemed best equipped to navigate Clarke's dark world – and what he was showing her beggared belief.

Clarke was extremely isolated. He had a complex relationship with his father and few other outlets – no colleagues, no friends, no partner. His connection with the world seemed entirely virtual – posing as a variety of avatars, he engaged with other faceless posters, sharing disturbing images and bitter thoughts. Helen had seen others sucked into this sinister netherworld and she wondered how far gone he was. Was there anything restraining him now?

Not from the evidence in front of her. Hudson had taken her to the darkest corners of the web, penetrating special-interest groups who traded in sadism and brutality. The frequency of their posts, and the explicitness of the content, was breathtaking. If you could imagine a form of depravity, these guys could serve it up.

'These clips were mostly shot in Iraq,' Hudson was saying, as he pulled up another grainy scene of brutality. 'They're a specialist sub-genre – military-themed torture porn.'

'Nice . . .'

'The footage is pretty gruesome, but the guys seem to enjoy it . . .'

Helen's gaze was glued to the hand-held footage on the screen. A young Iraqi combatant was slumped against a chair, his arms secured with cable ties. The prisoner appeared to be unconscious, but this didn't concern his three captors, who were taking it in turns to beat him with a bicycle chain. Grimly, the whole scene seemed to have a relaxed, even jovial air, the three Army officers posing for the camera as they cracked jokes.

It was beyond repugnant, inexcusable, but perhaps was a consequence of the terror, paranoia and bloodlust that warfare generated. What was less explicable was the delight ordinary people seemed to take in these scenes, people who had never seen a battlefield, never experienced real fear or pain. The clip was framed by numerous comments from around the world, underlining the viewers' enthusiasm for both the imagery and the content. 'Another one bites the dust' seemed to be a popular refrain, many posters wishing they could have been present to join in. 'Helmanned2008' clearly felt this, outlining in explicit detail what *he* would have done to the helpless captive. To which many of his online associates had simply responded: 'Lol'.

'It's like they're commenting on *Love Island* . . .' Helen murmured angrily.

'Something for everyone on the net,' Hudson replied dryly. 'I can show you worse if you like.'

'I'll pass. Do we know who these other posters are?'

She turned to Hudson to find he was looking directly at her. They were huddled close to each other, hunched over her laptop, but he seemed unembarrassed to have been caught out, calmly replying:

'It's too soon. They are all aliases, with no obvious signifiers. We're cross-referencing the names with other investigations – if that doesn't throw anything up, we'll have to work out where and when they posted, see if we can get a workable IP address for any of them.'

Helen looked back at the footage, pausing it just as one of the captor's attackers was poised to strike again. The young man's face was already a bloody mess and Helen had no desire to witness any more.

'Has he ever arranged to meet with any of them? Are any of them local?'

'Once,' Hudson replied, angling the keyboard towards him and typing some more. 'But we don't think it ever happened. Clarke made the offer but his correspondent never replied.'

Helen digested the dialogue. Clarke had spotted a reference to the south coast in a post by Bushwhacker99 and had probed further, but without success, his online 'friend' apparently running scared of real-world contact.

Frustrated, Helen turned to Hudson again, only to find him appraising her once more.

'DS Hudson, I appreciate your enthusiasm and attention to detail . . . but I have to ask – do you make a habit of staring at your superiors?'

'Only when there's something worth staring at,' he replied happily, not breaking her gaze.

'Well, let me give you a piece of advice,' Helen replied quickly, concealing her surprise. 'The way to get ahead here is to see what others miss, to fashion new leads. So, keep your eyes on the prize, Detective Sergeant.'

'Absolutely, ma'am,' he replied, the ghost of a smile drifting across his face, as his gaze turned back to the screen.

They resumed their exploration of Clarke's online

activities, descending ever deeper into the sewer, but Helen found it hard to concentrate. She had intended to shame Hudson for his blatant interest in her, but he had been utterly unembarrassed, happily acknowledging his attraction. This was both irritating and oddly impressive – most men would have quailed under the force of Helen's disapproval. But he had met her gaze, refusing to be intimidated, while nevertheless maintaining a respectful distance. It was as if he was offering up an invitation, without once overplaying his hand. It was artfully done, which made Helen suspicious, but also pleased her. He was an attractive guy – fit, athletic, handsome – and she was flattered and surprised that he should be interested in her, given the difference in their ages. There was no way anything would come of it, of course, that would be grossly unprofessional and ill-advised. And yet, for a brief moment, Helen enjoyed the warm glow of his interest – it was seldom anyone plucked up courage to approach *her*.

It was a fleeting moment of positivity, something to keep her going through their grim task. And she was glad of it today.

78

'Why?'

The starkest of questions and the hardest one for Charlie to answer.

'Why would anyone do something like that?'

Charlie stared at the bewildered face on the small screen. The Skype connection to Durban was far from perfect, the sound dropping in and out, but she had managed to convey the basic details of his daughter's death to Bob Scott. The 55-year-old, who'd moved to South Africa with his wife five years ago, was clearly poleaxed, struggling to process the calamity that had befallen him.

'That's what we're endeavouring to find out. We have our entire team working on it. And, believe me, we won't rest until –'

'And you say this is linked to another murder?' Scott said, cutting across her.

'Yes, the circumstances suggest the two incidents are connected.'

'Dear God,' Scott continued, running his hand over his face, now contorted with distress. 'I never thought it would happen like this.'

'Sorry?' Charlie replied, not sure she had heard properly.

'Well, we . . . Lauren's mother and I suspected that this call would come one day. But this . . .'

He couldn't say the words – horror assailing him – so Charlie jumped in.

'Can I ask why you were expecting this?'

Scott gathered himself, wiping a tear from his eye.

'Lauren was our only child and we gave her everything . . . but she was a lost soul. Difficult, closed, angry. She . . . she was difficult as a teenager . . .'

He hesitated as if unsure whether to speak ill of the dead.

'. . . but she was even worse after that. Drink, drugs, self-harm, you name it. By the time she was in her early twenties, she was hooked on heroin. That's when things really started to go downhill.'

'Meaning?'

'Meaning she would steal from us, often coming to the house when she knew we'd be out. She would shoplift, beg, borrow to find money for drugs. And when that wasn't an option, she, well, you know . . .'

He didn't need to spell it out – Lauren's convictions for soliciting stared up at Charlie from the charge sheet in front of her.

'Why was this, do you think?' she enquired. 'Why the drugs, the self-destructive behaviour?'

Scott shrugged helplessly.

'Perhaps it was just her personality. Perhaps she was in with the wrong crowd. Or maybe it was just because that's how shitty life can be sometimes.'

Bitterness had seeped into his tone now. Charlie looked at his face, intrigued by the conflicting emotions distorting it. Bitterness, guilt, shock, but also a profound, heavy sadness.

'Had you spoken to her recently? Had she talked to you at all about her plans?'

'We last spoke around four years ago. It was better that way.'

Clipped and definitive. Charlie was shocked – and angered – by this curt dismissal of his own daughter. She had no idea their estrangement was so profound.

'Because?'

'Because it was too upsetting for everyone. She couldn't change, despite all our efforts to help her.'

'So you . . .'

Charlie didn't want to say 'cut her off' but couldn't think of how else to phrase it.

'Oh, don't think it was our decision, because it *wasn't*,' he said firmly, reading Charlie's mind. 'My wife would have kept in touch, she wanted to keep the channels of communication open, even after we moved here, but Lauren wouldn't have it. She severed contact with *us*.'

'Why would she do that? Presumably she still needed you, your support.'

'Our money, you mean.'

Another shot of bitterness, but almost as soon as he said it, Scott's face resumed its sad, weary demeanour.

'Lauren didn't like herself. I can't put it any other way. If I was being generous, I'd say she cut us off to *spare* us. She knew she was self-destructive, exploitative, deceitful. She knew all this and yet she couldn't stop, the drugs were too much a part of her life by that point.'

Charlie nodded, then responded:

'I should say that your daughter was clean by the end of her life.'

Once more, Scott looked at Charlie as if she had just smacked him in the face.

'She'd been to AA, NA, and had got herself together. She had a boyfriend and was making a go of things.'

Now the 55-year-old broke down, burying his face in his hands and sobbing loudly. The fact that his daughter had had a shot at redemption, only to be brutally murdered, was too much to bear.

'I'm sorry, I'm sorry,' he mumbled, but kept his hands clamped to his face.

Charlie watched him, her heart breaking for him. But she knew the worst was yet to come. It now fell to her to compound his misery by telling him that in other circumstances, if Fate had not intervened so brutally, he would have been a grandfather. But before she could do so, Scott spoke again:

'It's such a waste . . .'

'I know,' Charlie replied, her own voice thick with emotion now.

'Despite everything, she was a talented girl. She had so much potential.'

'I'm sure . . .'

'And we were proud of her. Not of what she became, but early on. When she surprised us with her A-level results, when she started university. We could see a *really* bright future for her then.'

The tears were streaming down his face, but Charlie's sympathy was now tempered by curiosity.

'Sorry, you say Lauren went to university? We didn't find anything on record suggesting she attended –'

'She didn't finish the course,' Scott replied, matter-of-factly. 'She dropped out after a year or so, then that was that.'

Charlie digested this.

'And can I ask which university she attended?'

'She stayed locally, so as to be close to friends and family. Southampton University had a very good reputation at that time.'

Charlie sat back in her seat, momentarily lost for words. An interview that had promised so little, except distress and grief, had suddenly provided her with a significant new lead.

A possible connection between Tom Campbell and Lauren Scott.

79

It had been a long wait, but at last her patience had paid off.

Having been jumped by Graham Ross earlier, and dressed down by Simmons, Emilia had been determined to get back on the front foot. Which is why she was now in the car park of the Premier Inn, watching Matteo Dominici scurry across the tarmac.

Her coverage of the New Forest Killer had been good so far – better than good – but it lacked anything that genuinely tugged at the heartstrings. Melanie Walton had been too traumatized to talk and had knocked back all enquiries. Lauren Scott's parents, meanwhile, weren't even in the country and her boyfriend had gone to ground. Emilia had seen the footage of him fleeing his flat this morning and had immediately set about making enquiries, texting the cleaners, porters and receptionists she knew at the local hotels, hoping the promise of some drinking money might loosen their tongues. Sure enough, her foresight had paid off, one of her informants confirming that a flustered Dominic had checked into the Premier Inn off New Road earlier that morning.

Emilia had raced down there, but on arrival was frustrated to find that Dominici had left again, almost immediately after his arrival. She cursed her lengthy chat with Simmons and her contretemps with Ross, was sure she could have snagged him if she'd moved a bit quicker. But, counselling herself to be patient, she'd set up camp in the car park, watching the predictable parade of businessmen, stag-do revellers and adulterers file past.

Eventually Dominici surfaced. Exiting a taxi, he hurried across the car park towards the service lift, presumably hoping to avoid any unwanted attention. But Emilia was one step ahead of him, sauntering towards him, so as not to excite his interest, until it was too late to avoid her.

'Matteo?'

He jerked his head up, startled. Emilia stepped directly in front of him, extending a hand.

'I'm Emilia Garanita. I wonder if I could have a minute of your time?'

'Who are you?' he barked.

'I'm from the *Southampton Evening News*. We've been covering your –'

He pushed roughly past her, continuing his progress towards the building.

'I know you're grieving, Matteo,' Emilia continued, hurrying after him, 'and that you deserve some privacy. But ignoring the press is *not* the answer. The best thing you can do is give me your side of the story, then all this will –'

'Go to hell.'

'I'm not trying to upset you. I understand your distress, I really do.'

Dominici walked more quickly, Emilia struggling to keep up.

'I just want to get to know Lauren a little better. She was a wonderful woman, I'm sure, and I'd like to give our readers a better understanding of her. To afford them a glimpse of the woman you knew and loved.'

'Where do you get off?' Dominici stopped abruptly, rounding on her. '*Pretending* to be interested in me, in Lauren?'

Emilia held her ground.

'I'm just doing my job, Matteo. I will quote you accurately

and I won't put in anything you don't want me to. Talk to me about Lauren, tell me about –'

'You'll get nothing from me. *Nothing.*'

He took another step forward, but as he did so, he spotted something. A man with a long lens was taking pictures of their confrontation from the far side of the car park.

'Who the hell is he?' Matteo roared.

'Don't worry about him,' Emilia said blithely. 'We just need some photos, so our readers can see how well you're bearing up.'

Emilia was glad she'd asked one of their photographers to join her. The photos of Dominici looking crazed with grief would be perfect for the front page. But their subject didn't seem to share her enthusiasm.

'I hope you burn in hell, you . . . you parasite.'

Stepping forward, Dominici spat in Emilia's face, a large glob of saliva landing on her left cheek. Instinctively, she took a step back, fearing she was about to be attacked, but Dominici now turned on his heel and disappeared into the bowels of the hotel.

'You ok?'

Darren Hall, her snapping colleague, had joined her.

'Never better,' Emilia replied, pulling a tissue from her bag and wiping the spit from her cheek. 'Get anything good?'

'You betcha.'

'Then you'd better send them through.'

Emilia headed back to her car, tossing the tissue into a nearby flowerbed. Darren's concern was not unexpected; nor was it welcome. The truth was that when she had her game face on, Emilia could handle anything. Many people would shy away from the aggravation, the insults, the abuse, but not her.

She actively *enjoyed* it.

80

He tried to keep his breathing steady. But the adrenaline was pumping and his hands shook as he laid the clothes out on the bed.

It had become his ritual now. The calm before the storm, a moment to gather himself. But it was more than that. It was the point when reality drifted away to be replaced by something different, something better. Picking up one of the heavy boots, he ran his finger over the thick, rutted sole. It was so hard, so certain. Every time he put it on he felt some of its confidence rub off on him – it made him feel strong, powerful, untouchable even. Holding it up to his nose, he breathed in its aroma – a heady mixture of leather and rubber.

Laying it down, he picked up his fatigues. They too were army surplus and in mint condition. His day-to-day clothes were always crumpled and dirty, but never these. They were immaculately clean and pressed – he loved the way the iron purred over the black fabric as he worked on them. They remained concealed in the aged wardrobe, behind moth-eaten coats and jumpers, and he lived for the moment when he could retrieve them, smoothing them out and admiring them, as he laid them out on the tatty eiderdown.

Impatience now mastered him and he slipped them on, revelling in the feel of the coarse fabric against his skin. They made him feel whole. They made him feel *real*. Closeted away in his tiny, gloomy bedroom, the indignities of the working day seemed increasingly distant, as if they belonged to someone else. The curtains were always drawn, keeping the world at bay, allowing him to fashion a different destiny for himself. This place had always been his sanctuary, containing the only things that mattered to him. His uniform, his trophies, his weapons. For him, this was the promised land.

Darting a look at his watch, he realized with a shiver that it was nearly time. Darkness was falling. It was a summons he could no longer resist, so, snatching up his balaclava, he stuffed it into his backpack and grabbed his jacket. Slipping it on, he pulled the hood up and hurried from the room.

This time he didn't turn towards the front of the house, but to the rear. If anyone had spotted him returning home, they would *not* see him depart, the stakes were too high to allow that. Opening the French windows, he slipped out into the yard. From here it was a short march to the back gate and he didn't hesitate, pushing through it as he hurried towards the Defender.

At the last moment, he paused, caution dictating he check that the coast was still clear. But there was no one around, he was quite alone. So, climbing inside the battered 4x4, he fired up the engine.

81

Joseph Hudson toyed with the key fob, flicking it back and forth. Helen could tell he was excited, nervous even, longing to turn the ignition and snap into action. Clearly, he was not a man who was good at waiting.

Osbourne had joined McAndrew out front, doubling up a necessary precaution now that night was falling. Helen had opted to join Hudson in a spot near the top of the rear alley, partly because it was her duty to babysit the new recruit, partly because she was intrigued by him.

'Tell me about the bike.'

Hudson stopped flicking and turned to her.

'Have you always been a solo traveller?'

Hudson smiled at the double meaning, then replied:

'Product of a misspent youth.'

Helen nodded. Her own obsession with bikes had started when she and her sister, Marianne, used to steal them as teenagers.

'I don't broadcast it, but I grew up in a travelling community.'

Helen said nothing, genuinely surprised. Travellers seldom joined the police, given the suspicion that still lingered on both sides.

'We were on the south coast, not far from Chichester. We didn't have cars, well, not all the time, so I grew up driving quad bikes, mopeds, whatever we could construct, cannibalize . . .'

'Did you enjoy it? Growing up there?'

'What's not to like about racing around on quad bikes?' Hudson replied happily.

'My sister and I, we only had the two wheels, but I know what you mean. It's the sense of freedom it gives you –'

'And of being in control,' Hudson broke in. 'Of going where *you* want to go. One day, I just took off and didn't come back.'

Hudson clocked Helen's reaction, continuing:

'It was nothing bad. I just knew what I wanted to do and that didn't fit with the travelling life, so I went to London and started over.'

Helen digested this. The parallels with her own life were striking, except that she had headed south to change her fortunes, while Hudson had headed to the capital. Personally, Helen had been glad to see the back of it.

'I met a girl, fell in love, got married. Then fell out of love, got divorced and was back to square one.'

'Right.'

'I was a mess, truth be told, but I always knew what I wanted to do and that saved me. Work's always been my escape, my salvation.'

Another parallel. The more Hudson talked, the more he seemed to surprise her.

'So I did my training and signed up. The Met didn't have many travellers applying to be coppers back then,' Hudson continued. 'So, they did a very thorough background check on me. Bit like you're doing now.'

It was said with humour. Helen smiled briefly and looked away, scanning the street for signs of life.

'We're a tight ship here. I like to know who we're dealing with.'

'Well, let me know when I've passed the test.'

Helen said nothing, a companionable silence descending, before Hudson continued:

'How about you? Ever go back to your old haunts?'

'Absolutely not. I hope they've bulldozed the place.'

'There's nobody there any more? No friends or relatives?'

'Anyone I ever cared for is either dead or in prison. But I guess you know that, right?'

Hudson didn't bother to deny it.

'The only person I know from that time is Superintendent Simmons. She did me a good turn back then.'

'Then you must be glad to have her at Southampton Central.'

Helen was pleased he hadn't tried to pry.

'I'd love to say I've had bosses who I'd throw down for,' Hudson continued amiably. 'But to be honest they've largely been timeservers or glory hunters. It's one of the reasons I've kept moving, to be honest, kept trying to find the right place for me.'

Helen laid a hand on his arm. Hudson looked up, surprised, excited even, by this affectionate gesture . . . only to find Helen staring straight ahead of her. Hudson followed her gaze and was startled to see a battered Land Rover Defender roar past them and away down the street.

Clarke was on the move.

82

They drove in silence. The tension that had gripped Hudson earlier had evaporated – he was now focused on the task in hand. He drove assertively but steadily, avoiding lines of traffic and dawdling drivers, while keeping a manageable distance between himself and the Defender. Tailing suspects was an art form – too close and you get rumbled, too far away and you lose them. Helen was pleased to see that Hudson knew his stuff, always keeping at least two cars between themselves and the Land Rover, but never letting Clarke out of their sight.

McAndrew and Osbourne were on the move too, trying to get ahead of Clarke, in case Helen and Hudson ran into trouble.

'We're on Swift Road, heading east towards the intersection,' Helen said into her radio. 'What's your position?'

There was a brief pause, then Ellie McAndrew came through loud and clear.

'We're on Western Grove Road, approaching the lights. We'll head east, unless you tell us different.'

Helen clicked off and returned her attention to the Land Rover. It was idling by the lights and she could just make out the silhouetted outline of Clarke's head. What was he doing? What was he thinking? It seemed strange that the man whose habits, whose predilections they knew intimately, was just in front of them. So close, yet just out of reach.

The lights changed and the Defender took off, lurching to the right and speeding away. Immediately, Helen snatched up the radio once more.

'Suspect has changed direction. He has turned right and is now heading south-east on Archery Road.'

Hudson raised an eyebrow. The coincidence of the name was lost on nobody.

But the Land Rover had changed direction again, reaching the next intersection and swinging left onto Weston Lane.

'Now heading north-east on Weston Lane.'

'Roger that. We'll take Archery Grove, see if we can stay ahead of him.'

McAndrew clicked off and Helen returned her attention to their quarry. Where was he going? He was currently heading *away* from the New Forest, towards the eastern fringes of Southampton. But perhaps there was method in his madness, the assertive driving and sudden changes of direction instinctively making Helen nervous.

'Do you think he's spotted us?'

'Hard to say,' Hudson said cautiously. 'He's driving pretty fast, but he hasn't tried to cut across the traffic or run a red light, which would be the obvious play if he wanted to shake us off. It may be that he's just a man on a mission.'

Helen sincerely hoped he was right. Losing him was one thing, being rumbled by him would be something else. He might drop off their radar altogether, if that was the case.

'Shit.'

Hudson braked suddenly, bringing their car to a halt inches from the vehicle in front of them. It appeared to have stalled, the young driver labouring to start the car. Ramming the gears into reverse, Hudson lurched backwards, then circumvented the small hatchback, swinging round and back into lane.

'There he is.'

Helen could see the Defender, but he was eight cars ahead now, and even as they spotted him, Clarke changed direction once more, swinging right onto the A3025.

'Is he heading for the motorway? That doesn't make any sense.'

Hudson said nothing, increasing his speed to catch the lights before they changed. Arcing round to the right, they joined the A3025 at speed – but the battered Defender was nowhere in sight.

'For God's sake,' Hudson growled, rapping the steering wheel.

'He must have turned off somewhere, he couldn't have got to the end of this stretch already.'

They were both scanning the road desperately for signs of Clarke.

'But which one?' Hudson asked, an edge in his voice now. 'There are loads of turnings off here –'

'Try Botley Road. He seems to be sticking to the major roads.'

'Which one's that?'

'Here, here,' Helen pointed, chiding herself for forgetting how little Hudson knew the area.

Flicking the indicator, Hudson swung the car across the dual carriageway and into Botley Road. To Helen's enormous relief, the Defender could be glimpsed at the top of the road, indicating left. Eschewing caution, Hudson hit the accelerator, pushing the car hard along the road, as Clarke's vehicle disappeared around the corner.

'Suspect is turning left onto the A3024, from Botley Road.'

'Roger that' was McAndrew's brief reply, the pair clearly struggling to keep up with their suspect's erratic movements.

'Why can't he just drive in a straight line?' Hudson grumbled, clocking that Clarke was indicating again.

Hudson was clearly worried now that they *had* been spotted, but surely Clarke wouldn't be indicating, obeying the laws of the road so diligently, if he feared he was being pursued?

The Defender waited for a gap in the traffic, allowing them to pull a little closer, then turned right into Linacre Road. And now, for the first time, Helen got an inkling of where he was heading.

'Just hang back a bit,' Helen cautioned, as they drove down the quiet suburban street.

Hudson did as he was asked and, sure enough, the Defender now slowed right down, before easing into a parking spot. Helen looked away from the car, pretending to talk animatedly to Hudson as they drove past, before pulling up at the end of the road.

'What's he up to?' Hudson said, killing the engine and turning to Helen.

'Hold on,' Helen replied, holding up her hand.

Clarke was on the move. Quietly shutting the driver's door, he retrieved something from the back of the Defender then, after a quick check of the street, darted down an alley next to one of the tall tenement buildings. And now, finally, Hudson got it.

'We're in Linacre Road,' he said, suddenly recognizing his surroundings.

'Exactly,' replied Helen, taking up the radio once more. 'He's heading for Lauren Scott's flat.'

83

He crept up behind her, laying his hands on her shoulders. Charlie flinched, turning sharply, but immediately caught herself, shaking her head at her own stupidity. Steve often massaged her shoulders when she was crouched over the kitchen table, buried in her work, but tonight she had been so engrossed in what she was doing that she hadn't heard him coming.

'How you getting on?' he asked, shaking his head at her, as he kneaded her shoulders.

'Slowly . . .'

'Anything I can help you with?'

'Believe me, you don't want to. Police work's not all it's cracked up to be.'

For once, this wasn't a polite brush-off. She usually kept Steve at arm's length from her work for reasons of security, but tonight she was saving him from disappointment. Since returning home, she had been glued to her laptop, breaking only to put Jessica to bed. She was investigating the possible university link between Campbell and Scott, running the rule over Southampton Uni's intake for 2008, when Scott matriculated. In Charlie's day, you had your matriculation photo, hung in pride of place on your parents' wall and your yearbook. For the modern student, by contrast, everything was online, which should have made Charlie's life easier.

And it was true she *had* found matriculation photos for both Lauren Scott and Tom Campbell, but not the overlap she'd been hoping for. Campbell looked different – his long hair and earring a far cry from the sober professional he later became – and it was interesting to see Lauren as a teenager, looking even more fragile. But she could find no photos of them together – no clubs, no amateur dramatics, no sporting events, no pub crawl poses. Campbell had joined two years *before* Scott and they appeared to have moved in different worlds, which was perhaps no great surprise. When Charlie was at university, first-years and third-years were different breeds, gauche, un-sophisticated, mindless on the one hand, serious, cultured and staring down the barrel of finals on the other.

The fact that they had both attended Southampton Uni-versity, albeit studying different subjects, seemed to be a legitimate connection, but after two hours' searching Charlie had found nothing of any value. She had a short list of names to check out, students who'd enrolled on the same course as Lauren, but that was the sum total of her findings thus far. Perhaps it was time to call it a day and check in with the rest of the team. They were currently out on surveillance – Char-lie sincerely hoped they were having more luck than her.

'Finished for the day, then?'

'Might as well. I'm not getting anywhere . . .'

'Good,' Steve replied, gently pushing his thumbs into her shoulder blades.

The knots in her back protested, then gave way, as he increased the pressure. Charlie closed her eyes and relaxed into it – she had spent far too much time hunched over a laptop and a massage was long overdue. Already she could feel the cares of the day drifting away – Steve had always been a good masseur, with a surprisingly delicate touch for a burly mechanic.

He moved his hands up now, rubbing the base of her neck. This area was, if anything, even more stiff than her back, which was saying something.

'That nice?'

'Hmm hmm,' Charlie murmured. 'Painful, but nice . . .'

Steve laughed and continued, keeping the pressure on for another minute or so, before sliding his hands downwards, brushing over the nape of her neck, her breastbone, eventually slipping down into her cleavage, gently brushing the sides of her breasts as he did so.

'Steve . . .'

'Shhh,' he replied. 'You've had a long day, you need to relax. Jessie's asleep – I just checked on her and she's away with the fairies . . .'

He bent down and kissed her neck, nuzzling into her, before nibbling her ear.

'Steve . . .'

Still he kissed her, running the back of his hand over her right nipple, which immediately stiffened. Charlie knew where this was going and part of her would have happily succumbed. But another part of her knew it had to stop.

'Steve.'

It was said more firmly this time. She gently plucked his hand away and turned to face him – to find him looking confused, even a little aggrieved.

'Sorry, I thought that –'

'You've nothing to apologize for, but I can't do this.'

Now Steve looked properly worried, making Charlie feel terrible.

'I don't mean *this*,' she said quickly, gesturing to the house, them, Jessica. 'Of course not. It's just . . .' She hesitated, trying to find the right words. '. . . I know why you're being so attentive . . . and I don't think I can do it.'

Still he regarded her, saying nothing.

'I know we talked about it and we said in time we would try for another child . . .' Tears were pricking her eyes now, all the frustration and emotion of the last few days catching up with her. 'But with everything that's been going on, with Jessie, with the case . . .'

She took a breath, before muttering: '. . . with Joanne. I just . . . I just don't feel I can.'

Steve was looking at her, baffled and hurt.

'I'm sorry. I really am. I know this isn't what you wanted, not what we'd planned . . .'

She was desperately hoping he'd say something to put her out of her misery, even if it was only recriminations and abuse. But Steve continued to stare at her, tight-lipped and angry, his sense of betrayal all too clear.

84

He hadn't even bothered to reprimand her. Gardiner's secretary had tipped Emilia the wink that Simmons had rung her editor's office following their confrontation and she had duly prepared herself for her second bollocking of the day. But her editor had said nothing. Was this because he knew Emilia's actions had helped put more heat under the story? Or was it because he was weary of trying to engineer behavioural change in his wilful employee? Emilia suspected it might be both. Whatever the reasons, he was clearly happy to let it slide. Nobody else put the cat among the pigeons like she did.

'I'm thinking we could run a sympathetic piece about Matteo Dominici and Melanie Walton,' she announced. 'The legacy of the New Forest Killer, the ongoing trauma of those left behind. Major on what they've lost, the plans they'd made, but also highlight their close brush with the killer. By all accounts, their partners were plucked from their tents, while they were both sleeping inside.'

Gardiner shuddered involuntarily. Emilia had never asked her editor whether he was a camper and wondered now if this was why he'd taken such a keen interest in this story.

'Sounds sensible,' Gardiner mumbled, staring at the photos of Dominici, in which the latter looked genuinely unhinged. 'How many pages do you need?'

'Eight?'

'Bloody hell, Emilia. I was thinking four tops. There *are* other things going on in Southampton at the moment.'

'But there's only one story. Short-change it at your peril.'

'Five then.'

'I'll take six and crack straight on with it. Got to keep the public informed, right?'

Reluctantly, Gardiner conceded, picking up the phone to his deputy editor, as Emilia gathered her things.

'Sally, it's Martin. Change of plan . . .'

Emilia left, concealing her grin. Sally Jones, their long-serving deputy editor, was not a fan and would be aggrieved to have to give her extra pages, but Gardiner had made his decision.

Skipping back to her desk, Emilia settled down to write. Six pages was a lot and if she wanted to dominate tomorrow's news agenda, to heap even more pressure on Grace and her team, then she'd have to work fast. She had barely started writing, however, when her phone started to buzz. She picked it up and was surprised to find that she'd received a text. Nobody sent texts any more.

'Good talking to you today. Fancy doing it again?'

It was not a number she recognized and she assumed by the tone that this had not come from Simmons. Which left only one possibility. Graham Ross wanted to continue, perhaps even deepen, their association.

Standard protocol dictated that Emilia pause now, perhaps discuss the matter with colleagues, evaluate the pros and cons of meeting a man she barely knew. But Emilia had never run scared, trusting her street smarts to keep her safe, so turning away from her colleagues she tapped in a reply:

'Where and when?'

85

What was he doing in there?

Helen had been standing in the dark street for nearly twenty minutes, hidden from view behind a pair of municipal bins that had been shoved into a narrow alleyway. From here she had a good view of the third-floor flat that Matteo Dominici shared with Lauren Scott.

She had not set eyes on Clarke since he dived down the alleyway next to the house, but she was convinced he was in the flat. The alley he'd disappeared down bordered the garden wall, which was old, crumbling and low enough for a man of Clarke's stature to scale. From there, had he accessed the back door? Or tried the fire escape? Joseph Hudson was in the next street, to the rear of the property, and had confirmed that a pull-down fire escape ran down the back of the building. What was the betting Clarke had used this to make his way to the third floor?

Yet, still, there was no sign of him. The lights hadn't come on, nor had Helen seen a torch beam. What was his plan? Had he gone to the flat to find something? Had he intended to surprise Dominici? If so, he would be waiting a long time, as Lauren's bereaved boyfriend would not be returning any time soon.

Helen peered out of the alleyway, darting a look up the road. DC Osbourne was positioned at one end of Linacre Road, in case Clarke somehow evaded them and made off on foot, DC McAndrew at the other, in case he made a break for his vehicle. Everything was in place – all that was lacking now was their suspect.

Turning her attention back to the flat, Helen screwed up her eyes, trying to penetrate the darkness. It was maddening to think of him in there, padding around unmolested. She was tempted to kick the front door in and race upstairs, but experience told her she had to let this play out, to let Clarke reveal himself through his actions. Still, she yearned to know what had drawn him to his victim's flat. What part of his fascination with, or anger towards, Lauren Scott had not been sated by her brutal killing?

She longed for an answer, a dozen scenarios ricocheting around her head, but there was no question of forcing the situation.

All she could do for now was watch and wait.

86

His eyes never left the house.

The fire escape at the back of the property had been pulled down and, looking up at the third-floor windows, Hudson was convinced he'd seen the shadowy form of Clarke pass back and forth a couple of times. What he was up to was a mystery, but one thing was clear. If Clarke retreated the way he'd come, then Hudson would be the first to spot him.

It was an exciting prospect, a chance to prove himself to Helen, to the rest of the team. He had acquitted himself well so far, driving forward the investigation into Dean Clarke, but he had yet to make a real difference. He had disturbed Martin, but not captured him. He had tailed Clarke efficiently, but would have lost him were it not for Helen's intervention. It was all good, but not good enough for an ambitious DS keen to make his mark.

Removing his baton from his belt, he checked his position once more, making sure he couldn't be spotted from above. The communal garden was neglected and he had had no trouble finding a hiding place – the overgrown mulberry bush concealed him completely, cloaking him in its vast shadow. He would be impossible to see in the inky gloom, now that night had fallen.

A sound nearby. Faint, but audible. Looking up, Hudson spotted movement. A shadow prowling, then descending. The figure was taking great care, measuring each step carefully, wary of making the slightest noise. Hudson assumed it was Clarke from his size, but it was hard to tell for sure – as the figure turned, he caught a glimpse of his face, but it was masked, only the whites of his eyes visible.

Gathering himself, Hudson double-clicked his radio, the prearranged signal for signs of movement, then turned it off. Extending his baton, he readied himself. Clarke was nearing the bottom of the fire escape.

Stepping down onto the spongy turf, the figure suddenly stopped dead, turning to look back up at the building. A light had come on on the second floor, spilling light onto the garden below. The intruder remained out of sight on the edge of the shadows, frozen in the act of fleeing. Hudson wondered what was going through his head – would he make a break for it or sit it out? – but the light was now extinguished, plunging the garden back into darkness.

Now the figure was on the move again, padding swiftly across the garden. He didn't seem to be carrying anything, was unencumbered, and Hudson wondered again what the purpose of this night-time visit was. Hopefully, they would soon find out – the retreating figure was only ten yards from him now.

Hudson tensed. He was in the shadows, but would soon become visible, should Clarke choose to look his way. But their suspect seemed intent on getting away, hurrying past the bush without a glance. Hudson knew this was his moment, so he moved in for the kill, laying a firm hand on the figure's shoulder.

'Dean Clarke. I'm arresting you –'

An elbow rammed into his ribs, knocking him backwards. But he had a fistful of Clarke's clothing and he pulled hard, to stop Clarke escaping. Again, the elbow flew towards him, but this time Hudson dodged it, Clarke's arm glancing off his flank. Now, however, his quarry twisted violently away from him, breaking his hold. Hudson saw his intention instantly – to vault the nearby garden wall – and slammed his baton into Clarke's right knee. The fugitive howled in agony, stumbling slightly, and Hudson pounced, grabbing his free arm and wrenching it up his back. But even as he did so, Clarke pirouetted, spinning around sharply and freeing himself once more. Hudson raised his baton again, expecting Clarke to flee, but to his surprise Clarke turned and barrelled straight into him, the top of his head connecting sharply with Hudson's chin.

Stunned, he fell backwards, landing in a heap on the turf. For a moment he was poleaxed, a million pinpricks of light flashing in front of his eyes, and he was too slow to stop Clarke climbing on top of him. He jerked his body violently, trying to dislodge his assailant, even as a wave of nausea swept over him. But Clarke would not shift, manoeuvring his knees to try to pin him down. He swung his baton hard, catching Clarke on the side of his head. His attacker emitted a low moan, so he struck again. And again. Except this time, Clarke caught the baton, twisting it round and ramming it down onto Hudson's throat.

Hudson gasped, the rigid metal bar pressing down on his windpipe. Already winded, Hudson now struggled to breathe. Clarke was pressing down with all his might, as if he wanted to snap his head clean off.

The nausea was growing, the pinpricks going crazy. Hudson continued to buck, but he was losing strength, suddenly robbed of energy and oxygen. He knew he had to get Clarke off him somehow, but his attacker was in the ascendant, bearing down on his victim, his eyes flashing with cruelty and desire. Was this the last thing he would ever see? Those manic, laughing eyes?

Things were going black now. He was drifting further and further from reality, towards unconsciousness, towards the end. Then suddenly, the pressure lifted, all at once. His attacker flew sideways, crashing to the ground next to him. Oxygen seemed to flood Hudson's lungs and he jerked back to the present, just in time to see Helen Grace hurdling him to engage Clarke. The latter was already on his feet, swinging a meaty fist in her direction, but Helen dodged it easily, catching his arm and using Clarke's own momentum to swing him around, jamming a foot behind his right leg. Surprised, Clarke pitched onto the ground, biting the turf hard. And now Helen was on top of him, pinning back his arms, cuffing him.

Hudson struggled up onto his elbows, but the fight was over. Half a second later, another wave of nausea swept over him, then everything went black.

87

He was walking in circles, going nowhere.

Having watched his son depart from the yard, Terry Clarke had stuck it out for another half-hour before calling it a day. He was going through the motions, chasing up invoices, making calls, but his heart wasn't in it.

Locking up, he had driven home, his thoughts dominated by his son's strange behaviour. What was going on? Where had this sudden aggression come from? He had never seen him so hostile before, had certainly never been *attacked* by him. Dean seemed like a coiled spring these days, primed to burst forth at any moment. Terry prayed he wouldn't be around when he did.

Pacing the floor of the living room, he shot another glance at the window. Where did he go at night? What was there to do in Southampton that could keep him out so late? He never smelt of drink, or perfume, in the morning, nor did he dress up – his one set of smart clothes hadn't been touched in weeks. Nobody ever rang his mobile or contacted him at the yard, so who was he with? What was he doing?

He realized now how little he knew his son. Things had definitely gone sideways since Nancy died. She was the glue that kept the family together and now Dean seemed to want to spend less and less time with his father. He worked hard enough during the day, but kept his distance, then vanished at night. It was as if the thought of spending any time in the family home was too much to bear. Yet *something* was driving him, consuming him. He seemed to spend every spare moment on his phone, though what he was up to Terry couldn't say. Once he had tried to open up his phone, desperate to see what was so interesting, but it was password locked and he had thought better of it. There would be hell to pay if Dean worked out what he'd been up to.

Terry Clarke ground to a halt. Try as he might, he couldn't settle, couldn't sit still. Part of him thought he should get out, go down the Hare and Hounds. This house, this room with its threadbare rug and stained sofa, was depressing him. And yet something, some instinct, was making him stay put, as if abandoning his home now would be to abandon the family.

So, he resumed pacing, but movement outside now caught his attention. Immediately, he froze. He couldn't make out the cars that were pulling up, but he could see their blue flashing lights. Hurrying to the window, he saw two patrol cars, flanked by more, unmarked vehicles. Even now, officers were emerging, hurrying towards the house, hammering on the front door.

But Terry Clarke remained rooted to the spot, leaning on the window, staring at the lights. He suddenly knew with absolute certainty that the walls were about to come crashing down.

88

'What's all this about? I really *am* in a hurry.'

Nigella Ware was the definition of a modern working mum. Smartly dressed, she was weighed down with bags and files, labouring to manoeuvre a bulky pushchair out of the front door. She looked tired and harassed this morning, distracted by her toddler, who was banging a toy on the roof of his pram. Charlie knew how she felt – a hard night with Steve, full of argument, distress and anger had left her feeling raw and unsettled – but she had to ask the questions.

'We're making enquiries about Lauren Scott,' Charlie replied, pocketing her warrant card. 'You may have heard about her in the news.'

Nigella's reaction told Charlie that she had.

'I'm trying to track down people who knew her at university. I believe you studied geography together?'

'Well, we were on the same course,' Nigella replied uncertainly. 'But we weren't particularly close.'

That was good enough for Charlie. She'd only had a short list of names to start with – all of whom had so far proved to be out of town or unable to help.

'We don't need you to make a statement or anything,' Charlie continued swiftly, aware that the volume of the toddler's protests was growing. 'I'm just trying to find out about her life around that time. I know she had some problems, that she dropped out early in her second year.'

'Look, I really didn't know her. I wasn't part of her scene . . .'

Charlie assumed she meant drugs, but didn't probe further. Ware was clearly keen to be away, but her conscience wouldn't let her shrug Charlie off just yet.

'. . . and she didn't hang out with the people on our course. Best thing would be to track down her housemates. She lived in a shared house in Portswood, I think.'

Ware had stopped now, the memories arresting her. Charlie's hopes suddenly rose – any progress, however modest, would be very gratefully received.

'Can you think of any names? Anyone she was close to?'

'There were a few . . .' she said vaguely. 'People moved in and out a lot, but I think she was tightest with Aaron Slater and Julia Winter.'

Charlie scribbled down the names.

'Not that that'll do you any good.'

Charlie looked up, alarmed.

'Aaron Slater shacked up with an American girl in his final year – he moved out there a while back. And Julia's in a coma.'

For a moment, Charlie was lost for words, so Nigella continued.

'At least, I think she is. She flunked her first-year exams and tried to kill herself. She was on a ventilator at South Hants . . . but to be honest I'm not even sure she's still alive. Now, if you don't mind, I really *do* have to go.'

Charlie let her leave – her little boy had started to wail in earnest now. Charlie knew how he felt. She always chased down new leads with optimism and determination, but this morning she was struggling to remain upbeat. Perhaps it was the legacy of her arguments with Steve, perhaps it was the opaque nature of this case, but her tangible lack of progress left her feeling flat and dispirited. Maybe she was over-reacting, maybe fatigue *was* poisoning her mood, but her inability to fashion a clear link between Campbell and Scott, to find any real overlap, indicated to her that the university connection might prove to be a giant dead end.

In a case that already seemed to have a pronounced lack of clues, she feared it would not be the last.

89

'You're going to have to talk to me at some point, Dean. So drop the act and answer the question.'

Dean Clarke stared at Helen, but said nothing. After a night in the cells, he had been passed fit for interview by a local doctor, who'd confirmed that his injuries were superficial. Fortunately, so were Joseph Hudson's, but Helen had still given him the morning off to recuperate. And, as Charlie was pursuing another line of enquiry and facing her own issues at home, Helen had pulled in DC McAndrew to join her. So far, however, Clarke had refused to engage with either of them or offer any explanation for his presence in Lauren Scott's flat. In fact, he'd refused everything – a lawyer, a phone call, refreshments – seemingly intent on frustrating the process by his silence.

'Look, I am happy to charge you without a statement. If that's the way you want to play it, that's fine. But I would like to understand why you were in the flat, Dean. Did you know Lauren Scott?'

Dean slowly shook his head.

'What about Matteo Dominici?'

Another shake.

'And yet you targeted their flat specifically. There were others which would have been easier to access – the back door to the basement flat was pretty flimsy and wasn't overlooked. But instead you made your way straight to the third-floor flat, forcing the window and spending half an hour alone in there. Why?'

This time there was no reaction. Just an unflinching stare.

'We found these in your possession,' McAndrew added, indicating an evidence bag containing several necklaces and rings. 'They're imitation, not worth much. I presume it wasn't their *value* that appealed to you, so why did you take them? Are they precious to you?'

Still nothing.

'I don't need to tell you that Lauren Scott was murdered recently,' Helen resumed. 'Shot three times and left to bleed out. What would you like to tell us about that? Why did you target *her* specifically?'

Now, finally, Clarke reacted, snorting slightly, as he shook his head.

'We know you have the propensity for this kind of thing. We've had a detailed look at your viewing habits, Dean, both on mainstream internet and the dark web. We're aware that you regularly post explicit images of violence under the aliases "2Helmandback" and "Helmanned2008".'

A little flicker of something now. Hostility? Fear?

'We also know that you buy and trade exotic weapons – knives, maces, crossbows. I take it this *is* you?'

Helen offered him a screen grab of a masked man, matching his build and shape in every way, staring down the sight of a crossbow. Clarke licked his lips, but refused to comment, breaking eye contact for the first time, as Helen continued to stare at him.

'Lauren Scott was shot three times with a crossbow, as was Tom Campbell. Both were abducted and transported in a Land Rover Defender, very much like the one you drove to Linacre Road last night. We're conducting tests on your vehicle now, looking for traces of blood, saliva, skin, as well as running tests on a coil of rope we found in the boot of the vehicle. You can see where I'm going with this, can't you, Dean?'

He did and clearly didn't like it.

'Out of interest, why did you string them up? What was the point of that? You've got us baffled.'

She said this with a smile, as if inviting him to confide among friends, but his response was terse.

'This is bullshit.'

'I'm genuinely interested,' Helen persisted. 'I've seen a few things in my time, but this is something . . . special. I'd like you to help us understand what's going on. What had Lauren done to you? What had *Tom* done to you?'

'I don't know these people.'

'But you do, Dean, in fact you know them intimately. So well that you could abduct and kill them without anyone noticing, not even the people who were sleeping next to them.'

'You've no proof of that,' he asserted, angrily.

'On the contrary, we have plenty of proof. Not just evidence of your violent, sadistic nature, your love of weapons, your regular night-time excursions . . .'

Another little flicker. This time Helen saw fear.

'. . . We also have your method of transport, your visit to Lauren's flat in search of – what? – trophies? keepsakes? – *and* evidence that you were stalking Tom Campbell in the days before he was abducted and killed.'

Now Clarke looked rattled.

'Following your excursion last night, we checked CCTV footage from the streets near Tom Campbell's house. We didn't find anything from the nights *after* his death, but look at these stills . . .'

As she spoke, DC McAndrew slid a black-and-white image of a Land Rover Defender across the table.

'Look at the number plate – it's your vehicle. And here, in this one, we can see your face . . .'

An angled shot revealed Clarke's face peering out of the

driver's window. Though half cloaked in shadow, it was definitely him.

'We have images from two different occasions when you parked up in Madeley Road,' Helen said quickly. 'Less than a hundred feet from where Tom Campbell lived.'

She let this land.

'You were stalking him, weren't you? Perhaps you were checking out his daily routine? Perhaps you already *knew* he was going camping and were waiting for your moment to strike?'

'No . . .'

'Then why were you there? What was it about Tom Campbell that so excited you? Or perhaps it was his fiancée who interested you, Melanie?'

'I've said I don't know them,' Clarke insisted.

'But I don't believe you, Dean. Unless there was some other reason you were in his street? In Lauren Scott's flat?'

Dean Clarke turned his face to the floor, repeatedly kicking the table leg. Helen watched him with growing satisfaction – he was obviously feeling the pressure.

'What had they done, Dean? Why them?' she continued. 'Tom was engaged to be married, Lauren was pregnant . . .'

Clarke stopped kicking.

'Did you not know that? She was two months pregnant, a little boy. She had her whole future mapped out, a happy little family. But you snuffed that out.'

'No . . .'

'And a judge won't look kindly on that. The baby had as much right to live as Tom and Lauren, so you're looking at three life sentences. Not to mention what you'll get for attempting to murder a police officer.'

Clarke emitted a strangled noise – halfway between a cry and a roar. He was on the rack now, so Helen moved in for the kill.

'My team are currently at your family home, tearing it apart, piece by piece. What's the betting they are going to find a crossbow? The same crossbow that was used to kill Tom Campbell, Lauren Scott, her unborn son.'

'Please stop this . . .' Clarke moaned, cradling his head in his hands.

'Then tell me why you did it. Why you murdered three innocent people?'

Clarke continued to moan and shake his head, but Helen wasn't finished:

'Tell me *why*.'

90

Joseph Hudson stared in the mirror, sickened by the sight in front of him.

His high collar barely concealed the livid bruising on his neck, which ran from his chin to his Adam's apple, and there was little he could do to disguise the cuts and scratches on his cheek. A generous application of foundation, which he kept buried in his medicine bag, had dulled the abrasions, but little more. Worse still, though his throat hadn't sustained any permanent damage, it was obviously enflamed, meaning his voice was hoarse and scratchy, drawing attention to his plight.

For all this, it was the damage to his reputation that really hurt. The cuts and bruises would fade, but his besting by Clarke would remain long in the memory. Sure, Clarke was a big guy, a man who had trained hard to keep himself in peak physical condition, but so was Hudson. Furthermore, he had had the element of surprise. He had had a hand on Clarke, had him by the collar . . . and yet it was *he* who had ended up on the floor, his own baton pressed to his neck, fighting for his life. There was a special kind of derision reserved for police officers who had their own weapons turned on them.

Of course, he might not be standing here at all, were it not for the timely intervention of his boss. On receiving his signal, Helen had headed to the back of the house to assist in Clarke's apprehension, but instead had had to vault the wall and race across the turf to save his life. This had left him shaken, but severely embarrassed too.

Not because she was a woman – he wasn't a dinosaur – but because he had wanted to impress her. He knew the team he'd joined was one of the best in the business, that Helen would be a demanding boss, and he had prepared accordingly, resolved to put his best foot forward. But on meeting her, on spending time with her, his determination to shine had only grown. She was impressive, no question, but there was a vulnerability too, which he found very appealing. They came from similar backgrounds, had clawed their way up to the senior ranks and both were currently on their own. He had allowed himself to believe she might be interested in him, but what chance of that was there now, when he had humiliated himself, allowing himself to be bested by a delusional fantasist, a nobody who dreamed of notoriety and bloodshed? Whatever Clarke had done in that forest, he'd been unarmed when Hudson tackled him and still he had won.

Which was why, as Hudson continued to stare at his battered face in the mirror, he saw not the bruises, nor the cuts, but his own shame staring back.

91

She chuckled to herself, revelling in her triumph. There were his details on the screen in front of her: Dean Clarke, thirty-eight years old, resident of Woolston.

Finally, she had a name.

News of an arrest had broken early this morning. Since then, Emilia had tried and failed to get any of her contacts within Hampshire Police to give her the inside track. How she needed an informer, a paid insider, at times like this. But recently she had failed to find anyone weak or desperate enough to take her money.

Which left her with a problem, one she was still pondering as she pulled into the car park of the *Southampton Evening News*. As she squeezed her Corsa into a tiny space, her attention was drawn to an RAC van dragging a vehicle away from the building and a thought suddenly occurred to her. If the police had a suspect, they would presumably be busy raiding his home, his place of work, searching for evidence of his guilt. And, given that both murder victims had been spirited from a campsite to a place of execution some distance away, they would no doubt be taking a look at any vehicles he might own too.

Hurrying into the building, Emilia dug out the number for Hampshire Police's vehicle reclamation unit, an outfit that generally spent its day transporting stolen cars to the police pound. Emilia had a contact there, a driver called Jamie Mavers, who'd helped her out before, and she rang him now.

'Yup.'

Mavers was not a man who bothered with pleasantries.

'Jamie, it's Emilia Garanita. How's tricks?'

'Good. You?'

'Never better. Look I need a bit of information. Have you guys picked up anything interesting in the last twenty-four hours? Maybe a four by four? Some kind of off-road vehicle?'

'Sure. What of it?'

'Can you tell me anything about it? There's fifty pounds in it for you.'

'Well, we picked up a Land Rover from Linacre Road last night. It was sent straight to Meredith Walker for tests.'

'Who did it belong to?'

'Don't know.'

'Can you at least tell me the registration number?'

There was a pause on the other end.

'I don't know if I should . . .'

'How about I double your money?'

'Fair enough.'

Moments later, Emilia was deep in the DVLA database. Within minutes, she had found both the vehicle and the registered owner. Now all she had to do was a bit of digging on his background and she would have her scoop. Who needed informants, when a bit of ingenuity could get you everything you need? As she began to surf, Emilia broke into a broad smile.

Sometimes she surprised even herself.

92

'This is your last chance, Dean. Tell me what happened.'

Clarke had said nothing for the past ten minutes, rubbing his face with his hands as he stared at the floor. He seemed almost catatonic. Helen feared he would either shut down completely or erupt in anger and frustration. She couldn't tell which, but she had to try and prise him open, if they were going to make sense of these baffling crimes.

'If you don't talk to me, I'm going to have to assume you are guilty. Then I will have no choice but to charge you – here, now – with three counts of murder, one count of attempted murder, assaulting a police officer, resisting arrest, breaking and entering, theft . . .'

With each offence, Dean seemed to crumple a little, the reality of his situation finally coming home to roost.

'Now we can get someone to sit in with you while we do this. A lawyer, a friend, your dad perhaps . . .' Helen let this last suggestion linger. He and his father had a troubled relationship, but he was all Dean had left. '. . . but there's nothing I can do to stop it. Once you've been charged, you'll be offered a bail hearing, but for offences of this magnitude . . .'

She couldn't threaten him directly with incarceration, but her meaning was clear. Clarke ran his fingers through his hair, staring at the ground and muttering to himself, as if caught on the horns of a terrible dilemma. Helen could see the individual beads of sweat on his forehead, watching now as one slid slowly down his right cheek.

'If I talk to you, I want your help . . .'

'Of course.'

'I can't go to jail, I can't be locked up . . .'

It was amazing how all his swagger, all his bravado, had suddenly evaporated. He seemed diminished in stature, looking child-like as he cradled himself.

'Well, I can't promise that, Dean. But what I will say is that things will go much easier for you if you co-operate. A swift, honest admission of guilt will go a long way to –'

'I didn't do it, any of it.'

'Come on, Dean,' Helen said, exasperated. 'You were doing so well –'

'I mean, I'm not saying I'm blameless, I've done wrong, I know that . . .'

'Then tell me about it. Help me understand.'

'It is me in those pictures. On Madeley Road,' he continued, nodding at the photos on the table. 'But I wasn't there for him. Campbell . . .'

'So why were you there?'

'I was casing a property.'

Helen looked at him intently, trying to read his tone.

'I robbed a house in the next road. But from Madeley Road I could access the back garden, get to it without being seen.'

'What was the address?' Helen asked, her scepticism clear.

'Fourteen, no, Sixteen Elm Road.'

'When did you do this?'

'On the day the second photo was taken. The eighteenth, I think.'

Helen looked to McAndrew, who clocked her meaning immediately, rising and hurrying from the room.

'And Lauren Scott? Why target her? You hadn't done any surveillance on *her* place.'

'Because I saw it on the news.'

'Sorry?'

'They were going on about this girl having been killed and they showed pictures of her other half leaving the flat, being hounded out of it, to hole up in a hotel somewhere.'

Helen watched him, an awful possibility now formulating in her mind.

'I'd had some bother on previous jobs, been surprised a couple of times, and I figured this was an easy touch. Nobody in the flat, quick in and out . . .'

'You really expect me to believe that you targeted a flat in Thornhill?'

'It's rough, for sure. But everyone has something of value, right? Except they didn't. Just cheap fucking imitation jewellery.'

'So you're telling me you've carried out a wave of these raids, stolen loads of expensive gear . . . and yet you live in a run-down house, have a poorly paid job. What do you spend all your ill-gotten gains on, Dean?'

But even as she said it, Helen knew.

'The weapons,' Dean whispered. 'Every penny I've made, I've spent on them.'

His body was shaking now, the relief of confession over-whelming him. But there was something else there too. Shame.

'So, let me get this straight. You claim to be an SAS solider, someone who has fought to protect this country, laying low our enemies, liberating the oppressed. But in fact you prey on your own, robbing the unsuspecting and vulnerable, feeding off their distress to fill your pockets.'

Helen knew she had to control herself, but her blood was up. She was riven with frustration and anger, ready to evis-cerate Clarke for his misdemeanours, but further attack was unnecessary. Dropping his head in his hands, he began to sob – huge, racking sobs.

Immediately, Helen's anger dissipated, shock and resignation replacing them. A knock on the window made her look up and there was McAndrew, looking sombre and concerned, nodding meaningfully. Helen exhaled, long and loud, all her disappointment flooding from her.

Dean Clarke was guilty. But he was not their killer. He was the serial burglar who had been terrorizing Southampton's homeowners for weeks.

93

'Are we absolutely sure?'

DC Edwards's question perfectly captured the desperation felt by the whole team. Charlie and Hudson had now joined them, playing their part in the fevered analysis, though Helen noted the latter's reaction to this latest setback seemed curiously muted.

'Clarke gave us a full list of the properties he claims to have targeted. It matches our records and, as only a couple of those addresses were in the public domain, it seems credible. Also, the descriptions given by some of the witnesses during the burglaries tally with Clarke's height, build, accent. And the tools he had in his Land Rover are staple kit for these kinds of job.'

The team looked depressed, but Helen had no choice but to put the final nail in the coffin.

'Plus, I've just heard from Meredith Walker. The tyres on Clarke's Land Rover are old Avons, but the tread pattern doesn't match those we pulled from the crime scene. They had a couple of patches on them, bodge jobs done some time ago, which doesn't fit with the evidence we recovered from the campsite . . .'

'So, we're back to square one,' Edwards concluded, disconsolately.

'No,' Helen countered quickly, keen to avoid deflation setting in. 'We have a good body of evidence, relating to the perpetrator's MO, the vehicle he uses. We also have an image of him that we can work with. But, yes, we have to look at other possible suspects, new angles. Until we've exhausted all of those, we haven't done our jobs.'

There were a few determined nods from the team, which cheered Helen.

'So, let's review where we're at. DC Osbourne, you were checking out a man who'd been kicked out of a local archery club.'

'He's in the Philippines with his sister. Flew out there ten days ago, so we can rule him out.'

Helen tried not to let her disappointment show.

'And what about other weapons obsessives?' she said, turning to DC Reid.

'Still a couple of names to check out . . . but no one who majors on crossbows. It's mostly firearms these days, every-one wants to be a gangster.'

'How are we doing on the phone number then? The one that was on both Campbell's and Scott's call history?'

'We tracked down the caller,' DC Edwards replied promptly. 'The phone number belongs to a Mrs Mavis Stemple, a retired teacher living in Freemantle. She's got MS and a bulletproof alibi, so I think it's safe to assume her SIM card has been cloned.'

Helen resisted the temptation to swear. Every which way they turned in this case they seemed to hit a brick wall.

'It doesn't get us any further forward,' Edwards continued, 'but the call pattern *is* interesting. There were several calls in quick succession a few weeks back, then they suddenly stopped, just before the murders.'

'Ok, we need to put a trace on that number. I'll get the relevant authority, you set the wheels in motion,' Helen replied, before turning her attention to Charlie. 'DS Brooks, how are we doing with Lauren Scott?'

'Well, I've been trying to get to the bottom of a possible university connection between Scott and Campbell. Lauren *was* at Southampton University, for a year or so, before dropping out –'

'How did we not know this?' Helen interrupted, surprised.

'She didn't complete her degree, didn't get the qualification, so it wouldn't have shown up in our initial sweep. Anyhow, her two closest friends from that time were an Aaron Slater and a Julia Winter. The former is in the States – I'm still trying to trace him – but the latter is in South Hants hospital. She's in a coma following a failed suicide attempt and won't be any help, but I've just spoken to her dad, who *has* agreed to talk to us. It may be nothing, but I'd still like to get to the bottom of Scott's breakdown. Her drug use really ramped up in her early twenties, so it seems worth investigating.'

'Ok, I'll accompany you,' Helen answered, happy to grab on to any lead, however small. 'In the meantime, get busy. DS Hudson will cover for me, but you know the drill. Review every bit of evidence, every statement from the campers and campsite owners, looking for anything we've missed. Also, let's widen our search for the Land Rover. Ring round local body shops and garages, see if anyone has serviced one of these vehicles, noticed anything odd. Check out stolen vehicles too – if traffic cams have picked up any Land Rovers that have been reported missing, I want to know about it. That car remains our best bet of finding our man.'

Calling the meeting to a close, Helen gathered her things as she prepared to follow Charlie to the hospital. The rest of the team were at their desks, reviewing their files, hitting the phones, running down leads. Despite the major setback that they'd suffered, Helen was heartened by the sight. The team had never let her down before and she didn't think they would now. For all that though, something troubled her, a nagging worry that wouldn't go away.

Throughout the briefing, Joseph Hudson had not met her gaze once, keeping his eyes resolutely fixed on the floor.

94

Emilia marched towards Gardiner's office, humming happily to herself. The desks were aligned in such a way as to form a natural corridor, leading directly to his door. In Emilia's mind, this had always seemed like a triumphal avenue, a place to saunter down when the wind was at your back. She felt that this morning – the buzz of a job well done – and she held her head up as she hurried towards his office.

She was on fire. There was no other way of putting it. Having divined the suspect's identity, she had researched hard and fast, before banging out 2,000 words on the unfortunate Clarke. He was clearly a guy who had nothing going for him – dreary upbringing, no prospects, a history of minor criminality and mental health problems, all of which seemed to have propelled him into some kind of weird fantasy world. Some might have found the images of him posing with crossbows and knives troubling, but she found them hilarious, laughing out loud at his military tattoos. As if this muppet would ever be accepted into the SAS.

Reaching Gardiner's doorway, she stuck her head into the office. Gardiner was in urgent conference with his deputy editor, Sally Jones, but looked up as she entered.

'I've sent you the piece on Dean Clarke. I don't suppose you've had a chance to look at it?'

She knew he would have read it, but wanted to enjoy her triumph.

'Yes, I've read it. And I've just pulled it.'

For a minute, Emilia wasn't sure she'd heard him correctly.

'I don't follow. I can back everything up, I've checked every fact —'

'Problem is, we've just heard that Clarke is no longer a suspect,' Jones said, with no little satisfaction.

'He's been charged with six counts of burglary,' Gardiner filled in. 'He's the guy who's been putting the wind up local homeowners recently.'

'But . . . I . . .' Emilia stammered, shocked that her morning's efforts had been wasted.

'It's not all bad though,' Jones continued. 'As you've done a lot of the leg work on the burglary story, it shouldn't be hard for you to knock up a new front page. Shall we say forty-five minutes?'

Emilia stalked back to her desk, cursing every step of the way. She hated being behind the beat and she loathed Jones's snide, victorious tone. Collapsing into her chair, she opened up her burglary notes and without thinking started hitting the keys. She was careless of the quality, there was no time to polish, and her mind was hardly on the task. She was still thinking of the New Forest Killer and how she could wrest back the initiative, how she could prove to everyone here that she really was the top dog. And now, as she typed, her eye fell on her mobile phone. Snatching it up, she scrolled through her contacts until she found Graham Ross's number. A moment's hesitation, then she typed:

'Are you free now?'

95

'I'm Detective Inspector Helen Grace. I believe you know my colleague, DS Brooks?'

'We've spoken,' Oliver Winter replied, nodding at Charlie as he shook Helen's hand. 'She said you wanted to speak to me?'

'If you can spare the time, we'd be very grateful.'

Even as she said it, Helen darted a look through the viewing window to the high-dependency unit. From here, they had a perfect view of Julia Winter, who lay immobile in bed, attached to an assortment of tubes.

'Perhaps a quick coffee? I don't like to be away from Julia for long . . .'

'Whatever you're comfortable with,' Helen replied, gesturing Winter towards the coffee bar at the end of the corridor.

Five minutes later, they were seated in the overheated canteen, three milky coffees sitting untouched in front of them. Winter was open and cordial, though he seemed distracted by his daughter's plight. He spoke carefully, a slight Swedish accent still coming through, despite his twenty-five years living on the south coast.

'Can I ask how long Julia's been here?' Helen said hesitantly.

'Around eight years now,' Winter replied calmly. 'She jumped, from Itchen Bridge. You probably know it . . .'

Helen did. It was one of Southampton's most notorious suicide spots.

'The doctors told me she wouldn't make it. She'd sustained

severe head injuries, had massive internal bleeding. But my girl is a fighter . . .'

He said it with pride, but Helen could see the sadness in his eyes. After nine years caring for his daughter, this handsome man's face was pale and lined.

'She survived, although in truth it's the machines that are keeping her alive. At first, they thought that that was it, that she would be in a permanent vegetative state, but I was convinced that she could hear me, could understand what was going on. So, we tried different ways to reach her and for a time we did manage to communicate.'

Winter read the surprise on both their faces and smiled.

'We found a way of asking her simple questions, reading her answers through brain mapping. Depending on her response – yes or no – a different part of her brain would light up. It really was the most wonderful thing, to be able to talk to her again.'

His emotion was palpable, his voice thick.

'And now?' Helen asked gently.

'She contracted pneumonia a few weeks ago. Now it's a constant battle to keep her comfortable, to keep her lungs clear, so we've had to put our conversations on hold.'

It was said with a wry smile, but he couldn't resist shooting another glance towards the unit where his daughter lay.

'If it's ok, I'd like to ask you a couple of quick questions about Julia's time at university. I believe she was a housemate of Lauren Scott?'

'That's right. They had a house together in Portswood. After Julia's accident, Lauren stayed in touch for a while, visited when she could. She was a nice girl underneath it all.'

'You've presumably seen the news.'

'Yes, I was saddened to read about it. Saddened, if not particularly surprised.'

'Because?' Helen replied, wrong-footed by his response.

'Because I always suspected it would end badly for her. Not like *that* of course, but still I did think that one day I would read about her in the papers.'

'What makes you say that?' Charlie asked.

'Because she was fragile. Because she attracted trouble.'

'Even then?'

'Especially then,' Winter replied firmly. 'I think it's the reason she and Julia were friends. Both struggled at university. Julia found it hard living away from home and drowned under the workload. Lauren barely bothered with her studies, she was just there to please her parents. But she fell into bad company, got into drugs, into debt . . .'

Helen leaned forward, intrigued now to be getting a fuller picture of the young Lauren.

'Neither girl was enjoying her life there, but they handled it in different ways. Julia bottled it up, Lauren went the other way. She just wanted to get off her head as quickly as possible. I liked Lauren, but I feared for her. She was just one of those girls who never seemed happy in her own skin.'

Once more, Helen's thoughts went back to Lauren's parents. Was it possible there was neglect there? Even abuse?

'Did Julia ever confide in you as to the root cause of Lauren's unhappiness?' Charlie asked, as if reading Helen's mind.

'No, Julia wasn't the type to share secrets . . . but I always felt that Lauren was lonely. Her parents were uninterested, or disapproving, I could never tell which. And she was an only child, so . . .'

'She was isolated, then?'

'I think she sought approbation, affection, where she could get it. And she wasn't the best judge of character.'

Helen nodded, digesting this.

'You say she hung out with a bad crowd. Can you

287

remember any specific names? People who might have sold her drugs, got her hooked on drugs?'

'Not really, it was nine years ago now. There was . . . an Aaron somebody, who also shared the flat with them.'

'Aaron Slater.'

'That's him. As to the others . . . Julia and Lauren were tight, but they seemed to change their friends almost as often as their outfits. Whenever I went to the flat there were always new faces there.'

'Do you think . . .' Helen said, unsure if she should continue or not. 'Do you think it's possible that Lauren's parents might have harmed her in some way, historically, I mean?'

'I don't know about that,' Winter said quickly. 'You'd have to ask them.'

Helen nodded and Winter, realizing he had sounded defensive, continued:

'Look, I never liked them, that's for sure. The couple of times I met them. But I can't speculate on their home life, it wouldn't be fair.'

'Of course.'

Helen looked to Charlie, but she shook her head slowly, indicating she had no further questions.

'There was one last thing,' Helen continued, opening her file and pulling a photo from it. 'I was wondering if you recognized this man?'

She offered him the photo of Tom Campbell. It was her final throw of the dice, a last-ditch attempt to salvage something meaningful from the interview. But Winter slowly shook his head, dashing her hopes.

'I'm sorry, no.'

'He may have looked a bit different back then. Longer hair, earrings . . .'

She offered him a second photo from Campbell's student days. And now, to Helen's surprise, a cloud seemed to pass over Winter's face. Troubled, he picked up the more recent photo and held the pair together for comparison.

'My God, that's Tommy.'

'I'm sorry?'

'That's what they called him back then. I'd never have recognized him from *this* . . .'

He looked up at Helen.

'And this is . . . ? Tommy was also . . . ?'

'Yes, Tom Campbell was murdered five days ago. Do you know him?'

'I only met him a couple of times, but sure I know him. Though I never knew his surname until now.'

He was staring at Helen, stupefied, but still managed to mutter:

'He was Lauren's boyfriend.'

96

Helen marched away from the hospital, Charlie matching her stride for stride. Having been downcast following their wrong turn with Clarke, both felt energized by their interview with Winter. Previously, they had feared that the brutal murders were the work of an unhinged maniac or dark spirit preying on innocent holidaymakers, but now they felt sure there was a concrete connection between the victims, a reason for these baffling murders.

'First thing, I want us to do a deep trawl on all their communications. Emails, calls, texts, DMs, WhatsApp, the works. We need to know if Campbell and Scott had had any contact in the last few months.'

'You think they may have rekindled their relationship?' Charlie enquired.

'Why not? According to Winter, they were pretty tight during her first year. She still lived here, he came to Southampton every day for work.'

'We should check local hotels — for room reservations, credit card charges . . .'

'Absolutely. It's imperative we know if they were still in touch, if they still had feelings for each other.'

'Do you think one of their partners could have been involved?' Charlie asked. 'If they were having an affair, for example?'

'Potentially, but I don't see it. They seemed genuine to me.'

'Totally.'

'Plus the evidence suggests that carbon monoxide had

been pumped in to incapacitate *both* parties. I don't think Dominici was faking it.'

'A rival then? Someone who took exception to their relationship?'

'Anything's possible, but we don't even know if they were in touch, so we need to keep an open mind. We should look at drugs too.'

Charlie turned to Helen, surprised by this sudden change in direction.

'Lauren had a history of drug abuse, but it really ramped up during her time at university. The same time she was dating Campbell. We know Tom Campbell had a possession charge as a teenager, and was lucky to escape an intent-to-supply charge. He studied biochemistry at uni, was in a druggie scene . . .'

'You think he was a dealer?'

'Could be. He would be perfectly capable of producing MDMA and acid in a laboratory. Synthetic drugs too. Spice and K2 took off around 2008, while he was already at uni.'

'And he would have had a ready market for it.'

'Exactly.'

They had now reached Charlie's car.

'Do you think that he could *still* be dealing? That that was the basis of a possible reconnection?'

'I doubt it. It'd be far too risky. He has a good job, a nice house. It would only be worth it if he was doing it big time, so we should check out his financials again.'

'But it *is* possible that he was still using. He certainly had an appetite for booze and good living. Lauren had been trying to get clean, but we know she had fallen off the wagon before . . .'

'Even if they weren't in contact,' Helen continued, thinking aloud, 'it's possible that someone connected to their student scene was involved in their murders. Someone who still lives locally . . .'

'We've been concentrating so much on Lauren, but perhaps if we pull apart Tom Campbell's student days, then we might find something. He was the first victim, after all.'

Charlie looked at Helen, a ghost of a smile creasing her lips.

'Too right,' Helen replied. 'Race you back to base.'

She headed towards her bike, then slowed and turned.

'And well done, Charlie. We wouldn't have got here without you.'

97

It had been a gamble. One which was now paying dividends.

It had taken Emilia ten minutes to get to Ross's flat in St Denys. En route, she had rehearsed how this might play out, testing again the wisdom of responding to his earlier invitation to meet. On arrival, she had texted a colleague, making clear where she was and hinting at what she hoped to gain from her off-the-record chat with the photographer. This was standard practice when entering an uncertain situation, and though it didn't give you any real protection, at least it afforded you peace of mind that you wouldn't vanish off the face of the earth. Emilia was not by nature timorous, she could fight her own corner, but the tragic case of Kim Wall was still fresh in her mind and it wouldn't do to go completely off the grid.

Ross had welcomed her warmly, playing host efficiently, while complimenting her on her work. He seemed particularly interested in her future ambitions and in their earlier exchanges she got the distinct impression that she was being interviewed for a job. Soon, however, she managed to take hold of the conversation, allowing him one cup of tea's worth of questions, before turning it back on him.

'So, have you always worked for Grace's outfit?'

'Not at all. I've worked all over the country. Belfast, Glasgow, Manchester, Leeds . . .'

'The things you've seen . . .'

'Indeed,' he replied happily, stretching as he did so. 'And yet every crime scene still takes you by surprise.'

'Because?'

'Well, they give you the basics when you're en route – domestic murder, drugs killing, sex crime – and you picture it in your mind before you get there. And often the scene you've imagined is basically correct, but it's the small details that surprise you. The things they've done to try to stay alive, the keepsake they are still holding in their hands, the way the body has been arranged after death. Every detail tells a story.'

Ross seemed proud of his knowledge, of his insight, so Emilia had moved the conversation on quickly, zeroing in on his current case. She was surprised to find that Ross was largely dismissive of Grace's efforts so far. Emilia had always struggled to find officers at Southampton Central who weren't in thrall to her.

'They went down a total cul-de-sac with this Dean Clarke guy,' Ross declared, once Emilia had made it clear she knew Clarke was in the clear. 'That guy is a thug, a wannabe soldier without the brains or know-how to do *that* . . .'

He gestured towards the graphic photos of the corpses that were spread out on the coffee table, incongruous next to the tea and biscuits. They had been awaiting Emilia on arrival, as if Ross was displaying his wares.

'Maybe he would be capable of abducting the victims, pursuing them, but I've no idea what convinced them that he'd have an interest in arranging the bodies like that.'

Emilia took a look at the bodies of Campbell and Scott hanging from the trees, then back up at Ross.

'What do you mean?' she replied, being deliberately obtuse, hoping to draw him out further.

'Well, look at it. The two victims haven't just been murdered, they've been humiliated, hung out to dry. Whoever did this might enjoy the hunt, but it's the end result that's important. It's the *display*.'

'What does it mean?'

'Who knows?' Ross replied, chuckling. 'But it's interesting, isn't it?'

He leaned in a little closer to Emilia, laying a finger on the image.

'Perhaps he wants to shame them, mortify them. Perhaps he hoped that the birds and forest dwellers would feed on them, the corpses slowly disintegrating over time. Perhaps he wanted to display his physical strength and power, in killing them and arranging them like that. Perhaps he just likes messing with our heads, but that's not even the interesting part . . .'

It was to Emilia, who was still struggling to identify a discernible motive for these murders, but she let it go.

'. . . what's interesting is the staging,' Ross continued, almost without pause. 'Look at the framing of it, the way the bodies stand proud, while being enveloped by the clearing. It's gruesome for sure, but it's actually quite artistic, even beautiful.'

He seemed enraptured by the image.

'And therein lies its power.'

He turned to Emilia.

'It's one of the best photographs I've taken and believe me I've taken a lot.'

'Do you have more of these?' Emilia asked, suddenly intrigued.

But Ross didn't answer directly. Instead, he rose and gestured her towards the back of the flat.

'Follow me.'

98

'We need to get under their skin.'

Joseph Hudson had a team of junior officers gathered around him, a couple of data analysts too. Following her visit to the hospital, Helen had tasked him with leading the digital trawl of the two victims' lives. She meanwhile had headed off elsewhere, which secretly he was glad of.

'We are looking for any sort of connection, any form of relationship. Romantic, sexual, commercial, harmless flirting, animosity, recrimination . . . anything. If they had contact we need to know about it.'

The team nodded, waiting for more.

'So . . . look at what they spent their money on, where they went, what they did for pleasure. We know now that Campbell and Scott were previously in an intense, romantic relationship. Let's see if any of the old fire remained. Drop everything else – this is your top priority now.'

The officers stared at him, eager but static.

'Well? What are you waiting for?' he barked, making one of the female analysts jump. 'Let's get on with it.'

The team rose to do his bidding, hurrying away. The startled data analyst retreated to her desk quickly, beginning an earnest conversation with her colleague as she went. Hudson was dismayed to see that she appeared to be upset. Perhaps she was just shocked, perhaps she felt his irritation was directed at her, either way he felt bad at having provoked such a reaction. He would have to talk to her later, see if he could make amends.

Marching over to his desk, he got stuck into his work. Helen had given him a specific, important, task to complete and he intended to get it right. Yet now he couldn't seem to focus, his gaze inevitably drifting back to the data analyst, who was still deep in conversation. Hudson had tried hard to make a good impression with the team, leading by example. But he still hadn't got the measure of them and now he had a black mark against his name.

Were they speculating that he was smarting from his encounter with Clarke? Or were they wondering if he was just brittle, unable to handle the stress of a major murder investigation? The thought made him seethe; he had handled plenty of big cases in his time. None of them as unsettling and unusual as this, but still . . .

He was tempted to roar at them, to order them to stop gossiping and get on with the job, but reining his fury in, he rose, walking over to the murder board. He stood in front of it, gazing at Campbell's and Scott's mugshots, and the scribbled writing that surrounded them. On the face of it, he was taking in the lines of enquiry, trying to piece together the connections. In reality, he was trying to gather himself.

Things had started well for him in what was unquestionably the most challenging posting of his career. Stepping into a dead officer's shoes is hard, former colleagues naturally struggling to accept a replacement. Doing it in a team led by such a demanding boss made it more difficult still. And yet he had performed satisfactorily at first, bonding well with both Helen Grace and Charlie Brooks and making some positive interventions in the case. But where had it led him? Clarke had been his suspect, but had proved to be a mere burglar. A nasty, violent one for sure, but a burglar nevertheless. Worse, he had been left battered, bruised and humiliated, following his altercation with Clarke. Were the team laughing at him now? Questioning him? More importantly, what was Helen Grace thinking? Was she regretting her decision to employ him? Was that why she had tasked him with digital drudgery, while she and Charlie headed off to conduct interviews?

Once more, Hudson felt the anger rising within him. And once more he tried to swallow it down. He had to get a grip on it. It was affecting his work, his judgement, and if he wasn't careful it would consume him.

As it had done before.

99

Melanie Walton stared at Helen in astonishment. What had started as a terrible tragedy was fast becoming a hideous, twisted nightmare.

'No, no, he never mentioned her name in my presence,' she eventually managed to reply.

Helen scrutinized her, weighing her up.

'I mean, Tom had girlfriends before, of course. But he didn't have much to do with them and he certainly didn't speak about them. There was one – Louise – who I met once. They had a brief thing when Tom was in his mid-twenties. But other than that . . .'

'You never asked him about his early days? His first love, his first serious girlfriend,' Helen replied.

'I may have done, at the beginning. But he didn't seem interested in discussing it. He wanted to talk about us, the future, which I was pleased about.'

Helen noted this, wondering why Campbell was so keen to gloss over his relationship with Lauren Scott. Was there a part of him – the old Tom – that he wanted to keep concealed?

'Does he have any stuff from that time? Photos? Year-books? Diaries?'

'Possibly, but if so it'll be hidden up in the loft.'

'Do you mind if we take a look?'

Melanie didn't seem keen. For a moment, Helen actually thought she might demand a warrant, which of course was her right. But then the fight seemed to go out of her and she mumbled:

'This way.'

Five minutes later, they were standing in the dusty attic. A single, naked lightbulb illuminated boxes of junk, dumped and forgotten. Melanie was keen to apologize for the mess, but Helen batted away her embarrassment, instead enlisting her help in locating Tom's university mementoes. It was hot, dirty work, but eventually they found a single box, containing a programme for a Summer Ball, a university scarf, some CDs, a single dented trophy for the men's tennis team and several packets of photos. Helen homed in on the latter, sliding them from their Snappy Snaps envelopes and flicking through them.

It was like stepping back in time. The photos were all dated, the retro digital font stamped on the bottom-right-hand corner. They seemed to cover all of his university career, but the ones she was most interested in came from 2008/2009, when he would have been in his third year and Lauren in her first.

Most of them seemed to have been taken during the summer term, when the weather was nicest and the post-exam celebrations were in full swing. Julia Winter appeared in a few, as did Aaron Slater – both were faces Helen had come to recognize now. But she was interested to note that the vast majority of the photos – and there were a lot – were of Lauren Scott. Lauren in repose, Lauren laughing, Lauren smoking a spliff, Lauren flirting with the camera. Helen could see why Campbell had been drawn to her – she seemed so delicate, so pretty, but with a slightly dangerous edge. It was natural sex appeal, a knowing quality, that men would have found hard to resist.

'Is it possible . . .' Helen said, choosing her words carefully, '. . . that Tom had resumed contact with Lauren?'

Melanie was standing close by, shooting concerned glances at the photos of the young, attractive woman.

'No.'

'You haven't had any concerns? Mysterious texts? Tom being unnecessarily secretive about his movements, about who he was with?'

'Absolutely not, I trust . . . I trusted him completely.'

Helen nodded, but Melanie obviously sensed disbelief, because she continued her passionate rebuttal:

'I *know* he was faithful to me. We were about to get married.'

'Of course. I understand that. But people are weak and sometimes past associations have an enduring power.'

'No, no, no . . . Tom would never have betrayed me like that.'

She was staring directly at Helen now, radiating hostility and anger.

'*Never.*'

100

'Are you kidding? Lauren would never do something like that. She *loved* me. And I loved her . . .'

Matteo Dominici was pacing the front room, running his hand through his unruly hair. The last couple of days – the loss of Lauren, having to identify her body, being pursued by the press – had taken their toll on him. He seemed to have aged – his face was more lined, the grey at his temples more pronounced and he seemed on edge. Charlie's probing questions about Lauren Scott had only exacerbated his anxiety, but she had no choice.

'You were never suspicious of her? Nothing she did made you even the slightest bit concerned . . . ?'

'If you knew Lauren, if you knew us, you'd realize what a ridiculous question that is,' he replied, witheringly.

'Because . . . ?'

Matteo gave Charlie a long, hard stare, then sat down on the sofa. Charlie was pleased he had finally stopped pacing. He had been working himself up, but now seemed to calm a little.

'Lauren and I met at an AA meeting. She had managed to knock drugs on the head, but was struggling to get dry. I had been drinking too . . .'

He hesitated momentarily, perhaps weighing up how much to share, then continued falteringly:

'My marriage had gone south, at about the same time my business ran into difficulties. I wasn't the only one who got stiffed by the downturn, but that didn't make it any easier, having to go back to work in the family restaurant. Anyway, after a year of self-abuse, I decided to clean up my act. And on the first day there I met Lauren.'

The memory seemed to cheer him slightly.

'The attraction was clear, but that's kind of frowned upon, so we took our time. Got to know each other a little better. And everything I learnt about her I loved. She was funny, cheeky, but also honest, kind, clear-headed. She had no illusions about life, she knew that you survived in spite of it, not because of it.'

'Why do you say that?'

'Because her parents were shits. Sorry, but there's no other way to say it. They were classic upper-middle-class parents – controlling, judgemental, narrow-minded. They had a clear view of what they wanted Lauren to be, but she didn't fit the mould. And they couldn't handle that, cutting off funds, kicking her out the house on a couple of occasions –'

'Because of the drugs? The drinking?'

'She was no angel, believe me,' Matteo retorted forcefully. 'But she was never cruel. Her parents couldn't handle the fact she was different, that she wanted to make her own choices . . . but in trying to clamp down on her, they drove her deeper into the abyss. The worse she got, the worse they got. But none of it . . .' He rapped the coffee table hard with his knuckles to emphasize his words. '. . . *none of it* was necessary, because all she needed was a little love. I gave her that – gave her everything I could – but I got back far more in return. She often said I saved her, but that wasn't true. I freed her. And her gratitude, her love, was boundless . . .'

He raised his head to meet Charlie's intrigued gaze.

'Which is why I know for certain that she wouldn't have hooked up with this Tom Campbell, or any other old flame.'

'I do get that, Matteo, and I'm sure you're right. You knew her better than anyone probably. But you can see why I have to ask the question — their connection cannot be a coincidence.'

Matteo shrugged, begrudgingly conceding the point.

'And it's why I need to ask one more thing of you. I know this will be upsetting but, so we can be absolutely sure what we're dealing with, I need to ask you to provide a DNA sample. We need it to check it against the baby to establish paternity.'

Matteo's expression was a mixture of surprise and horror.

'I have the kit here, a cheek swab. It'll only take a few seconds.'

Matteo Dominici didn't seem to be taking in anything she was saying. He hadn't even known that Lauren was pregnant until a day or so ago. Now he had to face the implication that the baby wasn't his.

'Do what you need to do,' he breathed eventually. 'And then piss off.'

The words shot from him, startling Charlie. She didn't hesitate, pulling the sterile kit from her bag and slipping on a pair of gloves. She tore at the plastic wrapper and slid out the test tube and swab.

'Right, if you could just open your mouth for me . . .'

Slowly, he obliged. Charlie set to work, wanting to get it over with. But there was no mistaking the change in atmosphere. As she probed, garnering cells from the inside of both cheeks, Matteo Dominici's eyes never left her, simmering with cold hatred. Whatever trust had been engendered previously was now gone. From now on, in his eyes, Charlie would always be the harbinger of misery.

101

She was drowning in death.

Having initially been coy about opening up his files, Graham Ross now seemed keen to share. Portfolio after portfolio appeared, each one filled with a plethora of new and disturbing images. Body after body, scene after scene, every indignity and cruelty which one human being could inflict on another was hidden away in Ross's back room.

It was a strangely intimate encounter. The small space had been converted into a dark room some time ago and, though it seemed to function fairly effectively, was cramped for two people. This was in effect his private work space *and* his main storage area, which meant that he had everything to hand, even if accessing it was not always easy. Emilia had had to stand back, move, change her position on a number of occasions, Ross brushing past her as he dug out yet more gems from his treasure trove. Emilia assumed these fleeting moments of contact were accidental, but she couldn't be entirely sure.

Either way, she didn't feel threatened, nor would she exhibit anything less than upbeat enthusiasm for the brutal collage of images on the table in front of her. Stabbings, gunshot wounds, strangulation, even a crime of passion executed with a broken Perrier bottle – all these were arrayed for her pleasure. There were even a couple of photos from the New Forest crime scenes that Ross appeared to have withheld from the official files. Emilia decided not to call him on that, focusing instead on the overall brilliance of his work.

'I've never seen anything like this before,' she cooed. 'I mean obviously you have to do the standard close-ups and so forth, but there is something about your other shots – the ones that encapsulate the whole scene – that have . . . an elegance to them.'

Ross seemed pleased by the compliment.

'Anyone can photograph the evidence,' he said, as if this was almost unimportant. 'It's what the scene tells you that's interesting. Sometimes the perpetrator is actively trying to communicate with you through the staging, sometimes he's not, but either way the story is there, if you're prepared to look for it. And if you capture it right, frame it right –'

'Then a picture is worth a thousand words.'

'Exactly. If you take in the room, the position of the body, the state of the furniture and ornaments in that room, the mirrors, the pictures, then you can see it. There was one scene I went to where the killer had turned all the family photos face down, because he was ashamed of what he was doing, didn't want his relatives to witness the unspeakable acts of brutality he felt compelled to perpetrate.'

'I read about that,' Emilia lied, sounding as authoritative as she could.

'There's more to you than meets the eye,' Ross responded happily, turning over another print of carnage for her to enjoy.

'Comes with the territory, I guess.'

Ross smiled but said nothing, continuing to leaf through the photos.

'How many bodies would you say you've seen?' Emilia continued, picking up an image of a nasty teen-on-teen stabbing.

'Two hundred or so. Maybe more . . .'

'And does it ever get to you?'

'Not really,' he replied, in a matter-of-fact tone. 'I've always been very disciplined about that, it's work. To me they are subjects. I want to record them to help the investigation obviously, but I also want to capture them as they deserve to be captured. I want to give their deaths a certain significance, a beauty even. There is something about the stillness of death that renders them a serenity, a sense of peace, which was probably lacking in their actual lives.'

'I can see that,' Emilia replied dutifully.

In truth, she didn't, or not wholly anyway. There *was* an elegance, an artistry to some of his shots, those from the New Forest especially, but in others it was hard to divine. A teenager lying face down on the street, a young mother strangled by her violent partner – all Emilia could see in these shots was ugliness and brutality. But she kept up her patter of approval, which pleased her host.

'I have more, but maybe we should save those for another time. They are part of my special collection.'

'I'd like that,' Emilia lied again.

'Then that's settled.'

She left shortly afterwards, still mulling on the significance of the afternoon's encounter. It could hardly have gone better – the more Ross approved of her, the more likely he was to expand on his theories about the New Forest killings, unpacking the significance and meaning of these intricately staged murders. But the question remained – what did he want? He had gone out of his way to charm her, to impress her. Yet he had not made his move, either professionally or personally. There was no doubt that he was reaching out to her, trying to draw her into his world.

But why he wanted her close remained as much a mystery as ever.

102

It had been nagging away at her, but now she wanted to know the truth.

'DS Hudson, have you got a minute?'

Helen had returned from Melanie Walton's house, clutching an armful of photos, to find the Incident Room impressively populated. The discovery of a concrete link between Campbell and Scott had been a shot in the arm for everyone and the team were working hard, trying to unearth further leads. DS Hudson, who usually prided himself on being the last man standing, had decided to depart early, however, using the cover of his colleagues to make a break for it.

Hudson stopped in his tracks and turned towards Helen.

'I've sent you an update on our digital trawl –'

'It's not about that,' Helen interrupted, gently. 'Shall we?'

She gestured to her office. Covering his discomfort, Hudson did as he was asked. Helen shut the door softly behind her, as he settled into a seat.

'How are you feeling?' she asked, crossing the room to her desk.

'Fine,' Hudson responded quickly. 'I mean the bruising is a bit unsightly but –'

'We've all been there. It'll fade soon enough.'

Hudson nodded amiably, but said nothing. He obviously wasn't going to volunteer anything, so it would be up to her to grasp the nettle. There were many other things she could be doing right now, given the intense pressure on the team, but this could not be ducked.

'And how are you in yourself? You must be feeling pretty shaken.'

'No more than you'd expect,' he replied, evasively.

'If you need to take a day off, or to talk to our on-site counsellor –'

'That won't be necessary. I want to be here, contributing.'

'That's funny. Because I got the distinct impression that you'd rather be *anywhere* but here. If it's last night's attack that's worrying you –'

'It's not.'

'Then what?'

Hudson said nothing, breaking eye contact briefly to look out of the window, before returning his gaze to Helen once more.

'You know, Joseph, there are some guys who might find it hard working for a female boss. Guys who might feel angry or embarrassed if said female boss helped them out in a tight spot.'

'Do I look like that kind of dinosaur?'

He did not. He looked like a sophisticated, modern police-man and a handsome one at that. But she wasn't going to give him the satisfaction of sharing that.

'Some people feel that way, can't help themselves,' Helen continued, unabashed. 'And that's a shame. Because we've all had our backs against the wall at times. I've had my life saved on more than one occasion by a fellow officer and I've never felt bad about it. We are a strong unit *because* we work for each other. And there is no circumstance under which an officer should feel they've let the side down, just because they picked up a few bruises. We are successful here because we put our bodies on the line and I will never fault an officer who exhibits that sort of bravery and selflessness.'

Hudson was about to respond, but Helen wasn't finished.

'So, go home, Joseph. Have a drink, a smoke, watch Net-flix, do whatever you do to unwind. Then come back tomorrow, ready and raring to go. We are finally making progress on this case and I need my best people around me.'

Hudson rose, nodding his agreement. She was pleased to see that he looked a little more at ease, as if a weight had been lifted from his shoulders.

'First thing tomorrow then.'

There was a bit of steel in his voice now, which gratified Helen.

'See you then, DS Hudson.'

Helen watched him go, satisfied with her evening's work. They *were* finally getting somewhere on this case, but there was much still to do. Slowly, they were beginning to put the pieces together, but there were more riddles to solve, and unseen dangers to confront, before they came face to face with their killer.

When that moment came, Helen wanted *both* her DSs by her side.

103

She stood alone, cloaked in darkness.

Her conversation with Matteo Dominici had taken longer than usual – she had laboured to placate him, to no effect – and by the time she left, there was no point heading back to base. Instead, she had driven straight to their forensic base in Woolston, dropping off Dominici's DNA sample personally. She wouldn't normally have done this – that kind of job was the preserve of a junior officer or, failing that, a courier. But such was the importance of a quick answer that she'd decided to transport it herself – if Dominici was *not* the father of Scott's baby, then a whole new line of enquiry would suddenly open up.

Now, however, she regretted her selfless diligence. It had kept her at work later than usual and she hadn't arrived home until just before nine. She had called prior to that, hoping to say goodnight to Jessica, to test the water with Steve, but her calls had been ignored. Was this done to punish her? To make a point? Or was it entirely innocent, Steve too caught up with Jessica to notice his buzzing phone? Charlie didn't know which and it unnerved her.

Opening the front door, she had stepped inside to find the house quiet and still. The hall light wasn't on, nor were the lights in the kitchen and living room. The usual happy buzz of their cosy downstairs space was entirely absent. In fact, the whole house felt cold and unwelcoming tonight.

Quietly mounting the stairs, Charlie started to panic. It wasn't possible that Steve had left, was it? Taking Jessica with him? No, that was crazy. Cresting the stairs, she was re-assured to see Jessica's door just ajar, the warm glow of her night light emanating from within. Steve would never do something so dramatic, so underhand. He might be difficult, but he was open and honest, even when furious with her. Besides, they weren't at that stage yet, were they?

Tip-toeing past Jessica's door, she crept into their bedroom. Steve was there, which was a relief, but he appeared to be asleep. The curtains were drawn, the duvet was up around his chin, his face turned away from her.

'Steve?'

No movement. Not even a change in his breathing.

'Steve, are you awake? I'm sorry I'm late . . .'

She petered out, knowing she wouldn't get a response. Either he was asleep and she was wasting her breath or he was still too angry to talk. Either way, it was a depressing state of affairs. She had so much she needed to tell Steve – from the exhilaration of their new lead to her distressing interview with Matteo Dominici. She wanted to have a glass of wine, to share her anxieties, to ask for a hug. But she would get none of these tonight – for the first time in ages she felt unwelcome in her own home.

Easing herself onto her bed, she pulled one boot off, then the other. Her left ankle was throbbing again – the swelling around her injury resolutely refusing to ease – and she felt dog tired. Perhaps she was getting old, but she had seldom felt this wrung out during a case. All she wanted to do now was sleep, to snuggle down in her bed and pretend for a few glorious hours that all was well in the world. Sliding off her shirt, trousers and underwear, she threw on her pyjamas, eager for the oblivion of sleep. But even as she lifted up the duvet, a terrified scream rang out from Jessica's bedroom.

There would be no sleep tonight.

104

His eyes roamed the gloomy woodland, searching for signs of life. Yet again the police search teams had been active, delving ever deeper into the forest, penetrating its hidden corners. They were getting better at the task – they were more circumspect now, more observant, their progress less crashing – yet they still had little chance of catching him. Nathaniel Martin had lived in the forest for eighteen months now and there was not a sound, not a cry, call or creak, that he did not recognize. Six officers moving in unison were thus easy to detect. He could hear them at half a mile's distance, maybe more, ensuring that he could be long gone by the time they stumbled upon his latest hiding place.

The teams had dogs now, which made things more complicated. They were no doubt using items from his former camp to give the dogs his scent and they had proved adept at following it. To counter this worrying development, Martin had started coating his clothes in foul-smelling mud, rotting flora, even fox faeces, but even these pungent additions couldn't conceal his presence. Had the police let their dogs off the leash, let them run free, then they might have caught him by now, but, thankfully, this was not how search parties worked. They kept their Alsatians on tight leads, tempering the zeal of their charges. As a result, progress was slow, giving Martin ample time to vanish.

This was his life now, remaining vigilant from dawn until dusk, day after day. And he would have been comfortable with that, maintaining an itinerant lifestyle, until his pursuers finally called off the hunt and the forest became his once more. But the forest *wasn't* his any more and he feared it might never be so again. Not while evil continued to hold sway.

Having spent a year and a half in glorious isolation, emerging only to ward off those who threatened the forest's existence, Nathaniel Martin now felt beset on all sides. First it had been the builders, developers and holiday-makers. Then the police, journalists, even the occasional gang of high-spirited teenagers, daring each other to enter the dangerous forest. And circling them was the quarry they were all seeking, a fleeting, malevolent spirit, who had brought death and disquiet to Nathaniel Martin's sanctuary. Martin had not seen him in the flesh yet, but he had felt his malign presence. And he had witnessed his handiwork – two dead ponies, mercilessly butchered and left to rot. The sight of the dead horses – beautiful, even when contorted by rigor mortis – had nearly broken his heart.

Was he at large tonight? Was his bloodlust about to stain the forest once again? Martin kept perfectly still, his eyes darting here and there, seeking out his sinister form in the bushes, the foliage, the long, dark shadows. He couldn't see anything untoward, any sign that he was abroad, but that didn't mean much. He hadn't seen anything those other nights either, when he took the lives of four innocent beings, before vanishing once more. Who's to say he wasn't out there right now, watching *him*?

The thought made Nathaniel Martin feel distinctly uneasy. Previously master of his destiny, unofficial king of this vast wilderness, now he was on the back foot as never before, surviving by his wits alone. This forest had been his friend, his salvation, but it was no longer safe. It seemed impossible, but it was true. His new Eden had become a place of darkness.

105

The morning sun crept through the grimy windows illuminating the still figure of Helen Grace. She was standing in front of the murder board, staring at the faces arrayed in front of her. At the bottom were Nathaniel Martin and Dean Clarke and, above them, Tom Campbell and Lauren Scott, flanked by Matteo Dominici and Melanie Walton. Helen's eyes flitted between the latter quartet, as if seeking hidden connections, but their faces stared back at her, enigmatic and lifeless.

She turned slowly to take in another set of faces. The team were assembled, crowding around her in a crescent shape, curious to know why they had been summoned to an early meeting. Helen had been standing in front of the board when they first started arriving, some of them no doubt wondering if she had been there all night. They were right, she had, grabbing a couple of hours' sleep on her sofa, before changing, washing and starting again.

Helen felt sure that answers were under her nose, but still she struggled to see a clear picture. And her mood had not been helped by an early-morning call from the Police Service Laboratory in Woolston.

'So I got the results of the DNA tests this morning,' she announced to the assembled officers. 'Matteo Dominici *is* the father of Lauren Scott's baby.'

There were mild groans from the team.

'This doesn't mean anything per se. She might still have been having an affair with Campbell or have renewed her friendship with him. Where are we at with potential crossovers?'

'Very little so far,' DC Osbourne replied, trying not to sound too downbeat.

'What does very little mean?'

'It means . . . nothing. We've not found any evidence that they were in contact by phone or electronic media, nor that they met in person. We've checked their movements – both on their phone diaries and on what CCTV we have available – and there's no correlation at all. Campbell rarely ventured into Southampton itself – he commuted between Winchester and Lyndhurst and that was it. Lauren frequented Thornhill and Woolston, where she had a job in Boots. Other than that, she made occasional trips to the city centre to go shopping, but they were brief visits and seem to tally with card transactions at H&M, Primark, Tesco's.'

'What about their internet searches?' Helen demanded.

'We checked out their phones, tablets and laptops,' Reid responded briskly. 'There's no history of either of them Googling each other's names, personal details etc. They obviously weren't Facebook friends and, in fact, no friend requests were ever sent. They appeared to be unaware of each other, despite their relative proximity.'

'What about links to other folk she might have known from that time?'

'DC Edwards and I went over that again this morning,' Charlie said, swallowing a yawn. 'Campbell kept up with a couple of people from his university days – a friend from the tennis team who now lives in Singapore and a fellow history student who lives in the West Midlands, but contact is intermittent at best.'

'And Scott?'

'Nothing,' Edwards spoke up. 'No contact with anyone from that time.'

'What about the calls from the cloned phone? Could *they* have been from an old acquaintance?'

'Possibly,' DC Edwards replied. 'But the call pattern doesn't suggest Campbell or Scott were kindly disposed to the caller.'

'Meaning?'

'Meaning the caller always contacted *them*, never the other way around. The first couple of times Campbell accepted the calls, then thereafter they go to voicemail, judging by the duration of the connection. And it's the same with Scott. She accepted the first call, then she lets the subsequent ones divert. Numerous calls go unanswered and there's never any attempt to return them.'

'So the calls weren't welcome? Were even threatening perhaps?'

'Makes sense,' Edwards agreed.

There was a murmur of excitement from the team.

'How are we doing with the trace?' Helen persisted. 'Is the phone still active?'

'It's still used, but is only on for a minute or so at a time, and then only once or twice a day,' Hudson added. 'No obvious links to a residential address, hotel or hostel. DC Osbourne is pulling together a site map of the connections to see if we can identify any clusters or patterns of movement.'

'Quick as you can, please,' Helen encouraged. 'In the mean-time, we need to go back over Campbell's and Scott's movements, spending patterns, communications, everything, to see if we can find any correlation – any marked response – to those calls. We need to know why they were made, what their purpose was and how – if – they impacted on Campbell and Scott. Above all . . .' Helen paused, before concluding: '. . . we need to find out who was making those calls.'

106

His eyes stole over the text, drinking in the details. He'd read all the local coverage and had now moved on to the nationals, snaffling a discarded copy of the *Daily Mirror* from a nearby table. Unsurprisingly, the paper had devoted four pages to the New Forest killings, rehashing all the known facts, but also breaking the news that two dead ponies had been discovered in the forest. They had gone into great detail about the bolts that were found in them, not to mention the advanced state of their decomposition, while modestly refusing to publish photos that were available on the internet, but 'unfit for a family newspaper'. It would have made him laugh, in other circumstances.

Turning the page, he came face to face with Lauren Scott, her coy blue eyes glancing at him through her fringe. He had always found her beguiling and he felt those familiar stirrings now, even though this morning her pretty face was framed by tragedy. According to the horrified journalist, Lauren had been pregnant, a fact that seemed to have created a sea change in the way her death was being reported. Whereas previously the tabloids had majored on her drug abuse and troubled family life, now they were busy making her into a saint. The one person you're never supposed to harm is a pregnant woman.

Turning the page, he now found himself pitched into celebrity news – more bed hopping at a Premiership football club – so quickly doubled back to the slaughtered ponies. As he did so, he glanced up, to find the café owner staring

318

directly at him. For a moment, he froze, the page lingering half turned, then quickly resumed his reading, dropping his eyes to the paper.

The place had been busy when he entered and he had been able to eat a decent meal and digest his paper in relative anonymity. Now, however, the café was thinning out and he was more visible, attracting the attention of the owner who clearly didn't like the fact that he had been sitting there for over an hour, hogging a table for four. He looked like he was about to make a move, to come over and challenge him, but there was no question of that. It would be crazy to linger, to excite attention, so slipping the newspaper inside his coat, he rose and hurried from the café, watched every step of the way.

107

'This'll be the death of us, all of us. You put *that* in your newspaper.'

Nigel Robinson jabbed his finger in the air as he spoke, forcing Emilia to take a step backwards. The campsite owner's blood was up this morning, and she could understand why, but she wasn't prepared to sustain an injury on the back of his righteous indignation. She valued herself a little more than that.

The truth was she didn't even want to be here, going over old ground by talking to the desperate owner of the Woodland View campsite, but there was a troubling lack of developments in the investigation – no new arrests, no new leads, no new bodies, nothing to feed the frenzy of interest this case had aroused. News that Lauren Scott had been pregnant had created a stir yesterday, but for once Emilia had been behind the beat on that one, Spivack presumably having kept that little nugget to himself to sell to the tabloids. She would have to have a word with him about that.

They desperately needed something new to say. Only a handful of hardy souls were heading to the New Forest these days – for obvious reasons – so there didn't seem to be any major threat to the public, disappointingly. And they had mined pretty much everything there was to say about the private lives of the victims, baby aside, but Gardiner had not wanted to go too large on this for fear of upsetting their readers. Stumped for other angles, they had opted for the devastating effect of the case on local businesses. It wasn't exciting, it wasn't original, but at least it was relevant, providing an insight into Hampshire life which the nationals couldn't hope to rival.

'The longer this case goes on, the longer the killer remains at large, the worse it'll be for people like me. It's not just my own future I'm thinking about. I employ people, lots of people. If I go under, what'll happen to them?'

Emilia nodded sympathetically, only half listening. Normally she would record an interview like this, but she knew exactly what Robinson was going to say before he said it. His pompous indignation and outrage were utterly predictable — even if she couldn't remember his exact quotes, she could make up something suitable. As he spoke, she was already composing the articles in her head. Five hundred words, full of alarm and anxiety, painting a worrying picture of the future for local businesses and the New Forest leisure scene. Who would want to go tramping through the forest now when you might stumble upon a crime scene? There would be the odd ghoul of course, plus those who were too ignorant or uninterested to follow the news, but Emilia suspected most campers would opt for Dorset for now.

Robinson was in full flow, berating the police, the council, Visit Hampshire and any other local body he could think of. Emilia pretended to jot down his thoughts dutifully, but she was, in fact, doodling. She already had the shape of her article mapped out and her thoughts had now started to drift to Graham Ross.

She had sent him a thank you text this morning, adding that she would like to meet up again soon. So far, she had had nothing back. He might be working of course, but still his silence unnerved her. She needed his insight, and possibly those photos he'd held back, but she was also thinking of bigger things. A book on the current case perhaps, even a retrospective of Ross's life in crime, incorporating his amazing treasure trove of images. The opportunities were there for the taking, if he was prepared to play ball. But would he? This was what continued to exercise Emilia, even as Nigel Robinson droned on in front of her.

Would Ross go on record about the killings? Allow her to use his insights about the staging of the murders? Even consider some kind of joint venture? It was a tantalizing prospect, but one which lay just out of reach. She knew nothing about this man or his motives, nor what it would take to seduce him.

Who exactly *was* the mysterious Graham Ross?

108

'What have you got on Campbell's movements?'

Helen and Charlie were hunkered down in her office. While Joseph Hudson was trying to locate a new signal from the unregistered phone, they were busy probing ever deeper into the lives of their victims. Having already sifted their personal lives to exhaustion, exploring past and present relationships with lovers, friends and family, they were now drilling down into their movements. Where they went, who they saw, how they reacted to these mystery calls.

'Nothing out of the ordinary after the first call,' Charlie replied, consulting a printout of Campbell's diary. 'He had a meeting the following day at Lyndhurst, which he presumably attended, as he emailed minutes of it to his boss later that day. He doesn't seem to have had much on in the afternoon, which is a little unusual, but doesn't necessarily mean anything. We'd have to call his PA to find out more.'

'What about after the second call?'

'Similar. He was supposed to be at HQ for a training session in the afternoon, which it looks like he attended, as he bought fuel at a nearby petrol station around lunchtime. What about Scott?'

'Same. She only took the one call, but she seems to have been in Woolston the next day, so presumably she went to work. Reid is trying to contact the manager of Boots to double-check.'

'And Campbell didn't make any unusual travel plans off the back of these calls?'

'Not that I can see. If he was unnerved by them, he certainly didn't seem minded to make a break for it.'

'What about calls?' Helen persisted. 'Did he call Melanie after having received either call?'

'No. In fact, his call log is pretty light for those days.'

Charlie looked up at Helen, pondering the significance of this. But Helen was ahead of her, her mind turning.

'Same with Scott, no calls to her boyfriend. So maybe both Campbell and Scott wanted to keep things quiet. Maybe they were alarmed by the calls, but they didn't want anyone knowing about them . . .'

'Could be . . .'

A thought was crystallizing in Helen's mind now. Quickly, she opened the file with Lauren Scott's bank statements in them, running her finger down the column until she found the relevant dates.

'Did Campbell make any unusual payments or withdrawals around the time of the calls?'

Charlie seemed confused, then intrigued, as she divined the thrust of Helen's thinking. Leafing through her papers, she ran her eyes down the long list of transactions. Esso, Pret A Manger, Superdrug, Reiss, Cellar Door Wines . . .

'This might be something.'

'What is it?'

'Well, the day after the first call, he withdraws £200 from an ATM. Which is an unusually large amount for him, as he almost always uses contactless.'

'Lauren Scott does exactly the same. Withdraws £200 the day after the call, again from an ATM. And believe me this was even more unusual for her – she was permanently strapped for cash. In fact, that withdrawal put her into the red, which would have meant bank charges.'

Charlie was already giving another long list of transactions the once-over, her instincts aroused now.

'And here we are again. After the second call, Campbell takes out another £200.'

She looked up at Helen, triumphant.

'You think they were being blackmailed?'

'Exactly. Lauren had less to give, so maybe gave up after one payment. Campbell paid twice, but the calls kept coming.'

'Right up until the moment they were targeted.'

'So maybe they refused to pay, told their blackmailer where to go . . .'

'And paid the price.'

It was an intriguing thought, one which instinctively felt right.

'Even so, it doesn't get us any further on, does it? We don't know where the pay-off was made, if it was made at all.'

'Not yet, but it may be that the location of the ATMs can help us. If there was CCTV in the area, we may be able to track their movements, see where they went.'

'Campbell's withdrawals were both made at a petrol station, so it might be hard to track his movements via CCTV, unless the exchange was made there. We might have to rely on traffic cameras.'

'Scott's was made at a bank, the Santander on Burgess Road. They would definitely have cameras there and it's in a CCTV-rich area, which . . .'

Helen rose from her desk: '. . . makes that a very good place to start.'

109

Within minutes, they were on the road. Leaving her bike at the station, Helen requisitioned a pool car, deciding it would be better to travel to the bank together. They could use the time to turn over the latest developments in the case, but Helen was also keen to assess her old friend's state of mind. She had been worried about Charlie since their chat in the smokers' yard.

'How are the nights?' she asked, as they swung onto Onslow Road. 'Any better?'

Charlie shook her head.

'I'm getting less sleep now than I was when she was a baby. They didn't put *that* in the brochure.'

'And there's no obvious reason why she's waking up?'

'Impossible to say. It may just be a natural thing, part of growing up, or . . .'

Charlie didn't seem in the mood to elaborate, so Helen didn't press her.

'And how are things with Steve?'

'Even worse. Sorry, Helen, I know I sound like the most depressing person on earth at the moment,' Charlie laughed, before falling silent once more.

'Do you think you might be? Depressed, I mean. Because if you are . . .'

'I think I'm tired, worried, grumpy and a little bit sad. But other than that, I'm great fun to be around . . .'

She smiled ruefully at Helen, who returned the compliment.

'But let's not talk about me – I bore myself. Let's talk about something more exciting.'

'Such as?'

'Joseph Hudson.'

'What about him?'

'Seriously?'

Helen angled a sideways glance at her friend, to find Charlie smiling at her.

'What?'

'Come on, Helen. You must have noticed how he looks at you.'

Helen said nothing, deciding discretion was the wisest course.

'He's like a fox in the hen house. And I swear he's been checking you out. I took a look at his terminal after he'd left for the day, he'd pulled up your entire career history.'

'Charlie,' Helen replied, warningly.

'I know . . . but I won't apologize for keeping an eye out for you. Especially after Gardam.'

'He's not another Jonathan Gardam. He's far too green, too up front.'

'So he *has* expressed his feelings for you, has he?'

'Don't be ridiculous.'

'Not that he needs to, it's plain as day.'

Helen shook her head, amused. But privately she was pleased that his attraction to her was obvious.

'And if *I'm* allowed to bend the rules occasionally,' Charlie continued, a little glint in her eye. 'I don't see why you shouldn't.'

Helen frowned good-naturedly, but didn't look at her friend, keeping her eyes on the road.

'I mean he's a handsome guy, young, athletic . . .'

'He's my junior.'

'I'm not saying you have to marry him. And I swear I wouldn't tell anyone.'

Charlie was being deliberately provocative, enjoying teasing her old friend. Helen was pleased to see that a little colour had returned to her cheeks.

'I'll admit he does seem keen.'

'Well, there you go then.'

'And it would be nice to have some company.'

'So?'

Charlie actually seemed quite excited, but Helen couldn't resist teasing her back.

'But it's not something I would ever consider.'

It was said with a poker face, but Helen's tone was playful. Charlie eyed her suspiciously, unsure how to read her. In all honesty, Helen didn't know either – she was unsure what she felt about Joseph Hudson, if she *could* ever go there. But if it helped cheer Charlie up, distract her from her own problems, then she was happy to play the game.

Further analysis would have to wait, however. They had arrived at Burgess Road.

110

The Santander bank was a curious mixture of the old and new. Housed in an elegant Victorian building, it should have had some majesty, some charm, but this was undone by the gaudy red signs and endless posters of Jenson Button. It was not like the banks Helen remembered from her youth – heavy, portentous, silent as a library. These banks were bright, breezy and remorselessly customer-focused, deputy manager Jane Harris hurrying over to meet them, scenting new custom.

'Can I ask what this is all about?' she asked, disappointed, once Helen had outlined the reason for their visit.

'It's connected to a major investigation we're running. I can't say more than that, I'm afraid. But your assistance could be invaluable – we're looking for internal CCTV footage from the third of June.'

It was said cheerily, and with a smile, but Helen's tone was laced with urgency. Harris seemed to falter, looking uncertainly at Helen, then Charlie, then back again, before she eventually replied:

'Then you'd better come with me.'

Having been eager to assist them at first, Harris now hovered over them, looking concerned. Perhaps she was worried some financial crime had taken place, something that might rebound on her, perhaps she was just unnerved by their presence. Either way, she lurked behind them, craning over their shoulders to see the staccato black-and-white images on the screen.

Helen tried to blot her out, giving her entire attention to the parade of customers hurrying to and from the cash machine. She was playing the footage at double speed, making the customers' withdrawals slightly comic, as they punched in their PIN numbers furiously, then retreated at high speed. It was strangely hypnotic, the to-ing and fro-ing of the customers in the bank's atrium feeling like the ebb and flow of everyday life, but Helen kept her senses alert searching for Lauren Scott.

People came and went. Men, old ladies, young mums, rowdy lads, then suddenly there she was. Helen had shot past her arrival, so paused the footage and wound it back. Yes, there was no doubt it was Scott – she was wearing a vest top and Helen easily spotted one of her distinctive tattoos. More significant, however, was the fact that she wasn't alone.

'Is that Campbell?' Charlie murmured, without looking up, keen to exclude Harris from the conversation.

'Too tall,' Helen said quietly in reply.

Both figures had their back to the camera, but it was clear that Scott's companion was too lean, too statuesque to be Tom Campbell. The hair was also too long, too dark and the man's whole bearing seemed wrong. He was stooped over Scott, standing unnecessarily close to her.

Helen slowed the footage right down, watching it at half speed now. The pair seemed to be engaged in some kind of earnest conversation, before Scott turned away to begin her transaction. Without sound, it was hard to tell for sure, but something about their interaction seemed unnatural. The man now laid his hand on her shoulder. Was this an act of affection? Or was he simply holding on to her, for fear she might run away?

Now Scott turned back to him and this time her discomfort was clear. She seemed distressed, even scared, handing

330

the money over to him quickly, as if she wanted to be rid of it. Helen watched intently, as Scott now tried to disentangle herself from his clutches. But the man held on to her, moving his face close to hers. Scott seemed to back away and a small struggle ensued, but then, darting a look around at the other customers, the man let her go. Scott didn't need a second invitation, pulling her bag onto her shoulder and hurrying from the bank.

Helen shot a look at Charlie, who nodded back. Returning her attention to the screen, Helen stared at the figure in the atrium, taking in his lean form, his strangely menacing presence. He appeared to count the money now, before thrusting it into his pocket and making to depart. As he did so, however, he looked around once more, checking perhaps to see if anyone had witnessed his altercation with Scott. As he did so, his gaze rose, sweeping the walls and ceiling, before alighting on the camera. For a brief moment, he was looking directly at them and, jabbing the controls, Helen froze the picture.

'Gotcha,' Charlie breathed.

But Helen wasn't listening, staring intently at the image. It was not the unpleasant sneer on his face that had silenced her.

It was the fact that she recognized him.

III

The cries of happy children filled the air, but he didn't look up. The scrubby ground he was traversing was uneven and littered with rubbish and, besides, he didn't want to be noticed. He was a regular fixture at the site now, but he hoped that by keeping his head down, by not engaging, he could pass unseen.

This was a fond hope, of course. The travellers who dominated this site were a close-knit bunch and the presence of an outsider was always going to excite interest. He had received the odd cat call, even the occasional question, but he'd dead-batted them and hoped that if he showed little interest in them, they would grow bored and leave him alone. Generally, he tried to keep his perambulations across the site to a minimum. Out of sight, out of mind.

Today was different, however. He had craved a proper, home-cooked meal – he had been living off tins for too long – and wanted to find a newspaper. So, he had risked a daytime sortie. It had not been unsuccessful, but already he was regretting it, the chatter rising as he hurried back towards his caravan.

'What you up to, mister? You got a girl in there?'

The female voice was young and taunting, revelling in the bawdiness of her question.

'Or a boy?'

This was met with peals of teenage laughter, but still he didn't turn, dodging a discarded beer bottle as he approached his caravan. He would have loved to shoot a volley of abuse back – he had never liked gypsies or whatever they called themselves – but there was no question of engaging with them. A wanted man is best advised to keep his own company.

That was the one saving grace of his current situation. He had chosen the site deliberately and it had suited his purposes perfectly. It had an abandoned caravan which he could claim and, furthermore, was well off the beaten track. Few would stumble upon it in the normal course of things and, if they did, would swiftly retreat, the man on the street having an ingrained suspicion of travellers. Just as importantly, the travellers themselves were unlikely to turn him in, their well-founded paranoia regarding the police making them reluctant to snitch on anyone, regardless of their crimes. Justice was something they dispensed themselves, and as long as he could avoid provoking their anger, he might avoid any complications. It wasn't the perfect bolt-hole, but it was as good a place as any for someone who needed to remain below the radar.

He had reached the caravan now and slid the key into the padlock. As he did so, he stole a glance over his shoulder. The gang of teenagers had lost interest and were busy cackling over something they were watching on their phones. He took the opportunity to appraise their leader. She was a well-built, curvy girl, of no more than fifteen, who always wore a regulation outfit of crop top and denim hot pants. She was too large for the latter, a roll of smooth pink skin hanging just over the top of her shorts, but somehow it suited her. She was young, inexperienced, but also fleshy and inviting, ripe for the plucking. He let his eyes linger on her, as the last rays of the setting sun fell on her skin, imagining what might happen if he could get her alone in his caravan.

For a second, he was lost in the moment, but suddenly she looked up. Instantly he tore away his gaze. Hungry as he was, there was no way he could encourage her, not yet anyway. So, ripping off the padlock, he retreated quickly into the mouldering caravan, shutting the door firmly behind him.

112

Graham Ross was a parasite, feeding off other people's misfortune.

Emilia often felt that way about herself, but Ross took this to a new level. He had spent most of his adult life surrounded by butchered children, murdered lovers, battered wives – face to face with them, rather than at a remove like her – and *still* he went back for more. Was this professionalism or something else? To Emilia, it was beginning to seem more like an obsession.

Having written up her campsite piece, she had swiftly diverted her attentions back to Ross, digging down into his personal history and career trajectory, searching for something she could use, even exploit. But the more she'd read, the more intrigued and concerned she'd become, as his passion for death became clear.

As Ross had intimated, he was a man who'd always been on the move. He had worked for a number of forces up and down the country – moving from London to Glasgow, then to Manchester, then Hampshire – without ever committing to one place. He could have signed up to work for a specific force at any time, but had taken advantage of the privatization of crime scene services to remain freelance, to keep himself at one remove from the people he worked for. Was this because of a natural shyness or was it something more deliberate?

From her conversations with him, Emilia suspected the latter. Ross was someone who appeared to view human beings at a remove, as if they were subjects to be observed through the viewfinder of his camera, rather than actually engaged with. Was it possible he found people repellent, that he had a streak of misanthropy running through him? If so, where did she fit in? Why was he so solicitous of *her*?

Whether he desired her, wanted her to promote his work or had some other, unforeseen agenda, there was no question that she was the exception to the rule. Ross viewed life as art, something to be captured and preserved, rather than experienced. She could see the appeal – the control you exercised over your subjects, the world in general – but what did this kind of life do to you? His whole existence was caught up in photography – he ran courses on the subject and even curated local exhibitions to add to his income – which must affect your ability to engage, to be a normal human being. Add to this the fact that his job necessitated him recording the bloody remnants of human beings, capturing them only after their hopes and dreams, their very lives, had been snatched away from them and, surely, you had the recipe for some kind of psychological or emotional dysfunction?

Emilia had pondered before whether he might be dangerous, whether he might even intend her some harm. Previously she had batted these concerns away, but they returned to her forcefully now. Everyone – journalists, members of the public, the police themselves – had been scratching their heads as to a motive for these crimes. But had Ross, wittingly or unwittingly, given her a clue? Perhaps the staging of the deaths was significant, but not because of some deeper meaning to the arrangement of the bodies. Perhaps it was the staging *itself* that was important for the killer, the 'beauty' of the kill sites an end itself. If so, was it possible that Ross himself was somehow involved?

It seemed unlikely and yet it was a thought that refused to go away. So, swallowing down her disquiet, Emilia continued her descent into the dark world of a man who'd spent his life with dead bodies.

113

He was a face without a name.

As soon as Helen glimpsed him in the grainy, black-and-white CCTV shot, she'd felt a jolt of recognition. Not from any of their main lines of enquiry – their hard digging into the lives of Nathaniel Martin and Dean Clarke – but from something altogether more peripheral. Leaving the bank with the CCTV tapes in hand, Helen had ferried Charlie back to Southampton Central, shutting the door to her office and pulling down the blinds, as she laid out a series of photos that had been taken nearly a decade ago.

When Helen had first taken possession of the plethora of snaps hidden away in Tom Campbell's attic, she had sought out images of Campbell and Scott, searching for confirmation of their relationship. But as she did so, her gaze had alighted on other players – fleeting images of Aaron Slater, Julia Winter, but others who appeared more regularly. And one of them – this man, their mysterious blackmailer – had registered strongly with her.

Some of the photos were domestic in nature – sweet, goofy images of Campbell and Scott in happier times – but most of them were exterior shots. Smoking in the park, dancing in the twilight, sunbathing, swimming – endless shots of carefree, bacchanalian times when alcohol and dope were plentiful. Their suspect was notably absent from the domestic shots, making Helen wonder just how good a friend he was, but he *was* front and centre in the scenes of revelry, a young, sarcastic, but undeniably attractive lord of misrule.

Helen had assumed he would be part of their crowd, a fellow student at the university perhaps, but so far their search had thrown up nothing.

'What about the graduation photos? Perhaps he joined late, did a condensed course?'

They had already looked at Scott's matriculation photo, as well as Campbell's, and even the year in between. They had found many of the others – faces that were prim and earnest in the official photos, gurning and drunk in Campbell's party snaps – but there was no sign of their suspect. Charlie pulled up Tom Campbell's graduation photo and examined it.

'No, he's not there.'

'Let me have a look, while you check out Scott's graduation photo.'

Helen pored over the faces, but already knew the answer. Charlie was unlikely to have missed their suspect's distinctive face, with its aquiline nose, high forehead and thick, chestnut curls. On cue, Charlie looked up from her own perusal and slowly shook her head.

'Could he be their dealer? We know they both took drugs.'

'It's possible,' Helen replied cautiously. 'But he seems too embedded in the group. He pops up numerous times, drinking, laughing, singing with their group. I can't see sensible Tom embracing his dealer so enthusiastically.'

'Plus Campbell might have been manufacturing his own drugs,' Charlie replied, torpedoing her own line of thought. 'Could he be a friend of one of the others then? Or a relative even? Brother? Cousin?'

'Maybe, but I don't see a resemblance to anyone else present. And if he's a friend, we'll have a hard time working out whose. He seems to be on good terms with pretty much everyone and short of getting the team to examine the entire group's Facebook history . . .'

'It may come to that.' Charlie shrugged, though clearly she didn't relish the idea. 'We could start with their late teenage years, because I'd say this guy looks older. Older than Lauren for sure, and probably older than Tom Campbell too.'

'We could do, but I think the connection is the university years. Campbell and Scott didn't know each other prior to enrolling at Southampton Uni. I think this guy came in contact with them there, otherwise why would he be black-mailing both of them?'

'So perhaps he was an ordinary Joe, who happened to share a flat with one of –'

'Or he was a member of staff.'

Charlie looked up at her, intrigued.

'You get loads of old dinosaurs working at universities, the jobs-for-life brigade, but you also get young lecturers, PhD students and the like. Charismatic, mature figures who seem very impressive to young students.'

Even as she said it, it felt good to Helen, given the age difference.

'Can we pull up thumbnails of university personnel going back that far?'

'Sure thing,' Charlie replied quickly. 'Southampton Uni have always been keen to showcase their personnel, show off their credentials.'

'Let's start with the 2008 roster, when Campbell matriculated.'

Helen rounded the desk to hover at Charlie's shoulder as she scrolled. The familiar Southampton University crest appeared on screen and beneath it all manner of weird and wonderful thumbnail photos, displaying some of the brightest minds in the country on subjects ranging from art history to zoology.

'Try chemistry first, Campbell's subject.'

Charlie sped through the faces, but no one resembled their subject.

'Ok, let's try geography, then. Perhaps Scott was the connection.'

Charlie scrolled once more. Faces flew by – a young Asian woman, a handsome black man with a shock of white hair, a matronly older lady.

'There.'

Charlie virtually shouted it, before checking her volume. Ceasing her scrolling, she clicked on the image, enlarging it. Helen leaned in, drinking in his features, before turning to Charlie, a smile of triumph etched across her face. Finally, they had a connection.

More importantly, they had a name.

114

'So our suspect is Caleb Morgan.'

Several of the team scribbled down the name, before returning their attention to the big screen. On it were two images – the CCTV still from the bank and one of Campbell's snaps from 2009. Blown up for inspection, there was no question that both were of the same man.

'He taught for four years at Southampton University between 2006 and 2010,' Helen continued, 'before moving on to Bournemouth University. He did three years there, then got out of tertiary education to teach at a number of sixth-form colleges. Interestingly, he was suspended from his last post, following a complaint from a female student.'

'That was last year,' Charlie expanded. 'Around the time the #metoo campaign really got going. Following the initial allegation, three more female students came forward, from other sixth-form colleges. He now has three outstanding warrants against him for sexual assault and sexual harassment, but he went to ground before he could be arrested.'

'Bloody typical,' DC Edwards groaned. 'How long has he been off the grid?'

'Nearly two months now.'

'Which is presumably why he was tapping up his old "pals",' McAndrew added. 'No one will employ him, he's being hunted by the police, presumably running short of cash, so he goes to Campbell, to Scott. Campbell pays twice, Scott once, then both reject his calls. Now he's high and dry.'

'Perhaps he took out his frustrations on his former

friends,' DC Bentham added. 'Maybe he wanted to destroy them, humiliate them?'

'It's a theory,' Helen agreed. 'And one I'm keen to put to him. So, top priority is to bring him in. Where are we at with his phone calls?'

Now it was Osbourne's turn to speak up.

'A couple of the phone calls were made in the city centre, nothing particularly interesting about them. The main cluster was made in an area east of the city near Horton Heath.'

He stepped forward, heading for the screen. Helen ceded her position, joining the rest of the team, as Osbourne pulled up Google Maps.

'The calls were generally made at different locations on Burnett's Lane. There's nothing much out there, but there *is* a bus route that goes to Southampton city centre, so he could have walked to Burnett's Lane from wherever he's hiding out, making the calls there, out of earshot perhaps.'

'So, if you wanted to lie low out there, where would you go?' Helen asked.

'Hard to say. There's Knowle Park . . . and some playing fields. But both are used frequently by school kids and local clubs, so it wouldn't be ideal.'

'Derelict houses? Disused buildings?'

'Not that we know of, it's basically fields and country lanes. There are very few residential properties and no industrial estates.'

'Forests? Marshes? Anything distinctive?'

Again, Osbourne shook his head.

'It's all pretty bucolic really.'

For a moment, a frustrated silence filled the room. Then a new voice spoke out:

'There is one place he could go. A place that wouldn't be on Google Maps . . .'

The room turned to look at Joseph Hudson.

'A few locals might know about it, but it's not officially recognized, so wouldn't show up,' Hudson continued, moving towards the screen. 'It's a travellers' camp – about a mile or so away from Burnett's Lane.'

Hudson had now switched the screen to Google Earth and was zooming in fast on a mass of shapes in the middle of a swathe of green. Slowly the images came into focus. First the borders of a field, then a scattering of caravans, then tiny people, moving about the site.

'How have I lived here all these years and not heard about it?' Osbourne asked.

'Because that's the way they like it. It's under the radar, off the beaten track, and the men and women who live there don't take kindly to the attention of strangers.'

Several of the team were staring, visibly curious as to how a newcomer could know so much about local travellers' sites, but Hudson ignored their scrutiny, turning to face Helen.

'If I wanted to vanish off the face of the earth, I'd go there.'

115

They bounced along the dirt track, their heads brushing the ceiling as the car lurched and bucked. Helen was behind the wheel this time, Hudson sitting quietly in the passenger seat, as she drove with purpose and speed. Night was falling and she was determined to have Morgan in custody before darkness consumed them.

They drove in silence, the sirens hushed and the blue light stilled. They were kicking up a cloud of dust as they sped along the track, but Helen was gambling that speed would win the day. There were five vehicles in total, and if they could surround the site before Morgan had a chance to react, they would have their man.

'Have you been here before?'

'No. Just heard about it on the grapevine. I still have friends in the travelling community, so . . .'

'I'm very glad you do.'

'Talking of which, it might be best if you let me do the talking when we get there. We'll get results quicker that way.'

'No problem. I'm happy to bow to your superior knowledge.'

Hudson glanced at her, but said nothing. Helen was pleased to see a little of his old sparkle had returned. Perhaps their past awkwardness was behind them.

Returning her attention to the road, Helen spotted the camp coming into view. Excited as she was to see it, she nevertheless felt a stab of nerves, which surprised her.

'You'd better radio around,' she said quickly. 'We're here.'

Moments later, the cars roared into the camp. Two of them branched off, skirting the perimeter of the camp in order to cut off any escape routes to the rear, while Charlie's and McAndrew's cars pulled up by the entrance. Helen brought hers to a halt a few yards short of the caravans, and she and Hudson exited quickly. Now the blue light was on the roof, accompanied by a couple of short blasts of the siren, to announce their arrival.

The effect was immediate, a gaggle of children and teen-agers melting away, even as a group of men materialized. They were heading directly towards them and looked suspicious, even hostile. Normally Helen would have confronted them, but this time she stepped back, allowing Hudson to approach them alone. This was his world, not hers.

She couldn't make out the words, but the exchange was heated. Hudson was endeavouring to put the travellers at their ease, pointing to a photo of Morgan, as if keen to point out that *he* was the target of their attention, not them. At first, they seemed uninterested, as if anything Hudson had to say would fall on deaf ears, but to his credit the young DS persisted and eventually one of them shrugged, pointing to a caravan on the periphery of the site.

Hudson turned and nodded to Helen, who hurried over. Immediately, the group of men fell away, as if fearful of contamination.

'He's been hiding out here for the last six weeks. Third caravan from the end.'

They were already on the move. As they walked, Helen retrieved her radio, summoning the others to join them. The team was quick to respond. She could see them emerging from between the rows of caravans, forming a suffocating circle around the dilapidated dwelling.

In under a minute, she and Hudson were outside Morgan's

bolt-hole. It was dirty and damaged, with a hole in the roof. Beyond that, it was hard to see much — stained sheets covering the windows, shielding the interior from view.

'No heroics,' Helen said, as she slid her baton from her belt. 'I want this guy in a fit state to be questioned.'

Nodding, Hudson did likewise. Helen counted down from three, then stepped forward, throwing her boot at the door. Immediately, the lock exploded, the door flying open. Helen didn't hesitate, hurrying in through the doorway. Hudson was behind her, but was surprised by her speed, so Helen entered the caravan alone, eagerly scanning the gloom for their suspect. Feeling something flying towards her head, she ducked, only to find it was a bare lightbulb, swinging in the breeze. Her heart pounding, she turned to face the main body of the caravan, expecting to see Morgan rearing up at her.

But the interior was empty. There was no sign of their suspect, few personal possessions and just a smattering of empty tins in the sink. In fact, there was nothing of any interest in the caravan at all . . . save for a series of newspaper headlines, cut out and laid out carefully on the dirty Formica table, announcing the brutal murders of Tom Campbell and Lauren Scott.

116

The glowing tent was a beacon amid the darkness.

Night had stolen over the campsite now and the scattered tents seemed isolated and unconnected. Earlier there had been a few exchanges between the smattering of campers who'd ventured out to this remote site, but now everyone had retreated to enjoy a night under the stars.

Silence pervaded the darkened camp, save for the crickets and the occasional bird. Watching on from the shadows, Caleb Morgan remained stock-still, taking in the scene. It was so peaceful, so still. Few present would have guessed that there was evil in their midst.

He had left his caravan shortly before dusk, taking the back roads as he journeyed towards the forest. He was well prepared, but still his pulse raced as he gripped the steering wheel. He shot occasional glances in the rear-view mirror, but in truth there was nothing to disturb him. He had everything under control tonight.

Nearing the campsite, he had parked up on the fringes of the forest, taking care to conceal his vehicle behind some dense foliage. Then, removing his gear, he had continued on foot, reaching the campsite in good time to make his preparations. An hour later, the sun had set, but not before he was in position, concealed in the shadows on the fringes of the camp.

He had watched with satisfaction as the fires were extinguished, the lights turned out, the tents zipped up. The stage was set now and with each passing second, his excitement grew. He fingered his weapon carefully, itching to use it, but reined himself in. There was no question of going too early, of giving himself away. Caution was the watchword tonight.

Turning his attention to the tent once more, he smiled at the scene in front of him. The illuminated tent looked pretty, even faintly magical framed by the inky black sky. A lantern illuminated the interior, he could see the flame casting shadows inside, but it was clearly starting to dim. Soon it would be extinguished altogether and darkness would reign.

Until then he would remain where he was, suppressing his growing excitement, waiting for his moment to strike.

117

Her fingers crept through the dirt, finally alighting on something solid.

Their initial search of the caravan had yielded little – the cupboards were bare, the wardrobe unused, even the broken fridge was empty. But as they had started to lift the seating and pull apart the fixtures, Helen had spotted something lurking beneath the sleeping berth in the corner.

Dropping to her knees, she had slipped on a pair of gloves and groped towards the dark shape. Now she had hold of it and she slid it carefully towards her, a battered holdall emerging from beneath the bunk. The newspaper clippings had already been bagged and removed, so Helen lifted the bag onto the table, sliding open the zip. To find a face staring back at her.

A short intake of breath, then Helen realized that she was looking at a mask. Widening the mouth of the bag, Helen eased it out, holding it up to the torchlight. The smooth leather surface shone, even as the torch beam danced over the metallic, zippered mouth. It was a BDSM staple – a spin on the classic gimp mask – but it looked strangely sinister tonight.

She handed it to McAndrew, who pulled a face, and continued to investigate the contents of the bag. There were some more newspapers, some tatty clothing and underneath these, a laptop and a phone. Intrigued, Helen placed them on the table and turned them on, pulling over an upturned crate to use as a chair. Seating herself, she stared at the phone. The wallpaper was a dull grey and was demanding a four-digit passcode, so she turned her attention to the laptop instead. There would be time enough for the digital team to crack the phone later.

The computer proved more fruitful. It too demanded a password, but on the metal frame surrounding the screen, a word had been scratched: Pompey75. Helen had seen this kind of thing before, stolen computers sold at market stalls and in lay-bys, with the previous owner's password provided for convenience. This one had presumably come from Portsmouth, given the password, and Helen was not surprised when her typing unlocked the computer, the desktop opening up obligingly for her.

There were few files and only the standard applications along the bottom of the screen, but Helen's gaze was drawn to the top-right-hand corner. The laptop had stirred itself and was now forging a link to the iPhone on the table, the latter drawing on its 4G signal. This, then, was how Morgan connected to the outside world.

Helen pulled up his internet history. She wasn't expecting much, but even she was surprised by the treasure trove of depravity that presented itself. With the exception of a couple of news sites, all the websites were pornographic. Gangbangs, rape simulations, pre-teens and all manner of violence and coercion. Most of the women and girls in the clips appeared cowed, whether genuinely or feigned, and it was clear they were designed for people who were aroused by others' fear and pain.

Rising, Helen gestured to Hudson to take a look and, crossing to the doorway, headed back out onto the site. As she gazed at the line of caravans and the curious faces of the onlookers, her mind turned slowly on their discoveries. Morgan was into extortion, possibly blackmail, but what else were they dealing with? He had been accused of sexual assault and harassment, but was Morgan more than the common-or-garden rapists Helen had encountered before? On first sight, he appeared to be a sexual sadist with an interest in domination and torture, but how far had he taken his fantasies? Was he now dangerously out of control? Preying on those who thwarted him, revelling in their agony and distress?

Gazing out into the night, Helen wondered where Morgan was right now. Only a handful of determined holidaymakers now haunted the forest, the majority having heeded the warnings to steer clear, but still it made Helen uneasy. Had Morgan left by chance tonight or was there a more sinister reason for his absence? Scott and Campbell had been dispatched, and there were no other numbers he regularly called, yet the fact remained that he was absent. As was the crossbow, and a battered Jeep Cherokee that witnesses from the site said he drove. Which made Helen wonder – was it possible he was going to strike again tonight?

And, if so, who would be in the firing line?

118

'I'm sorry, but I don't want to talk about him. I never want to say that man's name again.'

'I appreciate that,' Charlie gently tried to mollify her, 'but it is vital that we talk to Caleb Morgan, and anything you can tell us about him —'

'I've done this before. Five, six, seven times,' Alice Walker responded angrily. 'And where has it got me? He hasn't been picked up. You lot don't have a clue where he is, do you?'

The young woman was crying, fear mingling with her distress. Charlie wanted to comfort her, but before she could do so, a gruff, male voice came on the line.

'This is Alice's father. She's said all she's going to say, you've upset her enough. Don't bother calling back until you've made some *bloody* progress.'

Charlie was about to answer, but he hung up, cutting her off. Charlie sighed, long and loud. Having left Helen and Hudson to continue their search at the travellers' site, she and a couple of others had returned to Southampton Central to continue their investigation into Caleb Morgan — his personal history, family background, past misdemeanours. But they had made little headway, his accusers either irrevocably hostile to the police or unwilling to relive their experiences. In truth, given the failed raid on the campsite and lack of concrete information on Morgan's habits or whereabouts, they were no further on.

'Working late?'

Charlie jumped, startled, then turned to see Superintendent Simmons approaching. She was surprised, the station chief seldom setting foot in the incident room, preferring others to come to her. At first, Charlie had wondered if this indicated a lack of interest, but now she realized that the reverse was true – Simmons was extremely interested in their investigations, but trusted the team to get on with the job. This was a far cry from previous station chiefs and Charlie was glad of the change.

'Trying. Not that we're getting anywhere fast.'

'I wouldn't say that,' Simmons reassured her. 'We know Morgan's bolt-hole now. Maybe he'll return in time, in which case we'll be waiting for him. If he doesn't, we'll release his details to the press tomorrow. It'll be a lot harder for him to stay hidden then.'

'Let's hope so.'

'I've no doubt. So why don't you get off home, rest that foot of yours? It's getting late.'

'Maybe another twenty minutes . . .'

'Go on, DS Brooks. You look tired.'

Charlie smiled an acknowledgement, but her heart sank. She had touched up her make-up to try and make herself look less haggard, but obviously hadn't succeeded.

'Maybe I will then,' she conceded, but made no move to leave.

'Is everything ok? You've seemed a bit down of late.'

Now Charlie just felt embarrassed. She had never had a senior officer sound so concerned about her well-being before.

'Yes, I'm fine,' she replied, as brightly as she could.

Simmons nodded, but didn't look entirely convinced. And somehow her warm, concerned expression demanded more.

'My partner and I are just going through a bit of a rough patch . . .'

'I'm sorry to hear that. But it's not uncommon in this job, as you know.'

'It'll be fine, I'm sure. We just need a bit of time together, to talk, but Jessie isn't helping.'

'Your little girl?'

'She hasn't been sleeping. Night terrors.'

'I see.'

Her tone was knowing, as if she too had experienced these.

'We've tried to get to the bottom of it, to see what might be causing them, but . . . it's a mystery. And, believe me, we could do with a good night's sleep.'

'Have you tried singing to her?'

Charlie was so surprised by this response that she thought she'd misheard.

'I know it sounds daft,' Simmons continued, 'but it worked a treat with my eldest.'

'Right . . .'

'He had night terrors for nearly four weeks. It was around the time I'd just got promoted to DI and things were a bit fraught in our house. I was stressed out of my mind, truth be told, then someone suggested a song at bedtime and suddenly they stopped.'

Charlie was surprised, but also interested.

'And singing to them at night can really make that much difference to a child?'

'Sure, but it's not really the difference it makes to the child that's important, it's the difference it makes to *Mum*.'

Charlie stared at her, wrong-footed.

'But, anyway, I'm keeping you. I'm going home now and so should you.'

With that, Simmons left. Charlie watched her go, still trying to make sense of her advice. She had given it generously, but firmly, as if she somehow knew the cause of Charlie's unhappiness. Any help was welcome and yet still Simmons's words unnerved her. She'd assumed all along that the problem lay with Jessie, that something was worrying her, but now another possibility raised itself. Charlie had been anxious, guilt-stricken, even paranoid since Sanderson's death, a state of mind which had definitely affected the mood in the house. Was it possible that she was the root cause? That Jessie had picked up on her anxiety?

Had *she* been the problem all along?

119

Helen cast an eye towards the seventh floor, to the dim light that peeked from behind the blinds. She was sure Charlie was still up there – she'd just emailed Helen an update on their progress – and she was tempted to go up and talk to her, to check that she was ok. But tonight Helen felt like getting away from Southampton Central, to give herself a little time and space to think, so instead turned away from the building and mounted her bike.

Hudson had offered to return the pool car, so Helen took advantage of his generosity, pulling her helmet from her bike and sliding it on. Immediately, the sound around her diminished, even as her view of the world became tinted and softened. It really was strange, and perhaps worrying, how calming she found being at one remove from the real world. Flicking off the stand, she fired up the engine and roared away from the bike park, heading away from the scene of her frustration.

Morgan was out there somewhere, but continued to elude them. Helen was sure he was the key – the only person who linked Campbell and Scott, the only one who had reason to harm them, not to mention the imagination and depravity to dream up this exquisite form of torture. But where was he? Morgan was from Macclesfield originally, but seemed to have little contact with his parents, who still lived there. He had few friends locally, none of whom had stuck by him since his outing as a sex pest. And his down-at-heel existence at the traveller site strongly suggested that he had run out of other options, living alone and modestly, eking out what cash remained by buying out-of-date tins. She sincerely hoped that he would return to the campsite – McAndrew, Bentham and some uniformed officers were stationed there, hidden in a neighbouring caravan – but if he didn't, if he clocked their presence and took flight, what then? An APB and press release might help flush him out, but if he went to ground, their only other option would be to interrogate his previous movements via his phone signal, to see if there were any other places that he liked to frequent. But it was a shot in the dark and Helen knew it.

She was still brooding on these thoughts, when she noticed something. She was on the ring road again, following her customary route home, and once more a solitary biker had appeared in her mirrors, bearing down on her.

Dropping her speed, she examined her pursuer, satisfying herself that it *was* Hudson. She marvelled at his cheek, uncertain whether to be annoyed or impressed by his dogged pursuit and lack of reserve. Either way, she was not going to let him have things entirely his way.

Lowering her speed further, she let him pull closer. Then suddenly she yanked back the throttle, roaring away from him. Now Hudson *did* react, but Helen had a head start, accelerating away from her pursuer.

Now it was a straight race. It was late at night and the ring road was empty and inviting. Hudson's bike was more powerful than Helen's, but she was the more experienced rider and knew every bump of the road. She took the bends hard and low, straightening up occasionally to roar past trundling lorries, zipping past them as if they weren't there. If there were traffic patrols out, she would have some explaining to do, but tonight she didn't care, revelling in the speed, the thrill of the chase.

The race had now become a game of cat and mouse. Hudson would close on her, sometimes getting to within twenty feet of her, then Helen would open the gap once more. He would come back strongly again, at which point Helen would use trickery, slowing down and feinting as if to turn off, before roaring away again, once Hudson had dropped his speed. On and on they went, enjoying the duel, toying with each other, two riders in their element, utterly unconstrained by the scattering of vehicles they sped past.

Eventually, however, Helen decided to put him out of his misery. Hudson had fought a good fight, but had not managed to catch her. Magnanimously, she guided her bike into a lay-by, bringing the chase to an end. Pulling up beside her, Hudson removed his helmet, smiling happily, even boyishly, at her. Helen looked at him for a moment, then lifted her visor, their eyes meeting.

'If we do this, we do it my way,' she said firmly.

'Fine.'

'We don't talk about it with anyone and when it's time to stop, we stop.'

'Understood.'

'Good. Follow me.'

Flipping down her visor, she roared away. Hudson did likewise, the pair of them burning off into the night, heading directly for her flat.

120

The ramshackle building was as quiet as the grave. The girl who'd opened up for Emilia was obviously surprised to have a visitor this early and was virtually monosyllabic, answering Emilia's questions with a remarkable lack of courtesy or interest. Clearly, she was not a morning person.

'It's all online.'

'Not the information I'm looking for,' Emilia contradicted her.

'If you're interested in doing a course,' the girl drawled. 'You should go to www –'

'Actually, I'm a journalist. My name's Emilia Garanita – you may have read my articles about the New Forest Killer.'

That silenced her, which pleased Emilia. Having exhausted her online research into Graham Ross late last night, she had set off for his photography school at first light. School was perhaps a rather grand title for the collection of small workshops that he and his colleagues taught photography courses in, but it sounded better on the flyers. It was housed in a former gym, which had now moved on to a more fashionable area, and included a space for exhibitions, for local photographers or artworks with a Hampshire bent.

'What I need from you,' she continued, nodding at the teenager, who now looked a little cowed, 'is a simple piece of information. Did this man' – she handed her a piece of paper with Tom Campbell's name on it – 'ever attend a course run by Graham Ross?'

The girl hesitated.

'I'm not sure I should. I mean, I've only got your word that you are who you say you are.'

'Here's my card.' Emilia handed it over. 'And there's twenty quid in it for you, if you're quick.'

This seemed to decide the teenager, a free night of drinks too much to pass up for a task that would only take a few minutes. She scurried away, leaving Emilia to ponder the wisdom of coming here. It was a bit of a flyer, but as she'd wracked her brains for potential connections between Ross and the known victims of the New Forest Killer, the only thing she had come up with was photography. Campbell was mad about it – indeed the paper had published numerous photos he'd taken of his girlfriend and, more sinisterly, several snaps he'd taken of the New Forest itself. She knew from her digging that Campbell had done courses on photography locally, and sitting at her desk, looking at her Venn diagram of connections, the link had seemed a potentially viable one. Now, however, she was having doubts, suddenly fearing she had battled the morning traffic for no reason.

To still her anxiety, she stepped inside the exhibition space. It too was deserted, a hushed reverence filling the quiet space. Emilia walked through the display, absorbing the images around her.

The photographs seemed to be themed around criminality, not surprising perhaps given Ross's chosen profession. This particular exhibition was called 'Crime and Punishment' – from what Emilia could make out all the portraits were of convicted felons, beneath which were small signs, offering a potted summary of their lives and the punishment they had received from the state. She read a couple – they seemed to be neither critical nor damning of the felons, allowing viewers to make up their own minds about the subjects.

She continued to walk the line of faces. Some looked like downright wrong'uns, people you would cross the street to avoid. Others seemed more vulnerable, plaintive even, particularly the women, and Emilia found herself gravitating towards those. She knew from her own childhood how routinely people abuse and exploit those they deem weaker than themselves.

There was an African woman, who had been convicted of people trafficking, a British teenager who'd been banged up for aggravated assault, even a pensioner sent down for multiple counts of fraud. Some were funny, others were tragic – women with facial bruising and trauma lurking just behind the eyes. On she went, letting the stories, the faces, wash over her, until suddenly she came to an abrupt halt.

At first, she was a little confused, then she felt a shiver run down her spine. For staring back at her, looking younger, more naïve, yet strangely defiant, was the face of Lauren Scott.

121

Helen stared at him, watching the morning sunshine steal across his face. She had been lying here for several minutes, enjoying a brief moment of peace, replaying the night they had spent together. But now Hudson was beginning to stir, the warmth of the sun doing its work, meaning Helen would soon have to face up to the consequences of her actions.

Normally she would have bolted from such a situation, but today she felt strangely comfortable. Conversation had been minimal on their return to the flat, but their lovemaking had been relaxed and passionate, only coming to an end in the small hours. Helen had fallen asleep soon afterwards, Joseph's arm draped across her shoulders, and she'd woken just before eight, feeling oddly refreshed.

She had given the team a late start, to make up for their efforts last night, so there was no abrogation of duty lying here, even though the clock had just crept past nine. She knew she would have to be on the move in a moment, but suddenly felt determined to wring the last moments of pleasure from what had been a surprising, but pleasant, encounter.

Hudson stirred, muttering something in his half-sleep, then turned onto his other side, pulling the covers over him. He probably had forgotten where he was, imagined himself in his own bed, which underlined how strange it was for him to be *here*. This flat had always been the place Helen retreated to in times of trouble – when she was recuperating from injuries, when she needed to hide from the world, on Christmas Day when her sense of isolation was at its most acute – and it was somewhere she inhabited alone.

Her office at Southampton Central was deliberately bare; what existed of her life up until now was here. The books she'd read as a child, the few photos she still had of Marianne, the jewellery Grace Simmons had bought her for her eighteenth birthday, her first police uniform, pressed and hanging in the wardrobe. Others had attempted to penetrate this sanctuary before and had been repelled, but Joseph she had invited in and she didn't regret it. When they were in bed, rank, seniority, even the difference in their characters went out the window, as both sought excitement, affection, comfort and solace. And what struck Helen now as she looked down at her companion was not how weird it was for him to be here, but how natural it felt.

She was still pondering this strange anomaly, when her phone started trilling. Helen seldom slept without setting an alarm – she was used to its tinny, harmonic flourish – yet she cursed it today. It meant a return to real life, to the investigation, to anxiety, worries, fear and death. Switching it off, she slipped out of bed, readying herself for action.

Today was a day like any other day and yet it felt different. So, as Helen walked lightly towards the shower, she offered up a silent prayer for the brief slice of happiness she had been afforded. Perhaps she *wasn't* a lost cause after all.

122

Jacquetta was trying her best to be brave, to *own* her pain, but her distress was plain to see. It was visible in a dozen small signs – the rings under her eyes, her harshly bitten nails, her nicotine-stained fingers. Charlie had come to the interview with a slightly heavy heart – sexual assault cases were always gruelling and she wasn't sure exactly what they would gain from the conversation – but now she felt utterly ashamed of herself. What this woman had endured was terrible and she deserved all the compassion, attention and sympathy Charlie could muster. Her own problems were nothing compared to Jacquetta's.

'He was very charming at first. Inspiring, even. I'd never met a teacher like him.'

Jacquetta had initially rejected Charlie's request to talk, when she'd contacted her by phone last night. But this morning Charlie had received an apologetic text, her conscience obviously getting the better of her, and now they were huddled together in a café at the top of Jacquetta's road. She didn't want to stray too far from home and, having heard the gist of her story, Charlie could understand why.

'How old were you when he taught you?'

'Nineteen. I was redoing my A-levels and he made a real difference. I got a D in geography first time round, but that year I was predicted an A.'

'And what made him different?'

'He was surprising, clever, funny. He was more like a

friend than a teacher. He liked the same music as we did, the same shows.'

'And when did the lines between teacher and friend start to blur?'

'Pretty early on. But it stepped up a gear in the summer term. He used to message, call. Not just me, others too.'

'Did you ever meet up outside of college?'

'Sure. When the weather picked up, we'd meet at pubs, on the beach, we'd go for walks.'

'And were you aware that his interest in you had a sexual dimension?'

Jacquetta cast her eyes down, looking slightly ashamed.

'Sure. But I kind of liked it . . .'

'It's nothing to be ashamed of, Jacquetta. You've done nothing wrong.'

'I suppose . . . I suppose I was flattered. He was older, smarter, more sophisticated . . .'

Jacquetta petered out, picking at her nails.

'And the incident itself? Are you able to tell me about that?'

There was a long pause, followed by a heavy, shaky sigh.

'It was last summer. A group of us had gone to Tanners Lane beach. It was a full moon and we planned to stay up all night – our version of the Thai beach parties, I guess. It was his idea – Morgan's, I mean – but we were all up for it. Our exams had finished and we wanted to relax . . .'

Charlie watched Jacquetta closely. Each word was hard for her, as she took herself back to the seat of her trauma.

'Caleb was telling stories, playing his guitar, making jokes. He seemed very attentive – to me particularly – and I remember feeling high on life. Yes, there were drinks, some drugs too, but it wasn't that. It was the place, the atmosphere, the sun on our faces. It was such a release, after all those months of study.'

A fleeting, bitter smile.

'We stayed up until three, four, I don't remember, then we all went to bed. I had a tent of my own and crashed out there.'

She paused, her breathing becoming shallow and more rapid as the emotion rose to the surface. But she persevered.

'Next thing I know, he's in my tent. On top of me, kissing me. I told him to get off, that I didn't want it to be like this, but he wouldn't listen. He told me he knew what I wanted, which *wasn't* true . . .'

Jacquetta was shaking slightly now and Charlie was tempted to reach out to her, but the young woman had withdrawn, wrapping her arms around herself.

'I tried to fight him off, then I tried to scream but he . . . he put his fist in my mouth. I thought I was going to be sick, but he kept it there. Kept it there the whole time . . .'

She was staring at her feet, as if still in disbelief that something so awful could have befallen her.

'Afterwards, he kissed me on the head and said "goodnight". Like what we'd done was normal. The next day, it was as if nothing had happened. He was friendly, chatty, relaxed. I almost didn't believe it myself, except for the fact that he'd hurt me, that I was still bleeding.'

'So, you didn't talk to anyone? Your family, your friends?'

Jacquetta shook her head forcefully, looking stricken.

'I wanted to tell someone . . . but the longer I left it, the harder it got.'

'I understand.'

'Eventually one of the other girls he'd attacked came forward. And then I felt I didn't have a choice. I wish I'd said something earlier, I really do. If I had, then maybe some of those other girls . . .'

366

Tears were sliding down her face. Reaching out, Charlie took her hand and this time Jacquetta allowed herself to be held. So many emotions were playing out on her face – shame, distress, anxiety, fear, regret, but Charlie felt only one. Anger. For she knew now beyond all doubt that Caleb Morgan was everything they feared him to be. He was not the victim of a witch hunt, nor an opportunistic sex pest.

He was a seasoned, practised predator.

123

Alexander Newton fiddled with the letter opener, turning it over and over in his hands. He would have looked like a textbook villain, the thin knife twirling between his fingers, were it not for the fact that he was sweating.

'So Caleb Morgan was a lecturer here from May 2006 to January 2010?' Helen demanded, her eyes flicking from her notepad to the faculty head.

'That's correct,' Newton said cautiously. 'We had a rather large roster of staff back then, but since austerity kicked in . . .'

'And that was why he left? Cutbacks?'

'Partly.'

'And the other part?'

'Can I ask what this is about?'

The knife now ceased moving. If anything, Newton seemed even more tense than before. Helen had come to the geography faculty at Southampton University to get some further background on Morgan, to explore his relationship with Scott and other students in his care, but ever since she'd arrived she'd sensed something bigger, something unspoken, lying just beneath the surface of Newton's purposefully bland responses.

'I suspect you're aware that Caleb Morgan is wanted for questioning on three counts of sexual harassment and sexual assault.'

Newton nodded slowly.

'We're obviously working around the clock to apprehend

him, but we're also trying to build a fuller picture of his behaviour from the mid-noughties onwards, to see if he might be responsible for . . . other crimes. So, I'll ask you once again, what were the other reason or reasons you felt obliged to let Morgan go.'

'As I said, it was mostly because of the cutbacks –'

'You terminated his contract in the middle of the academic year, Mr Newton. You don't do that for financial reasons.'

Helen was staring directly at him. She could have gone on, but held her tongue, letting the heavy silence do its work. Newton squirmed in his chair, then replied:

'Look, I think perhaps I ought to have our lawyer present . . .'

'By all means. But that would mean I would have to make things official. Any interviews would be conducted at Southampton Central and I would have to caution you –'

'All right, all right,' Newton responded anxiously, unnerved by the prospect of being treated like a common criminal.

'So tell me,' Helen demanded firmly.

The letter opener was now replaced on the desk. Running his hand through his thinning hair, Newton eventually replied:

'We . . . we had some complaints. From female students. Nothing too serious, I should say,' he added quickly, 'but enough to be troubling.'

'What sort of complaints?'

'Flirting, inappropriate suggestions, a crossing of boundaries.'

'Did he attack anyone?'

'Dear God, no . . . but there had been some physical contact that was unwanted, which had caused distress.'

'How old were these women?'

'Eighteen, nineteen . . .'

'And what did you do?'

Now Newton paused.

'Well?'

'We talked to him, obviously. Issued him with a verbal warning. But it didn't seem to do any good. There were a couple of further complaints, so we felt compelled to take further action.'

'Meaning what?'

'We terminated his contract.'

'Did he deny that he'd acted in this way?'

'Not really,' Newton said, evasively.

'You *did* confront him about these further complaints?'

And now Newton broke his gaze, staring down at the letter opener once more.

'You *didn't*, did you?' Helen continued, aghast. 'You just let him go.'

'Look, it was very clear that discussion was useless. He had no interest in hearing what we had to say –'

'So, you just moved the problem on. Least said, soonest mended.'

Newton didn't try to deny it.

'He went on to Bournemouth afterwards. Did you ever talk to them about your concerns?'

'I wanted to . . . but the board felt it would be unwise.'

'Then shame on you.'

Helen rose to her feet, shaking her head in disbelief.

'Shame on you for letting this university put concerns for its own reputation above the welfare of its students.'

'I did what I could –'

'Bullshit. You did what was easiest.'

Helen knew she was overstepping the mark now, but her blood was up.

'So, here's what's going to happen. You are going to pro-vide me with everything – and I mean everything – that you have on Caleb Morgan. His relationships with friends, col-leagues, his past addresses, his full student list and most importantly details of every complaint that was made against him. This may help us avert further pain, but it will not spare you or your superiors. You haven't heard the last of this.'

Newton wanted to respond – to appeal for leniency perhaps – but Helen was already on the move. Marching through the door, she hurried back down the corridor, keen to get back to base to update the team. But as she marched across the polished wood, her phone started to buzz. Seeing it was McAndrew, she answered quickly, wishing her a cheery good morning. For once, however, her junior didn't respond in kind, simply saying:

'We've found him.'

124

Charlie clutched her mobile tightly in her hand as she hurried along the road. She'd had to park some way from the café Jacquetta had chosen, which allowed her time to reflect. On what the young woman had been through, on what her description of her ordeal told them about Caleb Morgan, but also on her own situation. Suddenly she felt very foolish – how minuscule her problems seemed by comparison, how weak she was next to the young woman who was battling hard to rebuild her life.

Charlie had suffered, that was true. But so had they all – Helen, Ellie, in fact every member of the team who had worked with Joanne. And at least they had friends, family to support them, unlike Joanne's mother, Nicola, who was having to face her ordeal alone. Charlie had tried to deal with her grief, her anxiety, as best she could, but what had she succeeded in doing? Pushing her lovely boyfriend away and upsetting her daughter. What right had she to be so self-indulgent when others were really suffering?

Stopping by her car, she massaged her aching leg, then pulled her phone from her bag. Quickly, she opened up WhatsApp and clicked on 'Steve'. This was their private conduit for pointless messages of affection, but it had been unused of late, which made Charlie sad. Their relaxed, easy relationship had always been the bedrock of her happiness. So now she didn't hesitate, typing swiftly and intently.

'Sorry for being such a nut job. I do love you very much and want us to be happy.'

It wasn't much, but it was a start. And Charlie knew she wouldn't be able to do any better, in the short term at least. Experience had taught her that often the most important things in life were the hardest to say.

125

'I'm not exactly sure what you're implying, Emilia.'

Ross's tone was even, but had an edge. The pair of them were tucked away in a booth in Carluccio's, a venue Emilia had deliberately chosen for their interview – populated enough to be safe, not busy enough to be overheard.

'I'm not implying anything. I'm just saying that I was surprised to find that Lauren Scott featured in your exhibition.'

'It's not my exhibition.'

'It's your school.'

'Dozens of photographers contributed to that exhibition. They selected the subjects, people who had criminal records or –'

'But you chose which images to display, right?'

'Sure. But I still don't see why that should be a problem.'

Ross was starting to get agitated now. Perhaps he'd assumed her text inviting him here was the prelude to a cosy chat. If so, he had been sorely disappointed, Emilia beginning her questioning almost as soon as the pleasantries were concluded.

'It's a problem because you haven't been frank with me. You made no mention of the fact that you knew who Lauren Scott was.'

'What makes you think I did?'

'Because the exhibition has been running for over a month. You must have come across her weeks before she . . .'

'Before she . . . what?'

'Before she died,' Emilia returned, defiantly.

Ross shook his head angrily.

'She was one image among a hundred. I didn't even take in her name when I was curating the exhibition. It was only in the last day or so that I made the connection.'

'And what about Tom Campbell?'

'What about him? Don't tell me he was in the exhibition too?'

Ross was trying to be withering, but there was unease behind his hostility now.

'You didn't tell me you knew him too.'

'I don't.'

'He enrolled on your course four months ago. Did twelve sessions.'

'Not with me, he didn't.'

'He was there every Friday afternoon, for nearly *three* months.'

'I have a roster of staff and I seldom teach there. I don't have the time.'

'Do you keep records of who takes which sessions?'

'Not formally, it's mostly cash-in-hand work. They tell me who they've taught and get paid for it. I trust them.'

'So we have no way of knowing for sure who took Campbell's sessions?'

'If I looked at my notes, I could tell you.'

'But we'd only have your word for it.'

'For God's sake, Emilia, what is this?'

Finally, his anger rose to the surface. He was staring directly at her, fire in his eyes. A passing waiter turned, alarmed by the sudden rise in volume, but Ross didn't seem to notice.

'I'm just trying to get to the bottom of your connection with –'

'There is no connection.'

'So it's just a coincidence, then?'

'Yes.'

'Well, I'm sorry, but I don't believe in them.'

She stared back at him, refusing to be cowed by his visible anger.

'Then consider this conversation over.'

He rose, shaking his head angrily.

'That's ok,' she shot back breezily. 'I have everything I need.'

Ross had taken a step towards the door, but now hesitated, a horrible realization dawning.

'You're not . . . recording this, are you?'

He glanced down at her phone. Emilia lunged for it, but she was too slow, Ross getting there just ahead of her. He opened it up, scanned the apps furiously, then finding there was no cause for alarm, tossed it back on the table. Emilia let it land without looking, determined to appear insouciant. Rattled, unnerved by her studied calm, Ross shot a look at her bag, then dismissing that notion, dropped his eyes to the table. He scanned the surface, then suddenly got it, dropping down quickly to look underneath. This time Emilia was ahead of him, snatching the small recorder away and depositing it in her jacket pocket.

'I wouldn't if I were you . . .'

Ross had taken a step towards her, but Emilia's gentle warning stopped him in his tracks.

'There's a lot of people here . . .'

Ross looked like he might lunge at her anyway, such was his naked fury, but at the last minute he thought better of it. Turning, he hurried from the restaurant, without once looking back.

Emilia let him go, before signalling to the waiter for the bill. She was trying her best to appear calm and collected, but her heart was thumping. The interview had not gone entirely as expected, but she had come through it unscathed and had some useful material to work with. Not a confession, nor even an admission that he knew the victims personally. But his failure to refute her claims and his tense, defensive body language was telling. She didn't have him in the bag yet, but Emilia was sure she now had her prime suspect on the run.

126

Helen stared at the corpse, scarcely believing what she was seeing.

A terrified dog walker had made the call just after nine thirty this morning and shortly afterwards the half-naked, brutalized body of Caleb Morgan had been discovered by uniformed officers. As with the others, he was hanging from the branch of a stout oak tree, in a small clearing to the north-east of the New Forest. Helen had been convinced Morgan was their killer, the key to unlocking this bewildering case. In fact, he was victim number three.

Helen was naturally stoic, never doubting that diligent detective work would carry the day, but even she felt a shiver of panic this morning. All her theories, all her preconceptions, about the motives behind this killing spree had now gone up in smoke, this unrepentant, sadistic sexual predator given exactly the same treatment as Lauren Scott and Tom Campbell. It didn't make sense. *None of it* made any sense.

'They found his jeep about a mile away, concealed in some foliage.'

Hudson had joined her, but Helen didn't even bother turning, her eyes still glued to Morgan.

'Then you'd better take me to it.'

Thick vegetation cast a large shadow over the rusty Jeep Cherokee, making it look forlorn and lonely. Helen and Hudson approached it in silence, having spoken barely a word during the journey. In other circumstances, they might have made careful reference to their night together, testing one another's reaction to it, but there was no chance of that today. Morgan's unexpected murder had put everything else on hold.

Slipping on her gloves, Helen teased open the driver's door. It was unlocked and, stranger still, the keys were in the ignition. Was this deliberate? Had Morgan left them there for a quick getaway? Or was there another reason for this oversight? Leaning into the body of the car, Helen noted a baseball bat lying on the passenger seat. She wondered if it was always there. Or had Morgan come here expecting violence?

She ran her hand over the soft fabric of the seat as she peered into the rear of the car, but there was nothing of any interest there, so she returned her attention to the cockpit. Now she did find something that warranted her attention – a small smear of blood on the rim of the steering wheel. She gently teased the edge of the stain with her little finger. It smeared easily, suggesting it was still fresh.

Her mind turning now, she looked at the dashboard, the windscreen, then the driver's window. And here again there were signs of a struggle. There were long smear marks down the window – thin, translucent marks, which looked very much like fingers dragging themselves across the glass, as if trying to get purchase. More interestingly, there was another small patch of blood at the point where the window and door met. This time there were a few hairs nestling in it, dark-brown hairs that matched Morgan's colouring. Suddenly Helen had a clear picture of what had happened. Morgan had been attacked in his vehicle, possibly as he was about to drive off.

'Are there any campsites nearby?'

'Nearest one is Alder's Edge. It's about half a mile away.'

379

Nodding, Helen got out at the driver's side and crossed to the back of the vehicle. Hauling open the boot, she found that it was empty. If Morgan had come here with camping gear, it was elsewhere now.

The pair marched briskly through the forest and ten minutes later they reached the campsite. Ellie McAndrew had beaten them to it, gesturing Helen towards a small tent sitting away from the other pitches near the forest edge.

'Owner says there were only four tents pitched last night. All the other owners have been accounted for.'

Helen walked quickly over to the tent. Bending down, she pulled open the tent flaps to find . . . nothing. The small tent was entirely empty, save for a lifeless lantern sitting plumb in the middle of the groundsheet.

'I guess he liked to travel light . . .'

Hudson was on her shoulder, looking confused. But Helen was already thinking it out. Though Morgan had been dispatched in the same way as Campbell and Scott, the manner of his abduction was different. He had no intention of camping here seemingly – he had no bedding, no food, no change of clothes – and how likely was that anyway, when he had a secure hideout at the traveller site? No, instead he had come armed with a baseball bat and a lantern, which would presumably have illuminated the interior of the tent for a while, before eventually extinguishing itself. This, and the fact that his 4x4 had been artfully concealed, suggested to Helen that Morgan had not come here to camp. He had come to lay a trap.

Which raised an interesting question. Was it possible that Morgan was *expecting* to be attacked?

127

'Do you think he knew his attacker?'

Superintendent Simmons's question was a good one. Helen had been pondering exactly that on her ride back to Southampton Central.

'It's got to be a possibility. He was a man in a corner – no funds, outstanding warrants for his arrest, no friends to speak of – yet his prime concern was to try and entrap our killer. Furthermore, he seems to have known that this guy was likely to strike again.'

'Is it possible that they were in it together then? That his accomplice turned on him? It might explain why they were in the car together.'

'Maybe,' Helen conceded, 'but from what we can gather from the travellers, he never had visitors, plus there's no evidence of regular phone calls to anyone. Also, it looks very much like he was attacked from behind in the car.'

'So the killer was lying in wait for him.'

'Looks that way. I think Morgan was setting a trap, but our man was one step ahead, setting an ambush himself.'

'But that would mean Morgan knew that the perpetrator would strike at Alder's Edge campsite. How could he possibly be privy to that if he *wasn't* in league with the guy?'

'Not necessarily. It might just mean that Morgan knew the killer would come to him. That he sensed he was being followed, stalked even.'

'But Morgan has been off the radar for weeks now. How could our perpetrator have found him?'

'He *has* ventured out during the last few weeks. To meet Campbell twice, Scott once . . . If our man was stalking those guys, then it's very likely he would have spotted Morgan, followed him home.'

'And you think Morgan had noticed something, realized he was under threat?'

'Well, there's no question he was on his guard. He'd cut out clippings from numerous newspapers regarding the murders of Tom Campbell and Lauren Scott.'

'And you think they alarmed him? Even though he had barely seen these guys since he left Southampton University?'

'Looks that way.'

'But why? Why would somebody target them *now*?'

'I don't know,' Helen replied, frankly.

For the first time since they'd resumed working together, Simmons looked a little downcast. They were seemingly no closer to catching the perpetrator than they had been at the start of this baffling case. Helen knew she had to say – to do – something to keep things on track.

'The answer lies in the past, I'm sure of it. Something . . . we don't know what yet . . . connects these three. Something Morgan felt able to exploit when times became desperate for him. Our only option is to dig deeper, to take ourselves back to that time, and work out what's driving this guy. If we do that, I have every confidence we'll find our man.'

She sounded more confident than she felt, but it did the trick, the customary smile now returning to Simmons's face.

'And I have every faith in *you*,' she responded generously.

Helen left shortly afterwards. She marched down the corridor towards the incident room, fired up to grapple with evidence once more, to tease a lead from somewhere, but as she was about to buzz herself in she heard someone calling her name. Turning, she was surprised to find the desk sergeant, Jerry Taylor, waddling towards her.

'Sorry to bother you, Detective Inspector. But you've got a visitor.'

128

'I'm sorry, Emilia, I just don't buy it.'

For the first time in their dealings, the journalist looked flustered, reacting angrily to Helen's knock-back.

'I don't know how you can stand there and say that,' Emilia protested. 'We've all been looking for connections between Tom Campbell and Lauren Scott and I'm giving it to you on a plate. Graham Ross knew them both.'

'You *think* he knew them both.'

'I'm sure he came into contact with them there and something about them, about their stories, propelled him to –'

'You've got no way of proving that. And, besides, it may be that he is telling the truth. Coincidences happen.'

'Why are you so sure he is *not* connected?'

'I'm not. And if you can bring me concrete evidence of his involvement, then of course we will act on it. But Ross has never struck me as a violent man. Strange, yes, but not violent. Plus, he's right-handed.'

'That doesn't mean anything.'

It did, of course, but Helen let that go, circling round to the crucial point.

'And, besides, what would be his motive?'

'He's lost it,' Emilia asserted, without hesitation.

'Sorry, Emilia, you're going to have to be more specific than that.'

'He's spent too long around dead bodies.'

'So have you and I. Doesn't make us killers.'

'But it's different with him. His profession . . . his craft . . .

necessitates that he obsesses on the corpses, the tiny details of their trauma, the exquisite torture of their deaths. I think he's lost any feeling for them as real human beings, they're just subjects to him, to be lovingly recorded, obsessed over, preserved for . . . for his personal pleasure, for posterity perhaps.'

'And you know all this because . . . ?'

'Because I've been to his flat.'

'Emilia,' Helen replied, genuinely shocked.

'I've seen his stash of images. It's like a museum to death, a testament to his calling. To him it's not about the human story, the personal tragedy, it's about the beauty of his work. Murder has become his art form, his very reason for being.'

'Everything you say may be true, but that doesn't make him a murderer. Perhaps he's just a passive recorder of other people's misfortune . . .'

'But think about the staging,' Emilia insisted, passionately. 'Think about how these bodies are found. They are not . . . dispatched, then tossed away. They are very carefully, even artfully, presented. They are a statement, a thing of beauty, that *has* to mean something . . .'

Now Helen paused. Emilia was right of course. But it still didn't mean her explanation was correct.

'I don't deny that,' Helen conceded carefully. 'But I can't see the motive. There would be many easier ways for Ross to achieve what you're suggesting without chasing people through the forest. I can't see him having the skill, the strength or indeed the prowess to carry out these murders. Furthermore, I believe the root cause of these crimes lies further back, long before Ross moved to Hampshire –'

'You're missing the point –'

'No, Emilia, *you're* missing the point. You are a journalist, not a police officer. I thank you for the information you've given me, but you will have to let me run with things from here. You do your job, Emilia. And I'll do mine.'

The journalist left shortly afterwards, still grousing. Helen bent her steps to the incident room, but, as she did so, Emilia's words continued to spin around her brain. Helen was convinced that she was wrong about Ross, but what she'd said about the staging of the murders was correct, it had to mean something.

The question was, what?

129

The photos were spread out in front of them, a kaleidoscope of youthful merriment and misbehaviour. The rest of the team were processing the hard intel from the Caleb Morgan murder – tracing the movement of his vehicle in the days before his death – but Helen had pulled Charlie and Joseph Hudson into her office for a private conference.

Helen had told McAndrew not to disturb them unless something major cropped up. She wanted their sole focus to be on their victims – Lauren Scott, Tom Campbell and Caleb Morgan – whose happy, carefree faces stared up at them from the desk. Campbell's keen interest in photography had provided them with plentiful images of the heady days the trio had spent together and they scoured them now, searching for hints, clues, anything that might help them forge a clearer view of their connection.

'So, do we assume from these pictures that Campbell and Scott were part of Morgan's set?' Charlie asked.

'Makes sense,' Hudson agreed. 'We know he liked to have a gaggle of younger students around him, to be the centre of attention, the instigator . . .'

'Campbell was older than Scott, but Morgan was older than *him*,' said Helen, pursuing the theme. 'Morgan was presumably a glamorous, charismatic, rebellious figure in Campbell's eyes.'

'Scott might well have been smitten too. Perhaps Morgan targeted *her*,' Charlie offered. 'I think he was the driving force behind these full-moon parties, engineering them so that he could prey on his victims. We know Lauren Scott didn't like camping. Perhaps there was a *reason* why she had an aversion to it.'

'Possibly, but look at the dates,' Hudson pointed out. 'Scott appears at several of these parties. And she looks happy enough. Why would she go back for more if she'd been attacked?'

'And why would she take his call now?' Helen added. 'Why would she give him money?'

'Perhaps he was trying to sex-shame her? We know he was desperate for cash, had nowhere else to go. Maybe he threatened to reveal that she'd been raped. He had nothing to lose by doing so, as he was already wanted by the police. He could even have done it anonymously online, if he wanted to remain –'

'Possibly, but there's no evidence she *was* attacked. And, besides, Morgan tried to contact Campbell too. I can't see Campbell giving Morgan *anything* if he'd targeted his girlfriend as you suggest.'

'He might have witnessed something though,' Charlie speculated.

'That seems more likely,' Hudson said, brightening suddenly. 'Maybe they were *both* witnesses to something. Or complicit in some way. That would make sense of Morgan's attempt to extort money from the two of them. If they were linked to something criminal or immoral that he could use to humiliate them, threaten their jobs, their relationships . . .'

This thought seemed to land with all three. The trio returned their attention to the photos, searching, searching, searching. Helen's eye drifted over Caleb Morgan, Tom Campbell, Julia Winter, Aaron Slater and numerous other faces, caught up in the wild, hedonistic scene.

'Julia . . .' Helen murmured.

Charlie looked up.

'What about her?'

'She was good friends with Scott. They were housemates, in fact. Yet she's hardly in these photos . . .'

Charlie and Hudson perused the images and realized she was right. There were countless shots of Campbell, Morgan, Scott and many others, Slater included, but only a handful of the winsome, beautiful Julia Winter. Reaching out, Helen selected them, laying out five photos side by side. In them, she seemed happy, intoxicated, as carefree as the rest of them. There was certainly nothing in these images to suggest that anything was wrong.

'The dates.'

Charlie and Hudson looked at the dates stamped on the bottom-right-hand corner of the five photos.

'They're all the same,' Charlie murmured. 'All these photos were taken on the same day.'

'Exactly,' Helen confirmed. 'I was thrown off because it looks like she's wearing different clothes, but that's just because she's taken her hoodie off in a couple of them.'

'Plus, she has her hair up at first. Maybe she literally let her hair down over the course of that evening,' Hudson added.

'Thirtieth of April 2009,' Helen said, reading the date out loud. 'Perhaps the date is significant . . .'

Hudson was already typing.

'2009, spring full moon . . .' he muttered, waiting for the search engine to do its work, '. . . was on the thirtieth of April.'

He turned to Helen, looking sober, yet excited.

'Julia doesn't appear at any parties after this, but the others do,' Helen thought aloud.

'And we know Julia attempted to kill herself roughly two months after this, having flunked her end of year exams. Her father said it was because of academic pressure, but . . .'

'But perhaps it was because Morgan attacked her.'

Hudson's words filled the room, suddenly seeming to make perfect sense.

'If her father found out, he would have had a strong motive to avenge himself on Morgan, on all of them in fact. Imagine what it would have done to him, knowing that his little girl had been the victim of this habitual predator . . .'

'Maybe he took matters into his own hands. Perhaps in the end . . .' Helen looked up at her colleagues as she concluded: '. . . the hunter became the hunted.'

130

'Baldur var en av de mest älskade av alla gudar. Odins son, gudstjänstemannen och den välvilliga trollkarlsgudinnan Frigg, Baldur var en generös . . .'

His tongue slid over the words, enjoying their familiar cadence. Oliver Winter had lived on the south coast for nearly twenty-five years now, but he'd never lost his accent, nor his love of his mother tongue. Often, when he was with his daughter, he would read to her in Swedish, taking great delight in retelling the old myths, talking to her in a language only they understood.

He knew that the nurses thought him odd. Some, he suspected, thought him mad, endlessly reading and talking to a young woman who appeared frozen, offering no reaction to his endless prattling. But *he* knew she could hear him, was listening to what he was saying, and that was all that mattered. Never mind that her health was failing, that she was fighting a losing battle against the spread of pneumonia. She was there, with him, hanging on his every word.

Today, however, this cosy idyll was not to go unchallenged, for as Oliver turned the page, his mobile rang loudly. Immediately, heads turned, the nurses angered by his oversight in not having it on silent.

'Sorry, sorry,' he muttered, placing the book on the bed and hurrying towards the doors.

Pushing through them, he looked at the Caller ID. It was a foreign number, not one he recognized, and he hesitated for a moment, before pressing accept.

'Hello?'

'Oliver, it's Alice.'

His heart sank.

'Oliver, can you hear me?'

'Yes,' he replied, without enthusiasm.

'I've been trying to get hold of you. Have you been getting my messages?'

'Yes,' he conceded.

'Then why haven't you got back to me?'

'Because there's nothing to say.'

He was tempted to hang up there and then, but something made him hesitate – perhaps some vestige of politeness or maybe just the desire to enjoy his ex-wife's anger and distress a little longer.

'You've got no right to shut me out like this.'

'I've got every right.'

'She's my daughter too –'

'No, Alice, she *was* your daughter. She's mine now.'

'Whatever happened in the past, she's my flesh and blood.'

'How convenient that you remember that now. It didn't seem to count when you abandoned her . . .'

'Please, Oliver, don't be like this . . .'

He smiled at her anguished tone, pleased that he could still hurt her.

'And, anyway, I've told you before she's too sick to receive visitors. Especially people she hardly knows.'

'That's why I need to see her. If there's even the slightest danger that –'

'She has everyone she needs right here.'

'I'm not going to beg, Oliver.'

'I'm glad to hear it. Save your energy, go back to your new life. Your husband, your child. How are they, by the way?'

'Missing me.'

There was something knowing in her tone, which immediately alarmed him.

'What do you mean?'

'I'm here, in England. In fact, I'm outside your house right now. Do you still leave your spare key under the flowerpot?'

'You get away from there,' Oliver breathed, suddenly furious. 'You stay away from me, from us . . .'

'Sorry, Oliver, too late. I'm here, with a letter from my lawyers, and I am not going back to Sweden until I get what I came for.'

She paused for a moment, enjoying her advantage, before concluding:

'I want to see my daughter.'

131

He was a wanted man, a rapist and sex pest called Caleb Morgan. Even her dull-witted colleagues had had no problem prising *that* information from the uniformed officers, who seemed keen to trumpet their achievement in discovering the long-term fugitive.

Following her unsatisfactory interview with Helen Grace, Emilia had returned to work in a dark mood, only to find that the story had moved on again in her absence. A third body had been found in the New Forest. Cursing herself, cursing life, Emilia had resigned herself to the fact that her colleagues would be writing tonight's front page, settling down instead to apply herself to the more important task of identifying the perpetrator.

Grace had poured cold water on her idea that Graham Ross might be responsible and her casual dismissal of the idea had rattled Emilia, but she wasn't prepared to give up yet. So, she set about trying anything she could think of to find a link between Ross and the third victim, Caleb Morgan. But so far she'd found nothing. She had called the girl at the photo school, double- and triple-checked the names of those appearing in the 'Crime and Punishment' exhibition and conducted every imaginable online search to unearth a link between the crime scene photographer from Scotland and the lecturer/sex offender from Macclesfield, but she had come up with a blank. Was it possible that her instincts had failed her? That she had been wrong all along?

If so, she had shot herself in the foot in grand style. Ross had been angling to give her the inside track on the investigation, in the hope perhaps of a fruitful collaboration further down the line. But she had blown any chance of that with her seemingly ill-founded allegations.

Thoughts of his sinister collection drove her back to her search once more. There was not much to be salvaged from the wreckage of the last twenty-four hours, but the one thing Helen Grace had conceded was that the staging of the murders was significant. Emilia was convinced of this too, and sensing that Grace was at a loss for how to explain them, she resumed her hunt for answers. If she could cast some light on these strangely theatrical murders that would be something – something to hold over her colleagues, not to mention Grace herself.

Her initial searches were uninspiring, her key words throwing up hideous ISIS-style hangings. Moving on from terrorist- and military-related atrocities, she went further back in time, searching for significance in the manner and public nature of the deaths. This took her into the world of medieval torture, of a time when the punishment of crime was delivered more 'imaginatively'. But still there was nothing that fitted the bill exactly, causing her to wonder if there *was* no precedent, if the killer was just a twisted one-off.

Frustrated and angry, she was on the cusp of giving up, when suddenly she chanced upon an image that stopped her in her tracks. She had clicked on it more in hope than in expectation – it was on a site which explored Viking beliefs and rituals – but now it had her full attention. It was a cruel, unsettling image, but one which made Emilia's heart thump.

It was a carbon copy of Ross's crime scene photos.

132

'"Oliver Winter joined us from our Stockholm office in 1991, where he had worked as a compliance officer."'

Helen was on Bahcon's official website.

'"He now leads our Compliance Unit in the UK, his brief covering all aspects of engineering across our network of –"'

'Any mention of family?' Charlie interrupted.

'Just says he lives locally.'

'I'll check the National Archives,' Hudson suggested, typing quickly. 'If he got divorced over here, there should be a record.'

Helen returned her gaze to the official photo on the company web page. In it, Winter looked purposeful and contented, a far cry from the careworn individual she had encountered at the hospital.

'Here you go. A petition for divorce was filed in 1993, and was granted soon after. So, Winter and his wife, Alice, come over here at the beginning of the nineties. Julia must already have been on the scene.'

'She would have been a year old,' Charlie replied, flicking through her notes.

'Perhaps the marriage was already in trouble, or maybe Alice just didn't like living in a foreign country . . . ?'

'Could have been very isolating,' Helen added. 'If she was at home alone bringing up the baby. What does her Facebook page say?'

Hudson was already on it, a lovely picture of Alice, her husband and her teenage daughter, filling the screen.

'She lives in Stockholm with husband Peter and daughter Lilly. Says she's lived there her whole life.'

'She's blanked it out, it's like she never even came here. So the move to England, the marriage, was a mistake . . .'

'But when she goes back home, the baby stays here,' Charlie added.

Helen looked at her colleagues. This was their most intriguing finding so far. Had Alice Winter willingly given the baby up? Or had she been pressured into it? Was her desire to erase her past due to guilt, shame or something else?

'Must have been strange back then, a mother choosing not to live with her child . . .'

'Still would be now, though no one would say it to your face,' Charlie commented ruefully. 'Let's see what he has to say about it all.'

Charlie now pulled up Oliver Winter's Facebook page. Immediately, a profile photo filled the screen – a beautiful snap of a young Julia, aged perhaps fifteen or sixteen, laughing on the beach.

'She was a pretty girl,' Helen said, a touch of sadness in her voice.

'And he certainly loved her.'

It was true. Winter's posts were sporadic, but had a common theme. They were an extended roll call of Julia's achievements and virtues: her victory in a short-story competition, her success at Grade 5 cello, her swimming gala triumphs, her endeavours to raise money for Cancer Research.

'Never writes anything about himself, does he?' Helen observed.

'No, it's all about her . . .'

'What does he say around the time of her suicide attempt?'

Charlie scrolled forward, only to find a sudden jump in the time line.

'Very little,' she replied, taking in the details. 'He posts early in her university career. Look, there's a picture of the pair of them at her matriculation.'

They feasted on the image of a happy, proud father with his daughter.

'Then nothing for . . . almost a year. After that, he mentions her accident – he used the same phrase when we met him – and gives updates on her progress.'

Charlie flicked through them. Initially stunned and sober, the posts gradually became more positive, Winter speaking glowingly of her progress, even her ability to communicate with him, before becoming darker again as her condition deteriorated suddenly.

'He's pretty pissed off,' Charlie murmured, almost to herself, as she read his most recent posts.

'With whom?' Helen asked.

'Everyone. Initially he just gives the facts – hospital-born pneumonia – but then starts firing off at anyone and everyone. Doctors, nurses, life, God, his ex-wife of course.'

'"I hope that heartless whore is happy with her new life",' Hudson said, reading over her shoulder. 'That's a nice touch . . .'

'No mention of Campbell, Scott, Morgan, though.'

'Hardly likely to be. Either they're unconnected and thus irrelevant. Or he *did* set out to harm them, but decided against giving them prior warning.'

'Either way, we need to talk to him,' Helen said, rising. 'You stay here, dig out as much as you can about the nature and timing of Julia's suicide attempt. I'll find Winter.'

Helen snatched up her keys and made to leave. But as she did so, her phone buzzed. Removing it from her pocket, she was surprised to discover that she'd received a message from Emilia Garanita. It was short and sweet, reading: 'Killings are Viking sacrifice. See Uppsala.'

Surprised, Helen crossed back to her desk. Turning the laptop towards her, she googled 'Uppsala sacrifice' and immediately a selection of thumbnail images sprang up on screen. She clicked on the first one, keen to see what Emilia had meant by her cryptic text. Even as she did so, Hudson and Charlie gathered around, intrigued and confused by her sudden about-turn.

For a moment, time seemed to stand still. The pencil sketch on screen showed a half-naked man, hanging upside down from a tree. There was a small crowd around him, some of whom seemed to be involved in his execution, others merely staring at the pool of blood gathering on the forest floor beneath him.

'It's called "The Blood Sacrifice",' Helen murmured, speed-reading the text. 'It was the ultimate form of atonement for those who had sinned.'

Helen read on, devouring the details.

'Uppsala was the one place this kind of sacrifice was witnessed first-hand, by a travelling merchant. Where is that?'

Hudson had pulled up Google Maps.

'Central Sweden, north of Stockholm. But it's only a few miles from Haga . . .'

'Where Winter was born,' Charlie added, picking up on Hudson's thread.

'Presumably he would have known about these myths, then. Been told about them when he was a boy perhaps?'

And now, as Helen said this, another thought landed. Typing quickly, she pulled up another image, maximizing it so that Charlie and Hudson could see. It was a photo of a Viking helmet, perfectly preserved in a Stockholm museum, and the sight of it silenced them all once more. There were no horns on this helmet, like in the comic books of old, just a smooth, metal skull cap, with a cross-piece to protect the cheeks and nose and above it two huge, ghostly eyeholes.

133

Helen burst through the doors and hurried across the atrium. Ignoring the scrutiny of the hospital receptionist, she marched towards the lift bank. She had already visited the high-dependency unit and knew exactly where to go.

Less than a minute later, she was traversing the dull-grey linoleum that led to the unit entrance. People looked up as she passed, intrigued by her urgency, but she paid them no heed. As she approached the double doors, an elderly woman walked through, holding them open for Helen, smiling sympathetically at her. Helen returned the favour and disappeared inside.

There were only a handful of beds in the unit. Visits were strictly regulated, given the severity of the patients' conditions, but the hours were more generous, presumably due to the chance of a sudden turn for the worse. Oliver Winter had been stationed by his daughter's bed when they visited earlier in the week, but to Helen's surprise he was nowhere to be seen today. Julia lay alone and unconscious in her bed, her only company the steadily beeping machines that were keeping her alive.

'You've just missed him.'

Helen turned to see a young nurse approaching.

'Are you a relative? If so, I'm going to have to ask you to sign in –'

'Detective Inspector Helen Grace, Hampshire Police,' she informed the nurse, retrieving her warrant card.

'Oh, I see . . .'

'I need to have a word with Mr Winter. Are you expecting him back?'

'Normally, he never leaves during daytime visiting,' she replied, recovering her smile. 'Well, not until we kick him out, anyway. I'm not sure what happened today. One minute he was here, then the next he was gone. One of the other nurses said he got a phone call, that he'd had to go home urgently, but we were to call him if there was –'

'He didn't say if he was coming back then?' Helen interrupted gently.

'Not that I know of, sorry,' the young nurse replied, shrugging apologetically, before casting a glance over her shoulder. 'Anyway, I'd better get back to my duties.'

Helen sent her on her way, frustrated by Winter's absence, but intrigued by the nurse's testimony. How was Winter reconciling his attentive care for his daughter with his work schedule? He was senior management, but seemed to spend entire days, perhaps even the whole week, at the hospital. Was he on compassionate leave? Had he quit? More importantly, had the young nurse unwittingly cast a penetrating light on the timings of the crimes?

Helen was increasingly convinced that Oliver Winter had initiated these murders, perhaps even carried them out himself. He knew the area well, having lived here for twenty-five years, and was a trained engineer, presumably capable of designing and constructing homemade weapons. If their theories were correct, he also had a strong motive for wanting to harm the three victims. If they *were* right, if Winter was their perpetrator, then his nocturnal sorties suddenly made perfect sense too. They had assumed that the killer chose the cover of darkness to facilitate his attacks, or because he had a job that kept him occupied during waking hours. But maybe there was a very simple reason why these murders took place at night.

Because love kept him here during the day.

134

She paced to and fro, drawing hard on her cigarette. Alice Winter had known this moment was coming – that she had to confront it head on – but still her impending reunion with her former husband left her feeling nauseous and tense.

Their marriage had been short-lived and a mistake. She was only twenty, barely more than a child, when she'd met Oliver in a Stockholm bar. She was a country girl, dazzled by his confidence, his sophistication and charm, so much so that she'd got swept up in their whirlwind romance, marrying him six months to the day after they first met.

While they'd been living in Sweden, things had been ok. Oliver expected a lot and could fly off the handle, but they were happy enough. Then she'd fallen pregnant and, shortly after that, while she was still struggling with baby blues, they had moved to England. No discussion, no hesitation, they had just followed Oliver's career ambition and suddenly she found herself living in Southampton with a small baby. She barely saw anyone during the day and Oliver was moody and monosyllabic at night, the new job proving more stressful than he'd expected. Alice didn't speak English and in the pre-Facebook age it was easy to lose touch with family and friends back home. In truth, she'd been miserable from the day they landed.

Oliver had been shocked at first, when she'd told him she wanted to go home, but responded with characteristic decisiveness. He told her she could go, if she wanted, but he would be staying in England, with Julia. Then it was her turn to be poleaxed – he was so clinical, so precise in his destruction of their marriage – but in truth a part of her was relieved. She had never planned on being a mother so young – she felt trapped, helpless, a failure. And though it broke her heart when baby Julia looked up at her with love in her eyes, their split presented her with an unexpected opportunity: the chance to start again. Of course, when it came to it, she hesitated, trying to negotiate a compromise agreement with Oliver, but he was implacable. He would get full custody of his beloved daughter and Alice would get her freedom. So, shamefaced, she had returned to her family and had been living with the guilt ever since.

'Get the fuck away from my house.'

She was jerked from her memories by her ex-husband's voice. Tossing her cigarette in the gutter, she turned to face him.

'Believe me, I don't want to be here, Oliver. But you haven't given me any choice.'

'Bullshit.'

'I've messaged you countless times, asking you how Julia is, where she's being treated, but you never respond.'

'We had an agreement, Alice. I thought you understood the terms.'

Alice stared at him. He was older, gaunter, but somehow harder too. He'd always had a twinkle, but this was gone now, replaced by something altogether more disquieting. He had never been overtly violent in their marriage, though he had lashed out on occasion, but he seemed far more intimidating than she remembered him.

'Things change, Oliver,' she responded bravely, refusing to be cowed. 'I made mistakes, lots of them, but I'm older now, more mature. And if Julia, *our* daughter, hasn't got long left, then I want to see her.'

'To make your peace with her?' he replied, sarcastically.

'To tell her I love her, yes.'

She felt tears coming, but shook them away, refusing to give him the satisfaction.

'Well, I'm sorry, it's not going to happen.'

'I have a letter from my lawyer – a *British* lawyer – applying to Hampshire family services for an emergency access order.' She handed the letter to him. 'Now, you can fight it, but you'll lose. In which case, they may choose to review custody arrangements.'

But Oliver just shook his head, tearing the letter in two, before stepping forward to open the front door.

'You're not seeing her.'

'Yes, I am,' she challenged him, raising her voice.

'Not while I still have breath in my body.'

'I have come from Sweden to see my daughter,' she protested, grabbing hold of his arm, as he tried to brush past her. 'And I am not going home until I've done so. So, you'll stay here and talk to me. We are *having* this conversation, Oliver . . .'

She was virtually shouting and now, for the first time, her former husband seemed to hesitate. He looked around him, clocking a couple of local residents across the road, who were staring at them unapologetically.

'Inside,' he barked.

Grabbing her by the arm, he propelled her inside the house, slamming the door shut behind them.

135

'There's no way we can allow you access.'

The consultant stood directly in front of her, blocking her path.

'She is in a stable condition, but that's the best that can be said for her. She's been suffering from acute pneumonia for several weeks now – her lungs are shot, her immune system is compromised.'

'But her father visits her daily.'

'Under strictly monitored conditions and –'

'Even so, he's in there every day, talking to her. And he swears blind she is capable of understanding and even responding.'

'It's true that Doctor Ellis has had some success in com-municating with her –'

'Exactly.'

'But that was when Julia was in better shape.'

'And it's your opinion that me talking to her will *directly* endanger her life?'

Now Baines paused.

'Well, no, I can't say that for certain. But try to understand that her body is basically shutting down. We are keeping her alive in the hope that we may see some improvement, but honestly it would be a miracle. In reality, we are looking at a managed decline.'

'Which makes it even more important that I talk to her. I believe she was the victim of a very serious crime nearly a decade ago, a crime which she is probably the only remaining witness to.'

'I'm sorry, I can't allow it,' Baines insisted, shaking his head. 'The stress of being interviewed by a police officer, of reliving past trauma . . . well, I've no idea what the effect on her might be. And as her father isn't here currently –'

'Another reason why I need to interview her *now.*'

The consultant paused, the implications of what Helen had said striking home. He had no idea what crime Oliver Winter might, or might not, be accused of, but his imagination was running wild. Helen noticed beads of sweat pricking his forehead.

'Look, I will be as brief as I can,' Helen continued. 'And I will make every effort to avoid distressing her. But I do need to talk to her.'

Helen was staring directly at Baines and, finally, after a long-fought battle, she began to see some understanding in his expression.

'So, please, page Doctor Ellis. Do whatever you have to. But we need to do this *now.*'

136

'How does it work?'

Helen was cocooned in the HDU with Dr Louise Ellis. The room had been cleared of visitors and they were alone, save for Julia, who lay just out of earshot. The young woman, who had numerous tubes attached to her arms, now had electrodes attached to her forehead and temples too.

'It's a system that was trialled in the States for victims of road traffic accidents with severe head injuries. These were people in permanent vegetative states – they were unresponsive, the hospitals were angling to turn off life support, but tests proved that many of them *could* still hear what was being said to them. More than that, they could process it and respond.'

'But how do you understand what they're saying? How can they respond in terms we recognize?'

'They can't. Or at least, they can't form sentences, but they can give a simple "yes" or "no". Basically, different parts of the brain engage, depending on the kind of thing you're thinking about. If, for example, you're thinking about doing something active – running, dancing – the cerebrum at the front of your brain becomes active. If you're thinking about something visual, like a beautiful sunset for example, then the cortex at the rear of your brain engages.'

'So you ask a question,' Helen clarified, picking up on this, 'and if she wants to answer "yes" she thinks about running, and if she wants to answer "no" she imagines a sunset?'

Dr Ellis nodded, gesturing to a high-resolution monitor to the side of Julia's bed.

'The screen illuminates whichever side of the brain she's engaging. It's not foolproof, but it's been pretty effective. She and her father had quite lengthy conversations in the past. More recently, it's been one-way traffic of course, him talking to her, which I didn't think was necessarily a good idea. When you're in a bad way, you need all the help and encouragement you can get, but it can be very stressful to be bombarded with information which you have no control over.'

Helen glanced at the young woman, who looked so peaceful in her hospital bed. It did seem cruel to disturb her, but Helen had no choice, so turning to Dr Ellis once more, she said:

'I'm ready.'

Helen sat close to Julia, perched by the side of the bed. Dr Ellis stood to the other side, hushed and discreet. Clearing her throat, Helen began:

'Hello, Julia. My name is Helen Grace. I'm a police officer and I'm here to help you.'

Helen looked to Dr Ellis, who nodded to her to continue.

'If you do not want to talk to me, I'll understand. Just signal "no" and I will leave you alone. But I know you have suffered, now and in the past, and I think there is perhaps a lot you could tell me, if you were able to do so.'

The monitor, the ghostly shadow of Julia's brain, remained lifeless, but Helen persisted.

'I'm currently investigating some very serious crimes. Three people have been killed, people you know. Tom Campbell. Lauren Scott. Caleb Morgan. Now I'm sure it must be surprising, even upsetting, to hear those names again, but I'd like to ask you some questions about them. If that's ok with you?'

Still nothing. Concerned, Helen looked anxiously at Dr Ellis again, only to find her nodding meaningfully at the screen. Helen returned her gaze to the monitor to see the front part of Julia's brain flare briefly, before receding to grey once more. It was odd how beautiful it looked – the vivid flash of green before the return to monochrome.

'Thank you, Julia. Now we know these people were your friends, that you lived with Lauren for a time. But I think they may have harmed you in some way . . .'

Helen hesitated for a moment, before continuing:

'About two months before your accident at the bridge, you all went to a party. A full-moon party in the New Forest. We believe that it was instigated by Caleb Morgan and that he had a particular purpose in mind. Julia, I want to ask you if Caleb attacked you that night?'

There was a long, long pause, then the front of her brain lit up once more. Helen felt a rush of emotions – a charge of excitement that finally they were making progress, tempered by deep sadness for Julia. She had been barely more than a girl when the attack took place.

'Did he rape you?'

Another affirmative. Helen felt her anger growing, but she swallowed it down.

'Did Lauren and Tom witness the attack?'

This time the rear of her brain lit up. Helen hesitated, momentarily wrong-footed, then continued, feeling her way:

'Did you tell anyone about your ordeal though? You lived with Lauren. Did you tell her?'

After a brief delay, the front part of Julia's brain glowed.

'Did you tell the police?'

Seeing Julia answer 'no', Helen pondered her next question, then asked:

'Did Lauren tell you not to?'

A resounding 'yes', the front portion of Julia's brain flaring strongly this time. Now a picture was starting to emerge – the attack, the devastation afterwards, but also an attempt by Lauren Scott, possibly Campbell too, to limit the damage. Perhaps they'd been in thrall to Morgan, perhaps he'd had some hold over them. Either way, they had apparently fought his corner, turning on Julia when they should have helped her.

'And does . . . does your father know about this? The attack? The attempt to silence you?'

Another affirmative.

'I know this may be hard for you to answer honestly, but we really need to know the truth, Julia. Did your father . . . do anything about it? Once he found out what had happened to you?'

For once, the screen remained blank.

'You were the victim of a gross injustice, Julia. Caleb Morgan should have been arrested and tried, Lauren Scott and Tom Campbell too possibly. But revenge is not justice. Because innocents suffer. Lauren Scott was pregnant, she had a partner who loved her, Tom Campbell too, people who are grieving now, who are suffering just like you. So, please, if you know, tell me. Did your father murder Caleb Morgan, Lauren Scott and Tom Campbell?'

Another excruciatingly long pause, then the front part of Julia's brain glowed green. Helen breathed out, long and slow. So here, finally, was the answer to the riddle that had been perplexing them for so long.

Having wondered previously what Oliver Winter talked to her so earnestly about, day in day out, she had begun to ask herself whether he might have 'involved' Julia in his scheme, telling her of his actions in the hope of assuaging his guilt and providing her with some sense of satisfaction, of justice.

410

But it was one-way traffic, as Julia hadn't had the opportunity to respond, which was why Helen asked one, final question.

'And would you like it to stop, Julia?'

Helen looked from the girl to the screen. A second later, the front of her brain flared bright green.

137

'Enough!'

He spat the word out with unconcealed venom.

'You've said what you came to say. And I've given you my answer. There's nothing for you here, so go.'

He took her by the arm, but Alice shook him off. They had been arguing for the best part of an hour, but she wasn't finished yet.

'Look, Oliver, I know seeing me is painful, that what I'm asking you makes you feel angry. And if you want me to say that I messed up, that I treated her badly, then I'm happy to do so. I was wrong to do what I did.'

She had tried threatening him with legal action, she had appealed to his strong sense of morality, arguing that she had the right to see her own daughter, but nothing had cut any ice with him and she had grown tired of repeating herself. Her only hope now was to play his game, to abase herself in the hope that he might soften his stance.

'For a mother to abandon her child like that . . . I can make excuses about my youth, my state of mind, but none of them would make it any better.'

She didn't believe this – she *had* been young and he *had* bullied her into a bad decision – but she felt it was what he wanted to hear.

'And believe me, Oliver, I have regretted it ever since.'

'So much so you found yourself a brand-new family.'

'What else was I supposed to do? There was nothing for

me here – you'd made that very clear – and I still had my whole life ahead of me.'

'So why now? Why come back now, when you have your nice new life? Why come back to this?'

'We've been through this,' Alice replied, failing to conceal her exasperation. 'I have a daughter, a daughter who had no idea that she had a half-sister until recently. For her sake, I had to come –'

'You shouldn't have told her.'

'But how could I not? Julia is her flesh and blood. She's *my* child.'

'No, she's *my* child. You gave up any right to her the day you left.'

His words cut deep. Alice desperately wanted to respond, to justify herself, but he talked over her.

'I'm the one who brought her up, who educated her. I took her to dance classes, pony clubs, I told her about periods, I comforted her when she got dumped. *I* did all that, not you.'

'Oliver, please . . .'

'I got her through her exams, helped her get into university and when . . . and when she had her accident, *I* looked after her. I've been looking after her for nine years, Alice.'

'I didn't know about her accident, I didn't know about any of it.'

'Because you didn't care. Because you didn't ask.'

'You would have told me to go to hell.'

'And I would have been right to do so. You're weak, Alice. And selfish. She was better off without you.'

Tears pricked Alice's eyes. Oliver's words stung, partly because she suspected he might be right. But she refused to be cowed, there was too much at stake.

'If you'd told me she was struggling, if you'd told me what

happened, I would have come back, of course I would, but you deliberately kept it from me.'

Oliver laughed, long and bitterly.

'You kept it from me to hurt me. Just like you're trying to hurt me now.'

'You have no idea,' he replied witheringly. 'No idea what suffering means. With your nice house and your lovely family . . .'

He was staring at her intently, in a way that made her feel distinctly uncomfortable. Having been furious with her earlier, now he seemed like he was enjoying himself, enjoying her distress.

'I have spent every spare moment by Julia's bedside. Caring for her, talking to her, communicating with her. Giving her reason to live. I have sacrificed my own happiness, any chance of another relationship, even my job. And you know what? I did it happily, willingly, because I *love* my daughter, because she needs me.'

'I know that, Oliver, and I am so grateful to you –'

'And do you know why she needed me, why she was hurting so badly?'

'Because she was struggling with her work, like you said. Because she failed her exams –'

'Because she was raped.'

Alice stared at him, stunned. She felt like she'd been hit in the stomach, like she couldn't breathe.

'Raped by an animal who preyed on her naïvety, her youth.'

'No, Oliver . . .'

'This was a girl, *my* girl, who had her whole life ahead of her. She was bright, and caring, and funny, and beautiful . . . and he took that all away.'

'I don't believe you, I don't . . .'

But she *did* believe him. The naked fury in his eyes was not an act.

'I didn't know at first, she never told me. But one day I came home to find a farewell note, next to her diary. It was all in there, believe me, but I only read a few words before I was out the door. I had a sense of where she might be going, but I didn't get there in time.'

He was breathing heavily, as if the emotion might explode from him at any point.

'I saw her . . . I saw her on the bridge. I called out to her, but I was too late.'

In spite of everything, Alice reached out to him, grasping his arm. What Oliver was telling her was beyond awful – and it broke her heart.

'I held her while we waited for the ambulance, kneeling there on the road. I thought I was going to lose her.'

'But you didn't, you saw her through it.'

'And maybe I shouldn't have done.'

'Don't say that. You did the right thing.'

'Did I? Nine years she's been in that bed. Suffering all sorts of indignities, all sorts of procedures, and for what? She's lying in that bed now, her lungs filling up, drowning in her own mucus . . .'

'Please, stop,' Alice cried, unable to bear it.

And to her surprise, he did, his anger and distress suddenly seeming to burn itself out.

'You shouldn't have had to deal with this alone.'

'Who was I going to call? You?'

It was said with vicious sarcasm, but she ignored it.

'The police. You should have gone to the police.'

'Really? When she was in a coma, unable to talk, unable to confirm what had happened?'

'You had the diary.'

'And he had two friends, two *accomplices*, who were pre-pared to say it never happened, that Julia was making it up. Do you think we would have got justice?'

'But it's the police's job –'

'To protect rapists and liars. I wasn't going to put her fate in their hands. Julia is mine, she's always been mine.'

For the first time, Alice felt genuinely unnerved. There was something in his intensity that scared her.

'What about if we go to the police now? You have the diary, we could do it together.'

But Oliver shook his head.

'I mean it, Oliver. I can stay for as long as it takes. Make sure this man is questioned, charged.'

'You're wasting your time.'

'How can you say that?'

'You're too late.'

Such was the tone of finality that Alice now paused.

'I don't understand.'

'You never did.'

'Where is this man? What's happened to him?'

'He's dead.'

It was said so calmly that for a moment Alice was speech-less, before she gathered herself sufficiently to respond:

'The others, then? The ones who lied. Surely they can be –'

'They're dead too.'

Now Alice froze. There was a hint of triumph in his tone, but surely such a thing was impossible?

'How did they die, Oliver?'

But her former husband just stared at her.

'What have you done?'

Still nothing.

'Please, Oliver, you're scaring me. Tell me what's happened.'

He continued to stare at her, enjoying her discomfort. The atmosphere seemed to have been sucked from the room – it was hushed, tense, febrile – but now the heavy silence was broken by a nagging, insistent sound. The sound of sirens.

Immediately, Oliver reacted, rushing to the window and peering outside. There was no doubt that the sirens were getting louder, getting closer. Turning, he hurried towards the door, but Alice reached out, grabbing hold of his jacket.

'Tell me. Tell me what you've done.'

He flung out an elbow at her, smashing her in the ribs. But still she clung on, despite the agony that seared through her. He struggled to escape her grip, grabbing her hair as he tried to wrench her off. But this was one battle that she was determined not to lose.

Suddenly she *had* to know what her ex-husband had become.

138

She roared down the street, bringing her bike alongside Hudson's vehicle. As she'd sprinted along the hospital corridors, Helen had called Charlie, relaying Julia's damning testimony. Her friend had snapped into action and by the time Helen made it to her Kawasaki, the team had been deployed.

Helen had wasted no time burning across town to Upper Shirley. The sound of sirens grew louder as she neared Winter's home address and, picking out Hudson's car, she'd slid in just behind him. His flashing lights cleared the way for them both, making progress swift. Now they were approaching the family home, and signalling Hudson to take the front, Helen peeled off, swinging around one corner, then another, into the adjacent road.

Counting the houses down, she came to a skidding stop outside Winter's back gate. Killing the engine, she leapt off her bike and rattled the door handle. She wasn't surprised to find it locked, but didn't hesitate, placing her foot on the wrought-iron handle and hauling herself over.

She landed deftly on the other side and was quickly on the move once more. Without breaking stride, she pulled her baton from her belt, extending it fully, as she hastened towards the rear of the property. Something told her Winter would not come quietly.

She was now at the back door. Reaching out, she made a grab for the handle, but before she could do so, the door was yanked open. Instinctively, she raised her arm, as a burly form hurtled towards her.

But it was only Joseph Hudson. He looked flustered and disappointed, which told her everything she needed to know.

They were too late.

139

'I didn't know what he was doing. I didn't know anything about this.'

Helen was inclined to believe her. Alice Winter was deathly pale, except for the smear of blood on her mouth and cheek. The upturned furniture suggested a struggle had taken place, as did the bloody tissue clamped to her nose.

'I came to see my daughter,' the shocked woman insisted. 'I knew she was in hospital, that she was in a bad way . . . but . . . but I didn't know that she'd been attacked, let alone that Oliver would . . .'

She petered out, still struggling to process her recent discoveries.

'You had no contact with your husband since you left this country?'

'No. I tried to call him, my lawyers tried to call him . . .'

'And he never told you about Julia?'

She shook her head sadly.

'He wanted her to himself. And wanted to punish me perhaps.'

It was cruel, it was unpleasant, but it made sense.

'Was he ever violent towards you?'

'Occasionally, but nothing bad.'

'So he's never done anything like this before?'

'Of course not. But he did National Service in Sweden – men had to back then – so he would have known about combat, about camouflage techniques.'

'I see. And did he hunt during your marriage? Or go on a shoot?'

'No, but he did back in Sweden. When he was a little boy, his grandfather used to take him. They would hunt elk with bows. That's illegal now, but back then –'

'So, he would have known how to use a bow,' Helen interrupted. 'How to use a crossbow, specifically?'

'Of course,' Alice replied, matter-of-factly. 'His grandfather had several, swore by them, and when they'd finished for the day, he would give it to him to clean it. Oliver loved that bow . . .'

Helen stared at her, as Alice concluded:

'. . . and he knew every inch of it.'

140

He walked on, heading ever deeper into the sanctuary of the forest. He had known this moment would come and, though he had been rattled by the sudden unravelling of his plans, following Alice's arrival, he now felt oddly calm. He had long ago imagined how this would play out and he was ready.

Pausing, Winter laid down his heavy rucksack. He stared for a moment at the still, quiet woodland, enjoying the feeling of satisfaction these surroundings gave him, before opening his pack and pulling out the contents. The sun was dipping behind the horizon now, its final, golden beams peeking through the lower branches, which meant the time was right.

For the past nine years, his life had been consumed by suffering. Utter, heart-wrenching despair, punctured by bouts of furious, frenzied anger and moments of total weariness. His days he had devoted to Julia and they had been wonderful, but also awful, seeing the hollow remnant of his daughter lying comatose on the bed in front of him. But this was nothing compared to the anguish of the nights, when the crushing loneliness took hold, when he had no company save for his regrets, his bile and his despair. He would try to connect with Julia, spending hours in her bedroom attempting to harness her goodness, her positivity, her grace, but with each passing year he found it harder to still the voices growing inside him.

So he'd sought out her attackers, her betrayers, on Facebook, on LinkedIn, on Twitter, devouring the details of their lives. He'd learnt about their tribulations and setbacks, but also the accompanying highs – new homes, cars, holidays, even Campbell's engagement. At first, he had been consumed with bitterness, that they should still be living, laughing, having fun, then later he became taken over by rage, as he learnt from local newspaper reports that Morgan had struck again, ruined more young lives. And as darkness fell, nagging, insistent demons circled him, demanding vengeance, demanding atonement. In the end, he had given in to them, embracing the change in himself.

After that, he spent the nights preparing, fashioning his bow, an exact replica of the one he'd enjoyed so much as a boy, preparing his battle armour. He had felt uncomfortable, even self-conscious at first, sliding on the dark leather which encased his torso, his arms, his legs, but over time he had come to thrill to the feeling of power and invulnerability it gave him. The hood too gave him comfort, concealing him from prying eyes, from anyone who might chance upon him in the gloomy forest, but it was the helmet, fashioned by his own hands in his workshop, which completed the change. It was simple, it was strong, but somehow it made him. It alone seemed to have the power to banish Oliver Winter and replace him with someone bigger, better, more powerful. When dressed for battle, there was no longer any doubt, any fear, any remorse. The dogged, diligent, caring man, who politely thanked his daughter's carers, even as they plotted to switch off her life support . . . that craven weakling vanished the moment the helmet descended.

Then he was something else. Then he was a child of the night.

141

She roared along the tarmac, her eyes glued to the road. Occasionally Helen would steal a glance in her mirror, but Hudson was already a speck in the distance, the blue flashing light the only part of his car that was still visible. She was breaking protocol by not waiting for him, but every second counted, now they knew that Winter was in the forest once more.

A stolen Land Rover had been picked up leaving the western edge of the city, before disappearing into country lanes. The vehicle, which had been taken from a car park in Woolston three weeks ago, was on the team's watch list and a traffic unit had been scrambled to intercept it. Half an hour later, an eagle-eyed officer had spotted the old 4x4, hidden in foliage near Burgate, on the fringes of the forest. The vehicle, whose boot contained an eight-foot length of rubber tubing, was unlocked, the keys still in the ignition. This latter detail told Helen all she needed to know. Winter had no plans to escape.

Was he intending to harm himself? Or make one last stand? Either way, they needed to engage him fast. Despite all their warnings, there were still people turning up at the forest, out of either ignorance or brazenness, not to mention the residents who lived near the fringes of the forest. If Winter was abroad now, they needed to bring him in. There was no sign of his crossbow in the house, his workshop or his vehicle, so they were assuming that he was armed and dangerous.

Two tactical firearms units were making their way to the

forest. She prayed they wouldn't need them, but feared they would. Winter had crossed a line, had a taste for death now, and it would be hard to bring him in by conventional means, especially in such unfamiliar territory.

Helen felt a tingle of excitement, even as tension gripped her insides. She was speeding towards their suspect, towards an uncertain and possibly violent conclusion to this complex case, but finally the perpetrator was in their sights.

The end was at hand.

142

He padded through the forest, taking care not to make a sound. Many times he'd walked these paths, first with Alice and their child, then later with Julia, and he knew them like the back of his hand. But they meant something different to him now. Previously, the forest had been a distraction, a break from the cares of the day. Now it was his sanctuary, his cocoon.

Some people found the huge branches that stretched overhead intimidating, even sinister, but to him they appeared like giant arms gathering him into the fold. The forest appeared to him now as a friend, no, more than that, it was an ally, a place where he could be what he needed to be.

Had he encountered Caleb Morgan in everyday life, would he have had the courage to strike him down? Campbell and Scott too? During waking hours, surrounded by the trappings of his daily existence, he felt uncertain, frustrated, impotent. But in the forest it was different. Here he could slough off any instinct for mercy and pity, giving in to anger and hatred. Killing those horses had been unpleasant, but necessary – an important step on the journey, as he honed his skills and grew into his new identity. Taking on the mantle of the hunter made him feel taller, stronger, untouchable, but it wasn't just that. The very nature of time seemed to change once he was under the canopy of these aged branches. Here time seemed to be on his side.

When he was closing in on his prey, when they were exhausted, desperate, time seemed to slow. He could take in every detail – the anguish in their eyes, the blood on their skin, their dirty fingernails, as they reached up to him imploringly. Seconds seemed to stretch – it was as if he saw the bolts in slow motion, bursting free of their constraints and arrowing through the air, before slamming into their quarry. These were the moments he savoured – the look of shock on their faces, as the lifeblood leaked from them.

He had experienced something like this before. But that experience had been less pleasant, the worst of his life. Having found Julia's suicide note, he had raced to Itchen Bridge, convinced she would head there, as others had before. Had the traffic not been so bad that day, had he arrived home a few minutes earlier, then maybe he would have caught her. As it was, he got to the bridge just as she climbed over the safety railings. He had called to her, shouted and screamed, but she seemed not to hear him. He saw her take one careful step on to the ledge, then another. He was sprinting, but somehow wasn't going fast enough, his legs moving in slow motion. He was screaming. Surely she would hear him and stop? But instead she simply let go, hovering uncertainly on the edge for an eternity, before spreading out her arms and taking flight.

He had never known time to warp like that, to taunt him with the possibility of reaching her, only to dash his hopes. Since then he had enjoyed this strange, magical experience a number of times, in this place, his night-time playground.

People would judge him. Call him psychotic, deranged, but their deaths had felt *right*. It was an evening of the score, a father's duty. He would not apologize for it, nor would he bow his head and offer himself up for arrest. He had never had any plans to flee justice, to avoid the bloody reckoning, and he was determined to do this on his terms.

This whole, sorry story had started in the forest years ago and tonight it would end there too.

143

Ignoring the pain in her leg, Charlie sprinted across the tarmac, ducking low to avoid the blades. Helen had arrived at the forest, connecting with the tactical units who'd been scrambled there, and was now beginning her search. But before she'd done so, she'd called Charlie, telling her to head to the heliport. Night was falling now and the area they had to search was vast – they would need their eye in the sky if they were to flush Winter out.

The pilot opened the door and Charlie clambered inside, strapping herself in. This was only her second time in the police helicopter and the noise, energy and power of the machine were exhilarating. In under five minutes, they would be above the New Forest, firing their beam into the darkness. The helicopter's light was intensely powerful and would startle the forest dwellers as it raked its depths. Would it catch Winter in its beam? Once he was in view and they could monitor his progress from the air, there would be no escape for him.

'Ready?'

Charlie nodded, giving the pilot the thumbs up. Immediately, he hit the throttle, the blades whirring deafeningly above, and seconds later the whole aircraft rose into the air, wobbling momentarily above the launch pad, before swinging away into the night sky.

144

His car bounced over the turf, skidding to a halt just short of the forest edge.

Helen's Kawasaki was parked nearby, flanking the tactical support units' vans, but there was no sign of the woman herself. Cursing, Hudson slammed the door shut and walked towards the bike. He had done his best to keep up, but it was an uneven fight and he had lost sight of her on the ring road. Driving even faster, he'd hoped to rendezvous with her before the hunt began, to be in the thick of the action when Winter was finally caught, but she hadn't waited. How he wished he'd had his bike with him when the call had come in, rather than his cumbersome pool car.

Another vehicle had now pulled up and Hudson saw DC McAndrew climb out, followed by Osbourne. The others were close behind and soon they would all be deployed, penetrating the deepest corners of the forest in search of Oliver Winter. Hudson had no doubt their chief suspect was in there somewhere, which made him extremely nervous. Winter had retreated there for a reason, knowing full well he stood little chance of escaping capture in the real world. Out in the open, all manner of means could be deployed to bring him in, but the forest was his terrain. Within its confines, he would have the advantage. Even experienced police marksmen would be out of their depth, unfamiliar with its hidden paths and secret hiding places. What would that mean for them? And for Helen?

'What do you want to do?'

McAndrew and Osbourne had joined him.

'Do you want to wait or . . . ?'

Hudson looked at McAndrew, then beyond her to the other cars now pulling up. It was a tough call – the whole team were here, but they were unarmed. Ideally they would wait until the chopper was deployed, until the third armed unit joined them. But that was on its way from Bournemouth and would take nearly an hour to get here, which was why Hudson found himself saying:

'We go in.'

Gesturing to the others to follow suit, Hudson set off, McAndrew and Osbourne falling into step close by. It was risky, it was probably foolhardy, but Hudson could see no other way.

Helen was out there in the forest, facing down a sinister, unseen danger and there was no way he was going to abandon her to her fate.

145

'Stay close.'

Her hushed command had an instant effect, the armed officers closing ranks once more, pushing forward in a tight arrowhead formation, with Helen at the tip. In normal circumstances, they would have led, as they were best placed to neutralize any immediate threat to life, but tonight was different. She was glad of their presence, but the young officers seemed jumpy, even a touch nervous, disconcerted by the all-encompassing darkness and the constant, low-level movement around them. And while she would need to call on them if they confronted Winter, she didn't want them on point should they stumble across an errant camper or forest dweller. For now, she would take the lead, being their eyes and ears as they hunted a brutal killer.

They had started from Burgate, on the western fringes of the forest, and pushed into the interior. Heading east, they had stuck to the paths, fanning out on occasion, before resuming formation, constantly scanning the gloom for signs of life. It was possible that Winter might skirt the edges of the forest, keeping out of sight, but still able to flee its confines if necessary, but something told Helen that he would head deep into the interior, taking refuge in the dark heart of the forest.

On they went, treading carefully over fallen branches, avoiding the numerous holes that littered the forest floor. They kept their torch beams low, keen to see what was directly in front of them, without advertising their progress.

Looking at the tiny beams, pin pricks by comparison with the monumental darkness of the forest, it was hard not to feel like they were looking for a needle in a haystack. But it was too late for second thoughts now. They had committed to a course of action and Helen knew they had to see it through.

She marched on, sliding her radio from her belt as she did so. Teasing it on, she turned down the volume. In the far distance, she could just make out the dull thud of the police chopper. Soon it would be time to check in with Charlie, to co-ordinate their sweep of the forest, but she would not do it yet. Any sound might alert Winter to their approach and she dared not risk that, when he already had a huge advantage.

They walked on in silence, swallowing the occasional curse as their feet hit a hidden root or rabbit hole, searching diligently for their quarry. The forest, which had been close-knit thus far, suffocatingly close at times, now seemed to thin out and to her surprise Helen thought she could see light ahead.

Increasing her pace, she moved towards it, only to find that it was moonlight, filling a small clearing. The moon was full tonight and illuminated the space below brilliantly, making the clearing look eerily beautiful, but also dangerous – it was open ground surrounded on all sides by shadowy woodland.

'Easy now . . .'

Helen held up her hand and the team slowed. Carefully, Helen stepped out into the clearing. But her entrance provoked no reaction, no movement of any kind, and cautiously the rest of the team joined her. They held their line, alert to any sign of threat, but seeing none they pressed on, emerging into the stark moonlight.

Instinctively, Helen was keen to be away – they were

sitting ducks out here. She hurried towards the far side of the clearing. She was twenty feet from the cover of darkness, now ten, now five . . . Breathing a sigh of relief, she raised her torch beam towards the dense brush once more. To find a pair of eyes staring directly at her.

'Here.'

Immediately the team swung their weapons that way, their torch beams zeroing in on their prey.

'Armed police. Lay down your —'

But before the lead officer had completed his warning, the owl had taken fright, leaving its perch and flapping wildly as it made its escape. Raising their weapons, the officers turned to Helen, who signalled her apologies and gestured to them to continue. They did so without a murmur, focused on the task in hand.

Helen was glad of their professionalism, of their determination, but whatever confidence she projected, the incident had done little to raise her spirits, or indeed her hopes. Her heart was thumping, her nerves jangling wildly, and she suddenly felt very vulnerable. The forest was so vast, so full of life, so swathed in darkness and mystery, that suddenly she sensed threat at every turn. Perhaps Winter was staring at them right now, readying himself to strike. There would be no warning, no tell-tale gunfire, just the savage impact of the bolt, as it tore into them. Helen had never felt so defenceless, so exposed before, fearing that each step might be her last.

But they had no choice, so on they went, searching remorselessly for a phantom killer who refused to reveal himself.

He reached out a hand, then suddenly pulled it back again. Even now, when he had come so far, risked so much, he was unsure if he could go through with it. It was a pathetic sight, a grown man hesitating to enter an aged phone box, but still it felt wrong, like he would be betraying himself by touching it.

Summoning his resolve, Nathaniel Martin took a step forward and hauled the heavy iron door open. It relented easily, revealing a grubby interior which reeked of urine. The occasional tourist stopped to use this relic of the pre-mobile era – Martin had spotted them several times – but mostly it was used by drunken farmers or teenagers keen to leave their mark on the proud red landmark.

Stepping inside, Martin let the door shut. The smell was even stronger now and immediately he felt assailed by a wave of claustrophobia, a growing nausea. He knew that if he hesitated now he would lose his nerve, that he would turn and retreat to the forest, so taking another step forward he plucked the plastic handset from its cradle.

Immediately, he heard the gentle purr of the dialling tone. For a moment, he was rocketed back to his teenage days, when he used to call his girlfriend in stolen moments away from the house. But those pleasurable memories were at odds with the bitter present and he wrenched himself back to the task in hand.

He had debated long and hard about what to do. He had vowed never to engage with the world, had certainly never thought he would willingly use any kind of technology again, but what was the alternative? He had known for a while now that there was something malign in the forest. But until tonight he hadn't known what – or rather who – it was.

He had left his camp for the evening, taking advantage of the darkness to check his traps. The forest had been unusually quiet tonight and in other circumstances he might not have heard him, so gentle was his footfall. But his senses had always been sharp and he had been on his guard for search parties. Straining to hear, he was sure he could pick up the gentle sound – trump, trump, trump – of someone approaching. Immediately, he had withdrawn, concealing himself in the depths of a yew tree. For reasons he couldn't explain, his heart was suddenly thumping, fear seizing him, but he kept stock-still, even as the figure crept past. Nathaniel didn't get a good look at his face – he appeared to be wearing a mask – but he couldn't miss the crossbow that he cradled. Barely daring to breathe, he'd watched as the figure walked on for another fifty feet or so, before sitting down to rest by Cooper's Lake.

Instantly, Nathaniel was on the move. The figure's back was turned to him and he took full advantage, picking his way through the forest. He kept going for half a mile, maybe more, moving swiftly, before doubling back and heading for the forest edge. From here it was a short stroll to the phone box.

Breathing out, he raised the grubby receiver to his ear. He had hoped never to do this again, but the evil abroad could not be ignored, so pulling DS Brooks's crumpled business card from his pocket, he began to dial.

147

She should have felt like a god, but in fact she just felt sick. The helicopter was circling the forest in lazy arcs, firing its high-intensity spotlight down onto the woodland. Charlie was in the box seat, afforded a view of the national park that few were lucky enough to see, but she wasn't in the mood to enjoy it. In the darkness, the huge swathe of forest looked sinister, like a blot on the landscape, prompting Charlie to imagine all manner of threats lying within. More pressingly, for her at least, the wind was strong tonight, buffeting their light craft, making it judder and buck. Charlie was not prone to motion sickness as a rule, but wave after wave of nausea swept over her, unremitting, remorseless.

She clung to the roof strap, hoping that she would manage to see the night through without vomiting. Such a lapse would be not only embarrassing, but also extremely unpleasant for her and the pilot, crammed together in the small cockpit. So, overcoming her nausea, she tried to concentrate on her job, scanning the woodland below for signs of their suspect.

But it was proving harder than she'd hoped. When she'd done this before, they'd been shadowing a fleeing suspect on the roads. Then it had been easy to pick him up – the electric-blue Vauxhall standing out like a sore thumb, as it tore around a suburban housing estate. Furthermore, it had been easy to predict where he would go, the roads looking like a Lego construction from above.

But woodland at night was a different prospect. Stay too high and they couldn't see enough. Descend too low and suddenly the forest canopy came alive, waving violently in the down draught of the rotary blades. Even when they got it just right – no easy task in the gusting wind – the spotlight wasn't foolproof. Its powerful beam illuminated much, but also created vast shadows. On more than one occasion, Charlie thought she'd seen a fleeing figure, only for it to evaporate like a mirage when she pointed the beam directly at it. She was wondering now if she was starting to imagine things, so tight were her nerves wound tonight.

'Do you want to go around again?'

They had completed one circuit of the area to the north and her pilot needed fresh instructions. Charlie was pondering what to do next – should they head south towards Helen or cut east? – when suddenly her phone started vibrating. Pulling it from her pocket, she looked down at the caller ID. It was a local number and one she didn't recognize, so she pressed reject, keen to keep the line clear. Turning to the pilot, she replied:

'I think we should head –'

But now her phone started up again. This time she answered, albeit with ill grace.

'Yes?'

'Detective Brooks, it's Nathaniel Martin.'

Charlie wasn't sure she'd heard properly over the noise of the blades.

'Sorry, who?'

'Nathaniel Martin, we met a few days ago.'

'Yes, of course . . .' Charlie replied falteringly, stumped as to how to respond.

'I'm sorry to bother you . . .'

He was speaking slowly and in an exaggeratedly polite manner, as if talking to another human being was dangerous, exotic or both. But there was a hint of urgency in his voice too, as he concluded:

'. . . but I have information that you might find useful.'

437

148

'Are you sure it was him?'

Helen had asked Charlie to repeat herself a couple of times, but she still didn't believe it.

'Yes, definitely. He talked about our encounter, knew who I was. And he was only calling me because he had my card.'

'Do you believe him?'

'I've no reason not to. He sounded genuinely angry and concerned. He loves the forest, the ponies.'

'And where did he say Winter was?'

'He last saw him resting by Cooper's Lake. It's a small lake that feeds off Latchmere Brook.'

Helen's torch beam moved over her map.

'I've got it,' she said quickly.

It was in the most remote part of the forest, which was precisely where she had led the team. This was where the first murder had taken place, was perhaps where Winter felt safest – it made sense that he would have retreated here.

'I'm about five minutes from it. Hold a position to the east, until I radio you to move. I don't want to frighten him off, now that we have the advantage.'

'Roger that.'

Helen clicked off, radioing the news to Hudson, before turning to face her armed officers once more.

'Right. Cooper's Lake. Quick and quiet, please.'

They hurried through the forest, hurdling the obstacles which lay in their path. Their torches were on their lowest setting, but such was the strength of the moonlight that the going was fairly clear. So far everything had been against them, but suddenly it felt as if the wind was at their backs.

Helen powered forward, challenging the others to keep up. She had felt on the back foot for most of this investigation, pursuing numerous false leads and dead ends. Now she felt energized and excited. Winter had eluded them for days, but at long last they had a concrete lead, a chance to bring this violent, sadistic killer to book. Helen prayed he had stayed put, or if he'd moved on that he wasn't travelling fast. If he eluded them now, it might take hours, even days, to pick up his trail again. He had already proved himself adept at blending in with the fabric of the forest.

On she surged, marvelling at how the forest seemed to open up for her. Previously it had tried to thwart her, tearing at her clothes and skin, leading her down blind alleys. But now it appeared to make way for her, presenting her with clear, open paths and well-lit vistas. On she went, barely breaking sweat, her pace steady and strong, only now realizing that she had opened up a lead over the rest of her team. Slowing down, she held up her torch beam for them to follow, then resumed her headlong charge through the gloomy woodland.

But as she did so, her foot caught something. Suddenly she felt herself plunging forward, off balance and out of control. She expected to hit the ground hard, but to her horror now felt herself falling. Her hands lashed out desperately, hoping to find some kind of purchase, but clutched only air. Moments later, her shoulder collided with something hard and she seemed to spin around, jerking violently in a dizzying 180. Now she *was* on the ground, but her descent had not slowed, she was skidding fast backwards down some kind of slope. Brambles tore at her, branches whipped her face, but she seemed to be picking up speed, rather than slowing, then suddenly she came to an abrupt halt, the back of her head hitting something hard and unyielding.

She lay there, too stunned to move. For a moment, she thought she was going to faint – the pain in her head was unbearable – but she willed herself to stay conscious. She dared not black out here.

She tried to rise, but immediately fell back again, overcome by nausea. Instinctively, her hand went to the back of her head. She was alarmed to feel fresh blood. Was any other part of her injured? Groggily, she rotated her hands, then her feet, before running her hands over her ribs. She didn't think anything was broken, yet every part of her hurt and she wasn't even sure she could move. Which made her feel distinctly uneasy.

Now, up above, she saw movement. Tiny lights dancing to and fro. To her horror, she realized that they must be the torch lights of her colleagues. But they seemed to be up in the sky, miles away from where she was. Screwing up her eyes, she tried to focus on the darkness in front of her, and only now did she get a sense of just how far she had fallen. She must have plunged a hundred feet or more, utterly failing to see the steep slope in front of her. Now her support unit was at the top, desperately searching for her, while she lay in a heap at the bottom swathed in darkness.

Had they even seen her fall? Did they know she was down here?

'Help.'

Her voice was weak and croaky.

'Help!'

She tried to shout, but she had no air in her lungs. Above her, the torch beams were moving around frantically, as if conducting some mad dance.

'I'm here.'

This was a bit louder, her desperation raising the volume. And for one thrilling moment, she thought they'd heard, the beams suddenly ceasing their wild activity. But then to her dismay, she saw the beams moving off in unison, heading away from her.

'Wait . . .'

But it was too late, they were gone. For a moment, Helen lay there, despairing, before suddenly remembering her radio. This filled her with hope and from nowhere she found the energy to scramble onto her hands and knees. She grasped at her belt . . . only to find her radio was no longer there. Nor was her baton. Panicking, she thrust her hand into her pocket, but the map was gone too. And her torch? That was presumably buried or broken on the slope above, as she could no longer make out its beam.

Struggling to her feet, Helen looked around her. But she could make nothing out, save for the outline of the swaying trees and the sound of the whistling wind. Her sturdy leathers had saved her from serious injury, but that was about the best that could be said for her in her predicament.

She was shaken. She was lost. And she was now alone in the forest.

149

He remained motionless, only his eyes moving as he watched her pick her way through the undergrowth. She was clearly disoriented, constantly changing direction as she tried to get her bearings. At one point, she had been heading directly for him, forcing him to recede further into the shadows, but then she had thought better of it, finding an easier path elsewhere.

If Fate was smiling on him, she would connect with her colleagues and move on, yet still she lingered, as if riven by indecision. She clearly did not know these woods as well as he did, but her ignorance might yet cost him dear. If she decided to stay put until her colleagues located her, he would effectively be trapped, the moonlight too strong for him to risk making a break for it.

How had they found him so quickly? It didn't make any sense. He had retreated to the woods a matter of hours earlier, driving hard into its depths, staying well away from the beaten paths. He had kept his pace up, pausing only to rest and refresh himself at Cooper's Lake, before moving on once more. He had covered another half a mile at best, before he'd spotted them – torch beams away to his left, high up on the ridge. At first it was just one, which seemed to wobble, then plummet, as its unfortunate carrier pitched over the edge. Then several more followed – six, seven, perhaps as many as eight pin pricks of light dancing at the top of the slope. These had been more cautious, eventually moving away, leaving their fallen colleague alone.

From his hiding place in the shadows of a tree, Oliver Winter had watched the prone figure scramble to her feet. He could tell from her hoarse cries that she was female, but it was only when she returned to her full height that he realized that it was Grace. She had impressed him during their conversation at the hospital – her intellect, her determination – and, besides, she was instantly recognizable from her biking leathers, even in the gloom of the forest.

Somehow she had tracked him. It seemed impossible, given that he'd had no idea himself that he would end up here, but she had managed it. Perhaps they had found the Defender and taken a flyer that he would head to the deepest point in the forest. If so, they had got lucky. They could have had no idea that this was where his beloved daughter had been attacked all those years ago.

Still she made no move to leave. In fact, she was now standing stock-still, straining to hear, hoping perhaps to pick up the sounds of her colleagues on the wind, giving her a direction to head in. And then he thought he heard them. A slow rumbling, like dozens of feet haring through the forest. But that was crazy, it sounded like a small army . . .

Now the sound became a little clearer and for the first time he realized it was coming from *above* the forest. It wasn't a human noise at all, it was mechanical. He could make out the thrum, thrum of the rotary blades and now in the distance he glimpsed a thick beam of blinding white light.

This decided it for him. He could avoid a troupe of disoriented police officers, but there would be no hiding from a helicopter. Slowly, he reached down to his side and slid a bolt from his quiver. Silently, smoothly, he slid it into the flight groove, raising the bow until it was pointing directly at Grace.

She had concerned him when he first met her. He'd had

no doubt then that she was a dangerous adversary and so it had proved. Whether through her own enterprises, or Alice's intervention, she had worked out that he was responsible for the recent murders. Having done so, she had tracked him here, cornering him in this ancient forest, denying him the chance to say goodbye to Julia. His plan had always been to confirm to Julia that justice had been done, then dedicate himself solely to her care during her last few days. But Helen Grace was going to stand in his way, and so she would have to die, along with any of her colleagues who tried to intervene.

He stared down the shaft of the bolt. Helen Grace was directly in his sights, unaware of the danger she was in. He took his time, slowing his breathing, lowering the sight line slightly so that the barb would slam into her back. This would puncture her lungs, possibly her heart, and would propel her to the ground. Then it would be a simple matter of finishing her off, before turning his attention to the other aggressors.

Grace moved slightly now, taking a step left, and briefly his sight line was blocked. For a moment, he felt a shiver of panic pulse through him, but then she took half a step back in the other direction, craning up to look at the sky. And now he didn't hesitate.

Taking a small step forward, he checked his aim once more and pulled the trigger.

150

Acting on instinct, Helen threw herself to the left. As she did so, something shot past her, landing with a heavy thud in a nearby tree. Hitting the ground, Helen rolled sideways, springing up on to her feet. Her first instinct was to see what had clipped her – angling a look behind her, she caught sight of the barb sticking out of a tree trunk – then she turned her attention to her aggressor. But he was nowhere to be seen.

Dashing behind a nearby tree, Helen flattened herself against the trunk. Without knowing it, she had been seconds from death, distracted by the bright lights in the sky. It was only the tiny, faint crack of a twig snapping, presumably as Winter steadied himself to shoot, that had warned her of the imminent peril she was in. She had no way of knowing for sure it was Winter, but her senses were heightened tonight, her body tensed for danger, and without thinking she had taken evasive action. She gave thanks that her reactions were as sharp as ever – had she been a second slower she might be lying face down on the forest floor right now.

How had Winter found her? They were some way from Cooper's Lake. Had he chanced upon her? Seen her fall? Or had he stalked her to this point? Whatever, the fact remained that he now had her pinned down. The barb had penetrated deep into the trunk, suggesting he had shot from close range. There had been a forbidding bank of foliage, and a couple of yew trees, behind her. This placed Winter approximately thirty feet away – not good odds for her, given that she was unarmed and had little cover.

Inching around the tree trunk, she strained to hear. But the forest seemed to be alive, groaning, whistling, laughing even. Furthermore, the sound of the helicopter was getting ever louder, making it virtually impossible to hear the rustling of foliage, a killer's measured creep. Taking a chance, she inched round still further, darting a look towards Winter's last position.

A loud gasp nearby. Helen yanked her head back sharply, the speeding bolt flicking her hair as it sped past and away into the darkness. Her heart pounding, Helen leaned back against the tree, clinging to its security. There was no doubt he had her totally pinned down. All she could do was wait and hope that the helicopter would scare him off, before he had a chance to loose off the fatal shot. But even as Helen darted a look skywards, she saw the helicopter moving away from her.

'No, no, no . . .'

It made perfect sense, of course. The helicopter would be heading for Cooper's Lake, searching for Winter. But this was no help to Helen in her desperate plight. She looked on, as her last hope of salvation turned away, a feeling of fear stealing over her. What chance did she have now against a remorseless killer?

One thing was certain – there was no point sitting here waiting for death to come to her. If she was going to perish in this lonely stretch of forest, she would do it on her terms. A small, fallen branch was at her feet and she picked it up carefully now. Then, taking in a huge gulp of oxygen, she hurled the stick to her right, before darting off in the opposite direction.

She broke cover, sprinting for her life. For a second or two, all was quiet. Then she heard a rush of air. Another bolt shot past her, crashing into the undergrowth beyond. This

446

miss emboldened Helen and she sprinted on, ducking low to take cover behind a hedge, before hurtling on once more. Ahead she could see a faint path, curving around out of sight behind a line of bushes. If she could get there, she would be out of Winter's sights and then –

The impact knocked her clean off her feet. Having been charging directly forward, she now found herself flying sideways, crashing in a heap on the forest floor. For a moment, she was breathless, seeing stars, then suddenly the pain consumed her. Craning around, she saw it – a savage, bloody wound in her shoulder, from which the shaft of the bolt protruded.

Behind her, she could hear skittering footsteps, so Helen struggled to her feet. She had to get away. She could still run and if she could make it to cover . . .

Her right leg gave out beneath her, a second bolt slamming into her thigh. This time she lost her balance, pitching over and landing face first in the dirt. Spluttering, gasping, Helen tried to haul herself up, but a sharp boot connected with the side of her face and she pitched onto her back.

And even as she lay there, helpless and bleeding, her attacker loomed above her. Oliver Winter was dressed in leather body armour, a hood concealing a dull metal mask with two huge, sinister eyeholes. He didn't speak, simply loading his final bolt, before aiming the bow at her throat.

151

He tore along the path, his torch beam strobing the darkness. He saw shapes, branches, even the occasional pair of blinking, yellow eyes deep in the undergrowth, but there was no sign of Helen or Winter.

'Helen?'

Hudson skidded to a halt, calling her name.

'Helen, can you hear me?'

But there was no response, save for the roar of the wind. The weather was worsening, becoming wild and desperate – a fitting match for his mood. He and McAndrew had paired off, sending Osbourne and Edwards in one direction, Bentham and Lucas in yet another. Prompted by Charlie, they had descended on Cooper's Lake from different angles, expecting to find Helen and her team there, possibly with Winter already in custody. But when the disoriented armed officers had eventually arrived, there was no sign of their leader. They had lost Helen.

Hudson hadn't hesitated, tearing off in the direction they had come from, McAndrew labouring to keep up. Hudson hadn't spared her, keeping up a relentless pace, searching desperately for any sign of their missing colleague. Helen was alone in the forest now, with a brutal killer in close proximity, and Hudson was determined to find her. She had saved his life and he was determined to repay the favour.

'Helen? Helen, can you hear me?'

He was careless of the volume now. If he found Helen, great. If he scared Winter off, so much the better. The only thing he had no care for now was his own safety. While Helen was in peril, everything else was immaterial.

Yet still she didn't answer. Slowing, Hudson shot an anguished look at McAndrew, but she just shook her head, clearly as desperate as him.

'Helen? Please, if you're close by . . .'

He petered out, suddenly feeling utterly deflated. He had no idea which direction to go in, nor what might be happening to her. Was it possible that they might not find her in time? That she would become Winter's next victim?

It was too awful a thought to contemplate, so, signalling to McAndrew, Hudson resumed the hunt, plunging into the darkness once more.

152

'Please, Oliver, you don't need to do this.'

But the mask stared back at her, silent and expressionless.

'I'm not the enemy here . . .'

Winter lowered his face to the bow, staring directly down the sight line towards her.

'I know you've suffered, I know Julia's suffered. But it's over now. The people that ruined her life are gone. There's no need for further bloodshed.'

His finger squeezed the trigger.

'Please, Oliver. Just take off your mask, so we can talk . . .'

Now Helen heard a soft chuckle from behind the blank mask.

'You'd like that, wouldn't you?'

'Yes, yes, I would.'

'Buy yourself a little time. But it won't make any difference. Either I finish you off or you bleed out on the floor.'

Helen stared at him, trying to control her anguish. She knew she was bleeding heavily from both wounds – she could feel blood seeping through her saturated leathers – and she felt dizzy from the pain.

'I just want to talk, that's all,' she replied breathily. 'I understand why you felt you had to do this, why Morgan and the others needed to be punished –'

'Do you?' Winter shot back witheringly. 'And how do you know that?'

'Because I know what happened to Julia. I spoke to her today.'

Now Winter seemed to hesitate.

'What do you mean, you spoke to her? The hospital won't allow . . .'

'I forced their hand.'

'Bullshit.'

'Dr Ellis helped me. I asked Julia about you, about the murders. She never wanted any of this, she wants it to stop.'

Winter said nothing, shaking his head violently.

'And I know for a fact that she wouldn't want any more blood spilt. And surely *she* is the most important person in all this?'

'Of course she is. And do you know why?'

Helen looked up at her aggressor, who now leaned in towards her.

'Because she was the one that suffered. Do you know what it's like to suffer?'

As he spoke, he placed the toe of his boot on the bolt in Helen's leg, pressing down hard. Helen gasped, agony ripping through her, even as vomit rose in her throat. The pain was excruciating and her hand grasped his foot, attempting to wrench it off. But still he pressed, harder and harder . . . before suddenly relenting. Helen gasped in relief, clamping her hand to the gaping wound. But Winter wasn't finished yet.

'You have no idea what she went through. What that animal did to her.'

'I know that he raped her. That he –'

'He destroyed her.'

The bitterness, the bile, was pouring from him now.

'She left her diary, did you know that?'

Helen tried to answer, but the pain in her leg robbed her of breath.

'When she wrote me her farewell note, she left her diary. I've carried it next to my heart ever since . . .'

To Helen's surprise, Winter now raised his bow, reaching inside his jacket to remove a small diary from the breast pocket.

'Read it.'

He tossed it at her. She caught it with her left hand, looking up at Winter to see if he really meant it. He responded by raising his bow. Balancing the book on her stomach, Helen flicked through the early pages, straining to read in the moonlight. They were from October, November, December 2008 and were scattered with brief entries, recording Julia's excitement and anxiety at starting university.

'You know which date to go to,' he said quietly.

Even as he spoke, he cast around them, searching for signs of the helicopter, of potential rescuers, but there was nobody. They were quite alone. Flicking to April 30th, Helen started to read. Her vision was starting to swim, but she focused hard on the dancing words, trying to take in their meaning.

'Went to the woods. Full Moon party.'

Unlike her earlier entries, which had been verbose and gushing, this entry was terse and cold. Helen could well imagine why, the young woman presumably still in shock after her horrific ordeal. She flicked forward.

'Caleb had been attentive all night. Just after midnight, he suggested a game of hide and seek, just me and him. I agreed. I said "chase me" and ran off into the woods . . .'

Helen jumped a few more lines. She was feeling dizzy and had no desire to dwell on the details.

'I told him I wasn't interested. I pushed him away. But he hit me in the stomach. Next thing I remember I'm on the ground. My face is pushed into the floor, I have dirt in my mouth, I can taste the rotting leaves . . .'

Helen dropped the book to the floor, unwilling to read any more.

'Read it!' Winter roared.

'I don't need to read it. I'm sure Morgan denied it ever happened. That the others covered for him –'

'She told her *friend* . . .'

He said the word with such anger that Helen flinched.

'Told Lauren what had happened. And guess what? She told her boyfriend.'

'Who'd provided the drugs for the full-moon party . . .'

'Who'd provided the drugs for the party,' Winter confirmed bitterly.

It was just a guess on Helen's part, but it suddenly seemed to make sense. Campbell would have been worried about what might come out during a rape case, as no doubt was Scott, who'd sworn to her controlling parents that she was no longer taking drugs.

'Next day, Lauren told Julia that she didn't believe it had happened. That if she went to court they would say she wanted it, that it was consensual, that she had been all over him.'

Winter was virtually shouting now. To Helen's surprise, he suddenly reached up, ripping off his mask and tossing it into the undergrowth. She was alarmed by what was revealed – Winter's face was contorted with rage, years of pent-up fury bursting forth.

'They betrayed her . . .' he breathed fiercely.

It was true, they had. But it had come at a cost – Helen was now convinced that Lauren's self-hatred, her descent into hard-drug addiction, had been prompted by guilt over her treatment of Julia. Not that Winter wanted to hear that now.

'They betrayed her in the worst way possible,' he continued.

'Yes, they did.'

'Just like *you* have.'

'That's not true, Oliver.'

'How am I going to say goodbye to her now? How am I going to tell her I love her?'

His face was still set in anger, but sadness was also punching through now. He looked bereft, even hollow.

'Look, Oliver, if you co-operate I'm sure we can arrange –'

'Bullshit. This is the end of the line.'

It certainly felt like it. Helen's vision was swimming worse than ever, darkness creeping in from the edges. She felt the strength flowing from her, as if she might pass out at any time. But Winter showed no mercy, gripping the trigger once more.

'Time's up. For both of us.'

He lowered his eye to the sight line. Helen tried to keep her eyes open, tried to focus, casting around for any means of deliverance. And now she saw that her right hand still rested on her thigh, wrapped round the offending bolt. Instinctively, her grip tightened further.

'Goodbye, Helen. See you in the next world,' Winter concluded, taking a step forward.

Pain had always been Helen's friend, something she could channel. So, gritting her teeth, she ripped the bolt from her leg. Immediately, a huge plume of blood spurted up into the air, spraying them both. For a moment, Winter froze, but Helen didn't, lurching forward and slamming it into his thigh.

Winter roared – a sustained, bloodcurdling roar. He stumbled slightly, staring at the offending bolt, then, enraged, raised his bow once more. But Helen was quicker, wrenching the bolt from her shoulder. As more blood splattered her assailant, she plunged the bolt into his knee.

This time his agonized scream virtually deafened her. Winter fell backwards, dropping his bow, as his hands went to his knee. Now Helen scrambled to her feet, staggering drunkenly towards her foe. Alarmed by her approach, Winter tried to right himself, but Helen snatched up the discarded bow, bringing the butt crashing down on to his chin. There was a horrible click, as his jaw broke cleanly, then Winter hit the turf and lay motionless.

Helen swayed above him, battered but triumphant. Then, turning away, she cupped her hands to call for help. But as she did so, the world seemed to spin violently and she crumpled to the ground.

153

'Is she going to be ok? What's going to happen to her?'

The questions crept into Helen's consciousness, but at a remove. The voice sounded like it was miles away, at the end of a distant tunnel.

'Look, I know you can't promise anything, but I just want to know what we're dealing with . . .'

The soft voice sounded familiar. With enormous effort, Helen tried to open her eyes. The light was blinding, but she persisted. She'd expected to find herself prone on the forest floor, but she now saw that she was travelling at speed along some kind of corridor, Charlie by her side.

'Charlie?' she croaked.

Immediately, her friend cast a desperate, hopeful glance in her direction.

'Helen, it's me. You're in South Hants hospital. You've sustained some injuries, but you're going to be ok.'

She didn't sound convinced. Images came back to Helen now – Winter, the crossbow, those awful wounds. Helen knew she must have lost a lot of blood, the question was whether she still had enough strength, if her body still had enough fight, to make it through whatever operations she was about to endure.

'Everything's going to be fine. You'll be back on your feet in no time.'

Her voice shook as she spoke, tension undermining Charlie's attempt at a brave face. But Helen had no strength left to worry. What would be would be.

'Winter?' Helen murmured.

'In custody,' Charlie reassured her. 'Although he might need a trip to the dentist. I think you bust half a dozen of his teeth . . .'

Helen was about to respond, but another voice now intervened. Helen saw a young Asian woman, kind but solemn, looming above her.

'We're about to take you into theatre now, Helen. So, say goodbye to your friend. You'll need to conserve your energy . . .'

Helen raised a hand, too tired to talk. As she was wheeled through the doors, she looked back one last time, to see Charlie watching her anxiously. This was nothing new, the pair of them had been in this position many times before and Helen recognized the fondness and concern on her friend's countenance that she had come to treasure. Helen took in her face for a second, drinking in the emotion. Then the doors swung shut and she was hidden from view once more.

154

He wrenched open the door, revealing the dark space within. Oliver Winter hesitated, turning to Hudson as if waiting for a formal invitation to enter, but the latter was not in the mood to play games. Grabbing the prisoner by the collar, he shoved him into the back of the police van, before following him inside. Moments later, the doors were secured and they were on their way.

Tearing through the woods, Hudson's heart had skipped a beat when he'd heard a bloodcurdling cry echoing through the night. Following the direction of the cry, he'd stumbled into the clearing and been horrified to see two figures lying on the ground. Ignoring Winter, he had fallen to his knees beside Helen, desperately checking for a pulse. He had found one, thank God, and before long she was in the air ambulance, on her way to South Hants hospital.

Winter's injuries were less severe. Having been given the all clear by the police doctor, he had endured some emergency dental work, before finally being passed fit for the trip to Southampton Central. Hudson had volunteered to accompany him, determined not to let the multiple killer out of his sight until he was safely behind bars. He had caused too much anguish, shed too much blood, for them to take any chances.

DC McAndrew was in the cab with the driver, leaving Hudson and Winter alone. Hudson had expected the killer to be downcast, even penitent, but in fact the burly Swede seemed far from cowed, refusing to say a word to anyone and looking at them – Hudson especially – with a mixture of amusement and disdain. It was as if he was too far gone, as if the loving father had been permanently replaced by something darker and more disturbing.

Hudson felt eyes on him and looked up. Winter lolled on the bench opposite, his body jogging back and forth in time with the van's progress, staring across the divide. Hudson met his gaze, refusing to be intimidated. Winter looked a mess, his face bruised, smears of blood still clinging to his stubble – an odd frame for the bright white dental implants that now graced his mouth.

'How's your friend?'

His cracked voice made Hudson jump. He had barely spoken a word in two hours.

'Is she going to make it?'

'Shut your mouth.'

There was no question about it, Winter seemed *amused*. It made Hudson's blood boil, but he reined in his fury.

'She surprised me, you know.'

'Enough, Winter.'

'She was stronger than the rest, more resourceful.'

Winter was watching Hudson closely, clearly enjoying his discomfort.

'I thought she would die like the rest. On her knees, begging for mercy.'

'If you want to confess, Winter, save it for the station.'

But Winter waved his hand, to signal that they were way past that.

'But Grace . . . she wanted to fight. Stupid really, when she was unarmed and alone.'

'I'm not going to tell you again.'

But Winter laughed, flashing his new teeth at Hudson.

'I gave her two bolts. I would have given her a third. I *wanted* to give her a third.'

Hudson glared at him, saying nothing.

'Still, maybe the first two will do the job. She lost a lot of blood, was in a *bad* way . . . You never know, if you're lucky you might be in line for a promotion before the night is out.'

Winter had no time to react, Hudson bridging the space between them in a heartbeat, ploughing a fist into his stomach.

'Jesus Christ —'

Fear suddenly flared in Winter's eyes, but it was too late, Hudson dragging him off the bench and throwing him to the floor. Climbing upon his prone victim, Hudson punched him in the stomach again, once, twice, three times.

'What the hell . . . ?' Winter gasped.

But he wasn't allowed to finish, Hudson hauling him up and slamming him back onto the bench, his back crashing into the side of the van. Now Joseph Hudson moved in close, pulling the startled Winter towards him.

'If anything happens to her, anything at all, I *will* come for you . . .'

They were nose to nose now. Hudson could see a bead of sweat trickling down Winter's face.

'And I'll finish the job.'

Hudson maintained his grip for a moment, revelling in Winter's discomfort, before suddenly releasing him and returning to the opposite bench. Hudson's heart was thumping, his head buzzing — he wanted to scream and shout, to tear the van apart — but he was not going to compromise himself, would not let Winter score that small victory. So instead he sat on the bench, staring directly ahead.

Winter looked flustered and scared, fearing perhaps that Hudson would come for him again. But already he was receding from Hudson's consciousness. He had no time for this killer, this pathetic little worm, spluttering and gasping on the bench opposite.

His thoughts were all with Helen.

155

She pushed the door to and rested her head against its cool surface. It had been a horrendous night and Charlie felt utterly exhausted.

She had been determined to stay with Helen, but Superintendent Simmons had arrived to dismiss her, taking on the role of nightwatchman herself. She knew how close Charlie and Helen were, but she had a special bond with her protégée too and, reluctantly, Charlie had allowed herself to be convinced. Tonight had been a gruelling experience – up in the helicopter, trying to suppress her feelings of nausea as they swept the forest in search of Winter, and she felt utterly spent – tired, dirty and emotionally wrung out. Nevertheless, she had resisted Simmons's urgings long enough to receive encouraging news from the operating theatre – Helen was stable now and would pull through – before bending her steps for home.

Now as she looked around at the familiar surroundings of her house, Charlie felt enormous relief. She and Steve had had a good chat following her apologetic text and they seemed to be on the road to recovery. Jessie too had been a little better, sleeping through last night, and it was just possible that Charlie might get some rest. Something which was sorely required.

But as she crept up the stairs she was surprised to find the diminutive figure of her daughter waiting for her.

'Hey, what are you doing up?' she asked, concerned, shooting a look at her watch. 'It's nearly midnight.'

She feared she knew the answer, and wondered why Steve was not already on the scene, but to her surprise Jessie replied:

'Couldn't sleep.'

'Why not?'

'I'm hot . . .'

'Well, we can soon fix that,' Charlie said, guiding her daughter back into her bedroom.

Helping her back into bed, Charlie lifted the covers up to her waist and switched the table fan on, angling it in her direction. The cool breeze seemed to please her daughter, who snuggled down with her bears and closed her eyes once more. Heeding Grace Simmons's advice, Charlie sat down next to her, stroking her hair as she started to sing.

'Hush, little Jessie, don't you cry. Mummy's going to sing you a lullaby . . .'

Within a minute, Jessica was asleep, the very image of innocence and serenity. Charlie stopped singing, staring at her daughter with tears in her eyes. But they were not tears of sadness, or even anxiety, but happiness.

Perhaps there was no need to be afraid after all.

Epilogue

156

'So how are you feeling?'

Helen Grace considered for a moment, before answering. 'I feel . . . good.'

'I'm very glad to hear it. You gave us all quite a scare.'

Grace Simmons said it with a smile, but Helen knew that her mentor *had* been worried, visiting her every day, until she was finally discharged. Helen had lost a lot of blood in the forest and endured two arduous operations to limit the damage done by Winter's bolts. Thankfully, these had been successful and though Helen had sustained some muscle damage and scarring, the doctors had assured her that she would make a full recovery in time. Which was why she was back at work, albeit on desk duty.

A month had passed since that dark night in the New Forest. And though snapshots of her struggle with Winter still plagued her dreams, Helen did feel in a good place. This was partly down to her natural resilience, but mostly down to the solicitous care of her team. Simmons had continued to mother her, popping round to her flat on a number of occasions. Ellie McAndrew had also paid a visit, with gifts from the team, as had DS Hudson, clutching an armful of flowers. But it was, of course, Charlie who had been her greatest support, appearing regularly with home-cooked meals, magazines, even a Get Well Soon card from Jessica, which had made Helen cry.

It was not hard to recuperate with this kind of support around you. Indeed, the principal problem had been stopping

465

Helen from returning to work – she had never been good at kicking her heels. Somehow Charlie had prevailed on her, however, persuading Helen to give her body a rest for once. For all that, it felt good to be back in Southampton Central, primed and ready for work.

'I don't want you overdoing it. Things are pretty quiet at the moment, so why don't you take the opportunity to catch up on some paperwork?'

Helen raised an eyebrow.

'I mean it, Helen,' Simmons continued firmly. 'If you go throwing yourself around, chasing the bad guys, you'll end up doing some permanent damage to that shoulder. And I have no intention of sending my best officer to the knacker's yard.'

'I'll see what I can do. Perhaps there's a cold case I could look into, though it's not really my style . . .'

'I'm sure you can find *something* interesting. I don't want you working too hard.'

This was a constant refrain from Simmons and Helen knew not to interrupt.

'I know you like to lead by example, but one day you'll put yourself in the line of fire and run out of luck. I know I can't stop you doing what you do best . . . but, please, don't make this place, the things you do here, your legacy. There is more to life than work.'

Simmons stole a glance at the photo of her late husband and two strapping sons, which stood proudly framed on her desk. Helen glanced at it too – it was a photo which always brought a smile to her face.

'I know,' Helen conceded. 'And I'm working on it . . .'

'I'm very glad to hear it.'

Simmons paused for a second, looking back up at Helen and appraising her.

'You more than anyone deserve a little happiness, Helen. So, don't run from it, *embrace it.*'

As Helen walked away from Simmons's office, she felt more optimistic, more determined than she had done in ages. The fears and doubts which had gripped her for years seemed to be falling away, proving to be meaningless phantoms after all. She would heed Simmons's advice – she would seize the day and try to be happy.

But there was something she needed to do first.

157

The corridors were quiet this morning. South Hants hospital was usually chaotic and noisy, nurses and porters chatting and joking as they wheeled their charges around. Today, however, the wards seemed peaceful and hushed, as if a respectful silence was being observed.

Helen padded along the sixth floor, lost in thought. While she'd been recuperating, she'd kept close tabs on Julia Winter's condition, hoping against hope that she would make some improvement, that she would manage to fight off the pneumonia that was laying her low. But, to her immense sadness and frustration, the young woman's condition had deteriorated. Doctors were now unable to communicate with her, her brain function had flat-lined and it was only the drains and the ventilator that were keeping her alive. Doctors had urged Alice Winter to consider withdrawing life support and, after much soul searching, she had agreed. Which was why Helen was here. It was not a duty she was looking forward to, but one she felt bound to honour.

Charlie was already in the viewing area, looking at mother and child through the window. She turned briefly as Helen joined her, before returning her attention to Alice and Julia.

'Poor girl. That anyone should have to end up like that . . .'

Helen nodded, giving her friend's arm an affectionate rub.

'It seems so cruel, so arbitrary, that some should thrive and others, who've led a perfectly blameless life . . .'

'I know,' Helen agreed, as Charlie petered out. 'It's such a waste.'

They continued to stare at the couple, watching as Alice removed a hair from her daughter's face, before exchanging a couple of words with the attending doctor. As she did so, Alice spotted Helen, and gave her a brief, meaningful nod. Helen was moved to see tears pricking the bereft mother's eyes.

'I'm not sure I can watch,' Charlie murmured, her voice shaking.

'We'll do it together,' Helen reassured her. 'Alice will need our support afterwards.'

Charlie nodded, but said nothing. It was true – hard as this was, Helen was glad they were here. Alice's husband and daughter had journeyed over from Sweden to be with her, the latter spending some valuable time with her half-sister, but they had decided against attending today, deeming it too upsetting for young Lilly. Alice would feel so many conflicting emotions when it came to it – grief, emptiness, guilt – and she would need someone with her.

Alice and the doctor had now ceased their conversation and Helen could tell by the solemn look on their faces that the moment had come. Alice darted another brief glance at Helen and Charlie, before returning to her daughter's bedside.

Helen tried to keep a grip on her own emotions, as she watched Alice pick up Julia's hand to kiss it once more. The grieving mother held it tight, stroking it gently, even as the tears slid down her face. Instinctively, Helen laid a hand on Charlie's shoulder, drawing closer to her. And there they stood, watching the distressing tableau in front of them, reflecting on a life that had been cut short by tragedy and lamenting all that might have been.

158

They walked away in silence, deeply moved by what they had just witnessed.

Julia had passed away peacefully in her mother's arms, bathed in love and affection. The young woman was now at peace, which was something, but it still left both of them feeling hollow.

Swallowing their own distress, they had done their best to comfort Alice, who had borne up remarkably well, given the circumstances. She was obviously devastated and full of regret, but she had also treasured her time with her daughter and was grateful that she'd been with her at the end. In an act of amazing generosity, she had earlier made contact with her former husband in prison, asking if he wanted to apply for compassionate leave to be with his daughter today, but he'd refused, perhaps too ashamed to face her.

Alice had now left the ward and was on the phone to her husband, chatting soberly but positively about the arrangements that needed to be made. It was a touching scene – Alice clearly wanted to make up for past neglect by ensuring Julia was given the send-off she deserved – but it was not their place to linger, so Helen and Charlie had discreetly departed.

Walking back to Helen's bike, they said little, both knowing how the other was feeling. Occasions such as these were always upsetting, but nevertheless gave meaning to what they did, underlining that people mattered, that individual lives meant something and were worth protecting. Helen just wished she had known Julia earlier, when she might have made a real difference to her, and she suspected Charlie felt the same.

'Are you heading back to base?' Charlie eventually asked, as they neared Helen's Kawasaki.

'Better had,' Helen replied, wearily. 'I've got to begin the hunt for a new crime scene photographer, now that Graham Ross has decided to move on.'

'He's only got himself to blame,' Charlie replied, shaking her head ruefully. 'If you lie down with dogs . . .'

'My thoughts exactly. I've also got a month's worth of paperwork to catch up on, so . . .'

'Don't overdo it.'

'I'm fine, honestly. I'm eating properly again, sleeping well, everything is boringly normal.'

'I'm pleased to hear it,' Charlie responded, smiling. 'You could do with a bit of normal in your life.'

'And how are you?' Helen asked, changing the subject. 'How's Jessica?'

'Much better, thanks. We've had three weeks of undisturbed sleep, so fingers crossed . . .'

'And Steve? Everything ok between you two?'

Charlie paused, uncertain how to answer, which worried Helen. But to her surprise, Charlie now broke out into an even wider smile.

'Actually, things are good. Better than good. I'm pregnant.'

'Right,' Helen said, momentarily stumped. 'I didn't know that you . . .'

'I wasn't. I didn't plan for it, wasn't ready for it, but accidents will happen.'

'Well, then I'm very happy for you.'

'Thank you. We're both really pleased,' Charlie replied, laughing at the cosmic craziness of it all. 'I guess it was meant to be.'

Helen hugged her, giving her old friend a kiss on the cheek, before letting her go. Helen watched her walk away, feeling both excited and moved. Charlie had been through so much recently, Steve and Jessica too, and they deserved some happiness. It cheered Helen enormously to think that there would soon be a fourth member of their family, bringing fun, noise, happiness and chaos to their loving household. The last few months had been so dark, so challenging, but finally the sun was beginning to shine on them, promising better things for the future.

It was a timely reminder that amid all the death and suffering, there is always life.